A Little Help
from Above

A Little Help from Above

Saralee Rosenberg

AVON BOOKS
An Imprint of HarperCollins*Publishers*

HarperCollins books may be purchased for educational, business, or sales promotion-
al use. For information please write: Special Markets Department, HarperCollins
Publishers Inc., 10 East 53rd Street, New York, NY 10022.

FIRST EDITION

Designed by Rhea Braunstein

Library of Congress Cataloging-in-Publication Data

Rosenberg, Saralee H.
    A little help from above / Saralee Rosenberg.
        p. cm.
ISBN 0-06-009620-9
1. Mothers and daughters—Fiction. 2. Loss (Psychology)—Fiction.
3. Sisters—Fiction. I. Title

PS3618.O833 L5 2003
813'.54—dc21   2002027486

01 02 03 04 05 RRD 10 9 8 7 6 5 4 3 2 1

To Susan Keusch and Dan Rosenberg,
our little help from above

With love to my hero and husband,
Lee

Acknowledgments

I am grateful to the professionals I bombarded with questions and who were so generous with information, ideas, and inspiration. Larry Gordon, Dr. Jeff Zola, Dr. Heidi Rosenberg, Andrea Peyser of the *New York Post*, and Leor Warner, the astrological genius from L.A.

I could not have begun to understand the complex medical, legal, and psychological issues brought on by DES without the help of Nora Cody, Sally Keely, Cynthia Laitman, Joan Barnes, and Jenny Margolis. I am also indebted to the numerous other DES daughters who willingly came forward to share their stories, fears, and triumphs. They and their families are towers of strength and courage who deserve our compassion and prayers.

So glad to have Risa Sidrane, Pat Hanley, Fern Drasin, Lenore French, Sue Zola, and Judi Ratner as dear friends, readers, and perennial sounding boards. Wouldn't want to be taking this journey without their guiding lights.

I am eternally grateful to my sister, Mira Temkin, the first person to recognize my writing ability. I had to pay her a quarter to read my short stories, but she loved them enough to refund her fee. Her words of praise and encouragement have never failed to light the fire.

I would still be writing in the basement, lonely and undiscovered, without my dear agent and friend, Deborah Schneider. Her support and encouragement were unwavering, even when prospects looked dim. She has my eternal gratitude. Getting to work with a talented editor like Lyssa Keusch was a gift. She nurtured, she nudged, but mostly she cared. If you love this book, we both have her to thank.

My parents, Doris and Harold Hymen, love my writing but love my story even more. I got married, had kids, and found a way to make a living from home. Even better, now they can *kvell* at the bookstore. "My daughter wrote that." Thank you for the devotion and encouragement.

To my other mother, Rita Rosenberg, hugs and kisses. You read every word and ask for more. Your love and reassurance mean everything to me.

My children, Zack, Alex, and Taryn, are my divine inspiration, the reason I laugh, love, and live. Nothing lifts my spirit more than when they bring me coffee and whisper encouraging words, "You're almost done, right?"

Finally, to my husband, Lee, my heart and soul, my rock. Twenty-five years and still ticking. It doesn't get any better than this.

PART I

You Can Go Home Again
(if you remember the key)

June 1998

Chapter One

"Bagels! Who wants hot bagels?" David bounded through Shelby's apartment door, slamming it shut with the heel of his sneaker. "You up, hon?" he called from the kitchen.

I am now, hon, she almost yelled back. Instead Shelby lay motionless, hopeful Mr. Get-Up-and-Go would do precisely that. Why would a guy finally relieved of his dog-walking, diaper-changing responsibilities be up and out so early on a Sunday?

"I also got fat-free muffins," David hollered, his mouth full of nova and cream cheese.

Bagels? Muffins? Was he joking? After three months of dating, you'd think he'd have noticed that those calorie-clogged, carbohydrate killers never passed her lips. Or, at least had some inkling women in their late thirties didn't maintain taut, 115-pound bodies by eating just because the sun happened to rise.

"I know you're up." David poked his head into the bedroom. "You're not snoring."

"I don't snore. I have hay fever. Remember?" She would have said it sweetly if not for the shorts. The same damn shorts she'd just tossed in the cleaning lady's rag bag.

"What?" David looked down.

"Didn't I throw those out?"

"C'mon, Shel. They're so comfy. Be a sport."

"Can't. Where I come from, hairy men with large prostates don't wear threadbare shorts that went straight from El Salvador to the $9.99 table at the Champion outlet!"

"Well excuse me if they don't say Prada."

"Very funny. What happened to that nice pair I bought you?"

"I hate green. And they ride my crotch."

Better them than me, she thought, watching an exasperated David slink back to his Bagelfest. Shelby rolled over, depressed by two epiphanies. All men were created equal, sadly. And, bad batches were not limited to poorly manufactured clothing. Relationships also came in defective lots. How else to explain the run of dismal luck she'd had this year? Four different men. Not one of whom would pass muster with Inspector #36.

Gregory had been Harrison Ford handsome but a trifle too married. Next came Marc. And his mother. Such nice people, but between them they carried more baggage than a skycap at O'Hare. Then there was Donald, a fifty-six-year-old commodities broker, who was all too happy to let Shelby blow out his late wife's Neiman Marcus charge, provided that she didn't limit her blowing to the store. Donald was followed by David, who came into her life via a blind date arranged by one of Shelby's colleagues at the *Chicago Tribune*.

Things with David had begun on a promising note. He was sweet, funny, generous, and well trained by his ex-wife to pick up his socks but leave the toilet seat down. Trouble was he had little if any sex appeal. No physical attributes that made her heart beat faster. Or at all.

Ultimately what soured Shelby was the speed at which David had latched on to her as if she were prey in his Penis Flytrap. She worried there might not be time to escape before his poisonous grip rendered her limp and breathless. "Death by strangulation," is what the coroner's report would read. At least that's how the scene played out in her recurring nightmare. The one where she married David, moved to the suburbs, and drove the Wednesday car pool to ballet.

"Guess it's that time of month again," David, the ovarian expert, handed her coffee. "Want me to sing to you? That's what I do when Marissa wakes up cranky."

"I'm not cranky. Just stop feeding me, okay? Bagels go right from my lips to my hips."

"Not if you work them off." He nuzzled her neck.

"You're not going to leave me alone, are you?" She pushed his sweaty body off her.

"Afraid not. It's a beautiful June morning, you're a beautiful blonde, and no matter how badly you behave, when we're together, I feel inspired and alive."

Normally Shelby longed for men to speak tenderly and with reverence, but it was too late for David. She had already made the discovery he was less a man than a medical miracle. A male of the species born with a brain, but no spine. How else to explain the mind-set of a successful attorney who baby-sat his two children, so their mother, his ex, could shop courtesy of his credit cards, then see her boyfriend, Mr. Marriage Breaker?

"Could we please not confuse a hard-on with personal growth?" Shelby yawned.

"Party pooper," he groaned.

"Sorry, but I really want to go back to sleep so I don't have to think about my problems."

"What problems?"

"Name it. Relationship problems. Work problems . . ."

"We have relationship problems?" He gave her a tentative, puppy-dog face that made Shelby want to hit him with a rolled-up *Tribune*. Luckily for David the phone rang.

"Don't answer that," she ordered. "It's probably Rhonda wanting to know if you're coming over to blacktop the driveway."

"Okay, if this isn't PMS, what is?" he muttered on his way back to my kitchen.

"Fine. It's PMS." She stared at the ringing phone. Putting up with Men's Shit.

Should she answer or let the machine pick up? If it was her editor calling with a story for her column, she'd want to know. But what if it was someone who could aggravate her?

"Yes?" she tried sounding annoyed in case it actually was a call for David.

"Oh, my God. Oh, my God. Oh, my God."

Shelby shot up so fast the room spun. She only knew one person who spoke in triplicate when she was having an anxiety attack. "Lauren?"

"Don't hang up. Please don't hang up. I know you're not speaking to us, but don't hang up," she sobbed. "There's been a terrible accident. Everything's a mess. You have to come home."

"Stay calm." Shelby instinctively shifted gears into reporter-speak, a habit she'd developed early in her career, more to mollify herself than the victim. "Who? What? Where?"

"Mommy and Daddy," Lauren was choking, her breath dry from hysteria. "They were out jogging this morning when some freak of nature in a landscaper's truck smacked into them. A witness said the guy tried to take off, but his truck was wrapped around a light pole."

Shelby inhaled the news, instinctively categorizing it by level of importance. Even by her jaded standards this was a big story. If her father died before they reconciled, it would cost her thousands more in therapy. As for the woman Lauren insisted on calling Mommy, the jury was still out.

"Shel-bee," Lauren whined. "Are you listening? Did you hear a word I said? Daddy just suffered a severe head wound, his lungs are collapsed, his ribs are fractured, his neck is sprained, his spleen is ruptured, both legs are broken, maybe his hip, too . . . Shelby, the doctor said he might not make it. You have to come home."

Shelby's pulse raced. Fly to New York? Today? But she had tickets for a Cubs game, not that she cared much for baseball. Trouble was, this outing had nothing to do with drinking beer and eating peanuts, heaven forbid. It was about sitting in the *Trib's* sky box. It was about getting nine blissful innings to discuss ideas for her popular column with the paper's top brass.

"Are you there?" Lauren wept. "Say something. Anything."

"You're serious? They really jog?"

"Yes, they jog," Lauren gasped. "What kind of question is that?"

"I'm sorry. It's just that this call is coming as such a shock."

"Oh, and like when my phone rang at eight o'clock this morning I was expecting to hear from an Officer Padowski?"

"Are they in the hospital?"

"No, the Holiday Inn. Of course they're in the hospital!"

"Which one?"

"Shelby, what is wrong with you? You know which one. Please don't do this."

Shelby shivered. As a former beat reporter she'd witnessed tragedies strike randomly and without warning every day. Just not to her. Somehow she'd been lulled into thinking she'd been given immunity. Call it professional courtesy for journalists. But obviously she was as vulnerable as everyone else, and what a quandary that represented. For no matter who was lying in Long Island's North Shore University Hospital right now, she was never going back there.

"Shelby, you have to come home. I'm scared. What if Daddy dies?"

"They're not going to let him die. You think North Shore wants it on record they lost yet another Lazarus?"

"But you'll come home anyway?"

"What about Eric?"

"Are you kidding? And miss a day of rehab? Daddy just got him back into Betty Ford."

"I don't know. I'm on deadline now. Maybe I can clear my calendar for later in the week."

"Clear your calendar?"

"Hello?" Shelby was stunned to hear a dial tone.

"This is what happens when people don't sleep late on Sundays." Shelby rummaged through a closet for an overnight bag. "They get hit by trucks. But does anyone ever listen?"

"There ought to be a law." David watched a possessed woman start packing. "You're doing the right thing, you know."

"Oh good. Be sure to include that in my epitaph. 'Here lies Shelby Lazarus. Not the selfish bitch you thought.' "

"Don't be so hard on yourself." He stroked her hair. "Hey. Should I come with you?"

"No need. I'll be back by tomorrow night." She deposited one bra into her bag.

"I can't believe how well you're taking this. My wife would be downing Dylan's Ritalin."

"Ex-wife." Shelby cringed. "She's your ex-wife."

David shrugged. "Anyway, I thought you said your mom died when you were a little girl."

Shelby took a deep breath. "She did. Then a year later my father married my aunt." She removed her new Lilly Pulitzer dress from its hanger, staring curiously at the reincarnated version of the crisp, colorful shift her mother had once worn.

Back in 1969, Sandy Lazarus, a size-five fashion plate via her Bonwit Teller charge card, was the first to show the ladies-who-lunched at the Shelter Rock Country Club what their fashion sisters in West Palm were wearing. Certainly not those dreadful muumuus the gals at her club donned to camouflage their middle-aged girth.

Up until now, Shelby had no idea why she'd purchased the designer dress for herself. Lord & Taylor had been singing its historic, socialite praises, yes. But for a hard-core customer of the other Taylor in the family, Ann, the lime green elephant print was a far cry from Shelby's usual and customary wardrobe. Anything black. From top to bottom her closet was strewn with the requisite funeral-ready, career girl clothes. Who would recognize her in shocking pink? No one. Which made it perfect to wear around her old home town of Manhasset Hills, Long Island.

"So let me get this straight." David knew Shelby liked it when he invoked the name of her popular column. "Your father married his aunt?"

"No. He married *my* aunt. My mother's younger sister." Shelby threw in a pair of running shoes in case there was time to jog. Although given the circumstances, it would probably be wise to find an indoor track. "Lauren calls her Mommy. To me she'll always be Aunt Roz."

"You never mentioned having a sister." David followed Shelby into the bathroom.

"Really?" She grabbed the matched set of cleansing, exfoliating, and moisturizing products from the medicine chest. "What about a stepbrother who's an alleged drug dealer?"

He shook his head. "And you call yourself an ace reporter?"

"What's that supposed to mean?"

"C'mon, Shel. When you told me the story of your life, you left out two of the most basic, fundamental facts. A) you have a family and B) you haven't spoken to them in years."

"Guilty as charged, Your Honor."

"And yet, you're dropping everything to go home?"

"Am I on trial here?" Shelby applied lip color without so much as a quiver, all too aware David was looking for signs of frailty so he could finally play prince to her damsel in distress.

"No. But you've got to admit it sounds bizarre. Why aren't you speaking to them?"

Shelby blinked. This wasn't a road she could go down. At least not with a man who idolized his parents and would never dream of violating the fifth commandment.

"Doctor, I believe I've hit a nerve." He smirked too quickly.

"No. I've got a flight to catch, remember? Did you check the weather like I asked?"

"Yes, my lady." David knew a dead end when he careened into one. "According to the Internet, New York's got lots of rain in the forecast."

"Just great! My own boyfriend prefers going on-line instead of reading the *Trib*."

"Sue me." He shrugged. "Maybe while you're away I'll join AOL-ANON."

Shelby sighed. If only David was as handsome as he was amusing. "Have you seen my good umbrella?"

"In my car." David followed Shelby out. "But you're in luck. Mine's in the closet."

"Not that ugly, crappy Totes you got free with your JC Penney raincoat!"

"Jesus, Shel." He watched her tear through the closet looking for designer protection. "It's not like the Guccis are on border patrol."

"I'm sorry. It's just . . ."

"I know. It's okay." David lifted her chin. "I'm worried about you."

"Don't be."

"You sure I can't drive you to O'Hare?"

"Positive." She brushed a bagel crumb from his face. "I'm fine with a cab."

"Is there anything I can do? Call your boss? Water the plants?"

"No need. The last one died Tuesday."

"Your boss or your plant?" He pulled Shelby to him. "Can I at least give you a hug?"

"Sure." She shrugged, not expecting the warm embrace to feel so good it nearly broke her momentum. "Shoot. I still have to call the office and cancel out on the Cubs game. What do you think I should tell them?"

"I don't know. I'm generally partial to the truth."

"Sounds like a plan. But I can't do that. I never share my personal life at work."

Or anywhere, David thought as he watched Shelby head down the hall to the elevator. "I'm sure you'll think of something." He waved. "I hear TB is making a comeback."

"Such a kidder." Shelby chuckled before stepping into the elevator.

Not this time, he thought. For David was painfully aware he knew virtually nothing about his new love, and it wasn't for lack of trying. Even after their most intimate moments he could only get Shelby to reveal small, meaningless nuggets. She wasn't just playing her story close to the vest, she was playing it under lock and key. Even a private investigator on his law firm's payroll came up emptier-handed than expected. "Lady's done a damn good job covering her tracks." The investigator shrugged when he threw a half-page dossier on David's desk. "She may be a great reporter, but she's a lousy source."

So, David remained in the dark. Precisely where she wanted him. And everyone else.

Chapter Two

Would you look at Shelby? She gets a frantic call to fly home and her only concern is charging through the airport in search of coffee. I was happy with a fresh cup of Maxwell House, but not my daughter. The only blend good enough for her is Viennese-roasted and overpriced. Make that a grande! Such mishegas *with the coffee. In my day, no one would dream of spending three dollars for hot water with a spritz of caffeine and a spray of foam.*

Not that I didn't expect the world to change in the thirty years since I'm gone. Still, I barely recognize the place. Day spas on every corner, miniature telephones you carry in your pocketbook, and so many racy television programs. I do happen to love that Sex *and the City. I just couldn't imagine calling my mother, may she rest in peace with me, and saying, "Ma, come over. Let's watch four young gals on TV discussing multiple orgasms over breakfast." It's all so different.*

Then again, some things never change. Like stubbornness, pettiness, and families who fight. Like mine. Basically good people at heart, but always bickering and finger pointing. This one said this, and that one did that.

Shelby is the worst. Defiant. Judgmental. Always standing on her little soapbox. So it comes as no surprise that she's not on speaking terms with her sister, her father, her stepmother, or her stepbrother. I suppose she has her reasons. But on the other hand, she wasn't any easier to deal with as a child.

I remember one time when four-year-old Lauren was searching frantically for Barbie and Ken. Poor dear had spent all morning setting up the den for the big wedding when she realized the bride and groom were miss-

ing from her dollcase. Naturally, she assumed Shelby, the tyrant, had hidden them on purpose. And, naturally, ten-year-old Shelby denied the charges, screaming at the top of her lungs that she didn't take the stupid dolls, but if she found them first she was going to cut off their heads so they could never get married.

At the time I wondered if she was projecting the angst of my younger sister Roz, who was trying to manage her first trimester morning sickness. Had Shelby figured out that the nausea had less to do with the pregnancy than the fact that her aunt was thirty-one, broke and single?

Regardless, Shelby had to look no further than me for proof that marriage and family could be wonderful. In fact, back in 1969, I was Sandy Lazarus, queen of the good life. Loving wife. Devoted mother. Our home in Manhasset Hills, Long Island, was to die for (although I never expected literally). We had the first built-in swimming pool on the block, a Jaguar in the driveway, membership in a private country club, and shares of stock in some little computer outfit that my husband wouldn't stop yapping about. "What does IBM make?" I wanted to know. "Money!" he laughed.

And then without warning it was all over. By the end of the year, Larry had wealth but no wife. A limited edition car, but no one for whom he could open the door. Two beautiful little girls, but no mother to pick out their clothes each morning.

Naturally it was a difficult time for the family, but especially for Shelby. Not only did she have to cope with the loss of her mother, but her best friend, Matthew Lieberman.

When we first moved to Majestic Court, I was thrilled to discover a family three doors down with a baby the same age as Shelby. Little did we know that putting two toddlers in a sandbox would be the start of an inseparable, ten-year-long friendship. A friendship that surely would have continued if not for the fact that Matty was uprooted to California, the casualty of a dreamy-eyed father who thought Hollywood needed another agent.

It seems the night before the Liebermans moved, Matty pulled Shelby behind the snow-covered azaleas in our backyard, hugged her tightly, and kissed her on the lips for what felt like an eternity. Then he promised that whatever happened to him, he would love her forever.

Shelby was devastated. If this was true love, and she was certainly feeling something, did it mean she would turn into a sissy like Lauren, who brushed her dolls' hair for hours and spoke of nothing other than bridesmaids and china patterns? She never found out. After Matty moved, she never heard from him again.

Is abandonment why my darling daughter is thirty-eight and as single as a sock in the dryer? Why her most committed relationships so far have been with Mr. Sushi and the dry cleaner?

Her therapist says it's because she has many issues to resolve. I say name three people who don't. He says it's fine to choose a career over family. I say Golda Meir had one hell of a big job, and she somehow managed to have a husband and kids. He says she still has time to work things out. I say enough is enough. I have to do something.

Yes, I know that meddling with destiny is a big no-no up here. And with good reason. If all of us entry-level souls had the power of divine intervention, the universe would be inextricably altered.

But this is my child we're talking about. My precious firstborn. And herein lies a universal truth that is even more powerful than the laws of God and eternity. It's the law of motherhood. Whether dead or alive, our job never ends.

"Excuse me." Shelby hailed a passing cart the airlines used to transport the elderly. "I've just thrown my back out. Could you possibly take me to Gate 21?"

"Hop in, lovely lady." The gentleman smiled. "I don't often get the pleasure of escorting a pretty young thing."

"Thank you." She tossed her gear in back, wondering how different her life would have been had she been born plain-faced or obese. "No cup holders?" She held on to the paper mug.

The driver raised an eyebrow. "It's a cart, dear. Not a BMW."

"I knew that." Shelby smiled, suddenly concerned he'd recognize her from the paper and typecast her as one of those overpaid media snobs who expected royal treatment. Which she did.

Still, it had been so exciting when the *Trib's* advertising department plastered her likeness all over billboards and city buses. Even if she didn't yet understand the downside of fame. Which translated to having to behave nicely in public. Virtually overnight she'd lost the freedom to blow off windbags, vent on incompetent store clerks, or in today's case, unload on a sadistic driver who thought he was traversing the Autobahn.

"Gate 21." Mr. Leadfoot jammed the brakes. "Take care and have a nice day."

Shelby felt the hot coffee splash under the lid, wincing at how close she'd come to wearing it. "Thanks again." She winked. Okay, people are watching. Wave bye-bye to the nice man.

She grabbed her gear off the cart, took one look at the packed waiting area, and shuddered. The only empty seat was next to a screaming infant. Good God. The least a parent could do was sedate their whiny kid before subjecting the public to their offending racket.

Little did Shelby know a baby's cry could be so ear-shattering, it could drown out the sound of her name being called. A second, louder attempt did, however, catch her attention.

"Shelby? Is that you darling?"

Suddenly she was face-to-face with a face she hadn't faced in ages. Which hadn't been long enough. Even the baby sensed the storm warning and miraculously piped down. "Ian?"

"You look wonderful. What has it been? Five years?" the tall, dignified-looking man leaned in to peck her cheek.

"Where *does* the time go?" Shelby gritted.

"Looks like we're on the same flight, isn't that peachy? Plenty of time to catch up on the good old days and, in the meanwhile, you'll watch my bags while I make a pee-pee. You do look wonderful." He kissed her hand.

Pee-pee? Where were the airsick bags when you needed them most? Shelby watched Ian McNierney, the British import, scurry off to the men's room, his sixty-year-old Continental swagger still making ladies' heads turn. He was the only straight man she'd ever worked for who was more proud of his ass than his dick.

Suddenly she felt lower back pain. Not the stress-induced, premenstrual ache she could tame with Advil. Not even the throbbing muscle pain she felt after her personal Nazi trainer forced her into a few too many reps on the hip extension machine. No. In her professional opinion she was experiencing the eye-popping, fist-clenching, flare up of the sciatic nerve.

"Shit!" She tried holding back the tears as she ransacked her pocketbook. Why now? God help her if she hadn't packed her prescription pain reliever. Otherwise, she'd be spending the flight in the aisle, rocking on all fours. But there they were at the bottom of her bag. She downed two with the last sip of coffee and closed her eyes.

"Serves you right for lying about your back," Granny Bea Good suddenly interrupted her thoughts. A terrifying phenomenon, given her maternal grandmother was currently residing on Planet Alzheimer's. Shelby squeezed her temples. Jewish guilt not only traveled fast, it traveled far. How else to explain the ability to receive a message transmitted fifteen hundred miles by a woman who hadn't had a lucid thought since the Reagan administration?

"I know I shouldn't have misled the driver," Shelby relayed back. "But I only had two choices. Tell a small, white lie, or miss the flight." Oh God. I'm hearing voices and answering them. Could this day possibly get any worse?

Yes, actually. United announced a slight boarding delay just as Ian returned to the gate area. The thought of having to make small talk for more than a minute almost made her bolt.

What would they discuss? His burgeoning portfolio? His Pulitzer prize? Again? Surely he'd mention his latest sexual conquests. She winced. If there was a merciful God, Ian had finally concluded he was too old to chase every underage girl who had two legs and a skirt.

In all her years as a journalist, never had Shelby encountered a colleague as repugnant or loathsome as Ian McNierney. But having been forced to work under him, even figuratively, had made matters worse. In fact he had caused her such intense angst she considered suicide. Or binging. A choice she fortunately never had to make because he fired her. "Here's a little pink slip for your lingerie drawer," the Brit bastard sneered over drinks one evening.

In retrospect, he'd done her an enormous favor, unwittingly catapulting Shelby's career into an income and recognition stratosphere that garnered frequent mentions in her alma mater's *Columbia Journalism Review*. Still, there'd be no forgiving or forgetting Ian's abusive, employees-are-prisoners, management style.

And yet as he approached, he not only appeared haggard, but forlorn. His once piercing gray eyes looked as drab as cardboard. His fashion savvy still said *GQ*, but gone was the towering model's body to carry them off. It almost seemed laughable he'd ever represented such a threat to her integrity and dreams.

So why couldn't she help wonder how he was faring? Last she'd heard Ian had gone to work for fellow countryman Nigel Moore, alienating and harassing unsuspecting colleagues at the *New York Informer*, a new daily paper so racy, it often made the other tabloids in town look like church bulletins.

"Ah, there you are." Ian tossed a fellow passenger's bag onto the floor so he could squeeze in next to Shelby. "Have you thought of me? Have you missed me?" He took her hand in his and gazed into her eyes.

She almost vomited on his Harrods' engraved cuff links. "Oh yes, darling. In fact all these years I've wondered if I'd stayed at the *Free Press*, would I have been the next Mrs. McNierney?"

"You've made my day." Ian swooned, bringing her hand to his heart. "I feel complete knowing Shelby Lazarus yearned for me. A headline if ever there was one."

"Really? I prefer this headline: HORSE'S ASS MISSING; BRIT EDITOR CLAIMS RESPONSIBILITY." Shelby snorted. "Frankly, after the way you treated me back in Detroit, you deserve nothing short of death by castration. In fact, thanks to you, I always carry a knife."

Ian slowly released the clutch on her hand, then let out a laugh so boisterous it made his paunch jiggle. "My dear Shelby. Did that feel good giving me the what for? Do it again," he winked. "You know how I like 'em feisty."

"You are a sick, sick man."

"No longer. You must believe me. I've changed."

"Oh good. The world needed one less psychopath in heat."

"That's over and done with, I assure you."

"And the narcissism?"

"I think only of others."

"Ah, but have you remained faithful to your wife?"

"Please, Shelby. I said I was a changed man, not a saint. Matter of fact," he whispered, "I flew in just yesterday to rendezvous with a lovely new lady friend. God bless Viagra."

Shelby stood up and grabbed her bag. "You know what, Ian? I've had a fairly crappy day so far. Which puts me in the dubious position of asking a large favor of you."

"For you dear, anything," he crooned in his mother tongue.

"Good. Here's the drill. We need to pretend we never met. We're total strangers. Got it?"

Shelby didn't await his reply. First-class passengers were boarding, and although she was not among them today, she prayed to the God of Aviation that the gate agent would recognize her and allow her to board early.

Moments after takeoff, Shelby found herself in a surprisingly relaxed state. The narcotics, or whatever was in those little blue pills that kept her sciatic nerve in check, were performing admirably.

More importantly, the source of her pain, Ian, was nowhere in sight. Adding to her good fortune, her seatmate, a lady advertising executive from J. Walter Thompson, was cordial without being chatty. Everything was perfect, save for the fact the woman had sprayed her Guerlain fragrance too liberally. Didn't matter. Soon Shelby would drift off to a serene place where nothing and no one could penetrate her thoughts. Not David, not Lauren, not Granny Bea Good, and mostly not Ian, the scum.

Or so she thought, until her senses were suddenly jolted by whiffs of a strong scent. A male scent she guessed fell into the Polo family. Where was Ms. Guerlain? She opened her eyes and jumped upon discovering Ian in the seat beside her.

"What are you doing here? I told you to stay away from me! Where is my friend?"

"Easy there, lass. The lady is fine. I simply asked if she would be a darling and switch seats for a few minutes. And, bless her soul, she was quite nice about it."

Shelby closed her eyes and leaned back. "What do you want from me?"

"Actually, I had an epiphany during the cocktail hour," he announced, raising his plastic wine cup. "I said to myself, 'Little Shelby is quite the dandy reporter now. She should come back to work for you.' "

"Work for you? I don't want to be in the same hemisphere as you!"

"Come now. You've got to be bored silly at that little hometown paper, diddling every day with that column of yours. I've read you on-line and you carry on like a Mike Royko wanna-be."

"For your information, the *Trib* is the seventh largest circulation paper in the country, and I am honored to be compared to Royko. The man was a legend."

"Yes, yes, of course. But I'd think you'd be tickled to be in New York with the big boys."

"Why, Ian. You of all people should know size doesn't matter." She winked.

"Touché, my dear. Jolly good one. But if it's the high regard of your colleagues you desire, then you know as well as I, you're just snot in a tissue until you make it in New York."

"Oh, and like my colleagues would envy me if I joined your little rag? The only reason you have any readership at all is because the front page uses small words and big tits."

"Quite right, but maybe you'll be a tad less judgmental when Uncle Ian lets you in on a little secret. Last month I ran into your friend, Irving Davidoff, at the ANPA convention, and he was discussing your work."

"I'm sure it was all good." Shelby's pulse quickened. Hopefully. The *Trib's* tyrannical executive editor was better known for shouting obscenities than singing someone's praises.

"Oh, yes, he's quite fond of you. Although he did mention possible changes coming."

Her back stiffened. "Oh, that," Shelby said. "Every few years they bring in another high-paid consultant to redesign the paper, and no matter what, it still looks like the *Trib*."

"Actually, I believe he was referring to personnel changes." Ian coughed.

"Really?" Shelby pretended to stifle a yawn. "That's old news, too. Features and Sports let a few stringers go. I hear you get bigger shakes at McDonald's."

But, she knew full well what Ian was getting at. The biggest thing circulating at the paper for the past month were rumors of a shakeup. Not that she'd felt threatened. Only once had she received a terse note from Mr. Davidoff, and that was merely to suggest she limit her derogatory remarks about Chicago's deputy mayor. A woman Shelby subsequently discovered was the mayor's lover. And Mr. Davidoff's. Fortunately, that incident was long forgotten. She prayed.

On the other hand, even she'd had an inkling the novelty of her column was starting to wear thin. Hadn't the promotion department canceled the reorder of WE LOVE SHELBY bumper stickers? Oh God. Was Ian, the slime, implying he knew something she didn't?

"So as I was saying"—Ian waved a hand in front of her to regain her attention—"I'd think you'd jump at the chance to work under me again."

"You've got a better chance of being struck by lightning twice on the same clear day."

"Come now. We musn't live in the past. You'd have a very bright future with me."

"I'd rather cover the crime beat for the *Long Island Pennysaver*."

"Oh, me too. I love those juicy exposés on juvenile delinquents who knock over birdbaths. But wouldn't you rather be doing real in-depth reporting? Perhaps a multipart series? . . ."

"On what? The new spring line of animal-print condoms?"

"I like it. I do." Ian growled. "It's got that certain panache."

"You are such a lowlife."

"True. True. But the package I'd offer you would more than make up for that."

"Let me put this into words you'll understand. I hate you with every fiber of my being."

"So, you'll think about it?" Ian winked.

"Not even if you castrated yourself."

"Excellent then." He stood up and crawled over Shelby's feet to return to the aisle, his ass lingering in her face for just that extra moment. "Here's my card, darling. Call me."

Shelby's stomach churned. She knew this man to be many things, but not a fool. When it came to having a nose for news, a sixth sense for impending disasters, no one had his impeccable instincts. Ian McNierney was the prophet of doom.

She remained composed until she found her way to the lavatory. There, in the privacy of a two-by-two box, she grabbed a stiff paper towel and let out a wail. Was Mr. Davidoff going to have his henchmen take away her baby? Hadn't they been the ones to personally credit her column for revitalizing the stagnant Metro section? Yes, she was aware their once lavish praise was waning. But that didn't necessarily mean they were losing interest. Did it?

She would never forget the fanfare she'd received when "So Let Me Get This Straight" first appeared. Billed as the average man's revenge on inept leadership in government, education, and business, Shelby Lazarus demanded explanations from powerful people when they screwed up, and got them. But not just explanations—results!

Soon she was a star, winning over readers from Cabrini Green to Kennilworth. Then one day she was asked to speak at a civic association meeting, which led to a radio producer from WGN inviting her to cohost "Voice of Chicago." That enticed producers at Channel 7 to have her do a segment on the local evening news, which led to a chance to throw out the first pitch at Wrigley Field. Finally, she was summoned for the ultimate coup, a guest appearance on *Oprah*.

On the other hand, the more of a celebrity she'd become, the more she worried her enemies would try pulling back the curtain, revealing she was hardly the friendly, altruistic wizard the *Trib* liked to promote in its ad campaign. Not that she blamed herself for having a greater appreciation of good copy than of the poor slobs whose troubled tales she told.

Then again, so what if her job was history? If the *Trib* was stupid enough to fire her and pay out the remaining two years of her contract, word would spread faster than a computer virus. If Shelby Lazarus was available, every Pulitzer prize-seeking editor in America would go after her. Trouble was, none of their offers would come with the guarantee of celebrity. Or, the promise of being able to walk into Morton's on a Saturday night without reservations, and still be seated at an "A" table. Unless, perhaps, it was Morton's in Dubuque.

Shelby's eyes welled up. She couldn't bear the idea of having to scale Mount Journalist again. Not when she'd already paid her dues. Kissed endless asses. Proved her ability to increase circulation at every damn paper for which she'd ever worked. Honestly, was it too much to ask to be excused from all this bullshit? She was a goddamned Neiman Fellow! Surely that entitled her to be removed from the list of sacrificial lambs begging for mercy from the great King Consultant.

And now, just when this year's crop of prospective Pulitzer prize nominees was being considered, just when she was at the most vulnerable point in her career, she was missing out on a golden opportunity to cement her relationships with her bosses. All because some stupid, illegal-alien gardener had turned her father and aunt into target practice.

For the first time in years, Shelby realized only one person would know how to comfort her. Would know how to quiet her demons and make things right. "Dear God," she wept, "don't let my father die."

Chapter Three

Oy. *This isn't going well. Yes, I admit the accident with Larry and my sister, Roz, was my idea. Although believe me, I never expected it would nearly kill them. All I was trying to do was create a little excitement that would get Shelby, Lauren, and Eric to come running home. I figured if they came together in a crisis, they'd realize how nice it was to be a family again, then I could rest in peace like I'm supposed to. But noooo. Everyone has to have their own agenda.*

And by the way, who was that awful Ian fellow? I haven't a clue where he blew in from, but I do know he ruined everything. My plan was to have Shelby sit next to that nice woman in advertising so somewhere over Cleveland they could strike up a conversation. Then Shelby would discover the woman had a single brother who was a successful bond trader with a ski house in Vail. Instead, out of nowhere, this Mr. McNierney shows up, gets Shelby all worked up and good-bye nice lady with the brother. I swear I didn't see it coming.

Maybe this is why the higher powers frown on divine intervention. Unless you know what you're doing, that's some big margin for error. It reminds me of that margarine commercial where a booming voice warned people not to fool with Mother Nature.

I do suppose if any old spirit had the power to pluck loved ones from danger or hand them a royal flush in Las Vegas, life on earth would be as idyllic and carefree as it is here. And no one would learn a damn thing! That's why, in everyone's life, there are times when they are burdened with pain, adversity, sorrow, and struggle. It's pretty much the only way to get their undivided attention.

On the other hand, speaking as a mother, there is only so much wait-

ing and hoping one can do from this plane of existence. I know it seems as though the years on earth fly by, but here on the other side, eternity is more than a catchphrase. We have endless time to rest in peace. Trouble is, who can be at peace knowing their family is estranged? Lauren refuses to speak to Eric until he cleans up his substance abuse problem, Larry is fed up with Shelby's confrontational style, and Shelby is so furious with the whole gang, she severed her ties completely.

That's why I thought, let there be an accident. What better way to pull them away from their spoiled, self-indulgent worlds than to stick a major life-altering crisis under their noses?

Not that I was really convinced they'd fully understand this call to arms. Then again, I was hoping they'd surprise me. Which reminds me of my last conversation with Larry. He asked if I would prefer to be buried or cremated, and I said, "Surprise me."

Shelby exited the Northern State Parkway at Shelter Rock Road, just as she'd done hundreds of times before. Still, she never expected her rental car would somehow magically maneuver through the familiar streets as if it had been programmed like a VCR. Up the hill to the stop sign. A quick left, then a right, and she'd be back on Majestic Court. She could do this. Thomas Wolfe was wrong. You could go home. As long as you remembered to bring your key.

"Shit." She smacked the steering wheel. "How could I have forgotten my house key?" Shelby felt the sting in her hand, but at the same time became preoccupied with the stately, well-manicured homes before her. How ironic that the houses in the neighborhood had been built around the time she was born, and her first thought was how well preserved they looked. Was that how people spoke of her?

Number sixty-eight was up another block on the left. It would be so great if there was still a key in the coffee can, underneath the bathroom sink, inside the pool cabana. But then what good would that do? She'd still have to get past the alarm. One step at a time, Shelby tried to maintain her composure. Knowing Daddy, he probably hadn't changed a lightbulb in ten years, let alone an alarm code. Probably everything was exactly as it had been.

So much for that theory, Shelby slammed on the brakes. She must have driven right past her house because she suddenly found herself in front of the brick colonial where her best friend, Matthew

Lieberman, had lived. Then which one is mine? She put the car in reverse and counted backwards by three. "Oh God. That's *my* house?"

To say it bore no resemblance to the home of her youth misses the point entirely. Gone were the brown wooden shingles, the small picture window in the living room and the vanilla concrete where she and Lauren played hopscotch. Now the facade of the house had a sleek, contemporary stucco finish, two enormous columns, and a magnificent circular driveway of red brick and stone. Complementing the front was a landscape design right out of *Architectural Digest*, with no money spared on exotic shrubs and specimen plantings.

Suddenly it occurred to her this might no longer be *her* house. After all, a lot could have happened in the two years since she'd spoken to her father and Aunt Roz. Maybe they'd finally joined their empty-nester friends, who said, "To hell with high maintenance. Let's get a waterfront condo!"

That would be so typical of them to move without sending a forwarding address. Shelby smirked. Yes, it had been her idea to sever the relationship, and she still felt her decision was justified. But wasn't it a child's birthright to have last dibs on all remaining possessions before the estate sales ladies slapped price tags on your junk?

To hell with it. Shelby pulled into the driveway and headed up the steep incline to the side of the house. If some other family lived here now, she'd just say she had no idea hers had moved. And if they were as dysfunctional as everyone else, they'd surely understand. But no need to explain anything to anyone. There was her father's baby blue Jaguar XKE, a classic edition he once joked he wanted lowered into his grave. Was he crazy wishing a *ken a' hora* on himself like that? In the meantime, at least it was still his home, which gave her the inalienable right to break in. Question was, whose dilapidated Toyota was parked next to Blue?

Shelby got out of the car and followed the sounds of a loud Latin beat coming from the backyard. On tiptoes she could just peek over the top of the gate, where she glimpsed a young Spanish man sleeping on her father's custom-built chaise lounge. Someone's been drinking my tequila indeed, she shook her head, suddenly wondering if David thought she snored as loudly as this guy. Impossible. Standing next to him you wouldn't hear the Long Island Railroad coming!

She was tempted to waken the man when she noticed that the side door of the house was open. All that worrying about getting in had been such a waste. She wouldn't even have to knock.

"Hello," Shelby called when she entered, immediately taken aback by the enormity and beauty of the renovated kitchen. When did Aunt Roz acquire taste? Shelby was so captivated by the state-of-the art appliances and gleaming ceramic tiles, she jumped when the door from the basement opened and a young girl appeared.

"*Hola*," the girl said from behind a laundry basket full of folded clothes.

"*Hola* back. And who might you be?" Shelby asked while trying to estimate the amount of gold hanging from the girl's ears and neck. "Are you the weekend girl?"

The girl stared at her feet and shook her head no. "My sister. She works for the Mrs."

"Oh. So you come to do their laundry?"

Again the girl indicated no.

"Does Mrs. Lazarus know you're here?"

"My sister. She says it's okay I come. The Mrs. is no home on Sunday."

Ah-ha! One thing hadn't changed. The time-honored tradition of her father and Aunt Roz spending Sundays at Shelter Rock Country Club was still alive. "So let me get this straight," Shelby couldn't resist using her trademark line. "Your sister, who doesn't own this home, gave you permission to break in, just so you could do your laundry?"

"I no take nothing." She looked into Shelby's eyes for mercy. "Just a little soap."

"What a relief. The burglar's happy with clean sheets and towels. How did you get in?"

The girl carefully laid the basket down, dug into her pocket, and produced a familiar-looking key.

"What about the alarm?"

"My sister says not to worry. They no fix it."

"This sister of yours is quite a sharpie. Pity I won't be meeting her because here's what has to happen. You're going to give me the key, then give her a message. Tell your sister she is not to return. *¿Comprende?* No more job-ee. She's history. *Adios.*" Shelby wished she'd paid better attention in Spanish 101, but her limited command of the language seemed to be doing the trick. "Leave before I call the cops, and take Mr. Siesta with you!" Shelby opened the screen door to make sure she followed orders.

The girl handed Shelby the key and took off for her car, shouting to her husband to get up. "I no take nothing, Mrs.," she made one final plea in Shelby's direction.

I'm not a Mrs., Shelby wanted to yell back. Why did people automatically assume a woman who'd reached a certain age was someone's wife? Speaking of wives, what would her father say when he discovered *his* wife was so lame she had no idea their housekeeper had an open door policy? To their door?

And who said I didn't have a sense of humor, she thought as she watched the duo shove the laundry and the boom-box into the trunk of the Toyota? This situation was hilarious. Here her father was none other than Mr. Dri-Kleen himself, the founder and owner of the largest chain of laundromats and dry-cleaning stores in the entire Northeast. And yet total strangers preferred doing their laundry in the privacy of his basement. Did they have a thing against using quarters?

Shelby waited for them to hightail it out of the driveway before walking through the house on a reunion tour. "Whoa"—she grabbed on to a chrome-and-glass banister leading into what was now a sunken living room—"I've heard of homes settling, but not this much."

Admittedly, she loved what they'd done to the place. The furnishings were eclectic yet tasteful. The muted gray-and-beige color combination was subtle yet stunning. And the modern art hung gallery perfect, which could only mean one thing. They'd hired a Miracle Mile decorator, and there went Shelby's inheritance!

With hands on hips she surveyed the whole room. Was this her house or an ad for Fortunoff's? Gone were the humble wing-backed chairs, the velvet sofa with permanently attached slipcovers, the end tables with family photos, and what she had always viewed as the ultimate centerpiece of the room, Granny Bea Good's Steinway baby grand.

Oh God. The piano was gone. Suddenly Shelby felt an emotional attachment to an instrument on which she had never done more than bang out the beginning of "Chopsticks."

For years Aunt Roz begged her to take lessons, but gave up

when she realized if the request came from her it was a moot point. Still, Shelby would feel sick if something as precious, as beautiful, as friggin' expensive as a Steinway, had been auctioned off to the highest bidder.

I'm not so sure I want to see the rest of the house, she thought as she trudged up the long staircase to the bedrooms. Or what used to be the bedrooms. When she was growing up, the first door on the left was a combination Eric's room and shrine to the Yankees. Now it was a sleek, home office with something resembling a computer on the desk. But she must be mistaken. Her father couldn't use the microwave, let alone operate a sophisticated piece of technology requiring eye-hand coordination. Still, she hoped whoever had sold it to him had also sold him on the concept of a modem. Then she could check her e-mail and get to work on her next column. This was perfect. She'd call in sick, and no one would ever know that she left town.

Across the hall was Lauren's room. Or what was formerly her room. The walls had been blown out, creating space for a white marble and granite bath leading into the master bedroom. Shelby gently rubbed the imported Italian tiles and fixtures on the his and hers vanities when a noxious thought occurred to her. Who needed a Jacuzzi tub and bidet unless they were having sex? Gross! She shut the door in hopes of shutting the idea from her mind.

The guest room was the next surprise. Unless she threw a mattress on top of the treadmill, there was no place to sleep here, either. But who cared? The official Lazarus home gym offered the latest, greatest equipment and a mounted television, too. She was goddamn Shelbylocks. Everything was just right. First she could work, then she could work out.

Still, she wondered what they had against guest rooms. I guess after you piss every one off, you never have to worry about putting them up for the night, she thought as she walked to the end of the hallway. God willing they'd had the good sense to keep her old room intact for company, because she certainly wasn't sleeping in their bed.

As she reached her old bedroom, she suddenly felt anxious. Why was her door closed when all the others were left open? The reporter in her found that disturbing until she twisted the handle, peeked inside, and discovered the reason.

Her once beautiful room was now a veritable warehouse of Lazarus archives, with packing boxes stacked from floor to ceiling. Where was her white canopy bed? Her antique rocker and armoire? What right did they have to dismantle her room without her express written consent? She wasn't in the state of New York. She was in the state of shock.

Thankfully, she realized one familiar item remained. The pink-and-creme floral Laura Ashley wallpaper she and her mother had picked out at the D & D building in Manhattan was still looking classic and elegant. She remembered how her father had carried on when he'd found the bill. But the only bill Shelby and her mother cared about was the Bill who spent several days hanging the delicate paper.

Shelby looked wistfully at the rubble. Should she sift through it on a digging expedition? She was a reporter, not an archaeologist. On the other hand, maybe she'd unearth some profound discoveries that would shed insight as to why her family life had ultimately un-raveled. But what difference would it make now? The contents of her childhood had already been reduced to three boxes and an A & S shopping bag. Game over.

Just as she was about to close the door she noticed her name scribbled in magic marker on the side of a box that once contained a shiny new G.E. toaster oven. As she reached for it, she tripped over a table fan from sleepaway camp and stooped to retrieve it. She blew off the thick coat of dust and found a faded heart in nail polish with the initials SL and ML. Matty Lieberman, of course. Her one true love. Until the rat fink moved to California and broke his promise to keep her in his heart forever.

Shelby tore open the box and made a mental note to search for Matthew Lieberman on the Internet again. The last time she'd logged on to a website that helped reunite loved ones, she'd located three males in the Los Angeles area with the same name. Trouble with them was they weren't old enough to drive, let alone propose marriage. Although one courageous kid suggested they meet. "No thanks," she e-mailed back. "I'm no Mrs. Robinson. I have pocket-books older than you. "

But now as she sifted through bags of mementos, it occurred to her that she might never find Matty. Never learn how his life turned out. What if he was married? What if he wasn't? Then again, why dredge up her past? The whole point of denial was never having to say you remember.

Ah, yes. Denial. Shelby was eleven the first time she heard the word used in association with her name. It oozed from the mouth of a child psychologist her father insisted she see after her mother died. "The man works wonders with grieving kids, Shelby. I think he can help you, too."

But after two months of Aunt Roz shuttling Shelby from Hebrew School straight to therapy, Shelby announced she'd had it with Dr. Israel's stupid, yellow beanbag chair and his invitations to visit his candy drawer. Did he really think she'd spill her guts in exchange for a handful of Sno-Caps? Shelby knew the score. The way he'd justify his outrageous fees was by running back to her father, spiral notebook flapping, and repeating her privatemost thoughts.

Fortunately for Shelby, the doctor was equally frustrated with her. In all his years in practice, never before had he given up on a patient. But this child was beyond his help. Defensive. Confrontational. "Da Queen of Da Nile," he declared.

Shelby remembered looking up *denial* in the dictionary. "An assertion that something said, believed, or alleged is false." *Exactly*. She slapped the page. Her father kept insisting she needed help, but he was wrong. If anyone should have their head examined, it should be him.

He was the one who fell for Aunt Roz's tricks and got stuck having to marry her. He was the one who packed up every picture of her mother and stored them in the attic so there were no sad reminders in the house. He was the one who totally ignored her and Lauren after Eric was born, acting as though his new wife's son was more important than his own biological children.

And what was so wrong with letting her deal with her pain in her own way? It wasn't that she never cried. She never cried in front of others. It wasn't that she was taking out her anger on Lauren by calling her names and smacking her around. She was just trying to toughen the kid up a little. Life in their house would be an endless barrage of insults and humiliation. She just wanted her baby sister to learn how to fight back. And, by no means was it that she'd lost interest in school or her friends. It's that they were clueless what it was like to experience such a profound loss. No amount of getting Barbie and Ken ready for the prom or getting picked by the teacher to clean the blackboards would change a goddamn thing.

Denial, my ass, she thought, then and now. I know the bitter truth better than anyone!

Still, not all of Shelby's recollections were depressing. When she uncovered a musty, brown envelope filled with ribbons for her prize-winning soccer, equestrian, and swimming achievements, she had to admit it was sweet of Aunt Roz to have kept the entire collection intact. After Shelby graduated and left home, she could easily have thrown them into the trash. Who would have blamed her for trying to even the score with the vindictive one?

And maybe if she'd been sensitive enough to save a bunch of cheap, meaningless ribbons, she'd also held on to her stepdaughter's other prized possessions. Sure enough, as she dug farther, she found a small box of award certificates and laughed. Maybe she would hang these in her office. For no one who knew Shelby Lazarus today would ever believe she'd once served as her youth group's social action chair, raising thousands of dollars to help the homeless.

Ah! And here was real proof of her once charitable demeanor. A personal letter from her congressman thanking her for her humanitarian efforts on behalf of Soviet Jewry. It was dated June 1969. Six months before her mother died. Shelby sighed. So fine. Maybe there was a correlation between losing her mother and losing all interest in benevolent acts.

Just as Shelby was about to close the box, she spotted an envelope labeled "Shelby—Spelling bees." Again she smiled. Perhaps she'd given up on being charitable, but never on English. In her youth she was considered the Zen Master of Manhasset. For six straight years she slew the competition at her elementary school's annual bee. And yet this achievement paled in comparison to the time she skewered her arrogant, testy principal.

She wondered if Dr. Dellarusso had ever forgotten the day he dared embarrass her in front of the student body and their parents. Certainly she would always remember being called up to receive the award for winning her sixth and final bee, while the sadist mocked Shelby for being, ironically, the daughter of Mr. Dri-Kleen. "How does he spell that again?" The evil man laughed.

Rather than take the punch, Shelby got up and challenged the squat, little man to a spelling dual. Dr. Dellarusso wiped his brow and politely declined, citing the need to get on with the program. But when Larry Lazarus, Mr. Dri-Kleen himself, stood up and insisted the man take on his daughter, the audience applauded wildly and the judges consented. Ten minutes later a castrated principal bowed to the champion when he failed to spell *obsequious* correctly.

Suddenly, the sound of a car door slamming stopped Shelby's nostalgia train. She ran to the window, thankful she was in the room called Lookout Point, the only place upstairs offering a view of both the front and side of the house. Whenever Shelby whistled Daddy and Aunt Roz were back, Eric and Lauren would have just enough time to get rid of the joints and throw towels under the door to keep the sweet, telltale aroma from escaping.

She looked out, gasping at the sight of a gleaming, black sedan parked next to Blue. With the bright sun in her eyes she couldn't be certain, but it looked like a limousine. Or for a second, in a scary sort of hallucinatory way, it resembled a hearse. Which made her heart pound. Up until now she'd refused to consider the possibility that she'd come home to bury another parent.

The thought immobilized her. As did the idea that Aunt Roz might be in a coma, in which case the baton would be handed to her, the oldest child, to make all those morbid, grown-up-type decisions. Street clothes or shroud? Open or closed casket? Graveside or funeral chapel?

Suddenly she felt so dizzy she had to grab hold of a dusty floor lamp. She wasn't good at this sort of thing. Track down a source? No one ever eluded her. Demand answers? There wasn't any story she couldn't get to the bottom of. But jump in and be the mature adult who knew intuitively how to handle these situations? That's what parents were for, dammit!

Chapter Four

"Hello?" a man called out from downstairs.

Shelby raced out of her room and flew down the stairs into the kitchen, startling a stocky man with dark eyes and even darker curls. "Who are you?" she tried to catch her breath.

The man smiled. "Who em I?" he said with an Israeli accent, thick as desert air. "I'm Avi Streiffler. Are you Shelby?"

He knew her name? "Yes. Are you from the funeral home?" Her heart pounded.

"The funeral home?" Avi seemed more confused than Shelby. "I don't think so."

She sized up the man's black suit and dark shades. "Then you must be my father's driver."

"Once in a while yes." He laughed. "But all the time I em your sister's husband."

"Her husband?" Shelby was stunned to hear the words. When had Lauren remarried?

"It's a year next month." He easily read her mind. "Phew. That was some big party we had. We wanted to invite you, but no one thought you'd come in. Would you have come in?"

"I don't know." Shelby looked away, stung by the revelation the score was now a lopsided Lauren two weddings, Shelby none. And from the looks of this creep, how long could the marriage last? A year tops? Man. It would totally suck if her sister was already on to husband number three before she'd gotten to walk down the aisle at all. Not that she was feeling any pressure.

So you're the famous Shelby." Avi squeezed her so tight her back cracked. "We're family." He rested his head on her shoulder.

Shelby pulled away, certain she knew the difference between familial love and lust.

"My God. It's hard to bee-lieve you and Lauren are sisters." The bulge in his pants proved her point. "You're blond. She's dark. You have eyes as green as the Mediterranean Sea. Hers are brown. I think. You're tall and thin. She's . . . not. You won't tell her I said that?"

"Trust me, your secret is safe." Asshole. "So. Have you seen them?"

"Oy, my God, it's unbee-lievable what heppened." He smacked his hands together to demonstrate the impact. "I don't know what I would do if they were gone." He sat down at the table and began to sob. "They're my Ameriken family. Could you make me tea?"

Tea? What did she look like? Betty Crocker? On the other hand, what excuse did she have not to oblige? She wasn't rushing off on a story assignment. She didn't have whiny kids pulling at her leg. "Sure. Where's the tea thing?" she asked innocently.

He looked up in amazement, his tears suddenly evaporating. "You mean the kettle?"

"I guess. I don't know. It's been years since I drank the stuff."

"Never mind." Avi got up and headed to the fridge. "They have iced tea."

"How did you know I flew in?" Shelby followed him.

"I didn't."

"Then why are you here? Shouldn't you be at the hospital?"

"I just was there. What about you?" Avi shut the fridge with his foot as one hand held a can of iced tea, the other, packages of deli meat.

"Maybe later," she mumbled as she calculated the calories on his plate of roast beef, corned beef, mayo, and rye. How she used to love the salty taste of cold cuts on fresh, chewy bread. Now she wouldn't consume that many calories in a week, although it dawned on her she hadn't eaten today and was feeling a wee bit hungry. But obviously given what Avi was feasting on, Roz's kitchen remained a veritable carbohydrate convention, unsafe at any speed.

"What ken I do at the hospital?" Avi built a mile-high sandwich. "Am I a doctor? No."

"So you figured what the hell? I'll go over to their place and have lunch." Shelby opened the refrigerator to assess her limited options. Whoa! Fat free yogurt? Where am I?

"Exactly. And to catch a little of the Mets game before I get my four o'clock at JFK."

"Aren't we the concerned next of kin?" Shelby found fresh salad, too. Maybe Roz finally wised up that the AMA wasn't kidding about the connection between high cholesterol and strokes.

"What did you say?" Avi looked up, his large nose peered through his drinking glass.

"Nothing. How's Lauren?" Shelby closed the fridge. She'd eat later when she was alone.

"Lauren is Lauren," he shrugged. "She's completely hysterical. You kent even talk to her."

"What do you expect? Her parents were almost killed."

"You seem to be taking it okay," he yawned.

"You know nothing about me," Shelby snarled. Stop looking at my legs, you oversize, oversexed buffoon.

"I know what I know." Avi turned on the TV. "Lauren says yure an emotional misfit."

"Me?" Shelby bellowed, hands on hips. "What about her? What is she this week? An Orthodox, vegetarian, Feng Shui, tree hugger, who's trying to save the whales in Kosovo?"

"What ken I say? She has a big heart." He channel surfed for the Mets game.

And a big wallet, Shelby thought. "And, what do we know about you, other than you drive a limousine and are obviously unaware of something called fat grams?"

"You want to know about me?" He chomped down on the sloppy sandwich with gusto and a wink. "I'm a musician. One day my songs will be famous on the radio. Like Billy Joel."

"Uh-huh," Shelby watched Avi devour his food. "And until then you make airport runs?"

"You never know," he shrugged. "Maybe tomorrow I pick up Madonna. Lest week I drove a second cousin of David Geffen. I said to her, 'Give David my tape.' "

Avi's wishful thinking was interrupted by the phone. They looked at each other. Who would answer? The estranged daughter or the freeloading son-in-law? He blinked first.

"Guess who's here?" He managed to take another large bite.

A moment later he returned his attention to Shelby. "It's Lauren. She says to come right over to the hospital. They're both still in surgery."

Shelby shook her head no.

"She says no," Avi repeated to Lauren. "She wants to know why not?" he asked Shelby.

Shelby grabbed the receiver. "Hi, it's me. I came in, okay? But, you know damn well why I can't go over there. I figured I'd man the fort here. Make phone calls. Order dinner . . ."

Shelby stared at the phone, stunned to hear a dial tone for the second time that day. "Does she ever finish a conversation?"

"What?" Avi was already engrossed in his stupid baseball game.

"Oh, crap." Shelby looked over at the TV. Avi wasn't just watching any game. It was the Mets versus the Cubs. The very game she would have been at if not for this nightmare. Her heart sank as she studied the crowd for signs of backstabbing colleagues fawning over her bosses.

"It's not so bad." Avi winked. "The Cubs are only down by a run."

"I could give a rat's ass what the score is," Shelby yelled, heading back upstairs. "And next time you see your darling wife, tell her to go fuck herself and that horse she likes to ride in on."

"Maybe you should tell her." Avi chugged the last of his drink. "If I know my darling wife, she's on her way over."

Whoever said that opposites attract never met my daughters. From the start, the only thing these two girls had in common was a last name. Larry shrugged it off to the six-year age difference, but Dr. Spock he wasn't. In my opinion, the problem was karma. Simply, Lauren came into this life as the chalkboard; Shelby, the fingernails..

Shelby was ambitious and organized. Lauren wouldn't be able to find her shoes if they were already on her feet, and she wasn't about to get up and look for them either. Shelby was a straight "A" student, Lauren brought home the occasional "C," which was a relief since the rest of her grades were generally below that. Shelby was the world's youngest women's libber, ready to burn my bra, as she wasn't old enough to have one of her own. Lauren lived in a deep fantasy world that included a husband, two children, and a yearly vacation at the Fontainebleu Hotel.

Then again, Lauren was the one with the big heart. If asked for the shirt off her back, she'd easily give you that one, and two others. Shelby would gladly give up her shirt, too, but only after she cooked up a way to get it replaced with a more expensive one that matched the new pants.

Lauren was the one with dozens of friends, most of whom thought our refrigerator was community property. Shelby was so particular about who monopolized her time, she more often than not chose to stay home and read. Lauren was the one who would feel your pain. Shelby was the pain.

So I guess I'm not surprised the girls never found common bonds as adults, either. It was really no different for Roz and me. We argued about everything, to say nothing of the rivalry.

Don't think I didn't know how crazy my sister was about Larry. As soon as he and I started dating, it was obvious she had a crush on him. The first clue was she always managed to be home when he came to pick me up. The second clue was she was always dressed nicely when he arrived. Hair set? Check. Lipstick on? Check. Big old girdle in place? Check. It was as if she'd hired herself to play the understudy, ready to perform in the unlikely event the star of the show suddenly quit. Or died.

But Larry was smitten with me. She knew it. I knew it. And she knew I knew it. For her own sake I begged her to stop making a fool of herself. Why would this man be interested in roly-poly Roz, a little girl six years his junior, when he could be seen with me, a petite blonde with brains who my best friend swore filled out a sweater better than Doris Day?

Looking back, the only thing we ever did agree on was we both wanted to live my life. And ultimately my little sister got her wish. Before my body turned cold, she was living in my home, sleeping with my husband, raising my children, and driving my new, canary yellow Cadillac convertible with power windows. Which speaks volumes about playing the understudy.

Don't get me wrong. In a way I was glad that Larry married Roz. After all, she was family. I knew she would love and protect my girls as her own, plus she would make Larry proud on bowling night. Even better, her fast move automatically eliminated the competition, those awful, frosted blond divorcées at the club who thought they invented stretch pants and cleavage.

On the other hand, it is also true that when Lauren was born, my first wish was that she and Shelby would fare better in the sisters sweepstakes than Roz and I. Sadly, the irony has not been lost on me that history does appear to be repeating itself.

Oh, shoot! Look. It's Lauren driving down Community Drive like she's Maria Andretti in the Indy 500. She must be headed over to the house.

Slow down, honey. We've already had enough innocent pedestrians turned into projectile weapons today. Why don't they ever listen?

Shelby could not get over the fact the day had started as any other, yet here she was, hours later, in her old house on Long Island, seated at her father's massive, custom-designed desk. She also could not fathom what was he doing with a powerful computer and a cable line hooked up to his modem? Were his on-line needs so great he required an instant connection?

Only last week, ironically, she'd written a column about senior citizens afraid of using computers for fear of catching one of those mysterious, incurable viruses they kept hearing about. "Techno-chondriacs." Yes. That's what she'd called them. And although she hadn't said as much, based on her father's long-standing reluctance to embrace anything more high-tech than a cordless phone, she was certain he was a member of this low-functioning crowd. But obviously not.

First jogging, now computers. What was next for him? Honesty as a policy? And what's your screen name, Daddy? Shelby pondered. MeMeMe@AOL.com?

She casually leaned back in his immense black leather swivel chair to contemplate the new man her father had become, when without warning, she was nearly catapulted over the back. "Whoa." She grabbed hold of the wide arms to regain her balance. "This isn't a chair. It's a friggin' ride at Coney Island."

"That'll teach you to insult your father," the voice of Granny Bea Good piped in.

"Oh, shush," Shelby replied. "Stop defending him, okay? You know what he did."

"He's still your father."

"Fine. I get the point. Now go back to watching *One Life to Live*."

Shelby made sure her feet were planted firmly on the floor before resting her elbows on the cool surface of the desk. Which was precisely the moment she noticed the photo frame in the corner. On one side was a picture of a smiling Dad and Aunt Roz showing off their coveted bowling trophies. Opposite that, a picture of a giggling Lauren and Shelby holding rainbow lollipops the size of their sweet little faces. I remember that day. Shelby sighed.

It was taken B.C. Before the cancer. All Sandy had wanted was to surprise Larry with a nice, new picture of the girls on Father's Day. But Shelby and Lauren behaved so badly, the photographer threw a temper tantrum to equal theirs. Finally, his weary assistant handed the girls giant suckers, and bingo, they were as smiley-faced as child models. Pity no one snapped a picture after the lady took the suckers back. Now there was a photo op!

Although Shelby had to admit she and Lauren looked darling, it struck her as odd the only picture of her on display was one taken over thirty years ago. And Daddy accuses me of living in the past, she thought. The good news, on the other hand, was at least they'd finally had the good sense to get rid of that awful family photo taken the week Eric opened his ski shop in Vail.

Five years earlier, Shelby had flown out to Denver with Lauren, her father, and Aunt Roz for his grand opening, and if tension could power a plane, there would have been no need for a tail wind. In the span of a few hours the only topic of conversation was the skimpiness of the bag of peanuts since President Reagan forced the country to swallow airline deregulation. Yet hours later, when a photographer Eric hired yelled "money," they did what came naturally. They stood close and high-beamed their pearly whites.

If she were lucky, that photograph was now part of the rubble in her room, a sign of surrender from Aunt Roz that she'd given up perpetuating the myth they were one, big, happy family. The more likely scenario, however, was that Roz probably tossed the picture after realizing her darling Eric looked stoned, and she looked like a fat, middle-aged cow. Served her right for thinking she could pass herself off as Sophia Loren, just because she bought the same red, billowy ski bib after seeing the actress model it in *People*.

Shelby gently placed the photo back in the corner and picked up a silver Mont Blanc pen from its engraved caddy. As she stroked the cool barrel, she realized the pen wasn't the only thing in its proper place. The entire office was tidy and organized. A housekeeper's delight. But how had her father, the King of Clutter, managed such a feat? His office at the plant was legendary for being such a mess he used to joke about dying young, just so the cleaning crew could get a head start. And maybe find Jimmy Hoffa.

She'd always thought it sick that a man who lost his beautiful wife to cancer would take mortality so lightly. And yet her father thought nothing of joking about his death. But now, as Shelby studied his picture and looked deep into the gleam in his eye, she suddenly understood. In his lifetime he'd already experienced the loss of his true love, and with that loss, unspeakable grief. What then was left to fear? Nothing. Therefore, he could tempt fate at whim. Or so he thought. Maybe this accident wasn't as random as it appeared. Maybe he was getting a sign to stop joking around and start accounting for his sins. And maybe she was the one to tell him so.

Of course. She would send him an e-mail with her revelation. And if he was truly a changed man, he would gladly receive her message. But just as she turned on the computer, she heard Lauren call out. "Shel-bee?"

Shelby was tempted not to answer, although it was probably too late to hide. Better to get the formalities over with and move on to the fighting. Yet even before she could announce her whereabouts, the swivel chair spun around so fast she nearly got thrown off. "Jesus! This thing needs a seat belt." Then her eyes met her sister's, and she gasped. Lauren was easily twenty-five pounds heavier than the last time she saw her. And that was what, only two years ago?

"Good God, honey. How do you get your jeans on? With a pliers and a prayer?"

Now it was Lauren's turn to gasp. She cried out in anguish, nearly flinging a crystal desk clock if a fast-thinking Avi hadn't followed her into the room and released his wife's clutch. "Girls. Girls. This is how to behave?"

"I told you I shouldn't have called her." Lauren punched Avi's arm. "Didn't I say she was the meanest thing?" She sobbed on his shoulder.

"What did I say?" Shelby feigned innocence. "I was merely remarking it looks like you've put on a little weight since the last time I saw you. Don't be so touchy. Relax."

Lauren tried to speak but sputtered instead.

"Sh, sh, sh," Avi gently patted her back and glared at Shelby. "Ken't you see we're suffering? Our parents' lives are in jeopardy, and all you ken think about is the crazy scale?"

Our parents? Shelby did a double take. Did someone say *inheritance*?

Avi looked at his watch and pecked Lauren's wet cheek. "Avi Bear's got to go. I have a four at JFK and a six-thirty at Newark."

Avi Bear? Shelby felt a twinge of nausea watching Avi embrace her sister.

"You okay?" He wiped away her tears. "Try deep breathing. Get in touch with your chi."

"It won't help," Lauren cried out. "I can't deal with her and deal with them . . ."

"Be nice," Avi warned Shelby. "We're under terrible stress, she's on medication . . . "

Shelby signaled she could take it from here. "Go. She'll be fine. This is old turf."

Lauren's eyes opened wide. "Old turf?" She tried to storm off, but Shelby grabbed her arm.

"C'mon, Lauren. Stay. I'll make you some tea."

"I heard you don't know how." Lauren pushed Shelby away and ran down the stairs.

"Yes, but you do," Shelby followed. "I like that lemon zinger stuff you used to whip up."

Lauren's attitude softened, as it always did when Shelby made an effort.

But the only conscious effort Shelby could make was refraining from lecturing Lauren about her high percentage of body fat. Yes, it was a pity she'd inherited the short, stocky Lazarus gene, but all the more reason to diet. They'd have a little talk about vanity when Lauren was in a better mood. Now it was probably best to chitchat. "So"—she clapped—"how did you two meet?"

"Shel-bee! Aren't you even going to ask how Mommy and Daddy are doing?"

"She's not your mother. Must we go down this road again?"

"Why?" Lauren wiped her eyes. "Is it out of your way?"

"Yes, and we've been through this a million times. It's a simple concept. Roz is our aunt."

Lauren filled the kettle while taking deep breaths to settle her nerves. "You call her whatever you want, but to me she's Mommy. Okay? It's not my fault the woman who gave birth to me died when I was four, and much as I try, I don't remember her."

"Well I do, and trust me on this, Aunt Roz was a lousy consolation prize."

"Enough!" Lauren slammed the kettle on the stove. "Leave her alone, Shelby. Please."

Shelby sighed. Touchy, touchy, touchy. "Fine. Sorry. I'll start over. Tell me what happened. Tell me how they are."

But no sooner did Lauren try to bring Shelby up to date than the floodgates opened. Family and friends began calling and stopping by, each one hungry for information. How did the accident happen? What were the doctors saying about Larry's and Roz's prognoses? What could they do to help? Translated, should they send over dinner or dessert? A brisket or a babka?

"It's Dr. Gold," Shelby covered the mouthpiece on the phone. "I can't remember. Is he the dentist from the club, or that lunatic chiropractor from across the street who pees on his lawn?"

"Neither," Lauren interrupted her cell phone conversation. "I think he's Daddy's podiatrist. No wait. His proctologist."

"He wants to know if they were knocked unconscious."

Suddenly Lauren broke down like a '57 Chevy. "Daddy was. Mommy wasn't, poor thing. She was just lying there in her own blood, screaming for help. She couldn't even move her legs. Couldn't tell if Daddy was dead or alive. That's probably when she went into shock."

Shelby took a deep breath and repeated the story, grateful for her years of experience as a detached reporter who could deliver information without emotion. But after the first few calls it dawned on her that people weren't calling to offer comfort. They were calling to receive it.

"I know. I know. It's a nightmare. But don't worry Mrs. Kaplan. I'm sure they'll be fine."

"Yes. Such a terrible shame. It could be months before they rejoin the bowling league."

"No, really. Go see the movie. I'll leave a message the second I hear anything."

Or worse, they wouldn't hang up until Shelby agreed to consult with *their* doctors, presumably the only medical practitioners on earth who could save Larry and Roz.

"Really? Harold doesn't limp anymore. That is amazing."

"A healer? I don't think so. No, I'm sure he's the best, it's just not our style. Oh. I see. Lauren asked you for his name . . ."

In one sense, Shelby was grateful for the barrage of inquiries, as it gave her no time to think. On the other hand, as the grim details of the accident unfolded, reality hit hard. No amount of reporter's objectivity could negate the facts. Her father and Aunt Roz had suffered serious, life-threatening injuries and the next twenty-four hours were critical.

Chapter Five

"Is this the home of Lawrence and Rosalyn Lazarus?" a young boy in shirt and tie asked.

"Yes," Shelby replied. "Can I help you?"

"Ma'am, I'm Richard Rienzo from *Newsday*. Do you mind if I ask you a few questions about this morning's accident?"

This kid was a reporter? He barely looked old enough to deliver the paper.

"Sure. Come on in," Shelby led him into the living room and extended her hand. "I'm Shelby Lazarus. *Chicago Tribune.*"

The cub looked baffled. What didn't ring a bell? Chicago, or the *Tribune*?

"Whoa. They must be pretty important people if the out-of-town papers are here."

Shelby sighed. Had a village reported a missing idiot? "Hello? I'm family of the victims?"

"Oh. Got it. Actually, your name is familiar. Maybe later I should ask you about a job."

"Don't you already have a job? Isn't that what brought you here?"

"No, it's just a summer internship. But I'll be graduating from Ithaca next year and then . . ."

Jesus! A celebrated member of the press suffered a tragedy and the best *Newsday* could do was send over a kid who still needed his ass wiped?

"Okay. First rule of thumb, Richard. Never hit on a source. It could really piss them off. Particularly if they're in the middle of a personal crisis."

"Right. Of course. Sorry." He cleared his throat. "I'm sure this is very difficult for you. I'll need just a few more minutes of your time."

Shelby's heart raced as the kid sorted through his notes, rattling on in graphic detail without so much as a wince. "Lawrence Lazarus, sixty-five, and Rosalyn Lazarus, fifty-nine, while out on a morning jog, were struck from behind on Royal Lane, Manhasset, by the driver of a 1993 Ford pickup, a Mr. Juan Pedro Martinez, thirty-two. Both victims were rushed to North Shore University Hospital, where they remain in critical condition. It is believed Mr. Lazarus, found unconscious at the scene, suffered the most extensive injuries, contusions over 40 percent of his body, collapsed lungs, fractured ribs, a fractured hip, sprained neck, a ruptured spleen. Mrs. Lazarus suffered multiple abrasions of the head and chest, a fractured nose, broken arm and leg . . ."

As the kid droned on, all Shelby could think of was how bitter the medicine tasted when it was hers to swallow. Didn't this callous, mechanical moron with a pen understand he was speaking about her flesh and blood? How could he be so insensitive? And yet she knew better than anyone, learning to feel nothing came more easily than one would suspect.

"It's why they call it a *story*," Ian McNierney used to drum into her head. "It's not real. Unless, of course, you're the bloody victim, and then it's very real. But that's none of your concern."

"Who's at the door?" Lauren called out from the kitchen.

Clark Kent, Jr., she was tempted to say. "A reporter from *Newsday*," Shelby yelled back.

"Oh God." Lauren rushed in to peer out the living room window. "Not the damn media."

"Excuse me?" Shelby stood, hands on hips. "Do we have a problem with the press?"

"Sorry." Lauren blushed. "I forgot. But you understand, Shel. Who needs to be exploited at a time like this? You think Channel 7 is on their way over? Maybe I should go change."

"This is my sister, Lauren . . . what did you say your new last name was again?"

"Richard Rienzo from *Newsday*." He shook Lauren's hand.

Thataboy Richie, Shelby thought. Get over it. Who wants to waste time speaking to a lowly print journalist when the possibility exists they can see themselves on the evening news?

"Can you tell us anything about the savage beast who hit them?" Lauren wiped her nose.

"Yeah, did they arrest the guy?" Shelby piped in. "We heard he tried to flee the scene."

Richard flipped to the back of his notepad. "Actually, ma'am, the vehicle was impounded, but there was no immediate evidence of mechanical failure, although further testing will be done in the next few days. License and registration were valid, the driver had no priors, no DWI . . ."

"What about a green card?" Shelby sniffed. "Is the guy here legally? What do you bet he's halfway back to the Dominican Republic by now."

"No, ma'am. I just spoke to him a little while ago. He's over at the hospital. He's all shook up. This is the first time anything like this has ever happened to him. He owns the landscaping company, the truck, a nice home, he has a family . . ."

"I didn't see him at the hospital," Lauren said. "Was he hurt?"

"No, it seems he's there on a vigil now. He's very concerned about your parents."

"No, he's concerned about us pressing charges," Shelby said. "Why did he try to flee?"

"Actually, according to the police report, he was running for help. In fact, a witness corroborated that the man flagged down a motorist and used her cell phone to call an ambulance."

"I don't understand," Lauren cried. "If he's such a nice man, why did he hit them?"

"He said he was doing the speed limit but the glare from the morning sun was so bad he couldn't see a thing, and then boom! Until he got out of the truck he had no idea what he hit."

"The poor man," Lauren cried. "We have to talk to him, Shelby. Tell him we forgive him."

"Sure. Let's bring him a bottle of wine, too. Are you crazy? No contact, Lauren. I mean it. Next thing you know you'll be inviting him for Thanksgiving. Let the attorneys handle this."

Shelby then thanked the reporter for his time, making sure he understood he'd just been dismissed. Better to get rid of him before he remembered he wanted to pump her about a job.

"*Let's go tell him we forgive him,*" Shelby mimicked as she returned to the kitchen.

Lauren followed, then took one look at the feast on the table and couldn't resist. "Wasn't that reporter nice?" She nibbled from the tray of cookies.

"Lovely." Shelby watched her in horror. "Doesn't this feel really creepy to you?"

"No." Lauren attacked a platter of cold cuts and coleslaw from Ben's Kosher Deli.

"Well it does to me. People are treating us like we're already sitting *shiva*."

"No, they're just being nice." Lauren gobbled down two chocolate *rugalach*, spraying crumbs all over the clean, ceramic tiles.

"Look what you're doing." Shelby bent down to wipe up the mess. Same old Lauren. A balanced diet was a cookie in each hand. "You're being such a slob."

"Forget it. Maria comes tomorrow."

"Not if she's Maria, the housekeeper with the sister," Shelby examined her manicure.

At last. Something got Lauren to stop chewing. "What do you mean?"

"I mean when I got here, I found some Spanish chick doing her laundry, and when she said she didn't work for the Mrs., but her sister did, and she said it was okay to be here, I told her to tell her very generous sister neither of them should bother coming back. Basically, I fired her."

"Oh God, Shelby. Mommy and Daddy love Maria. They know about her sister. She's been doing it for years. How could you just walk into someone's house and fire their maid?"

"First of all, it's not someone's house. It's my house. Sort of."

"Never mind." Lauren sighed. "I'll straighten it out with her later. Let's just get over to the hospital. Daddy might be in recovery by now."

Shelby shook her head no.

"What does that mean." Lauren imitated Shelby's head shaking.

"It means you know why I can't go there. I think I'll go find a hotel for tonight."

"That's ridiculous." Lauren tried to sneak a cookie behind Shelby's back. "Stay here."

"Where here? There aren't any extra bedrooms, no pull-out couches . . ."

"I know. They built a guesthouse out behind the cabana."

"A guesthouse? Are you serious? Who are they? Mr. and Mrs. Bill Gates?"

"No, but last year after Daddy sold the business they got a little antsy and decided to renovate the house. Then they got the idea to add on. Come. I'll show you. It's really cool. "

Her father had finally retired? Shelby was busting to know how much he got for the business, but before she could pump Lauren for details, the phone rang. Lauren rolled her eyes as if to say, who is it this time? Mrs. Epstein calling to see if Larry is a widower and in need of her famous potato kugel? Trouble was it wasn't a friend.

"Oh, my God," Lauren cried out, clutching the phone to her heart. "Daddy's in distress."

"Define distress."

"I can't," she whispered. "It's too scary to say."

Shelby took a deep breath. Was it all over but the crying? "C'mon." She smoothed Lauren's hair and gently hung up the phone. "I'll drive you over there. Maybe you can give blood."

Oh boy. This is never going to work. Shelby's been avoiding hospitals for almost thirty years, particularly North Shore. I doubt she's suddenly going to change her mind and walk through those front doors as if it's just some large, innocuous place to visit the sick. Not when she still holds them accountable for my death.

Lauren, naturally, was too young to remember my final days, but Shelby was wise beyond her ten years. No matter how hard Larry tried assuring her the doctors were doing their best to save me, she knew he was lying, and worse, she knew my doctor had screwed up. Frankly, she was right. Had my initial complaints been taken seriously by him, I'd probably still be on your side.

The year was 1969. One day I had two young children, a beautiful home on Long Island, a loving marriage and a lethal, unreturnable backhand, and next thing I know I'm in my gynecologist's office. It wasn't easy trying to follow Dr. Weiner's thick, German rambling about my test results, which were supposed to explain my recent problems with bloating and constipation. Finally, I heard the words, stage-three ovarian cancer. And something about his being very sorry. And surprised. Rarely did this deadly disease strike women so young.

But lest we forget, in the late sixties, when in spite of, or maybe because of all those burning bras, the medical community still viewed women as the hysterical sex. More times than not our concerns were written off as "kvetching." Which explains why half the gals in my tennis league had hysterectomies. Whatever ailed us, the cure was removal of the ovaries, and voilà, we were Henry Higgins's dream date.

The whole thing reminded me of that old joke. What's a Jewish girl's favorite wine? "I want to go to Florida!" So when I complained to Dr. Weiner I was bloated, constipated, and so very tired, he just shrugged and said in his native bratwurst, "It's nothink, Sandy. You haf vat I call One-a-Dayitis." In other words, there was no need to bother with medication or tests. All I needed was proper nutrition and a good multivitamin.

"And tell that cheap, bastard husband of yours to take you on a nice vacation," the good doc said. Little did I know, six months later I'd be taking the longest vacation of my life. Death.

Anyway, during those final weeks I was in and out of North Shore, Larry pleaded with Shelby to write me nice, cheery notes, rather than visit. But she wouldn't hear of it, carrying on until Roz or my mother drove her over to see me. It was then I saw firsthand what a keen observer she'd become. No matter how pleasant the nurses acted, no matter how bright a picture the doctors painted about this new treatment or that new drug, she saw through the whites of their lab coats. They knew nothing and did even less, save for that one compassionate nurse who kept upping my morphine drip when the pain became unbearable.

Now, of course, I can see Larry was right to want to shelter Shelby from all this. Ever since my death, she's been so terrified of anything medical, she once had to be put under for a bikini wax. And the closest she ever came to seeing a doctor was dating one. Heaven forbid this child of mine ever gets sick!

Shelby was glad Lauren's car was blocking her rental in the driveway. Now Lauren would have to offer to drive and be the one to deal with the lousy hospital parking.

"*Yes.*" Lauren clapped upon miraculously finding a spot in the always packed, three-story garage. "It's our lucky day."

Our lucky day? Are you serious? Shelby didn't budge.

"Shelby?" Lauren said in her imitation Ricky Ricardo accent? "I can't do this."

"What do you mean? Daddy's in distress. You have to go in."

"Actually I don't. Been there. Done that."

Lauren buried her face in the steering wheel. "You're kidding. Right?"

Shelby shook her head.

"Look. I know what happened here, but it was a really long time ago. And see? The place has totally changed. Can't we just pretend we're at a different hospital?"

Shelby peered through the windshield at the massive glass tower. It certainly didn't compare to the modest, two-story brick building she remembered as a child. But bigger was by no means better. To her, it remained the heartless, inept institution that got away with murder. If only someone had been writing an investigative newspaper column like hers back then!

"I don't expect you to understand," Shelby spoke softly. "You were a baby. But I was there every day. I saw how they let her suffer . . ."

"It's not even owned by North Shore anymore. They merged with Long Island Jewish . . ."

"You want to know how she really died?" Shelby cut her off. "They let the fluids in her body build up to a point where her intestines were blocked. Basically, they let her starve to death."

"I'm sorry." Lauren yanked her keys from the ignition and opened the car door. "I understand our mother's death was a senseless tragedy. What I don't understand is how that gives you permission to turn your back on your family when they need you most."

"Give me the keys and your pager." Shelby scooted over to the driver's side.

"No! Where are you going?"

"Over to the police precinct to find out what really happened this morning. I'll pick you up in an hour. Page me if . . . anything."

Tears rolled down Lauren's cheek. "Why does it always have to be your way or no way?"

"That's not how it is at all. You're simply doing what you do best, and so am I."

"I can't believe you're doing this to me." She threw the car keys in Shelby's lap. "I swear to God, if he dies, and I'm all alone up there . . ."

"Just go." Shelby waved her off. "He's not going to die."

"Oh, really? How do you know that?"

"Because. Only the good die young. Like in the Billy Joel song. Ask your husband."

Lauren's eyes widened. "That is the most asinine thing I've ever heard anyone say," she replied before slamming the door and storming off.

Vintage Lauren. Feel it, think it, never say it. Someone could get hurt. Most likely her. Did I say this wouldn't work?

As Shelby watched Lauren waddle off in the direction of the hospital's front doors, all she could think was how fat Lauren looked. Not that this was new news. Her sister had been up and down the scale so often, Weight Watchers created a program just for her. The Perpetuity Plan.

"Maybe it's not what you're eating, it's what's eating you," Shelby remembered suggesting upon learning Lauren's biology term paper was entitled, "Why Women Gain Five Pounds After Eating a Two-pound Box of Chocolates."

In hindsight, Shelby's well-meaning diagnosis was more of a turning point for herself than for Lauren. By spring break, Lauren had gained another ten pounds, and Shelby switched her major from psychology to journalism. "Helping crazy people takes too long," she said, sharing her revelation with her faculty advisor. "It's much easier to write about them and move on."

Not that it stopped Shelby from calling Lauren every few months to insist that she try her latest weight loss strategy. Finally, after stomaching an entire week of the no-fail, cabbage-and-lemon diet, Lauren begged for mercy. "Find someone new to torture, Shel. I'm never going to be you, and I'm okay with that. I still have a pretty face."

Which was Shelby's point. Lauren could have been a knockout if she didn't subscribe to Aunt Roz's, "what's one little piece of cake going to do?" attitude. Yet even with her weight issues, there were times Shelby was secretly envious of Lauren's natural attributes. She was the one who'd inherited those big, brown M&M eyes, the lush auburn hair, and the satiny, olive complexion that glowed even on dreary, winter days.

Still, if there really had been a contest, the judges would have declared Shelby the family's "it" girl. For she was the one fate chose to come in standard-equipped as a long, leggy blonde with a tiny waist and chiseled cheekbones. But Shelby also knew there was an unspoken truth. Sandy and Roz, two very different-looking sisters, had genetically predisposed the next generation of sisters to the same miscarriage of justice. One could stop traffic, the other wouldn't get arrested for standing naked in Times Square.

Poor Avi, Shelby thought. He probably met Lauren when she was in one of her svelte, size-ten cycles, never imagining she'd blow up to have an ass shaped like a couch cushion. No wonder he thought I was so hot.

She flipped down the sun visor to reaffirm her stunning good looks in the mirror, then practically jumped out of her own flesh. Gazing back in the reflection was the shadowy image of her mother's face. Shelby punched the sun visor up and clutched her shirt. Was she so tired she was seeing ghosts? She closed her eyes, hoping to erase the eerie vision in the glass.

It was one thing to have occasional make-believe conversations with Granny Bea Good, her Jiminy Cricket. It was quite another thing to be spooked by your dead mother at the very place where her life had ended.

Suddenly she was reminded of the time Ian McNierney, speak of the devil, handed her a bizarre assignment when she first started working for him. "Find Detroit's top psychics and clairvoyants, and see what they're predicting for the nineties." He'd grinned.

Assuming this was some kind of hell week prank, Shelby submitted her first draft, a piece she cleverly entitled, "Boo!" Never did she expect Ian to attack her for allowing cynicism to seep through the words. "Mock readers, mock me," he bellowed. "But then I should have guessed you'd be daft on this subject. You're living proof, education is the bane of enlightenment!"

Shelby had never forgotten Ian's stinging remark, not because he'd attacked her elite American schooling, which he insisted had left her void of original thought. What had been far more disconcerting was this brilliant man's unshakable belief that humans could communicate with the dearly departed, and learn about the future from them, too.

Total lunacy was her reaction then and, his little psychedelic trip notwithstanding, now. If it was true those who passed on had the ability to communicate with loved ones, why hadn't her mother appeared before today? Surely she had to know Shelby still mourned her loss, still drifted in a sea of uncertainty without her loving presence.

She quickly rolled down the window, flush with neurosis and in desperate need of air. What to do next? Lauren was no longer in her line of sight, so it would be pointless trying to catch up to her. Yet she knew she had to get the hell out of the car, for it was no longer a safe haven.

With her heart racing, she jumped out and began to pace. Should she, could she, walk through those hospital doors? Her rapidly palpitating heart answered no. Nor could she just drive off, either. If she looked in the rearview mirror and saw her mother's reflection again, she'd surely floor the gas pedal, crash through the brick wall, and hurtle the car in a downward spiral to parking level one.

Then panic set in. What if from now on every time she looked in a mirror, her mother's ghost appeared? How would she put on makeup? And what was she supposed to say to Ernest at Hair Georgio next time she was due for a trim? "Could you please drape a towel over your mirror?" Even worse, with every workout studio at the gym totally mirrored, would she now have to cancel her membership? She could only imagine the scene if her mother showed up at her spin class. Shelby's stationary bike might become airborne.

It'll be a living nightmare. Shelby bit her lip. For as much as it would be nice to know her mother was watching over her, she wasn't prepared to play peekaboo for the rest of her life. On the other hand, at least this little call from Graveland had occurred when she was alone and not while she was at the office. No doubt her cronies would have toasted her meltdown, for up until now it was only a rumor Shelby Lazarus felt human emotion.

The thought of work suddenly gave her a new, desperately needed focus. She'd only left Chicago this morning, but in the paper trade, every minute you were out of touch was an eternity to the editor trying to reach you. She tore open her pocketbook, reached for her cell phone, and called in for messages.

So much for thinking she was important. The only calls were from David begging to hear how she was managing, and one call from her friend Risa, asking if Shelby was done with David, could she give his number to a friend who was ready to start dating again?

Shelby couldn't decide whether to laugh or cry. Was the dating pool so dry that even an overweight, bald guy without a spine was valuable currency? As she looked around the crowded parking lot, it occurred to her the problem with men was they were no different than parking spots. The good ones got snapped up right away, and the only ones left were disabled.

Just as she was about to dial David's number, a car stopped and a middle-aged man with a bad toupee honked, then pointed at her spot. "You leavin'?" he mouthed.

She was about to blow him off when something stopped her. "Uncle Marty?"

The man rolled down his window, yanked off his sunglasses, and squinted until his sun-drenched eyes adjusted to the dark garage. "Oh, for Christ's sake. Shelby? Look, hon. It's my niece, Shelby. You remember my wife, Bonnie, don't you?"

"I certainly do." Shelby grimaced. More like I've spent the past six years trying to forget how my mother's older brother dumped sweet Aunt Ellen for this stacked, blond-from-the-box *shikseh* with fake fingernails and an even faker ID. "If she was born in '61, I'll eat at McDonald's," Shelby whispered to Lauren at their wedding.

Bonnie peeked through the window, snuffed out her Virginia Slim, and waved hello. "Hi, hon." Her gum snapped. "How you doin'?"

How am I doing, you ask? You fat ignoramus? Excuse me. Aunt Ignoramus? Shelby knew the polite thing would be to walk over, but her legs suddenly turned to Jell-O while a magnet-like force glued her rear end to the car door. "I'm fine, thanks."

Uncle Marty didn't seem all that interested in following social graces, either. His hands remained clamped to the steering wheel. "Good for you. You came all this way to donate blood."

"Excuse me?" With all the garage noise in the background, surely she'd misunderstood.

"We got a call to come over right away. They said your folks needed blood. But you're definitely the better match. I mean 'cause you got all of your dad and maybe some of Roz."

Shelby nearly passed out at the thought of having a needle jabbed into her arm. "Nobody said anything about giving blood. I'm just here to support Lauren."

"From outside? Jeez, Shelby. Don't tell me you're still pulling that stupid, baby crap about not going into hospitals. You're a grown woman, for Christ's sake."

"And you're a moron if you think my father wants to be injected with the nicotine-filled blood of your *shikseh* wife who's wearing a cross so big she could probably be nailed to it!"

"Whad she say?" Bonnie stopped cracking her gum.

"Forget it." Uncle Marty waved in disgust before speeding off.

Shelby stood motionless, terrified, thinking that some migrant worker who swam here from Cuba was now waiting for her upstairs with a syringe and a basket of empty vials.

I need to collect myself, she thought as she opened the car door and collapsed in the driver's seat. She turned on the ignition, the radio, and the AC, rolled up the window, and leaned into the headrest. After a short nap she'd be fine. Back to her old self. The tough-minded, volcanic-spewing Shelby, who still believed polite conversation was entirely overrated.

Oy.

Chapter Six

"She's coming to." A nurse in blue scrubs pulled back the curtain. "Call Dr. G! Stat!"

Shelby's first conscious thought was she wished she didn't drool when she slept. Nothing was worse than waking up to a moist cheek on a soggy pillow. Or having to admit drool's cousin, incontinence, would inevitably be the next member of the Insult family to visit. Her second conscious thought was, what pillow? She didn't remember there being a pillow in Lauren's car.

Nor could she readily identify her bland, green surroundings. In fact it was not until she looked up and saw a bag of clear fluid hanging from a pole that it dawned on her she was no longer in Lauren's VW. Not even German cars came standard equipped with needles that could be lodged in one's forearm. Did she say needle?

A shrill, earsplitting scream suddenly echoed down the hospital corridor and an army of medical attendants came running. "Shhh. It's okay. You're going to be fine." An intern gently stroked her hand. "Dr. Glavin is on her way."

"Who?" a bewildered Shelby said, yanking at the white tape holding the needle in place. "Get this thing out of me! Since when do you take blood without getting someone's permission?"

"No, no, honey." A nurse with wash-and-wear hair pushed Shelby's hand away. "We're not taking blood. We're giving you fluids intravenously, and we need you to finish the bag."

"What are you talking about? Get away from me. You have no legal right to touch me without my express, written consent! Wait until you hear from my high-priced attorney . . ."

"Shelby?"

Shelby looked up to see a striking, tall blonde approaching. Whoever this chick in a lab coat was, she looked like she'd be more at home with her sisters at Kappa Kappa Gamma.

"Hi. I'm Dr. Glavin. How are you feeling?"

"Fine. Great. Terrific. Now get this thing out of my arm." Shelby tugged at the tape.

"I wouldn't advise that." Dr. Glavin examined the amount of fluid remaining in the bag. "You were extremely dehydrated when I found you passed out in your car."

"Passed out? That's ridiculous. I just dozed off waiting for my sister to come back. Is North Shore so desperate for patients they have to canvass the parking lots . . ."

"Uh-oh. Looks like she's on to us. " Dr. Glavin winked at her comrades. "But how about sitting still for another few minutes until one of the residents can examine you?"

"What are you? An actress? 'Hi. I'm not a doctor, but I play one on TV.' "

Dr. Glavin smiled. "You don't remember me, do you?"

Shelby stopped fidgeting for a moment. This was someone she knew?

"I treated your brother a few years ago when he was in my rehab program. I believe you attended a couple of the family therapy sessions."

Shelby blinked. Family therapy? If ever good money had chased bad. But yes, she did vaguely remember the perky, blond shrink Eric fantasized about screwing.

"Whoa, whoa, whoa." Shelby held up her hand. "I pass out in a car and they call in a psychiatrist? Isn't that a tad judgmental? Just because my stepbrother is crazy doesn't mean . . ."

"It's nothing like that, Shelby. As I was pulling into the spot next to yours, I looked over and saw a woman fall over. When I couldn't unlock the car door, I called for help."

"So, you didn't know it was me?"

"Not until they found identification in your purse. Have you eaten anything today?'

"Coffee at the airport."

"Well no wonder. Can we get Ms. Lazarus a bagel with cream cheese and a large glass of orange juice?" Dr. Glavin asked the nurse.

"No need." Shelby nearly fainted again at the mere thought of scoffing down more than a thousand calories in one sitting. "There's a yogurt with my name on it at home."

"Oh my God, oh my God, oh my God." Lauren charged through the curtain. "What happened, Shelby? Were you driving when you passed out? Is my car okay? This is a nightmare." She burst into tears. "First Mommy and Daddy get rushed here, then you . . ."

"The car is fine. I'm fine, too, thanks for asking. I just need to get out of here before they schedule me for a lobotomy . . ."

"Miss Lazarus?" A wisp of a doctor entered, holding a clipboard bigger than his face. "I'm Dr. Rhouhani. I understand you lost consciousness in your car, and you suffer from anemia?"

"Anemia! Who the hell told you that?"

"I did?" Lauren looked down. "It's just. I don't know. You're so thin . . ."

"Oh, for Christ's sake. All of you get the hell away from me," Shelby jumped off the table, finally pulling the IV from her arm. "I'm fine. Okay. Look. I can stand. I can hop. I can fox trot." She grabbed Dr. Rhouhani's arm and swung him around.

"Shelby, we're only trying to help," Dr. Glavin cut in.

"I don't need help." Shelby stopped. "My father needs help. He's upstairs in distress. . . ."

"Actually, they've stabilized him," Lauren said softly. "But it's still very touch-and-go."

"Yes, I heard about the accident." Dr. Glavin patted Shelby's shoulder. "I'm so sorry. But tell you what. Why don't you two get something to eat in the cafeteria? Then I'll come get you the minute the doctors can speak to you."

"Thanks for the offer, but I'm heading home." Shelby looked around for her pocketbook.

"My sister has a whole phobia about this hospital," Lauren explained to the uninformed members of the group. "Our mother died here, and . . ."

"I'm fine." Shelby grabbed Lauren and pierced her with a shut-your-mouth look. "I just need to rest."

"And eat." Dr. Glavin winked.

"What are you?" Shelby bellowed. "The Food Police?"

"Come here, miss. I vish to check your vital signs." Dr. Rhouhani took Shelby's pulse. "Perhaps I should prescribe something to help you . . ."

"You want to help me? Find my damn pocketbook and point me to the nearest exit."

"We know this is very upsetting, dear, but before you can be released we need to follow certain procedures." The nurse pushed Shelby back onto the table. "Just let Dr. Rhouhani examine you, then you can sign the release form and be on your merry way."

"That's what's wrong with managed care!" Shelby screamed, as a blood pressure cuff was wrapped around her arm. "People in dire need of medical attention are left to die, while the perfectly healthy ones are held prisoner in ER's."

"Is she always like this?" Dr. Glavin whispered to Lauren, her psychiatric eyes lighting up.

"No. Usually she's much worse."

By the time Shelby was finally reunited with her pocketbook and declared free to leave, she was so drained she didn't have the strength to argue when Lauren grabbed her hand and said they were headed to the cafeteria. There they would eat and await word from Dr. Glavin as soon as the surgeons had news to report. At least for the moment the girls knew their father and aunt remained in critical, but stable condition. Still, no one was guaranteeing their survival. It was simply too soon to tell.

"Are you sure that's all you want?" Lauren eyed Shelby's near barren tray as they approached the cashier. "What about a nice muffin or a bagel?"

"There's no such thing as a nice muffin." Shelby paid for her apple and yogurt. "They're high-fat, high-carb, high-calorie time bombs that . . ."

". . . Taste so good, especially with butter and then you nuke them in the microwave . . ."

"Be my guest. But I, for one, like it when I can zip my pants in the morning."

"You are so mean." She jabbed Shelby's arm. "Why are you so mean?"

"Forget it. Let's go sit over by the window. In case we decide to jump."

Look. Shelby's inside the hospital. Granted it's only the cafeteria, but it's still progress. And see how nicely the girls are sitting at the table? They're not fighting, not stabbing each other with utensils. On the other hand, they're not talking, either. Shame is, I know Lauren has so much she wants to say but fears confrontation. Always did. Shelby, of course, thrives on confrontation. And given her lovely behavior with the hospital staff, I don't blame Lauren for lying low at the moment. Although there is one subject that's generally considered a safe zone.

"This is the first nice day we've had in almost a week." Lauren smiled at the view of sunlit trees. "It started pouring Monday night, and we thought it would never let up."

"Really?" Shelby stirred the last bit of yogurt. "Maybe that's why they were up and out so early."

"You're probably right. " Lauren smiled. "The thing is, rain was in the forecast for today, too, but then the sun came out. They must have gotten so excited . . ."

". . . They ran straight out. But, of course, it's been scientifically proven after heavy rains, the clouds burn off and the sun is extra bright. Sometimes blinding."

"So the man who hit them," Lauren bubbled. "It wasn't really his fault . . ."

"Are you crazy?" Shelby's eyes bulged. "Remind me to leave you home when we drag that stupid, son of a bitch into court. Of course he's responsible. The law says if you get behind the wheel of the car you have to compensate for any and all hazardous conditions regardless of . . ."

"You want another yogurt, Shel? They also have nice big salads, oh and the French onion soup looked really good. You used to love that."

Shelby still felt hunger pangs, but made a face so Lauren would see that there were people who eat to live, not live to eat.

"Lauren Streiffler? Shelby Lazarus?"

The girls glanced at each other, then turned around to see who was calling them. An overgrown, baby-faced man in blue surgical scrubs and glasses was searching the room.

Lauren stood up to signal their whereabouts. "Excuse me. Sir? Over here."

The doctor waved back, then started a quick trot over to their table.

"Who's he?" Shelby asked.

"I'm not sure. I guess one of the surgeons. You have good instincts. Does his face say good news or bad?"

Shelby, who certainly did pride herself on her ability to read people's faces, was nonetheless stumped. The man's expression was neutral. This could go either way.

"Hi, Shelby. How are you?" The unshaven doctor leaned over and kissed her cheek.

Lauren was not nearly as stunned as Shelby. She assumed all men treated her this way.

"You don't remember me, do you?" He looked at Shelby's puzzled expression. "Scott Rosenthal? Well, now it's Dr. Rosenthal. I'm a thoracic surgeon on staff."

Tic-tac-toe. This was the third time today someone from her past showed up unexpectedly. If only she'd known, she would have chosen her clothes more carefully. On the other hand, unlike Ian and Dr. Glavin, she was clueless as to who this guy was. "I'm sorry. Do I know you?"

"It's okay. It's been a lot of years. And I've put on a few pounds." He patted his stomach. "Anyway, when I saw who they'd brought in this morning I felt terrible. I just wanted to come down here and tell you we're going to do everything we possibly can to help your parents through this terrible ordeal."

"Thank you." Lauren smiled. "Do you have time to join us?"

"Of course. Of course." Dr. Rosenthal pulled out the squeaky chair next to Lauren's. "So how are you two holding up? You must be going through hell."

"Longer than you know," Shelby mumbled. "What can you tell us about their condition?"

"Well, I'll be honest with you. They both lost a lot of blood, and it's not that any one injury in particular was catastrophic; it's the cumulative effect of the multiple injuries that's putting them at such high risk. I'm sorry to put it this way, but basically it would be a lot easier to put back Humpty Dumpty. If they make it through the next forty-eight to seventy-two hours, I'm not going to say they're out of the woods, but it would certainly increase their odds of survival. The bad news is then they're looking at months, if not years, of physical therapy, pain medications, surgery . . ."

"Are you suggesting they'd be better off dead?" Shelby said icily.

"No, of course not. I just thought you should know the magnitude of the problem."

"Oh my God," Lauren began to sob. "This is so scary."

Dr. Rosenthal rubbed her back. "I know. But the one thing in your favor is we've got the best team of surgeons working on them. If anyone can save them, it's North Shore."

"Great! It's déjà vu all over again." Shelby bit her lip. "Same hospital. Same bullshit."

"Excuse me?"

"Nothing. Forget it. So what happens next?" Shelby took a deep breath.

"Actually, that's what I came to talk to you about. We'd like both of you to give blood. It could really make a difference, especially for your mom."

"She's not our mother," Shelby jumped in. "She's our aunt. I doubt our blood types would even match."

"Your father married his aunt?" Dr. Rosenthal raised an eyebrow.

"No," Lauren said. "After our mother died he married her sister. She's our aunt. Not his."

"Oh. Well, there's still a very good chance you'll be the same blood type as your dad."

"Sorry," Shelby examined her new choice of nail color. "I can't give blood."

"Why not, Shel?" Lauren pleaded.

"I'm anemic. Remember?"

"No you're not! I made that up so they'd be sure to take good care of you."

"You did?" Shelby blinked.

"It's okay," Dr. Rosenthal said. "Even if one of you gives, it will be a big help."

"But what if neither of us can give?" Lauren bit her lip.

"I'm sure there are other family members who . . ."

"Wait a minute," Shelby interrupted. "Why can't you give?"

"Because, Shel. I have . . . problems, okay? I'm taking all these different prescriptions and I don't think you can give blood if . . ."

"Is it those diet pills again? How many times have I told you that stuff is pure speed . . ."

"Could we not worry about this for the moment?" Dr. Rosenthal said.

"Fine. When can we see them?" Lauren asked, just as her pager sounded. "Shel, you have my beeper. Where is it?"

Shelby reached under her shirt to unclip it from her slacks. At least it hadn't been ripped off while she lay unconscious in this god-forsaken place.

"Shel-bee." Lauren pressed several buttons. "Why didn't you tell me I had messages? Avi paged me four times."

"Sorry. When I'm out cold I'm just not my usual, efficient self."

"Can I use my cell phone in here?" Lauren inquired.

Scott shook his head. "Too much interference. You have to go outside."

After Lauren excused herself, he reached for Shelby's cold hands. "You haven't aged a bit." He smiled. "You look wonderful. I mean, even with what you must be going through . . ."

Shelby retreated. Why did men always feel they had to touch her when they talked to her?

"I'm sorry." He sensed she didn't appreciate the gesture. "I didn't mean to be forward. It's just that . . . I can't believe you don't remember me."

"And I can't believe you care. Who are you anyway?"

"I made that much of an impression on you?" Scott chuckled. "Remember the boy who drove your father's Jaguar into a fire hydrant during the homecoming parade?"

Shelby blushed. Who could forget being the only Homecoming Queen ever to be in a collision when the entire town was watching?

"So you can imagine how shocked I was when I realized I was working on your dad. It was like, oh God, please don't come to until I've had a chance to make it up to you, sir."

"I think saving his life would pretty much even the score."

"And what about you? Do you have any interest in evening the score?"

"We have a score to even?"

"Well, let's see. Thanks to your insistence that I jump the parade route, I was grounded for three months, New York State nearly revoked my license, and my friends never let me live it down that I was the only guy in Manhasset High's history ever to get into an accident while driving five miles per hour. Now it's twenty years later, and I find out you didn't even know my name."

Shelby smiled. Poor guy was right. "Hey. How was I supposed to know my father would actually give up a golf game to watch me in the parade?"

"How was I supposed to know you didn't have permission to drive his car?"

"How was I supposed to know you only had a junior license?" Shelby's eyes narrowed.

"How was I supposed to know you told Barry Berman not to drive you?" Scott replied.

"He had a friggin' Ford Mustang, for God's sake," Shelby cried. "Was the queen not entitled to a car befitting royalty?"

Suddenly Shelby could not hold back. The memory of her father's scrunched-up face as he tried peeling red paint off his beloved Blue Jag made her laugh so hard, a tear rolled down her cheek. The relief felt awesome, as did the sound of Scott Rosenthal's equally loud snort.

"What's so funny?" Lauren returned. "I could use a good laugh."

"You remember when I was in the homecoming parade and some kid smashed Blue into a fire hydrant?"

Lauren nodded.

Scott waved his hand. "Hello again."

"Get out of here." Lauren punched his arm. "You did that?"

"Afraid so." Scott bowed his head. "But I was provoked." He smiled at Shelby.

"You know, Shel, if it wasn't for Mommy, Daddy would have killed you that day."

Shelby was curious enough to let the "Mommy" reference slip. "What are you talking about?"

"I mean she told Daddy she gave you permission to use the car. She even paid for the repairs herself from her mah-jongg winnings."

"You're kidding? Why?" Shelby couldn't believe this bit of news.

"Beats me. I mean the way you treated her, I thought she'd use it as a chance to get even. Then she went and took the whole rap. You didn't know that?"

"No."

"Sounds like an incredible lady." Scott sighed, just as his pager went off. "Uh-oh," he read the message and took a deep breath.

"What?" Lauren grabbed his arm.

"I'm needed upstairs. Sit tight, girls. And pray. Pray hard."

Chapter Seven

I know, I know. This little accident idea of mine is now a full-blown disaster, and you're hoping this is the part where I just flap my wings and make everything all better. Unfortunately, I'm so low on the spirit totem pole I have no wings. Most of us here don't. It's like the army. Anyone can join, but only a select few are deemed worthy enough to be called General.

You might call it a heavenly hierarchy. Only those who've evolved over many lifetimes and who have genuine empathy for human frailties ever reach the top pinnacle. These lucky souls are our Archangels, like Michael and Gabriel.

Here's something else you may not know. Miracles begin with the human spirit. Really. No prayers? No answers. Yes, I know Lauren is down on her knees, but she seems to be the only one, and you can't attract much attention with a single voice. For best results, there needs to be an entire chorus. And sincerity, too. It's simply not good enough to go somewhere to pray, then spend the time wondering if the woman next to you is carrying an expensive, designer handbag, or the knockoff from the street vendor who sells in front of Saks.

In the meantime, if it's divine intervention you want, don't look at me. I think I've proven that my supernatural abilities are limited. Remember the debacle in Lauren's car? I can't even reappear without causing my daughter to faint.

Funny thing is, I was so sure Shelby would take comfort in getting a glimpse of my smiling face. Oh, I know she's a cynic. Most people are until they've had their first enlightening experience. It's called an awakening. I just thought if she saw me, she'd know I was at peace and would have the *courage to enter those hospital doors. Which technically she did, although it was by way of a stretcher.*

Now you understand why I'm leery of helping my husband and sister recover. Given my track record, I'd only make matters worse. Frankly, the best I can do at the moment is to give my children the strength they'll need to carry on. Isn't that what a mother does?

Over the next few hours, Lauren became the self-appointed diplomat, shuttling between the third floor ICU and the cafeteria, where she reported in to Shelby. Occasionally there was new news, rarely was it good. Their father had lapsed into a coma, as the doctors suspected he might, and Roz was rushed back into surgery to try to locate the source of her internal bleeding.

In the meantime, Shelby lost count of the cups of coffee she drank. Nor could she remember if she'd switched to decaf. How could she possibly concentrate when a continuous parade of do-gooders was annoying her?

First came a visit from the hospital chaplain, a slight man in a dark suit who kept referring to Larry and Roz as Mother and Father, as if they were his family, too. Hard to believe this guy existed because he beat out a million other sperm, she thought, sighing.

The chaplain was followed by Dr. Glavin, who came to confirm that Shelby had eaten and that she felt no ill will after Shelby's little tantrum in the ER. To prove her point, she offered Shelby a personal escort to the third floor as soon as she felt up to the challenge. "We'll take it nice and slow." She smiled. "In the meantime, here's my card."

Shelby didn't get the chance to tell Dr. Glavin she wouldn't go to the third floor if she were escorted by the Mormon Tabernacle Choir, for the next visitor had already arrived. This time it was a nurse from the ICU who had just gone off duty. She offered Shelby her heartfelt wishes, and a new antidepressant a detail man had left last week. "If those were my parents up there, I'd take the blue one now and the red one at bedtime."

No sooner did she leave than Scott Rosenthal returned, not to share more gory details about her father and Roz, but about his recent separation. Let me guess, Shelby thought. Your wife wanted it all. The bottomless checking account, the big house, the fancy car, jewelry . . .

"How could I pay for everything unless I was out busting my hump?" he cried.

"Sounds like a Wynonna Judd song." Shelby shredded her napkin.

"No, this is. Love is grand," he crooned. "But divorce is two hundred grand. Anyway, what about you? I bet you're happily married."

"Yeah, I married a great guy. He owns a BMW dealership. We have two beautiful kids . . ."

"But no diamonds?" Scott studied her ringless fingers suspiciously.

"They're in the vault. Why be a target when I travel?"

"Uh-huh. But isn't your last name still Lazarus?"

"Well, duh. I use my maiden name professionally."

Suddenly Scotty boy remembered some important phone calls he had to return. Works every time, Shelby mused, watching him trot off with a sad face. At least now she'd get some time alone. Or not. She'd know those crass voices anywhere, she thought as she turned around to find Uncle Marty and Bonnie the Bimbo headed over. Who else would be grumbling loudly about the high cost of parking in the hospital lot?

"Someone shoulda told us Larry was in a coma and Roz was in surgery." Bonnie fluffed her hair when they reached Shelby's table. "We woulda come tomorrow, or the next day."

"Or you could not come at all, and use the six bucks for a pack of cigarettes and a beer."

"What's with the snippy shit?" Bonnie pouted. "Jesus, Shelby. We're your family."

"Let's not get into this, okay?" Uncle Marty glared at Shelby. "The meter's running. Call us when they're up and around."

"Does that mean if they're paralyzed we won't ever have to speak to you again?"

An older woman observed the couple leaving in a huff and approached with caution. "You must be Shelby." She smiled.

"Whoever you are, I'm begging you. Go away." Shelby rested her face on the cool table.

But when Shelby looked up, the woman was not only still there, she was seated.

"Let me guess," Shelby sulked. "You sell Avon. No wait. Long-term care policies."

"I'd probably make more money." She smiled. "But for now I'm a social worker on staff. My name is Irma." Irma patiently explained that she was there to offer Shelby counseling services during this difficult time. And although Shelby's initial reaction was to spout out a few nasty barbs, she suddenly felt too weary to be combative. So this was battle fatigue.

To say nothing of the fact that, in spite of the woman's drab, matronly appearance, she was sharp as a new razor. Somehow she'd gathered a dossier on the Lazarus family history, complete with names, dates, and confidential details so accurate, they stunned Shelby. And disturbed her.

"You have some nerve probing into our personal lives like that. What gives you the right?"

"Oh dear. I thought you'd be impressed. I mean because you're a professional reporter. Besides, isn't this what you do every day? Pry?"

Shelby would normally have engaged in verbal combat, but she was momentarily speechless. She hated arguing with someone when they were right.

"Besides, dear," the woman continued, "I didn't really do any prying. I merely spent time with your sister, and she was quite informative. A lovely girl. Very honest. And so open . . ."

"Like the Suez Canal," Shelby seethed. "The only secret she can keep is where she hides the M&Ms. But what's the point of all this? Don't you think I know my own life's story?"

"Of course you do, dear. I just thought you'd feel better knowing someone on staff was also aware of your special predicament."

"My special predicament?" Shelby mimicked.

"Yes. That the memory of this place haunts you. That it's difficult for you to be here."

"It doesn't haunt me," Shelby gritted. "It pisses the hell out of me! Besides, you shouldn't be playing the Clark Kent home game unless you've verified your story with a second source."

"Of course, dear." She cleared her throat. "That is why I also spoke to Dr. Weiner."

"How dare you? I hate that slimy, arrogant prick!"

"I'm sorry." The woman's eye twitched ever so slightly. "I didn't realize it would offend you. After all, he was your mother's doctor for so many years."

"Yeah, and the one who botched her diagnosis. Where'd you find him anyway?"

"I'm afraid that wasn't difficult either." She seemed sullen. "He's here. In the hospital."

"No way! You'd think a guy that incompetent would have been forced out years ago."

"He has lung cancer, Shelby. He's in as a patient, not a physician."

"Serves the fat bastard right." Shelby peered outside. "Besides, he's got nothing to complain about. He got to live a full life. My mother was robbed of hers in her prime."

"It was over thirty years ago, dear. They knew so little about the disease then. And your mother was so young. There was nothing to suggest . . ."

"Oh bullshit. If he'd been paying as much attention to her as his golf game . . . "

"Shelby, you may not believe this, but Dr. Weiner suffered terribly after your mother's death. He took it very very hard, and although he's not sure anyone would have picked up on the cancer in its earliest stages, he never stopped second-guessing himself. In fact, several years later he left the field, left his family, was treated for depression, moved to California . . . remarried . . ."

"He told you all that?"

The woman shook her head no.

"So? What? You're making this up as you go?"

"Of course not. Every word is the truth."

"Why should I believe you?"

"Because I lived through it with him." She deadlocked with Shelby's eyes. "I was Mrs. Weiner. The first one anyway."

Shelby's heart pounded. His wife? Over the years she'd only considered how her mother's death had affected her family, not his. But when she studied the woman's face, she recognized the look of profound sadness and suddenly realized they might somehow be connected.

"Did you . . . ever meet my mother?" Shelby asked softly.

"Oh yes, of course, dear. I worked in the office, and she was one of our favorite patients. But it wasn't until after she developed problem pregnancies that I really got to know her."

"She had problem pregnancies?"

Irma nodded. "If I recall, she had two miscarriages in between you and your sister."

Shelby was nearly rocked off her seat. Her mother had miscarried?

"You know"—Mrs. Weiner smiled—"you remind me so much of her."

"I do?" she perked up.

"Yes. I can't believe the physical resemblance. You even sound alike. Nice and loud!"

"Excuse me?" Shelby's tone changed.

"Let's just say your mother was a pistol. She didn't take crap from anyone. Especially my husband. I actually used to look forward to her visits because she always gave him hell."

Now Shelby beamed.

"In fact one time, I think you'll enjoy hearing this, she came in and all of a sudden I heard screaming from one of the examining rooms. I ran down the hall, positive my husband's temper had gotten the better of him. But when I opened the door, I nearly fell over."

"Why?" Shelby was on the edge of her seat. "What happened?"

"Your mother had grabbed him by the tie and was screaming in his face. He was practically choking to death, but she wouldn't let go. I had to unfurl each little finger . . ."

"That's the most wonderful story I've ever heard." Shelby clapped. "Do you remember what she was angry about?"

"Well I wasn't in the room, of course." Irma sighed. "But I believe it had to do with how bad she was feeling. She knew something was wrong, and all he probably came up with was his usual diagnosis, One-a-Dayitis. Eat better and take vitamins. That was his cure for everything."

"So she almost strangled him? That's incredible!"

"It was gutsy, that's for sure. In those days doctors were considered gods. Nobody questioned them about anything. Especially a woman. It was unheard of."

"But she was right and he was wrong." Shelby knew the rest of the story. "Dead wrong."

"Yes."

Shelby's eyes welled up. Maybe this was a cute little story to Mrs. Weiner, but to her it was a revelation. Her mother hadn't gone quietly to death's door. She'd practically killed a man with her bare hands while screaming for help. Suddenly she understood the families of murder victims who read the police reports and learned their loved ones had put up a struggle. It didn't change the outcome, of course, it just somehow gave people comfort knowing the victims had fought back.

"I thought you'd like that story." The embarrassed social worker smoothed out her skirt.

"What else do you remember?" Shelby said sweetly, wanting desperately to sit in this wonderful woman's lap.

"Perhaps another time, dear. I have rounds to do. But let's keep in touch."

"Of course." Shelby tried to hide her disappointment.

"There is one other thing," Irma stood up. "When I heard who they'd brought in this morning . . . I . . . this sounds awful. But a part of me was happy it was them."

"Are you serious?" Shelby felt as if she'd been stabbed.

"I know. It makes me sound like a monster, which I assure you I'm not. But you have to understand how much pain your family caused my family."

"Excuse me, but I think it was the other way around." Shelby sniffed.

"Forget it. I was wrong to say anything. Believe me, I am praying for their recovery."

"No wait." Shelby got up to reach for the woman's arm. "Please tell me what you meant."

Irma seemed surprised by Shelby's curious expression. "Well, you knew, of course, that your father sued my husband for malpractice and in the process destroyed his reputation."

Shelby shook her head no.

"Needless to say, the case dragged on for years."

"Then what happened?" Shelby asked, sorry she didn't have her notepad handy.

"In the end he was exonerated. So we thought, okay, now we're finally going to be able to get on with our lives. Then your father hit him with a million-dollar civil suit."

Shelby was clearly thrown. "I knew everything that went on in that house, and trust me, it was more than a ten-year-old should have to know. But I never heard a word about any lawsuit."

"Well believe it. It's why Bernard had a nervous breakdown. Even attempted suicide."

"I'm confused." Shelby collapsed in her seat. "My father refused to let me mourn, or even talk about my mother. Now you're saying during that whole time he was out for blood?"

"I apologize. I had no business telling you any of this. You've been through enough."

"No, it's okay."

"No, it was totally unprofessional on my part. I frankly don't know what got into me."

"Forget about it." Shelby shrugged. "I've been known to overdo it myself on occasion."

"It's just . . . I've always wondered if your father had let us move on, maybe Bernard wouldn't have left medicine. And left. . . ."

"You?" Shelby finished her sentence.

Irma nodded.

"Thank you for coming to see me." Shelby smiled wistfully.

"Of course." Irma bowed. "I'll check in with you again tomorrow, if you'd like."

"Great." Shelby watched her head out. "But not too late. I'm flying back to Chicago."

"Like hell you are," Irma muttered when she was out of earshot.

I may not know much, but of this I'm sure. When Irma Jean Weiner (nee Epstein) is returned to the safe, warm existence from which we all come, she will be ushered in by the angels and bathed with love. And she will be deserving. Not merely because she was compassionate and generous, but because she learned to use her native wit and intellect to overcome great personal problems. Albeit too familiar problems for a doctor's wife.

Hers was a textbook case. She not only put her husband through med school, she raised their two sons while Dr. Important built up a small practice that made him so instantly wealthy, he bought the damn building where only two years earlier he was just happy to be able to meet the rent. Oh, and did I mention his philandering and preoccupation with marijuana? He certainly gave new meaning to the expression high-and-mighty.

Anyway, here was Bernard M. Weiner driving around in his big BMW (just so he could show off his vanity plates boasting the same initials as the car) while Irma drove around town in a red Gremlin she shared with her son. Good old Bernie picked up on a moment's notice the instant he heard about a challenging new golf course somewhere in the Caribbean.

Irma was just happy he didn't hassle her when she flew down to Miami to visit her mother.

Then a few months after their younger son Brad's Bar Mitzvah, Dr. Putz left her for the proverbial young, shikseh nurse and moved to California, where fat, rich, Jewish, middle-aged men with blond babes were as indigenous as avocados. Irma cried for weeks, then cashed in her life insurance policy and returned to college. It took years, but eventually she got her master's in social work, found gainful employment, put her sons through college, then law school, married them off to two nice girls, baby-sat for her beautiful grandchildren, traveled, and occasionally had dinner with a nice widower she met at her granddaughter's nursery school picnic.

Then one day, good old Bernie's on the phone, crying that his second wife left him. As did his third. Most of his money was gone, burned by a tax shelter deal that went bad. And now the ultimate blow? Test results showed conclusively he had lung cancer. What should he do?

As far as I'm concerned, the guy got what he deserved, and I would have told him so. But Irma insisted he return to Long Island so she could care for him.

I know. You think she's a patsy. The Grand Martyr in the Fools' Day Parade. But don't be too quick to judge. What she really is, is wise. For in spite of her suffering, she came out on the other side of the experience having learned a valuable lesson. Bitterness only poisons the soul from which it stems. She would either be consumed whole by anger and resentment or move on.

Irma chose "B," which is one reason she will be found deserving of having eternal peace. And the other? You know that little chat she had with Shelby? I loved the part when she said I was one of her favorite patients. Ha! She hated me, and who could blame her? I was so smug, with my Louis Vuitton pocketbooks and professional manicures. Plus, I never had an appointment I kept. I'd call to change them two or three times, then arrive late with apologies to no one. And yet, you heard Irma. She made it sound as though she adored me.

Then that bit about how I almost choked Bernie to death? Never happened. Not even close because it simply never occurred to me to question him. I guess I was too self-involved and vain to think I could actually have a serious problem. Which, in retrospect, made me no better than he.

Still, you've got to love Irma for lying to win Shelby's trust. And for understanding the one thing Shelby desperately needed to validate was that her mother was a fighter. Just like her.

Now here's the ironic part. Irma's ex-husband is lying in North Shore where his days are numbered. Only one floor above my husband, whose days may also be numbered, depending on what God has in mind. That means the two men who had more to do with shaping my destiny, and whose own destinies were ultimately and dramatically altered by my death, are now under the very same roof as I when I was fighting for my life.

Honestly. Who's writing this script?

Oh, and something else. Irma was right when she guessed Shelby wouldn't be leaving yet. Somehow she sensed she wasn't going anywhere until she came to terms with both these men.

I do hope there's time.

Chapter Eight

When Shelby awoke the next morning, in a bed and a room that were completely unfamiliar, she only vaguely remembered why. Something about a bad dream involving an accident, a frightening visit to an emergency room, and a bunch of unfortunate reunions with people she didn't care for, or about. It reminded her of one of those Ann Tyler novels where one insufferably long day in the heroine's life took seventy-three pages.

Then she came to. She was back in New York among the people she was connected to by blood and ancestry. It wasn't a dream or even a decent novel. It was her damn life.

She opened one eye to slowly take in her surroundings and gasped. Surely this part had to be fictitious. Otherwise, she'd just spent the night in a place where a disciple of Martha Stewart had gone mad. Large, maple furniture and lemon yellow chintz were everywhere. Curtains. Dust ruffles. Tablecloths. Chairs and ottomans. Was she hallucinating again, or had Aunt Roz hired a decorator who was legally blind?

Shelby inched out of bed to begin a full examination of what she now recalled was the guesthouse. It was more akin to a studio apartment, but she had to admit there was a certain coziness to the place. She especially liked the airy feel of the floor-to-ceiling windows, and the plush, plum-colored carpet under foot. Welcome to Hotel Lazarus, she thought as she made her way to the private bath, which boasted a Jacuzzi tub and a closetful of velvety towels. If there was also maid service, she might never leave.

Question of the day was, why didn't she have any recollection of how she'd gotten here? As if that never happened before, she mused. But this time she was certain alcohol had played no part. Maybe if she took a moment to collect herself, the details would surface.

Shelby was beckoned to a massive, leather chair in the corner, which looked perfectly comfortable save for the bright, yellow gingham throw pillows tucked inside. What decent decorator would mix twentieth-century Haddassah with *goyishe* country chic?

As she tucked her legs in, it occurred to her she was still unsure how she ended up asleep here, but she now knew what woke her. A bird convention had assembled outside the window near the bed, and they were so insanely loud, Shelby surmised they were either planning to overthrow the government or visit the in-laws in Miami.

So how *did* she get here? Oh, yes. Avi had come to the hospital to retrieve her and Lauren, as neither felt up to driving home. At the house, he dug into a brisket dinner a neighbor left for them in the refrigerator, then took off into the night for a last-minute airport run.

Shelby then remembered Lauren guiding her down the lighted path to the guesthouse. Once inside, she'd turned on a small Tiffany lamp, pointed out the bathroom and the phone, mentioned something about a migraine, then quickly said good night.

Now as she stared at the clock on the night table, reality time registered. It was 8:23 A.M. Monday, June 23. The day after the most horrific headline of her life had run: LARRY AND ROZ GET HIT BY A TRUCK; BUT SHELBY'S LIFE IS OVER! Right. The accident. A sudden queasiness churned inside. Had anything happened during the night? Surely Lauren would have woken her if they'd died. Trouble was, and she was even sickening herself thinking this, she really didn't know what to wish for. She only knew what it was too late to wish for.

It was too late to wish her number was unlisted so that Lauren wouldn't have been able to notify her of the accident. It was too late to wish that her father and Aunt Roz were still sedentary couch potatoes so they would have been sleeping instead of jogging. And, it was especially too late to wish that her father never married Aunt Roz at all. Not merely because Shelby detested her cheap, unkempt appearance, but because she was so tired of explaining their unusual relationship .

"We're like a Jewish *Chinatown*," she cried to her shrink, taking creative license with the famous line from the movie. "She's my mother, my aunt, my mother, my aunt . . ."

But why wish for anything? The way her luck was running, if her ship ever came in, she'd surely be at the airport! The only thing left to consider were the "what-ifs."

What if they didn't survive? What if they did? Scott Rosenthal was probably right. Humpty Dumpty would be easier to put back together. They'd need round-the-clock care, months of physical therapy, operation after operation, pain medication, conferences with specialists . . . She'd seen this movie thirty years ago and knew the genre didn't guarantee a happy ending.

Only difference between the death of her mother and the survival of her father and aunt, was this time she wasn't as emotionally vested. Not since spending the past two years distancing herself from them, paying thousands in therapy bills to justify the decision.

It occurred to her that she might be entitled to a refund if she now had to pay for reverse emotional osmosis or additional hypnosis sessions. How else would she summon the empathy she'd need to stomach whatever happened next? Hold that thought, she groaned. Someone was at the door. "C'mon in," she called out. "I'm up."

Lauren peeked inside. "How'd you sleep?" she asked.

"Great," Shelby stretched. "You?"

"Not a wink. I think I was afraid to fall asleep in case the phone rang."

"And? Did it?"

Lauren shook her head.

"So that's a good sign. Right? They must still be alive."

"Oh my God, Shelby! What is wrong with you?" She turned and headed out the door.

"What did I say?" Shelby found her slippers and ran after her.

Lauren kept walking, refusing to answer.

"Get a grip on yourself, would you?" Shelby caught up just in time for Lauren to slam the kitchen door in her face. "I only meant that we should be happy . . ." She stopped short, taken aback by the sight of a tiny, black woman removing fresh cinnamon rolls from the oven.

"Care for one?" the woman delicately dropped a hot, melted bun on a plate.

I'd kill for one, she thought. "No thanks. They're loaded with fat, carbs, and sugar."

"I didn't ask about the food groups, dear. I just asked if you'd like to try one. They're your sister's favorite."

"What isn't?" Shelby sniffed.

Lauren's eyes welled up. "Stop it, okay? I can't take your being so mean to me right now."

"Fine. I just don't remember you being so touchy."

"Come here, baby." The woman offered Lauren a hug. "Shhh. There now. It's okay."

Shelby took a step back on the slim chance that she was going to be invited into the group hug. And what was with everyone treating Lauren like she was an emotional cripple? "I'm mildly curious." She tapped the woman on the shoulder. "Who are you?"

"Name's Maria." The woman began arranging the rest of the rolls on a ceramic tray.

"Name's familiar." Shelby copied the attitude. "Didn't I fire you yesterday?"

"Shelby!" Lauren cried.

"It's all right, baby." Maria stood erect, then looked straight at Shelby. "I have a saying. He who hires me is the only one who fires me. I've been with your folks a good number of years . . ."

Lauren ran to throw her arm around the woman. "And she's like family to us."

"You're joking. Someone would actually volunteer to be in this family?"

"She's all yours, dearie," Maria remarked. "I'll be upstairs. It should be safer there."

"Thanks." Lauren waved. "Oh, by the way. Avi and I will be staying in their room. Be a doll and strip the bed?"

"With pleasure, sugar." Maria reached for a dust rag and whistled out.

"Sugar, doll, dearie, honey child," Shelby mimicked. "You need insulin to be around her."

Lauren pulled out a chair and quietly munched on a sticky bun.

Shelby was all too familiar with the silent treatment in this house but as always, ignored it. "Why are you staying here? I thought you said you have a place."

Lauren bit her lip, tearing the remains of her roll into a few pieces.

"Oh please. Not this game. It won't play well at the funeral."

Lauren looked at her, her eyes still moist from the last cry. "Shut the hell up."

Whoa. Lauren used a curse word? "Fine. I'm sorry. Let's start over." Shelby spotted fresh coffee. She was saved. One large cup, and she could stave off hunger for hours. "Good morning. How are you? Have we heard from the hospital? Maria's here? Excellent. At least we'll get clean towels and mints on the pillow. Did you happen to notice she's black, but the one who was here yesterday was Latino? How can they be sisters? Sisters look alike. Like me and you."

Lauren tried to hide a smile. "Trust me. They're sisters, okay? Maria's the oldest of six girls. Kaneesha's the youngest."

"No way. The black one has a Spanish name and vice versa?"

"They're lovely people, that's all I know. Maybe they had the same mother and different fathers. Or, maybe they're like us and Eric. Different parents, but still a family."

Shelby bristled at the reference to their adopted, drug-dependent stepbrother, and out of disgust, grabbed the last bit of roll from Lauren's plate.

"What? Reporter Barbie's eating? Call a press conference."

"Good one." Shelby opened the refrigerator and grabbed a yogurt. "But for your information I eat plenty. I just stay away from all the crap."

"I could too if I used all my kitchen cabinets to store shoes and pocketbooks."

Shelby cleared her throat. She'd forgotten Lauren had once visited her place. "What can I tell you? I have very limited closet space. But at least I don't put on, oh say, twenty pounds a year?"

"Is that what you think? That I just sit here all day and pig out? For your information, there's a very good reason I look like this."

"You became a professional boxer and had to bulk up for the championship fight?"

Ding! Just as if the fight might really begin, the bell rang. Or at least the phone. Lauren and Shelby looked at each other. Who was brave enough to answer?

"Rock, paper, scissors, shoot?" Shelby poked Lauren's arm.

"Wimp." Lauren got up to answer. "Oh hi, Dr. Glavin."

Shelby groaned. "Tell her I just had a six-course breakfast. And good news. My arteries are starting to close."

"Shelby says to tell you she's feeling much better," Lauren said. "And thank you so much for your concern."

Shelby heard enough and headed back to the guesthouse. Hopefully the birds had found somewhere else to congregate, or she was going to turn into the Great White Hunter. For what she needed now was complete silence. It was important decision time.

It was nearly eight o'clock back in Chicago. Normally at this hour she'd be in her office preparing for a staff meeting, so in just a few minutes her absence would be apparent. Particularly since as VP, Cynicism, her job was to bring comic relief to the proceedings. No Shelby? No wisecracks. Not that the other reporters weren't thinking what she said. They were just too green and timid to speak up. God, they were graduating them young these days.

In any event she needed a plan. Not only had she not yet accounted for her whereabouts yesterday, she needed a better-than-average reason why she wouldn't be in today. Then again, would her managing editor give a shit? Sadly, yes. Walter Sipowicz was one of the rare breed of newspapermen with a big heart and an office that doubled as a confessional, remnants of his first career as a Jesuit priest. He was also as flexible as a gymnast when it came to story assignments. There were only two things that mattered to him. Honesty and good attendance.

Two things that meant a hill of beans to Shelby. So where did that leave her? Telling him the truth? Bad idea. She'd have to explain why she'd always led him to believe she was practically an orphan, with her only living relative a senile grandmother in a nursing home. How did you just suddenly remember you also had a father, stepmother, sister, stepbrother, and various crazy aunts and uncles?

Maybe she should go back to her original idea and send him an e-mail that she was sick. Then he'd never know she was out of town. But that wouldn't work. Walter was actually known to visit under-the-weather employees.

Shelby had no choice. She would have to lie. Maybe she'd tell him that she got a hot tip on a story coming out of New York that would be perfect for her column. Yes, that was it. She was following a lead that two Chicago aldermen were siphoning millions of dollars in coins from parking meters, and were using the money to buy into a new Donald Trump development. Lord knows it was probably true.

But more importantly, Walter loved stories that knocked politicians off their fat, Chicago arses, as he liked to say. And he'd be so proud of her dedication, that she cared more about her responsibilities as a journalist than going to a silly baseball game to rub elbows with Irving Davidoff and the boys.

Which two aldermen though? She tapped her fingers on the night table as she dialed the office. Were there any not already under suspicion for scurrilous acts of taxpayer betrayal? "Hey, Ginny. It's Shelby. I know Walter's in a staff meeting, but I need you to pull him out for a minute. It's really important . . ."

"Where the hell are you?" Ginny screamed. "I can't believe you of all people aren't here. It's just awful what they're doing!"

"Whoa, slow down. Start from the beginning. Who, what, where, when . . ."

It was another one of those times Shelby was sorry she asked. By the time she hung up, her hands were quivering, and her mouth was dry. These past twenty-four hours simply had to be a nightmare. Otherwise, her family was in the middle of a life-and-death crisis, and her employer had just gone on a Monday morning massacre.

Sixteen staffers were being reassigned, and twenty-two others were in the midst of getting walking papers, including the nicest guy in the world, Walter Sipowicz. Probably because he was the nicest guy in the world, Shelby bit her lip. How many times had she warned him not to be such a pushover? And what would he do for income? He had two kids in college and a wife just diagnosed with multiple sclerosis.

Shelby was taken aback by her feelings of concern. Was it a sign of aging that she was suddenly mellowing? Or was she just so frazzled from the events of the past two days that she wasn't quite herself? But enough about him. What was her job status?

Ginny said she heard a few rumors, but was more concerned with the fate of her own job, status unknown. "All I know is the newsroom looks like a front-page story: DISGRUNTLED PUBLISHER GOES ON RAMPAGE. Everyone's walking around in shock."

"Take down my number," the shell-shocked columnist said. "And call me back if you find out anything else." Not that she hadn't heard all she needed to know. Ian McNierney, the prophet of doom, had just hit another bull's-eye. Only yesterday he'd told her heads would roll, and even though she'd been privy to the same rumors, she'd been positive he was way off base.

Shelby was so deep in thought when the phone rang, she jumped, knocking her water glass off the table. No way could Ginny be reporting in with new news. They'd just hung up.

She took a deep breath. "Hello?"

"Shelby, it's Walter. Is that you? Where are you?"

"Yes, hi. I'm in New York. What the hell is going on?"

"As if you didn't know," he snarled. "No wonder you didn't show up at Wrigley yesterday. I just can't believe you left me in the dark."

"What are you talking about? I just happened to call in, and Ginny told me what was going on. I'm shocked."

"Bullcrap! You could have at least hinted not to throw out the Sunday classifieds."

"Walter, I swear on my life. I'm as shocked as you. The only reason I'm not in the office is yesterday morning I got a call from my sister that my father and stepmother got run over by some blind guy in a landscaper's truck. I ran to O'Hare and caught the next flight out."

"Shelby, I'm ashamed to say I called you my friend. First you deceive me, then you make up some horrible lie to cover up. You told me you didn't have a family, remember?"

"Actually, I do. I lied about that."

"So why should I believe you now?"

The guy had a point. "Walter, I swear on your favorite Bible. I didn't know."

"I really trusted you, Lazarus. But why should you care? You've still got a job. Bitch!"

Shelby stared at the phone. The only two people she knew who didn't have a foul mouth had both cursed at her today. Was there a full moon? "You said I still have a job? Doing what?"

"Hope you like the Internet, baby." He choked back tears before hanging up on her.

The Internet? Shelby groaned. Oh no. Not the digital publishing division. She hadn't worked this hard to suddenly have her fan base be all those fat-assed, pimple-faced day traders in cheap apartments who read her on-line.

"Miss Shelly? Miss Shelly?"

Shelby put the phone down, shuddering at the sound of her mispronounced name. It was bad enough the hired help couldn't get it right. But did Maria always have to sound as if she was in the remake of *Gone With the Wind*? She opened the door to find her sprinting over.

"My name is Shelby, okay? S-H-E-L-B-Y. Now what is it?"

"Come quick, Miss Shelly. Lauren got a call from the hospital. It doesn't sound good."

Shelby groaned, but started to follow the woman out. Then the phone rang. "Hold on. I have to take this." She ran back. "Be there in a sec."

Maria waited, hands on hips.

"Hello. Is this Shelby Lazarus?"

"Yes."

"This is Debby from Mr. Davidoff's office. Please hold the line for him."

Shelby broke into a sweat. Oh God. Why now? How could she remain composed when Maria, the domestic barracuda, looked as though she was ready to pounce?

"Shelby? Irving here. I understand you're in New York attending to a family emergency?"

"That's right . . ."

Suddenly Maria grabbed the phone. "Miss Shelly is very sorry, but there is a very urgent matter in the house, and she'll be needin' to get back to you." With that she hung up.

"How dare you?" Shelby screamed. "Do you have any freakin' idea who that was?"

"Child, I wouldn't care if that was the good Lord himself." Maria grabbed her by the hand. "Your sister is catatonic in the kitchen."

"Oh. So now you're part housekeeper, part psychiatric evaluator?"

Maria sprinted back to the kitchen with Shelby in tow, then pointed to what looked like a comatose Lauren in the chair. Tiny specs of tissue were stuck to her nose, and her body trembled.

"What happened?" Shelby tried assessing the seriousness of the situation by studying Lauren's face.

Lauren tried to speak, but was only able to moan. Then her breathing became rapid, and her skin tone began to match the shade of the pale gray floor tiles.

"Oh shit. She's hyperventilating. Get a paper bag," Shelby ordered. "No, get two."

Maria ran to the pantry and pulled out two large paper sacks from the supermarket.

"No, no, no!" Shelby said. "Small lunch bags."

"Mrs. L. doesn't keep anything like them around. Is plastic good?"

"Fine. Anything," Shelby realized her own breathing was fairly uneven. "Just hurry."

As Maria searched for Ziploc bags, Shelby watched her sister's body cross from listless to limp, just as it had when she was younger. She suddenly remembered overhearing Aunt Roz telling her father the pediatrician said this was Lauren's way of getting attention, but as Shelby studied her disoriented eyes, it occurred to her no one needed attention that badly. What if Lauren had been misdiagnosed, just as their mother had been when she was told her stomach problems were related to a lousy diet?

"Here." Maria handed Shelby the bags. And not a minute too soon. For the instant Shelby placed the bag over Lauren's nose and mouth, she vomited into it.

Maria quickly handed Lauren another bag, and for what seemed like an eternity, the only sound was heavy breathing. And a telephone ringing in the distance. Shelby looked over at the door until Maria shot her a glance that said if you go for it, you're going to have to get past me.

Finally, Lauren pulled the bag away.

"He died, didn't he?" Shelby looked down at her hands.

Lauren shook her head no. "There's a large blood clot by his brain. They have to get to it . . . before it bursts."

"Oooh, that sounds risky." Maria clutched her heart.

Lauren nodded vigorously. "He'll die if they don't, but they want us to know . . ."

"There's a good chance he might not survive the operation," Shelby finished her sentence.

Lauren looked at her with terror in her eyes.

"When?" Shelby said softly.

"They're prepping him now." She burst into fresh tears. "What if he dies on the table?"

Shelby cleared her throat. "Does Aunt Roz know?"

Lauren shook her head. "She's still in recovery."

Suddenly the room fell still, save for the rhythmic breathing of three women and a symphony of kitchen sounds; the ticking of the wall clock, the clanging of the dryer, the ringing of the damn phone in the distance.

"We'll get through this," Maria squeezed Lauren's hand. "The Lord will hear our prayers."

"Now for sure we're in trouble." Shelby stared outside. "He's done shit for us so far."

Maria gasped and quickly made the sign of the cross.

"Shelby!" Lauren pleaded. "Don't be like this. Don't give up hope."

"I haven't. But I'm sure as hell not putting my faith in God, or in the asshole doctors who can recite every feature of a new Mercedes 500SL, but are totally unfamiliar with pain and suffering. All I know is, whatever's going to happen to them is out of our hands."

"So that's it? We sit around all day waiting for the phone to ring?" Lauren whimpered.

"It's a lot better than pacing the halls, waiting for some crybaby doctor to tell us he tried his best, but it's all over, while he looks at his watch to see if he can still make his tee time."

"I'm sorry. We belong at the hospital," Lauren said bravely. "I'm going over there."

"Be my guest. I'm going to shower and change, then call my office. There seems to be a little problem at work."

"Well there's a big problem at home!" Lauren nearly choked. "Can't it wait?"

"No. In fact I'm probably going to have to fly back tonight."

"No don't." She reached for Shelby's arm. "You can't leave me alone here."

"You're not alone," Shelby said. "Maria and Avi are here. I'll come back in a few days."

"A few days?" Lauren looked over at Maria. "Are you telling me your stupid job is more important than your own family?"

"No, I'm saying there's not a damn thing I can do for them, so I might as well go home and find out if I even have a stupid job!"

Lauren stood up, clutching the tall arm of the chair for support. "I have something to say."

"Fine. But you're wasting your time if you plan to threaten me." Shelby folded her arms.

"It's not a threat. It's a promise." Lauren mustered her bravest face. "I'm telling you right now if you go back to Chicago today, we'll never speak again."

"Oh please." Shelby laughed. "You know how many times you've said that to me?"

"I mean it with every ounce of strength I have left." Lauren swallowed. "If you walk out on me, I'll never speak to you again."

"Now there's a line you've had a lot of practice saying!"

Lauren slapped Shelby's face so fast and hard, they were both stunned. "Go to hell!"

"Isn't that where I am? " Shelby ran for the door. Her cheek stung so badly her teeth hurt.

Maria shook her head as the Sisters Pathetic returned to their corners of the ring. Round one was over. God help them both.

Chapter Nine

Just before Shelby was connected to Irving Davidoff's office, she made herself a bet. If he wasn't puffing a soggy cigar, everything would work out fine. But if he was already chomping on a smuggled Havana import, it meant he was in a fetal position and all bets were off.

"You read the report." Irving blew rings of smoke so noxious, Shelby swore the cigar odor wafted through the phone lines.

Oh shit, she thought. It's all over.

"Circulation was hemorrhaging in the 'burbs. We had no choice."

"So let me get this straight." Shelby's heart raced. "After last quarter's audit bureau report, the suits in marketing brought in some upstart consulting firm with a nifty website, who got free rein to create their vision of the paper. Then the boy genius behind it, who's probably so young he's still writing thank-you notes for his Bar Mitzvah, told you the economy's good, people don't like controversy. They want stories that soothe the soul."

Mr. Davidoff's reply came in the form of a long puff and a cough.

"So that's it?" Shelby's voice grew louder. "We're going back to the soft stuff, like in the seventies, when the local network affiliates decided viewers needed happy news?"

"The numbers don't lie."

"I see. So let me get *this* straight. I busted my hump for a few years, put the Metro section back on the map, and now it's thanks for the memories?"

"For which you were very well compensated."

"And will continue to be well compensated," Shelby cut him off. "You want a great read? Take a look at my contract."

"Yes, yes. Legal's looking into it. But in your case we're not dealing with a termination. Exciting opportunities await you in the world of our digital publishing division."

"Over my dead body."

"Don't give me sour grapes, Lazarus. I find it unprofessional. Besides, whatever gave you the impression your column was anything but a sideshow? A novelty act?"

"Oh really? Is that what you told Royko, too?"

"Trust me, you're no Royko. Mike was a masterful writer. A genius of the ordinary and the sublime. You, frankly, are a loudmouth call girl with a cell phone and a pen."

Shelby was barely able to catch her breath when Mr. Davidoff continued.

"Besides, once our focus groups indicated readers were growing tired of your column's whining and carrying on, our decision was made."

"Trust me. So is mine," Shelby bit back. "I'll e-mail my resignation to you. Unless you find that unprofessional." She slammed down the phone.

Shelby closed her eyes to hold back any tears. For someone in the business of reporting bad news, she had still never learned how to receive it. She collapsed on the bed and slammed her fist into a pillow. Was there any aspect of her life that hadn't yet unraveled this morning? Let's see. Her personal life as she knew it was over, and now so was her career. Was she really such a selfish ogre she deserved not one day's happiness? Lots of people were far more hopeless and pathetic than she, but their lives didn't seem to be constantly undermined by catastrophe.

It seemed like an appropriate time to cry, and Lord knows Dr. Kahn would be proud to hear that his most stoic patient finally surrendered to her pain, finally got past her "fear of the tear." Trouble was, having cried buckets into her pillow every night after her mother died, she had been neither relieved of her despair nor offered closure. It was at that point that she'd decided never to cry again. Not even now when she knew a few good tears might manipulate Irving into submission.

Shelby tried envisioning a tearful scene in his office where she sobbed, pleading to keep her job. But given her take-no-prisoners approach to life, a more realistic dream involved her shopping at Kmart for masking tape and a gun, then holding Irv hostage while *he* cried for mercy.

Maybe the reason she couldn't just bring on the tears was that she felt more relief than sadness. She knew full well she was weary of faking compassion for the helpless lowlifes she wrote about. Most days she viewed them with apathy, if not total disdain.

Besides, whom was she kidding? She'd never had any regard for Irving's fear-driven, editorial judgment. "Have you seen the waffle man?" she would sing before he entered a room. So if she was nothing more than a call girl with a cell phone and a pen, he was the neighborhood pimp who never stopped looking over his shoulder.

And for all his talk about focus groups, Shelby knew the real bottom line. After 152 years in business, the *Chicago Tribune* was still suffering from an identity crisis. No matter how hard they tried to earn the same respect, credibility, and number of Pulitzer prizes as the *New York Time*s, they would never be anything more than first runner up.

"You wouldn't understand what it's like being number two," Granny Bea Good said.

Shelby shook her head, hoping to terminate the interruption. What was it about Alzheimer's patients that allowed them to tune into the conscience of loved ones?

"Ask Lauren what it's like always being in your shadow."

Shelby closed her eyes. This business of her beloved grandmother piercing her inner sanctum was so disconcerting she wanted to cry out to be left alone. On the other hand, once again, Granny had made a valid point.

Lauren did always seem to be in the middle of an identity crisis. In fact, she'd spent her entire life in a futile attempt to compete with someone whom she was destined to follow. Simply, Lauren would always be second. The second daughter, second fiddle, second-rate. Ditto for the *Chicago Trib*. Why even their hometown's nickname said it all. Second City.

Clearly these runner-ups should just accept their lots in life, and instead of fighting it, create their own unique identities. Like the *New York Informer*, Shelby thought.

The *Informer* never gave a damn what the *Times* was working on.

They'd developed their own brand of journalism, badass media. Which meant that they could go down dark, political alleys the *Times* wouldn't even be able to find on a map.

But what was she thinking? That she respected the raging tabloid? That she thought they could play as important a role in the political influence arena as the crusty *Times*? Apparently, yes.

Shelby got up and started rummaging through her pocketbook. She'd thrown his card in there yesterday. "Got it!" she said. Then before she even had a second to reconsider, she dialed the number.

"Ian McNierney, please. Tell him Shelby Lazarus is on the line."

My mother, Bea, lived for her soap operas. I swear the house could be on fire, but if As the World Turns *was on, they'd have to carry her out clinging to her beloved color TV. You don't believe me? After my father had a heart attack, the first thing she did at the hospital was pay the lady who turned on the sets in the rooms. Bea Goodman was not letting Sheldon's poor health prevent her from tuning in! When he died a year later and the rabbi set the funeral for 1 P.M. Friday? Don't ask. She said, "Rabbi, it's either Sunday or nothing."*

Me? I much preferred watching Bewitched. *At least the Stephenses made me laugh. Especially when dear, sweet Aunt Clara came for a visit. Talk about clumsy in the magic spells department. If there was a way to screw up, she found it. I never guessed that one day I'd be just like her. Every time I tried helping, I only made matters worse.*

I tried bringing my family together, and I nearly killed two people. I tried getting Shelby and Lauren on speaking terms, and instead they're at each other's throats. I tried arranging for the best doctors to be on call when Larry and Roz were brought in and what happens? The kid who cracked up Larry's car shows up in the OR with a medical license and a scalpel. And now my husband's in a coma.

In the meantime, poor Roz is in agony. Not from all her broken bones, from seeing herself in the mirror. After being booted like a football, then landing on concrete, she prays her plastic surgeon is as handy as he is creative. Her nose is broken, her cheekbones are fractured, and her face is disfigured from the abrasions. Trouble is the doctors can't do a thing about any of this until all the gravel is removed from beneath her skin with lidocaine. Which, trust me, will be so painful a procedure she's going to wish they left her bleeding to death on the street.

And she's the lucky one! Larry took the real brunt of the blow. Between the extensive fractures and broken bones, and the indeterminable amount of damage to his internal organs, even if he survives he'll never fully recover. God only knows what lies ahead.

As for Shelby and Lauren, not even divine intervention would help those two. They erupt on a whim like active volcanos, with hot lava spewing from their mouths. And that's just over who forgot to turn off the hall lights!

I do have an idea that would bring them closer together, but it's completely crazy. Then again, what I love best about the spirit world is we don't have calories, and there's no such thing as crazy!

It took Shelby four sleepless nights to summon the nerve to return to New York. And no sooner did she arrive, than she thought about running like hell before Lauren discovered she was home.

Not that Chicago had offered much relief, given that her day job no longer existed. Sure she'd been given options: A, take the job editing the *Trib's* newly expanded on-line edition, or B, leave it. Shelby chose B, as it seemed less demeaning, and thanks to the hefty severance package David negotiated for her, the pay was higher. It was the least he could do after dumping her.

Seems the Sunday of the accident, after Shelby left for O'Hare, David paid a visit to his ex-wife and begged to be taken back. As luck would have it, Rhonda was game now that her lover, Mr. Marriage Breaker, no longer found it pleasurable to be shacked up with the mother of two whiny, Ritalin-dependent kids. Besides, she really wanted to renovate the kitchen.

For a brief moment on her return flight to New York, Shelby wondered if she'd left Chicago too hastily. In her younger days she would have marched back into the *Trib's* executive offices and demanded to be reinstated. Afterward, she would have driven over to David's place, made love to him, and convinced him he was better off with her than his fickle, headachy wife.

Unfortunately, both scenarios made Shelby want to search the seat pocket for the airsick bag. She would rather open the emergency exit door at thirty thousand feet than have to grovel at work. As for David, who was she kidding? Sooner or later she would have broken up with him for health reasons . . . she was sick of him.

So here she was, back in Manhasset, just a tad shaky on why. Having spoken to Scott Rosenthal by phone every night, she knew her father had survived the operation to remove the blood clot in his brain, but remained in a coma. Aunt Roz was in great pain, but showed real staying power. Amazing that both had been at death's door and somehow managed not to answer.

Still, Scott was not one to sugarcoat their odds. "Each day is going to be just another crapshoot," he warned. "Another day of weighing possibilities versus risks." It would be weeks, possibly months, before either was well enough to be released. Not that Shelby envisioned herself playing Nurse Nancy while they convalesced from reconstructive surgery.

Maybe she'd look for a new job, not for the money, but to have a ready excuse in case Lauren felt she couldn't handle the burden of caring for Daddy and Aunt Roz alone. Besides, it would be foolish for Shelby to waste her first-class credentials when she was in the media capital of the world. And hadn't Ian McNierney been positively ecstatic when she called? He'd begged to meet for drinks so they could discuss exciting opportunities at the *Informer*. But was that what she really wanted? To be subjected, again, to the infantile whims of a crazy, maniacal editor?

One day at a time, she thought as she logged on to her father's computer, feeling a little like a Pavlovian cyberdog, salivating at the prospect of hearing the voice announcing she had e-mail. But alas she hit a snag. No password? No signing on. Good thing her father wasn't the creative type. He'd likely chosen something as obvious as his birthday or the name of his business. But when those failed to unlock the computer vault, Shelby grew anxious that he might be hiding something clandestine. Why else did one need a top secret password?

After trying dozens of combinations, Shelby had one last idea. He used to use her mother's birthday whenever he needed to create a code. "I need all the reminders I can get," he'd laugh. But it was such a long shot, she was completely thrown when she suddenly found herself logged on. Not that her breaking and entering effort had been worth the aggravation. She had only two e-mails, both from Walter, both a continuation of his ranting.

So much for getting him as a reference, she thought. Or any of her other former colleagues, either. Upon finding a number of her

Trib buddies on-line, she sent them instant messages and didn't receive a single reply. Which meant they'd already removed her screen name from their buddy lists or just didn't care to reply. The digital version of the proverbial slap in the face.

"The hell with them if they want to think I knew about this," she cried out. "I did not betray anyone." Still she was smarting. Not from the rejection, which was old news, but from the realization that computers could no longer be viewed as harmless hardware. At the touch of a button, they were more masochist than machine, able to inflict pain on relationships sans the guilt.

On the other hand, her father and Aunt Roz hadn't needed technology's help to destroy their relationship with her. They'd done permanent damage the old-fashioned way. By being thoughtless and selfish. But wait. Perhaps the computer could help patch things up. If she explored her father's files, discovered his memoirs with a special section on the worst decisions of his life, she might find it in her heart to forgive him. Wishful thinking? Perhaps. Violating his privacy? Definitely!

But what the hell? It would be fun. So fun in fact, one might not hear a car door slam.

"Shelby?" Lauren called from downstairs. "Is that you?"

Shelby froze. Did she have enough time to cover her tracks before Lauren found her? "No, it's the pope," she yelled back. "I'll be down in a sec."

But before Shelby could sign off, Lauren bounded into the room and hugged her. "I saw your suitcase in the kitchen. I can't believe you came back!"

"I said I would, and I did." She made the mouse dance as fast as it could.

"Oh God," Lauren studied her face. "You look awful. Have you slept?"

She shook her head. "I had to get a skycap for the bags under my eyes."

"Why didn't you call me? I would have had Avi pick you up at the airport."

"No thanks." Shelby was almost signed off. "He drove me to La Guardia, remember? And one trip with him was plenty. Apparently in Israel a red light is only a suggestion. Besides, didn't you tell me if I left, we'd never speak again?" Phew. Done.

"Oh. Right. Look, I'm sorry about all that. You have your own life. What did I think? That you'd just drop everything and move back here?"

Shelby flinched. The only time Lauren was this understanding was when she wanted something. "You need a favor, don't you?"

"No." Lauren's right eye started blinking.

"I knew it." Shelby wagged her finger. "Let me guess. They need my kidneys."

"Don't be ridiculous. It's nothing like that. We'll talk later." Lauren hugged her again. "I'm just so happy to see you."

"Oh my God," Shelby groaned. "It must be huge!"

"We'll discuss it later. First, I have something important to tell you. Come downstairs and I'll make us lunch."

"No thanks. I just had a yogurt." Which sure beat the last few days of gorging on Slim-Fast over ice. "But I will gladly take some of your famous tea." She trailed Lauren into the kitchen.

"Okay. First the good news." Lauren began to heat the kettle. "Daddy's vital signs have stabilized, and now all of Mommy's broken bones have been set."

"I know. I spoke to Scott Rosenthal several times. He kept me up to date."

"Really? I didn't know he called you." Lauren seemed genuinely happy.

"He didn't." Shelby cleared her throat. "I called him."

"That's great, Shel." Lauren beamed. "Anyway, I have to tell you something important I learned about Mommy. Something that came as quite a shock to me."

"Let me guess. You finally figured out she's not a nice person."

Lauren slammed the freezer. "I like her, okay? But I'm not talking about her. I'm talking about our real mother," she said quietly. "How she hated to betray Roz for her years as stand-in."

"Yeah, well. I bet I can top that," Shelby said excitedly. "I just found out something about Daddy that shocked me."

"Really? What?" Lauren tossed a package of frozen lasagna in the microwave.

Suddenly Shelby realized it might be a big mistake to tell Little Miss Goody Two Shoes what she'd done. "Nothing. Forget it."

"No. Tell me."

"Okay, but you have to promise not to get all crazy."

"Me?" Lauren pointed at herself. "I'm cool."

"Good." Shelby clapped. "Guess what Daddy's password is on his computer?"

"I have no idea. Dri-Kleen? His birthday?"

"Nope. Mommy's birthday."

"So? They're together almost thirty years. Why does that surprise you?"

"No, not Aunt Roz's birthday. Our real mother's."

"You're kidding. Who told you that?"

"No one. I figured it out myself. See, first I tried the usual stuff. Birthdays, anniversaries. Twenty-two different commonly used golf terms. But when those didn't work I suddenly heard a little voice say, 9-27-31. And voilà, I was in. Don't you think it's sweet he still thinks of her?"

"Yes. But I hate the fact you broke into Daddy's computer. How could you do that?"

"I don't know. I was bored. But wait. I discovered something else that was interesting."

"I don't care. It's wrong to invade another person's privacy."

"Oh please. Like Daddy's got such a high moral code?" Shelby waved as she sat down at the table. "Anyway, here's what blew me away. He has the *Tribune* on his list of favorite places."

"So?" Lauren placed a piping hot cup in front of Shelby.

"So, it has to mean he was reading my columns." She dunked the tea bag.

"Well, duh," Lauren said. "You don't think Daddy's proud of you? He subscribed to practically every paper you ever worked at, even though Mommy would get all crazy because they'd just accumulate and make this huge mess."

"Are you serious? He had the out-of-town papers delivered?"

"Yes, but then after he bought a computer, I showed him how to get everything on-line, and now he's like this addict. We just started calling him Computer Butt . . ."

Shelby was floored. The man who wouldn't pick up a phone to make amends after she told him she hated his guts still cared enough to follow her career?

Lauren smiled. "Does this mean you forgive him?"

"No. Of course not."

"Shelby, what did he do to you? He has no idea . . ."

"Like hell." Her pulse raced. "Just forget it, okay? What did you want to tell me?"

Lauren sat quietly at the table, poking the steam out of the lasagne. "It's very important, okay? So don't say a word until I'm done. Do you promise?"

"Whatever."

Lauren took a deep breath. "I found out what my problem is."

"No offense"—Shelby eyed Lauren's heaping plate—"but you have more than one."

"Stop it, Shelby." Lauren put her fork down. "I was referring to my fertility problems. Why I can't have a baby."

"That's easy." Shelby yawned. "First thing you need is a husband who's home at night."

"Would you please? My problem is not Avi. It's Mommy. The one who gave birth to me."

"You lost me." Shelby leaned in.

"I know. So let me explain." She wiped her chin. "I found out that she took DES when she was pregnant, and that's the reason my periods are so painful and why my uterus is T-shaped, and worst of all, why I keep having miscarriages. I've got the classic symptoms of a DES daughter."

Shelby felt faint. "Are you absolutely sure?"

"Yes."

"How long have you known? How did you find out?"

"It was weird, actually. See after you left, this Mrs. Weiner, one of the social workers at the hospital, was looking for you, and we got to talking, and one thing led to the other, and I mentioned this infertility specialist I was seeing because of my miscarriages, and she told me how her husband was Mommy's doctor, and how Mommy had several miscarriages, too, and how back then they thought DES was a good preventative for that. Then, when I told her about my other medical problems, she immediately got on the phone with this big muckety-muck DES specialist in Manhattan, and I ended up spending four hours in the guy's office, and after a zillion tests, he said, 'Lauren, unfortunately you're a textbook case.'"

"Unbelievable." Shelby fell back. "Where is the justice? We lose our mother to cancer, and now we find out thanks to the same asshole Dr. Weiner, we're DES daughters."

"Not you, Shelby. Me. Mommy didn't start taking DES until *after* you were born."

"Oh." Shelby resumed breathing, uncertain what had just scared her more. The idea she might never be able to have children, or the idea she most certainly could.

"Not that it should matter to you," Lauren continued. "You don't want to have kids."

"Excuse me, but just because I chose to pursue a career over a family doesn't mean that one day I won't want to experience the drudgery of motherhood."

"Well when would be good for you? When you're on Medicare?"

Shelby froze. It was true the years had gone by faster than she would have ever imagined, but plenty of women today had babies later in life. Certainly she still had a window of opportunity if Matthew Lieberman or an equivalent came along. Didn't she?

"Look." Shelby hesitated. "I know how much you want a baby . . ."

"Do you?" Lauren perked up.

"It's all you've ever talked about, so believe me I feel for you. I really do."

"Please don't pity me. I'm just happy to finally know what's wrong with me. All these years I felt like a freak. Remember how I'd catch every cold that went around, and you'd make fun of me for being such a weakling?"

Shelby didn't answer. Hopefully Lauren wasn't fishing for a soppy apology.

"See, I found out the reason I was always sick was because I had such a low immune system, which is one of the most common symptoms of DES. But that's not why I'm telling you this. Remember how well I took it after my first miscarriage?"

"Actually, if I recall, you lived on Absolut and Doritos for about two weeks. I'm not sure that qualifies as keeping it together."

"I didn't say I wasn't upset." Lauren blew the bangs out of her eyes. "But after I was done moping I thought, okay, no big deal, we'll just try again. And I was really upbeat. Really hopeful. Then a few months passed, and every time I got my period I'd freak out. Poor Alan didn't know what to say to me anymore. I mean we were trying all these fertility drugs, and I was blowing up like a balloon in the Macy's parade, and still nothing. After a while, neither of us could take it, and by the time he left me, I couldn't blame him. I was so crazy I wanted to leave me, too."

"Oh please." Shelby waved her hand. "He did you the biggest favor of your life. I mean he was a nice guy and everything, but c'mon. He turned out to be gay."

"I know, but he was such a gentle soul, Shel. And he taught me so much."

"About what?" Shelby snickered. "Coordinating your shoes with the right handbag?"

"Enough." Lauren got up to rinse her plate. "He happens to be a decent, thoughtful human being who still remembers my birthday every year, which is more than I can say for my only sister. Did you know last year he gave Avi and me theater tickets for our anniversary? Orchestra seats!"

"Really? That was generous."

"I guess." Lauren cleared her throat. "I think his boyfriend was in the cast."

Shelby bent over in laughter and clapped her hands.

"I really don't appreciate this right now," Lauren pouted. "So he was gay. He was a very good husband."

"Oh fine." Shelby tried to wipe away her smirk. "Keep going."

"Okay. Anyway, then I met Avi, and he was so understanding about my problems. He even learned how to give me the Perganol injections, and when I finally got pregnant we were so happy, but then I lost the baby after forty-two days, it was ectopic, and they told me then I might have difficulty conceiving again, but they couldn't tell me why, and I thought I would die."

Shelby felt a twinge of nausea for having teased Lauren mercilessly. "I had no idea."

"Of course not. You were too busy ignoring me."

"Listen . . ."

"No! You listen. Did you know I flew to Chicago to see you last year? And when I got to your office they said you were out of town, so I wrote you this whole long note?"

"I know." Shelby picked at a hangnail. "I just didn't see the point of answering you. The last thing I needed was to get involved in all the family *mishegas* again."

"So we're slightly dysfunctional. Name one family that isn't?"

"Sorry, but how many people do you know have a stepmother

who's also their aunt, a half-brother who's also their first cousin, an uncle who's so cheap he won't spend six bucks to visit his sister in the hospital . . ."

"Whoa. You mean stepbrother. You said half-brother. We love Eric, but he's not really related to us."

Shelby blushed. "Half-brother, stepbrother. What the hell difference does it make what we call him? He still fucked up the family tree!"

"Don't say that, Shel. He's trying very hard to turn his life around. In fact Dr. Glavin told me she called a colleague at Betty Ford and found out he's cleaning up very nicely this time."

"Well yippee." Shelby rebounded from her little slip of the tongue. "At a cost of $1500 a day, he damn well better be responding to treatment."

"You're just being mean because you're tired." Lauren stared out at the shimmery, blue pool. "I'm tired, too. Yesterday Maria found a half gallon of milk in the cabinet. I couldn't even remember taking it out of the fridge, let alone putting it away."

Shelby nodded. She understood the perils of sleep deprivation. Yesterday she'd gone for a run, completely forgetting she'd called Mr. Sushi for California rolls. Nothing worse than being greeted at the door by a delivery man who'd waited over an hour for his tip.

She was about to share this little anecdote when she looked over and noticed tears in Lauren's eyes. Oddly, she never looked more beautiful, with those exotic, baby browns glistening, and the sunlight jutting off her golden skin. In another era they would have called her a goddess. But by today's standards she would be written off as another fat Jewish girl not worthy of a second look. It was the media's fault. And, okay, obsessive women like me, she thought.

Regardless, she wanted to offer Lauren words of comfort, if only she knew any. Perhaps Lauren would just take solace from the warmth of the kitchen and the fact Shelby was ripping apart her napkin into hundreds of little pieces, just as they had done as kids. What fun it was to make this huge mess on the table, then walk away so Aunt Roz would have to clean up after them. Which she always did.

Honestly, Shelby thought. What was the point of rearing children if you were going to create indulged little monsters who had no sense of their limitations?

Maybe if the three Lazarus kids had gotten cracked across the face every once in a while, Eric wouldn't be strung out on drugs, Lauren wouldn't be so needy, and she wouldn't be so hell-bent on battling authority figures all the time. Not that she would ever openly admit this.

Lauren smiled at the sight of Shelby diligently shredding her napkin and sat down to join her. "Who's going to clean this up when we're done?" She got right into the rhythm.

"Maria," they suddenly burst into song. "I've just met a girl named Maria . . ."

West Side Story was the perfect tension-breaker, but when the music stopped, Lauren resumed where she left off, not missing a beat. "My life has been such a nightmare lately. I've had test after test, dozens of painful procedures, I live at the doctor's, it's hard for me to keep a job because I never feel well, I'm fat as a horse because of all the fertility drugs I take, which they now think might have hyperstimulated my ovaries . . ."

"Believe it or not I know what you're going through." Shelby stood up to stretch. "A few years ago I did this big series on DES daughters, and I couldn't believe what the pharmaceutical companies got away with. They dispensed DES like it was coming out of freakin' Pez dispensers, even after all the evidence proved it would permanently mess up women's reproductive tracts! But they were making millions off it, so what the hell? Finally, this group of DES daughters shamed Congress into appropriating funds for research and education, but by then it was blood money. Basically they left thousands of women to fend for themselves, and their stories are total travesties. Although a lot of them have sued and walked away with big settlements."

"I don't want to sue." Lauren wiped her eyes. "I just want to have a family."

"Don't be naive. You're a perfect candidate for litigation. We'll get yours and Mommy's medical records, then I'll help you find a lawyer who specializes in class action suits . . ."

"No. Suing is not the answer for me. I want to focus all my energy on having a baby."

"Fine. Do what you think is best. I just can't be of any help to you in that department."

Lauren looked over at Shelby, her face filled with despair. And there was that twitching eye thing going on again, too. Which set off a bell in Shelby's head. As a master of analyzing facial expressions, she could tell what people were saying when they weren't saying anything at all. This time, however, she prayed she'd gotten her signals crossed. "I saw that look."

"What are you talking about?" Lauren turned away.

"That blinking thing that happens to your eye whenever you're about to ask me a favor. How will I ever be able to tell if you're having a stroke?"

"I can't help it. It's involuntary, like a sneeze. But now that you mentioned it . . ."

"Oh my God," Shelby fell into her chair. "I was right. There is something you want."

"The odds of my having a normal pregnancy are very slim."

"Oh my God."

"I mean I could probably get pregnant again, but basically my cervix is retarded, and it's not likely I'd be able to sustain a pregnancy long enough to deliver a healthy baby. Plus, there's a good chance I would pass on the DES problems, so they don't think I should use my eggs. That's why a lot of women in my case are using . . ."

"Surrogates?" Shelby barely had enough oxygen to say the word.

Lauren nodded yes, her eyes pleading.

"Me?" Shelby pointed to herself. "Have you gone completely mad?"

"You wouldn't have to give me an answer right away. All I'm asking is for you to consider the possibility."

"No." Shelby pounded the table. "There is no possibility. How could you even come up with the self-serving, ill-conceived idea of using me?"

"On-line."

"You mean a chat room?"

"Sort of. I found this support group for DES daughters, and they were all talking about their sisters, and cousins, and friends and aunts volunteering to be their surrogates. So I showed Avi some of the things they said, and he immediately thought of you."

"Well sure. He probably thought it meant we'd have hot sex every month."

Lauren lowered her head and began to cry.

"I'm sorry. I didn't mean it like it sounded."

"Yes you did. But forget the whole thing. You're right. It's a ridiculous idea."

"Yes it is." Shelby shook in disbelief. On the other hand, at least she'd confirmed her impeccable instincts were still operating on all cylinders. She knew Lauren was up to something, although had she realized her sister was shopping for a uterus instead of a kidney, she would have been out the door in a heartbeat.

"But don't you think it's interesting that there's like this whole society of surrogates?" Lauren, the prizefighter, would not stay down. "Every year thousands of women bear children for others, totally out of the goodness of their hearts."

"Right. And the quick twenty grand they get plays no part in their decision."

"Fine. So a select few do it for the money. But my point is . . ."

"I know what your point is. But I'm not like those women, Lauren. I'm selfish, I'm vain, and believe me, the only doctor who's ever gotten that close to my vagina bought me dinner first."

"I know it's a big decision." Lauren reached into her pocketbook for a pamphlet. "But here's some information on surrogacy that could answer a lot of your questions. Will you at least read it?"

"Absolutely not." Shelby walked over to the window. "I wouldn't be a surrogate if you got Mel Gibson to fuck me. Sorry, Lauren. I'm not your girl."

"Avi's feelings are going to be hurt you know. He's going to think you don't like him."

"I don't like him." Shelby turned to her. "But wait a second. I might have an idea."

"Really?" Lauren pressed her hand against her heart.

"Yes. If all you need is a Rent-a-Uterus type arrangement, get Kaneesha or one of the other five cleaning sisters to do it. They probably pop out babies like toaster cakes."

"Shelby," Lauren gasped. "You are positively shameful. Haven't you ever had a dream?"

"No, but I've had my share of nightmares. And this one is at the top of the list."

"Fine. If that's how you feel, then this is the end of the discussion."

"I'd be eternally grateful."

"No wait." Lauren clenched her fist. "Rock, paper, scissors, shoot?"

Finally! I think I got a handle on this power of suggestion thing. All I did was come to Lauren in a dream, plant a tiny seed of an idea in her head, and boom, she ran with it like a quarterback on fire. I wonder if Shelby would be that receptive if I came to her in a dream? Nah, she'd probably think it was a nightmare and blame it on too much red wine.

PART II

Oh Baby

Chapter Ten

Given the surreal circumstances under which she'd returned home, Shelby was amazed at how quickly she'd transitioned from a pressure-cooker job into the gentle rhythm of unstructured days. A week ago she was worried her story reservoir had gone dry, as she was down to one measly lead about a South Side cop allegedly selling stolen cars on the Internet. Now her only newspaper-related concern was solving the *Times* crossword puzzle in less time than it took the day before.

A week ago she'd been romantically involved with David. Now she had a new love interest, a real bastard. His name was Pucci. Like David, Pucci raced over the minute he heard Shelby's voice, and he was a master at begging. Unlike David, the only way he could be with her was if he squeezed his tiny Yorkie body under the next-door neighbor's fence.

Trouble was, Shelby wasn't much of a dog lover. Sooner or later she'd need to seek the company of a two-legged friend. Would that mean returning to David? She did enjoy his razor-sharp humor and the way he turned Saturday night dates into all-out events. Frankly, no one else had ever flown her to St. Louis for a restaurant opening, or snuck her into a private party on Michigan Avenue, claiming she was Sarah Jessica Parker's sister.

But in all the time they went out, Shelby never thought of him, yearned for him, or gave herself to him. David may have been camp-director fun, but he had the sexual prowess of a neutered house pet. He may have been legally divorced, but his true love was still his ex-wife, Rhonda. And for the sake of unsuspecting single women everywhere, Shelby hoped the couple reconciled so he never came back on the market again.

But aside from losing her job and her lover, the biggest change in Shelby's life was that instead of chasing people, now she made every effort to avoid them. Particularly Lauren and Avi, who were pressuring her to warehouse their baby for nine months.

Fortunately, it was not difficult avoiding Avi, as it was only a rumor he was in residence. With so much pressing business at the airport, he was doing late-night runs, then getting back on the road by dawn. The only telltale sign he'd slept in the house was if the early edition of the *New York Informer* was left lying on the kitchen counter.

Shelby prayed Lauren never found out she was not only stealing the paper, but Maria's fresh-baked pastries. It came as a shock, but Shelby discovered she liked lounging in bed, reading the paper from front to back, and stuffing her mouth. It was a nasty habit, but only temporary, of course.

What surprised her even more than how much she liked Danish was how much she liked the *Informer*. It was brazen, entertaining, and totally irreverent. This morning's edition was a prime example. While serious folk were concerned with economic recovery and combating terrorism, *Informer* readers were lapping up a story entitled, "Whereist thou Shelby Lazarus?"

The gossip writer speculated the feisty, veteran journalist's fallout with *Trib* management came so unexpectedly there was no time to decide the fate of the thousands of leftover WE LOVE SHELBY bumper stickers. Rumor also had it staffers seemed particularly gleeful when opening their office windows to dump them into the Chicago River below.

Inquiring minds apparently wanted to know. Was Shelby Lazarus mulling offers at her Lake Shore Drive condo, or playing snookems in Tortola with the recently divorced publisher of the *Los Angeles Times*?

"Where the hell did they get this?" Shelby laughed, secretly delighted she'd been deemed newsworthy enough to be at the center of a whisper campaign. Yet deeply hurt her own sources never informed her the rich and handsome Jack Bennett was back in the single circuit.

In the meantime, it occurred to her Ian McNierney was baiting her, knowing if she saw the story she'd have to call him on it. But what would she say? That she was whiling away the day sipping iced tea by the family pool? That her only offer thus far was from the *Des Moines Register*, inquiring of her interest in editing their Sunday style section? Honestly. How much style could there be in a place where the women and the cows wore approximately the same size?

Perhaps she would call Ian to say she was back in New York, and thanks for the mention. But when would she find the time? Between answering the endless queries of concerned family and friends, attacking the *Times* crossword puzzle, working out, researching DES, and running errands for Maria, she was booked solid. Speaking of which, Maria had given her yet another grocery list and would inevitably carry on until Shelby delivered the needed household items.

"Who's working for whom here?" Shelby grumbled, as she pushed a mega-store cart through the produce section of Waldbaum's. It had been an amusing, little chore the first time she returned to the supermarket of her youth. Even though, just as with her house and the hospital, it bore no resemblance to the place she remembered. For sure the Waldbaum's of her past did not have a sushi bar, a photo-processing lab, or ten thousand items that would guarantee a serious relationship with a cardiologist. A whole aisle for chips, and another for cookies? Was it any wonder America was now the land of the obese?

"Excuse me?" Exhibit A waved from across the watermelon bin. "Don't I know you?"

Oh no, Shelby sighed. Not another day of "Shelby Lazarus, This is Your Life."

"I'm sorry." The big mama blushed. "I thought you were someone I grew up with."

"It's okay." She coughed. "I'm recognized all the time. I'm Shelby Lazarus."

"Oh my God. I thought so," she said, clapping. "I'm Stacy Rothstein. Well, now it's Alter." She flashed a wedding ring with so many karats, the other veggies were surely jealous.

Her maiden name sounded middle-class-Jewish familiar to Shelby, but there was no way they were the same age. This woman was old enough to have four whiny kids and gray hair.

"You don't remember me, do you?" She blushed, fully aware her late-model, extralarge body could have something to do with it. "From Shelter Rock Elementary?"

"I think so. You were in my . . ."

". . . Same class all the way from kindergarten to sixth. Then there was junior and senior high."

"Right. Sure. Stacy Rothstein. I remember you," Shelby lied.

"It's okay. I was really shy back then. I'm just glad my guys aren't like that."

"They're all yours?" Shelby gulped at the sea of sticky-faced critters.

"All mine." She beamed, wiping four little noses before Shelby could have even found a tissue. "Lee is my big guy, Zack and Alex are my twins, and this little cutie is Taryn."

"They're adorable," Shelby lied again, shuddering at the idea of caring for a whole litter.

"How about you?" Stacy smiled. "How many children do you have?"

"Me?" Shelby examined a green banana. This was why intelligent people stayed away from class reunions. They were so damn inhospitable. "None. I'm single." There. She said it.

"Really?" Stacy seemed taken aback. "You always talked about having a big family."

"No way!" Shelby grimaced. "You must be confusing me with what's her name. That girl who used to practically announce it over the PA system every time she missed her period."

"You mean Sherry Melnick?"

"Yeah. Sherry Melnick. Whatever happened to her?"

"I'm not sure. She showed up to our tenth reunion all cozy with some black guy she introduced as her boss. Then I heard she moved to India and changed her name to Swami Maharji."

"Never was the sharpest tool in the shed. But where did you get the idea I wanted kids?"

"I may not have said a whole lot when we were younger." Stacy laughed. "But I never missed a thing that went on. Don't you remember Miss Oberlin's monthly essay contests?"

"Vaguely." Shelby shrugged, wondering how banal an existence this woman must have if she still kept memories of third-grade writing assignments in her head.

"I'll never forget yours," Stacy kissed her daughter's head. "Because you always wrote about the same thing. How you wanted to be a famous writer and a mommy. In fact, once you said you wanted one child for every day of the week."

"That's ridiculous," Shelby snorted. "That wasn't me. I mean I definitely remember wanting to be a writer, but I assure you the last thing on my mind was wiping dirty noses." Oops, she thought when Stacy blinked. Perhaps there were times when smugness had its limitations.

"No, it was definitely you." The nose wiper fortunately didn't appear to take offense. "I remember because the contest always came down to you and Marc Silverman, and you never won."

"Yeah, but that was only because it was more a personality contest than a writing contest." Shelby stuck out her chin. "Everybody voted for Marc because his dad was part owner of the Knicks, and he could invite whoever he wanted to the games."

"Yes, but then for the last contest of the year, you got up there and read this beautiful piece about the true meaning of Mother's Day, and about how girls were so much luckier than boys because we got to have the babies, and all the girls were crying, and Miss Oberlin's mascara was running down her face . . . don't you remember that?"

"Not really." Shelby cleared her throat. "Did I . . . win?"

"Yes you won!" Stacy laughed. "That's why I remember it so well. After you got your little trophy, you went over to Marc and kissed him on the lips, and Miss Oberlin nearly fainted. I can't believe you don't remember . . ."

"It does sort of ring a bell . . ." A baffled Shelby stared at the watermelons. But it was before my mother died. Before my life was turned upside down, and I never saw anything the same again.

"To me it seems like yesterday." Stacy picked up the candy wrapper her son dropped. "I still remember who was in our classes, who liked who . . ."

Suddenly Shelby got excited. "Do you by any chance remember Matty Lieberman?"

"I remember his name," she replied. "But didn't he move away?"

"Yes. At the end of fifth grade . . ."

"Wait a minute. Wasn't he the kid who used to freak out Mrs. Dwyer by pulling the little wires out of his notebooks, then sticking them in his ear?"

"No." Shelby sighed. He was the one who kissed me in the snow and promised he'd love me forever. He was the one who wrote me love poems and pushed my bangs out of my eyes.

"You know who might know?" Stacy whipped pretzels out of her bag to feed the farm animals in the basket who were getting fidgety. "Do you remember Abby Cohen?"

"Sure. Dear Abby," Shelby nodded. Who could forget the school yenta?

"Well, she and her husband moved back here a few years ago, and now she works over at the Manhasset Press. Anyway, she started this thing called, 'Where Are They Now?' and every month she runs a picture of someone who grew up here. Then readers write in whatever they know. You wouldn't believe what some of the kids are doing. Remember Ross Greenblatt?"

"Yeah." Shelby puffed out her cheeks. "The only fourth grader who needed two chairs."

"Not anymore! He's in Hollywood now. He lost like a hundred pounds and changed his name to Darin something. He was on *The Young and the Restless* for a while. Or one of those."

"Wow. That's amazing. Okay, good. I'll give Abby a call. What's her last name now?"

"Rosenthal."

"Oh God. You're kidding," Shelby cried. "Is she married to Scott Rosenthal?"

"Yes, but he was a year behind us so I wasn't sure if you'd remember him."

"Oh, I remember him," Shelby rolled her eyes. "In fact, believe it or not, he's one of the doctors on my father and stepmother's surgical team."

"Really? I heard about the accident of course," Stacy said sadly. "How are they doing?"

"It's touch-and-go," Shelby said matter-of-factly. "We're taking it day to day . . . Oh no."

"What?" Stacy jumped.

"Nothing. Just my pager again. Our housekeeper thinks I'm her personal messenger." She shook her head as she reached under her T-shirt to read the critical message. Then she cried out.

"What is it?" Stacy reached over the watermelons for Shelby's hand.

"Oh my God." Shelby used her other hand to cover her mouth.

"Is everything okay?" Stacy panicked.

"Daddy's out of the coma," Shelby slowly repeated the message that blipped across the tiny screen, a ticker tape of vital information. "I can't believe it."

"It's a miracle." Stacy came around to hug Shelby, tears streaming down her eyes. "Maybe that means he's going to be fine. I'm so happy for you."

"Why are you crying, Mommy?" Alex looked up.

"Because my friend Shelby just got some wonderful news."

This is so bizarre; Shelby looked at Stacy's wet face. *A woman I haven't seen in over twenty years is crying for joy about a man she never met, while I'm feeling . . . nothing?*

"I really have to get going, but good luck with everything." Stacy waved good-bye. "And, I hope you find Matty Lieberman."

"Me too," Shelby whispered. *Me too.*

It's so funny. Here I am trying to use what limited powers I have to straighten out my daughter's errant, misguided life, and then without any tinkering on my part, she runs into a former classmate at Waldbaum's who just happened to remember Shelby once spoke lovingly of motherhood. Sometimes I get the feeling there's a grander plan than I'm privy to.

But if that's true, what's the holdup getting Shelby and Matty back together? I suppose it's that whole karma, timing thing. We choose rebirth in order to learn tough lessons. And sometimes the hardest lesson of all is learning to trust the wisdom of the universe. Not questioning what comes our way.

It's quite an eye-opener coming to terms with the fact the universe works on its own blessed timetable, and no amount of hoping and wanting will speed up the process. It's very frustrating, of course, but it probably seems whenever there's something you desperately want, something you're completely obsessed with, you can pretty much guarantee it's not going to happen at that time.

Later, when you've calmed down, opened your mind to other possibilities, lo and behold, the head banging ends, and doors magically open. Not necessarily the way you originally envisioned, and maybe not quite exactly as you hoped, yet somehow the circumstances seem right. Then you hear yourself saying, "It's amazing how everything worked out for the best."

Welcome to Universal Law 101. You can plan, plan, plan, but only that which is meant to happen, only that which is God's will, ever does. It doesn't explain why the people you hate most seem to have all the luck, but trust me, everyone has to pay their bill before checkout time.

As for Larry's miraculous turnaround? You see how powerful the unconscious mind is? Even in a comatose state, one can make the decision they want to live. God bless free will.

Shelby raced out of Waldbaum's parking lot, not because she was in a hurry, but because the rapid acceleration of Aunt Roz's new Lexus had her doing fifty-five before she was back on the street. Hopefully that shopping cart in her path hadn't made too much of a dent in the trunk. But there was one dent she had to admit was growing deeper. The dent in her heart.

How else to explain she was driving in the direction of North Shore instead of the house? It would have made so much more sense to go home, put the groceries away, then speak to Lauren by phone. So why was she driving in the opposite direction? It was a good question. Unfortunately, the driver behind her did not care to join her in thought, as he viewed the green light as his signal to lay on the horn.

I'll just run in for a minute, find out what the story is, then go home, she thought as she pulled into the infamous hospital parking lot. I wonder if any of those old essays from Miss Oberlin's class are still in those boxes in my room?

But the instant Shelby walked through the front doors with the other throng of visitors, she was whisked away by Mrs. Weiner.

"Lauren hoped you were on your way over." She held Shelby's hand as they made their way to the elevator. "It's an absolute miracle what's happening. No one can quite believe the turnaround. Your father is fully alert, lucid, has all his faculties . . ."

"Where are you taking me?" Shelby stopped. She was not a collie on a leash.

"I just thought we could go up to the waiting area to speak to the doctors. It's not anywhere close to the ICU."

"No." Shelby shook her head. "No. I don't do third floors. I'll wait in the cafeteria."

"Shelby, it's okay. I'll be with you the whole time. Don't you think it would be incredibly helpful if your father knew you were nearby?"

"No! My father would totally understand why I can't be up

there. Who do you think drove me twenty miles to another hospital when I fell off a horse and broke my arm? He did. Believe me, it'll be enough for him just to know I'm back in New York."

"All right then." Mrs. Weiner sighed. "But I really think you'd be fine if you just tried. You're not a child anymore."

"Thanks for pointing out the obvious." Shelby led them to the cafeteria. "But maybe you could explain something I don't understand. Why do you and every other do-gooder think you have to be the next Annie Sullivan before you can live with yourselves? Why is it you can't rest until you've found a social specimen you can write about in some psychobabble journal so the experts on human delineation can ooh and ahh over the findings at the annual convention in Cleveland?

Mrs. Weiner laughed. "You make a very good point, dear. I promise to omit your story at next year's symposium on head cases. But if I don't get nominated for best social worker of the year, it'll be on your conscience, not mine."

"Fine." Shelby found her safe-space table in the cafeteria and threw down her pocketbook and keys to reserve the territory. "I'm getting their lousy coffee? You want?"

Minutes later Lauren ran in, her face swollen from tears. "Can you believe it?" She hugged Shelby. "The doctors are calling him Miracle Man. They've never seen anyone come through a trauma like his in such a short time. And there's no sign of any brain damage."

"Have you seen him?" Shelby bit her lip.

"Seen him? I was right there! I was just rubbing his arm, talking to him about a million things, when I happened to mention the idea of you helping me have a baby, and . . ."

"You did what?" Shelby jumped up. "Why are you telling people that?"

"He's not people, Shel. He's Daddy. I mean, don't you think it's a miracle he heard your name and suddenly his fingers moved ever so slightly?"

"The only miracle will be if I don't kill you in your sleep . . ."

"Well I'm sorry if you can't appreciate what an awesome moment it was." Lauren turned to Mrs. Weiner. "At first I thought I was imagining it, but when I repeated Shelby's name, and his hand flinched, I screamed so loud, the nurses came running. They were scared to death."

"Isn't that something?" Mrs. Weiner clasped her hands in prayer formation.

"How could you say I was having a baby for you?" Shelby remained frozen in her tracks.

"Oh relax." Mrs. Weiner pulled Shelby back to her seat. "You can just deny it if he asks. "

"Yes, but you said you were going to talk to her," Lauren whispered to Mrs. Weiner.

"Not now, dear," she returned the whisper. "Let's focus on your father's recovery."

"Oh my God," Shelby yelled out to no one in particular. "Call Oliver Stone. We have a little conspiracy thing going on here."

"Shelby, calm down. There's no conspiracy. Lauren just happened to mention her idea about your being a surrogate mother, and I told her I'd be happy to share what I know about the process. I didn't say I would try to talk you into it."

"Yes, but you said you'd tell her why you thought it was a good idea," Lauren nudged her.

"We are changing the subject." Shelby banged on the table. "I will never, ever carry anyone's baby . . . other than my own." Had she really once said she wanted seven children, one for every day of the week? What the hell was that about? "This matter is not open for discussion!"

"Fine. You've made your point." Mrs. Weiner patted her on the back. "Now let's find out what else Lauren knows about your dad. Has your mother seen him?"

"No, she was down in X-ray, but they said she burst into tears when they told her, which was not a good thing because she has this fractured orbit in her eye . . ."

"Did you tell Daddy I was here?" Shelby interrupted, not interested in Aunt Roz's condition.

"Yes."

"And? What did he say?"

"Nothing really. But that doesn't mean anything. No one really knows how much he hears or understands. All we know is when Dr. Rosenthal asked him his name, he said, 'Larry.' "

"Larry," Mrs. Weiner repeated. "This is so great."

"Wait. It gets even better. With all the excitement about Daddy, I didn't get a chance to tell you Mommy's good news. The orthopedic team cannot believe how incredible she's doing, too. They said they've never seen anyone practically heal themselves before. It's as if somebody up above is orchestrating the recovery of the century."

"Isn't this wonderful news, Shelby?" Mrs. Weiner clapped.

"You betcha." Shelby examined her dry cuticles. She desperately needed a manicure.

"But here's the best news." Lauren was practically singing. "Even though Mommy's bandaged from head to toe, the nurses said we could wheel her into the solarium to have lunch."

"When?" Shelby's neck hair suddenly felt moist.

"Today. Now." Lauren smiled eagerly.

"But it's not visiting hours yet," Shelby stammered. "And it's such short notice for her. She probably needs time to get ready."

"Are you nuts? She's never been more ready for anything. She's dying to see you, Shel."

"Gee, I don't know. I was planning to run over to Frederico's to get my nails done."

"Oh please? You could do that anytime. I want you to be there to have the honors."

"What honors?" Shelby gulped.

"Feeding her, of course. It's going to be a while before she can eat on her own."

"You're kidding?"

"Well duh, Shel. The poor woman's got a broken jaw, both arms in casts, and a face that's all bandaged except for her right eye. They thought maybe we could start by spoon-feeding her some apple-sauce."

Spoon-feeding her? Shelby laid her head down and groaned. The last time she saw her aunt they'd had a vicious exchange of words, and Shelby polished off the fight by screaming, "Why don't you go shove a spoon in that big fat mouth of yours so no one has to listen to you?" Was this some kind of sick, cosmic joke that two years later she would be given the chance to insert said spoon?

Worse still, she shuddered at the prospect of Aunt Roz being helpless, as everyone would expect her to act the part of the dutiful daughter. To wipe her drool, wipe her brow, wipe her ass. Shelby would rather binge on a Big Mac than conjure up that image in her head!

Truly, the only way she would survive a face-to-face meeting with Aunt Roz was if she had enough time to build up the courage. Yes, that was it. She just needed an adjustment period, an opportunity to go through reentry, like when the astronauts returned to earth after a long mission.

On the other hand, maybe she was blowing this first meeting out of proportion. After all, it was just lunch. Like the dating service. Her only obligation would be to engage in polite conversation and decide if she could stomach the person enough to see them again.

Too bad there wasn't a special service that brought adult children together with their estranged parents, she thought. They could call it, "Just a Nosh." Forget the stress of making it from drinks through dessert. All one had to do was maintain civil conversation through coffee and cake. If they survived that, the next stop was early-bird brunch. Separate checks, of course.

"So? What do you think, Shel?" Lauren nudged her arm. "Should we go have lunch?"

"What floor is she on?"

"Fifth floor," Lauren and Mrs. Weiner said in unison.

"You've never been up there, dear," Mrs. Weiner winked. "It's a new wing."

"I don't know." Shelby started to sweat. "I'm not ready. I need more time. It's too soon . . ."

"Pretty please." Lauren reached for her hand. "I promise we'll stick to you like Velcro."

"Yes, and maybe we could even stop by to say hello to Dr. Weiner. He's on the same floor, and I'm sure he'd love the company."

"Are you out of your mind?" Shelby sprang up as if there were coils under her shoes. "He's the last person I want to see right now!"

"You're right," Mrs. Weiner stood up. "Bad idea. Perhaps another time."

"Only if it's to pull the plug on his life support," Shelby groaned, as Lauren and Mrs. Weiner locked arms with her.

"We're off to see the Wizard," a giggling Lauren sang, as they skipped to the elevator, their terrified prisoner in tow.

Chapter Eleven

Shelby didn't care if today was the grand opening of this hospital wing. Between the antiseptic-scented walls, and the floor's ammonia odor, it still smelled like good old North Shore. But mostly it still *sounded* like North Shore, what with the medicinal clatter accosting her the moment she stepped off the crowded elevator; the nurses' squeaky, rubber-soled footsteps, the endlessly disruptive pages blaring over the hospital PA system, and the off-key symphony of endless heart monitors. This was the reunion of sounds she'd hoped never to hear again.

But the one eerily familiar noise that truly brought Shelby back was the clanking of food carts rolling down the halls. How she dreaded hearing the orderlies' approach, knowing they would fly in to her mother's room with a tray full of bland, lukewarm mush under metal covers. Mush that would lie untouched until some indifferent attendant had time to take it away.

"See?" Lauren wiggled Shelby's hand. "It's not scary up here."

"And everything's different." Mrs. Weiner held on tight. "Right?"

"The only difference I see is all the WMJDs are gone."

"The who, dear?"

"The white, male, Jewish doctors," Shelby said, as a turban-headed Pakistani doctor rushed past. "Look around. The place is run by foreigners now. Incidentally, how do you pronounce names with six consecutive consonants?"

"I'm surprised to hear you speak that way." Mrs. Weiner held on to Shelby's arm as they power-walked the long corridors. "Shouldn't you have a reporter's objectivity?"

"I'm sure she's very objective when she writes a story," Lauren said in her defense.

"Let her carry on," Mrs. Weiner whispered. "As long as we just keep moving."

"Irma! Is that you?" a hoarse voice cried out from a room on the right.

"Yes, dear." Mrs. Weiner continued her fast pace. "I'll be back in a bit."

"Irma," the man cried out again. "Get in here. Now!"

Mrs. Weiner stopped abruptly, a knee-jerk reaction to her days as the obedient wife. "Hold on, dear." She patted Shelby's hand. "I'll be just a minute."

"Uh-oh." Lauren glanced at Shelby. "And we were doing so good."

"Relax." Shelby patted her cheek. "I'm not going anywhere. I think I can do this."

"Really?" Lauren resumed breathing.

"Sure. We're just going to say hello to her, feed her, then call the nurses to bring her back to her room. I can still have my hands in a bowl of marbles and suds in less than an hour."

"Shelby? Lauren?" Mrs. Weiner called from the room. "Could you please come in here?"

They looked at each other and gulped. Now it was time for both of them to panic.

"Come in for a minute, girls." Mrs. Weiner returned to the hall. "Dr. Weiner won't bite. He'd just like to say hello."

"Like hell I'm going in there," Shelby whispered. "I hate that son of a bitch!"

But before Shelby could choose the best getaway route, she and Lauren were ushered into the dying man's private room. Her first thought was how embarrassed she'd be if she hurled from the familiar, tainted smell of sickness.

"Hullo." The pale, thin patient waved shakily. "Thank you for stoppink by."

"Like we had a choice?" Shelby glared at Mrs. Weiner. This was such an incredibly bad idea. Yet she couldn't help but be thrown by the man's thick, German accent. For a person she'd spent a lifetime hating, ironically she knew very little about him.

"Here's who you were looking for, Shelby." Mrs. Weiner smiled, ignoring Shelby's puss.

"Excuse me?"

"Here's your WMJD. Although he was also foreign-born, so he might not meet your stringent qualifications."

Shelby's face reddened. Okay, maybe she had gone a little far mocking the foreigners in the hospital. Lord knows how many Eastern European Jewish doctors entered the country after the war, and what a travesty it would have been had they been denied opportunities in America.

"I don't have much time left." Dr. Weiner coughed and sputtered.

"How old are you?" Shelby stood firmly at the door.

"Seventy-three this August," he wiped his brow. "God willing."

"Well, that's a lot longer than our mother ever had."

"Shelby!" Lauren grabbed her arm. "Don't be rude."

"No, no, it's okay." Dr. Weiner waved. "She's angry vith me. Belief me. I understand."

"To be honest, I can't say angry sums it up." Shelby's wrath quickly converted to steam heat. "Not when I'm looking at a man who put his right hand on the Bible and took the Hypocrite's Oath. Thou shalt enter the practice of medicine with the sole purpose of milking it for the cash cow that it is . . ."

"Shelby, please." Mrs. Weiner put her arm around her. "He just thought if you two had the chance to meet . . ."

"That what? I'd sit here and listen to his crappy apology?" Shelby pushed her arm away. "Sorry. Apologies are for when you're late for dinner or you forget a friend's birthday. They don't count for shit when a doctor is so cavalier and inept, so terribly conceited and unfeeling, he destroys a person's life, then takes almost thirty years to express his deepest sympathies."

"Jost like the mother." Dr. Weiner smiled, shaking his finger in recognition.

"I'll take that as a compliment." Shelby stood, hands on hips.

"Of course." His chuckle quickly turned into a mucus-filled gag. Still, he held his hand up, signaling he had more to say.

"You say I was conceited? Uch! You're right. But not unfeeling. Never unfeeling." He looked into Shelby's angry eyes. "And not vithout regrets. You don't think I vished I could do better? But who knew? We were in the dark ages then. We didn't have the research, the tests . . ."

"Oh, please," Shelby cried. "I'm not a child anymore. I don't hold you accountable for what you didn't know. I hold you accountable for your arrogance and your contempt. When my mother came to you in pain, you told her to stop *kvetching*. You blew her off, Dr. Weiner. And six months later she was dead. Now I'm supposed to forgive you just so you can die with a clear conscience? Give me a break!"

"Shelby, stop!" Mrs. Weiner ran to her ex-husband's side. "You're upsetting him."

"No, no." He waved. "Let her get it out. It's good to get things out."

"I think we should go," Lauren whispered. "Mommy's waiting for us."

Shelby nodded in agreement and turned around.

"Wait. Please," Dr. Weiner called out. "I vant to finish."

"Maybe another time, dear." Irma fluffed his pillow while signaling the girls to leave. "This wasn't one of my better ideas . . ."

"Listen to me." He tried to sit up. "You don't think I cried at the sight of your mother's small, ravaged body? At the sight of you beautiful children clinging to her? I was devastated, believe me. But I never turned my back on her. I consulted with anyone I thought knew something about her cancer. I called the universities, the drug companies, I even flew to Tijuana to get her the Laetrile therapy. Ask Irma."

Shelby and Lauren stopped.

"It's true." Mrs. Weiner stroked his arm. "He was also one of the first physicians to use marijuana to control pain and nausea."

"I gave her from my best stash." Dr. Weiner winked.

Lauren looked at Shelby in disbelief. Their mother had smoked joints?

"Toward the end he made sure she was so high she felt nothing," Mrs. Weiner said. "And believe me, that was very risky. He could have been arrested. He could have lost his license . . ."

"It's a lovely story." Shelby smirked. "Very compelling. But did it ever occur to you, Dr. Weiner, that none of your Superman heroics would have been necessary if you'd just listened to her?"

"Okay, that's it. I've heard enough." Mrs. Weiner started to show them out. "You want to spend the rest of your life wallowing in pity and hatred? Be my guest. But you have no right to come in here and be heartless."

"She's not heartless, Mrs. Weiner." Lauren held Shelby's hand. "She's in pain. And this was your idea. Not ours."

"Out, out, out." Mrs. Weiner began shooing them.

"Irma!" a ferocious-sounding Dr. Weiner growled. Everyone jumped. "Please." He started to cough up blood. "I want to hear what she has to say."

"No, dear," Irma bravely defied him. "You have no idea what she's really like, and . . ."

"You don't know"—he tried catching his breath—"from having your mother torn from your arms when you're a mere child. We do." He pointed to the girls and himself. "What I wouldn't have given to shake my fist at the barbarian who killed mine."

"Oh my God." Lauren placed her hand over her heart. "Your mother was killed?"

Dr. Weiner nodded, then pulled up the left sleeve of his hospital gown to reveal his German phone number. The six-digit tattoo brandished in his arm by the Nazis. "Not just my mother. My father. My aunts, uncles, cousins, brothers, sisters, friends, neighbors. Believe me," he whispered, "I know about loss. About suffering. Bergen-Belsen never leaves you."

Shelby and Lauren looked at one another, too stunned to speak. Too moved to hear the cheerful cries of a child running down the hall.

"Papa, Papa! Today was Moving Up Day at school and the man said I could have red Jell-O." An exuberant five-year-old zoomed in and jumped on the bed. "Now I don't have to eat yours!"

"Justin!" Dr. Weiner tried to hug his beloved grandson but got tangled in his tubes.

"Oooh, Justin, be careful. Move down this way, sweetie." Mrs. Weiner lifted him. "How's Grandma's big graduate?" she kissed his head. "Kindergarten here we come."

"Hi, Mom." The boy's father strode in, holding a bag of toys and a sack of bagels. He walked over to his mother, kissed her cheek, then his father's. "How you doing, Dad?"

"Fine. Fine." He managed to smile. "Just doing some reminiscing."

"You took the day off?" Irma took the bagels from her son.

"Sure. How often does one's son graduate nursery school?" He patted Justin's head.

"Not graduate, Daddy. Moved up. When's the Jell-O coming, Papa? I'm hungry."

"Soon, dear." Grandma smiled. "Go find Papa a wheelchair? He's waiting for his ride."

"I'm sorry," Brad said as he watched Justin scramble off the bed and out into the hallway. "I didn't know you had company. Hi. I'm Bradley Weiner."

"Hi." Lauren smiled meekly, and extended her hand. "Lauren Streiffler."

"Hello." Shelby smiled, but decided not to introduce herself in case the Lazarus name offended him. And what was with the dirty look from Irma? So I checked out her son. He's cute, but it's not like I plan to seduce him.

"Okay, well, I think we can get going now." Mrs. Weiner clapped. "We were just on our way to visit Mrs. Lazarus, dear. Take Daddy out, and I'll be back in a little bit." She patted Brad's shoulder. "Unless I happen to pass a friendly tavern first."

I swear on my previous five lifetimes I had nothing to do with what just happened. You think I'd want my daughters to be dragged into that old lion's den? What was Irma thinking? That the meeting would turn into a lovefest? A "Tuesdays with Bernie"?

Yes, I know all about the best-seller. With the possible exception of Oprah's Book Club selections, which only God was privy to and then sworn to secrecy, the libraries of the universe get advance copies of the books they know will fly off the shelves in the physical world so we can stay in tune with our loved ones.

But I digress. Listening to Shelby give Bernie Weiner a kick in the ass was one of my proudest moments as a mother. Not that I'm in favor of being rude to a dying man. It's just for the first time she's confronted one of her demons, and maybe now she'll begin to realize that harboring hatred and resentment wastes tremendous energy, our soul's most precious resource.

That's my hope anyway. Plus now that she's on a roll, it would also be a load off my mind if she finally came to terms with the two other people in her life she's neither been willing to forgive nor forget. My husband and my sister, of course, who as you know are conveniently lying in the same hospital as Dr. Weiner. Gives new meaning to the expression one-stop shopping!

"You are some piece of work, Shelby." Mrs. Weiner raced down the hall with what appeared to be a fairly decent tail wind.

Lauren tried to keep up, but Shelby simply stopped. Who was she kidding? She couldn't see Aunt Roz now. Couldn't make small talk with her other nemesis. Not after that mortifying, disconcerting encounter with Public Enemy # 1, Dr. Weiner.

"You go," Shelby grabbed Lauren's arm. "I can't. I'll just say something stupid, and everyone will get mad at me, and . . .

"It wasn't your fault, Shel. She never should have brought us in to see him."

"Yes, but she did, and now I'm spent. Just go. Tell her I'm coming down with a cold."

"But we're so close, Shel. Please?" she begged. "We wouldn't have to stay long."

"Sorry. I just remembered my horoscope said it was a bad day for relationships. "

"I thought you don't believe in that stuff."

"Suddenly I do."

"But Mommy's expecting you. What am I going to tell her?"

"How about the truth? Tell her Mrs. Weiner put her own agenda in front of mine, and it spoiled my big debut."

"Don't be like this," Lauren pleaded. "I hated what just happened in there, too. But I understand why she wanted us to meet him. He's not the big bad wolf you made him out to be."

"Sure he is, Little Red Riding Hood. You just didn't recognize him because he's wearing a hospital gown instead of Grandma's dress. Same shit, different designer."

"Well I disagree," Lauren said angrily. "But you know what? Nothing I say is going to change your mind, so go enjoy your stupid manicure . . . I hope you bleed."

Not bad. Not bad, Shelby thought as she watched Lauren venture off into the medicinal sunset. Admittedly her sister was weak in the comeback department, but brave on all other fronts. Still, for herself, she knew she'd made the right decision. She was going to need lots more time to prepare for her first encounter with Aunt Roz. Just as a general needed time to prepare for battle. The big dif-

ference, however, was in lieu of hand-to-hand combat and sophisticated weaponry, the only arsenal she'd have at her disposal were
pursed lips and under-her-breath commentary.

Maybe she'd go back to the house and rehearse, she thought as
she headed down the hall. But just as she passed Dr. Weiner's room,
she saw a confused orderly holding a bowl of red Jell-O.

"I believe they went for a walk." Shelby cleared her throat.

"Oh man. A walk? The kid wouldn't let go a me 'til I promised
to get this, and now he ain't here? I gotta get back to my job."

"I'll give it to him." Shelby shuddered. Acts of kindness were
such unfamiliar territory. But what the hell? She was only going to
leave it on the table and go.

"Thanks, ma'am." The young man smiled as he handed her the
bowl. "Tell the boy sorry they was out of whipped cream, but at least
it's red like he asked."

"No problem." Shelby slowly eased into the room, careful not to
let a drop of the slimy red blob touch her clean white shirt. Of
greater concern was why the attendant had called her ma'am. Good
God, was Mother Time knocking already? Did she need to be cozy-
ing up to a plastic surgeon for the return of her youthful appearance?
But who would operate on a woman who needed Valium for facials?
So absorbed was she, she didn't hear the ruckus.

"She's taking my Jell-O! The mean lady's taking my Jell-O."
Justin raced down the hall and into the room, colliding with Shelby
as she was setting the bowl down on the rolling tray table.

"Oh crap!" Shelby yelled, gaping in horror at the wet, red slime
running down the middle of her shirt. Her new, hundred percent
ribbed, Armani T-shirt that flattered her tight abs and probably cost
more than the kid's entire wardrobe. "Look what you did, you little
brat!" Shelby screamed.

"Please don't speak to my son that way!" Brad ran in. "I'm sure
it was just an accident."

"Why did you take it, lady? It was for me," Justin cried at the
sight of his treat on the floor.

"What are you doing in here anyway?" Brad tried consoling his
young son.

"Oh my God. I wasn't taking his freakin' Jell-O. I was doing him
a favor. The guy who brought it had to leave, and I was passing by,
so I said I would make sure he got it."

"Oh." Brad started to wipe up the spill with a tissue. "Sorry."

"And why are you calling me a mean lady?" she asked Justin. "What did I do to you?"

"My daddy says you're mean 'cause you made my papa cry."

"I made *him* cry? Ha! What about all the times he made me cry?" Shelby replied.

"C'mon, lady." Brad stood up, soggy tissue in hand. "Are you really going to stand here and argue with a five-year-old?"

"No. No, I'm not," Shelby took off, mumbling about the pointlessness of trying to be nice.

Now look at me, she thought when she reached the parking lot. I'm never going to get this awful mess out. Figures something like this has to happen the first time I don't wear black! And of all times for Mr. Dri-Kleen not only to have retired, but to be in and out of consciousness.

It'll be okay, she thought as she ransacked her pocketbook for her car keys. I can be home in five minutes and hopefully Maria remembers a few of Daddy's stain-removing tricks. Now where the hell are my keys? She dumped the entire contents of her bag on the hood of the car and then it hit her. She must have left them on the table in the cafeteria when Lauren and Mrs. Weiner whisked her away to see Aunt Roz.

"Shit, shit, shit!" She jumped up and down. She couldn't do it. She couldn't go back in there looking like a child who refused to wear a napkin. But what choice did she have? She threw everything back in her bag, then stormed off in the direction of the cafeteria, brushing past people without uttering a single, "Excuse me." If one more goddamn thing went wrong today, people were going to discover her testy side.

"Okay, break it up," Shelby yelled at the teenagers making out at her table. "And get your tongue out of his ear. Don't you know that's unsanitary? Now did either of you two kids find a set of car keys when you sat down?"

They shook their heads no. No point in coming up for air to talk to this bitch.

"Oh great." Shelby shot over to the cashier to ask if anyone had turned in a set of keys. The woman reached behind the cash register and retrieved a pair of men's sunglasses. "Sorry." She shrugged. "Try Lost and Found."

"Where's that?"

"Over by Admitting."

"Well, now that's real helpful as I'm personally familiar with the entire layout of this friggin' hospital!" Shelby yelled as she took off in the direction the woman pointed.

"Shelby!"

She turned around at what sounded like Lauren's voice. But that wasn't possible. She was upstairs spoon-feeding Aunt Roz.

"Over here, Shel," a beaming Lauren cried out. "Look who's here!"

Shelby looked over her shoulder, then gripped the top of a chair. A broken and bandaged Aunt Roz was being wheeled through the cafeteria with Lauren at the helm.

"The nurses said it was okay to bring her down." Lauren waved. "They thought a little change of scenery would do her good."

Ding, ding, ding. It was a left hook Shelby never saw coming, and now she was going down for the count. The fight was over. Lauren got her wish for a reunion and was declared champion. Goodbye composure. So long thirty-year moratorium on tears. It was Howdy Doody Nervous Breakdown Time for Shelby.

"Look, Mommy," Lauren cried as she wheeled Aunt Roz over to where Shelby had collapsed. "Shelby's so happy to see you she's in tears."

Shelby wailed even louder.

Chapter Twelve

"Hello, Shelby." Aunt Roz waved her arm cast, wearing her bravest face. What little of it showed through the bandages. "Thanks for coming."

Shelby looked up, bewildered not so much by the yards of white tape running the width and length of her aunt's body, but by the seated position from which she was taking it all in. It made her feel powerless to peer up from the floor at the Queen Mother on her makeshift throne. And what was with that trite, hackneyed expression, thanks for coming? First Dr. Weiner said it. Now Aunt Roz. It was eerily reminiscent of her mother's funeral when her father, numb in the receiving line, mechanically shook hundreds of people's hands. "Thanks for coming . . . thanks for coming . . ."

"Hello, Aunt Roz." Shelby wiped her eyes and stood up, hoping it wasn't necessary to kiss the woman, what with most of her face covered.

Fortunately, Aunt Roz did not appear slighted. For with her one good eye she was already focused on Shelby's dirty shirt. "What happened to you?"

"I was going to ask you the same thing," Shelby teased.

Lauren and Aunt Roz laughed. Only Shelby would be funny at a time like this.

"You look good, honey," Aunt Roz said. "A little too thin, and you could use a touch-up. But for your age, still a beauty."

"Gee, thanks." Damn straight I'm a beauty. Or hadn't you noticed every man's head turned when I walked by?

"So. How are you feeling?" Shelby knew it was a ridiculous question, but it was the best she could do in her shaken state.

"How do you think I'm feeling? Terrible! But at least, thank God, Daddy and I are still alive. I've always said as long as we can be together we'll be fine."

"And I've always said a good attitude is everything." Shelby smiled.

"Since when?" Aunt Roz sniffed.

"Oh no." Lauren held her breath. Was the war of words starting already? She counted to three, but miraculously, Shelby curbed her acid tongue. The cease-fire was holding.

"What are you doing down here?" Lauren whispered as she wheeled Aunt Roz toward a vacant table. "What happened to your nail appointment?"

"I couldn't find the damn car keys. That's what happened."

"Oh, God," Lauren could barely contain a smile. "With all the craziness in Dr. Weiner's room, I forgot to tell you that you left them on the table when we were down here with Irma so I just grabbed them. You must have freaked when you couldn't find them."

"Oh, please. It takes a lot more than lost keys to get me worked up." *If you only knew how close I came to jumping in front of a car because I couldn't get out of this place.*

"This okay?" A gleeful Lauren stopped at an empty table, hoping Shelby wouldn't be picky.

"Fine. Fine. Anywhere." Aunt Roz tried shifting in the confining wheelchair. "I'm just so happy to be out in the open, you could put me anywhere."

Don't tempt me, Shelby thought. Still, she managed to act gracious while wondering how long she could maintain her composure now that Lauren had abandoned her to cootchy-coo every baby in sight. Which left Shelby fending for herself when making conversation with Aunt Roz.

But after a few minutes of working in the trenches alone, Shelby realized it was getting harder to avoid the dozens of land mines, otherwise known as personal questions. For someone like Aunt Roz, who was so masterful at keeping her own secrets, it amazed Shelby that the woman had no clue others might also want the details of their life to remain private. Yet she pumped Shelby as if she were the last gas station for miles. Was she seeing anyone? Did she like her job? Was she seeing anyone? Did she have enough money? Was she seeing anyone?

It was one time Shelby would have welcomed listening to the woman drone on about her own problems. It would have been less exhausting than fending off every question with three-word answers. "I'm not sure." "I don't know." "Is that right?"

Finally, when it became apparent to Aunt Roz that Private Shelby was not going to share, she moved on. "You know what came in the mail a few weeks ago?" she asked.

"I give up," Shelby yawned. "What?"

"An invitation for your thirty-fifth nursery school reunion."

"That's absurd. I've never heard of such a thing. And who said you could open my mail?"

"It wasn't addressed to you, smartie pants. It was addressed to the parents of . . ."

"Well I hope you threw it away. I wouldn't be caught dead at something like that."

"Why not? You never know who'll be there. You could meet someone nice."

"First of all, I have no interest in finding out the kids who peed in their pants every day are now Internet billionaires. Secondly, I've gained at least a hundred pounds since then."

Aunt Roz shook her head. "Such a *meshugeneh* with the weight . . ."

"You hungry, Mommy?" Lauren finally rejoined them.

"I'm okay. Maybe a little water or juice. All those antibiotics make my mouth so dry."

"I'll go!" Shelby jumped up, delighted it was already intermission. A few more minutes of chitchat and she could be on her way. "Lauren, explain to her why nursery school reunions are a stupid idea."

"No, they're not," Lauren said. "That's how my friend Elise met her husband. And who knows. Maybe you'll run into Matty Lieberman."

Shelby stopped rummaging through her pocketbook for her wallet. "Why would you think I'd be looking for him?"

"Stacy Alter told me. I ran into her at Blockbuster yesterday."

Shelby winced. This was why she could never live here in Yentaville. On the other hand, Lauren might be right. Both Matty and she had gone to Temple Judea's Early Learning Center. Even if he hadn't registered to attend the reunion, he might be on their mailing list.

"Did you save the invitation?" Shelby coughed.

"I don't remember." Aunt Roz chuckled. "Check the desk drawer in the kitchen."

"Great. Okay then. Who wants orange juice?"

Shelby returned to the table to find Lauren and Aunt Roz in a huddle and suddenly felt queasy. There was something about the way those two connected that always led to trouble. It was more than a paranoid conspiracy theory, it was fact. Whenever they looked this cozy, a major storm was brewing. She could practically feel the Kansas dust kicking up.

"Here you go." Shelby took a deep breath, handing Lauren the juice cup. "You give this to her. I've already spilled one thing today."

"Sure." Lauren smiled. "This is working out even better than I expected."

"Oh, I know," Shelby whispered back. "I'm having a ball."

Then Lauren put the straw in Aunt Roz's mouth and lit the match that could have started another Chicago fire. "I was just telling Mommy about my problems because of the DES."

"Uh-huh," Shelby said. "Aunt Roz, do you remember anything about the pills our mother took?"

"Sure, I remember. She took them for almost a year, and Granny Bea would laugh because they were so tiny. Not like her high blood pressure medication, which could choke a horse. She'd say, 'What good are those? They look like candy.' But your mother took them every day while she was pregnant, and that's how we got our little Lauren. Such a beautiful *punim*."

"Thank you." Lauren smiled lovingly. "Anyway, I was explaining how the doctors have pretty much said it would be impossible for me to have a baby of my own and what a lot of women in my position do is use a surrogate."

"Uh-huh." Shelby shivered, signaling Lauren not to go down this road again.

"Personally, I think it's a wonderful idea." Aunt Roz nodded. "And so unselfish. Did you know even Abraham and Sarah used a surrogate? That's how they had their first son, Ishmael."

"Really?" Shelby searched her bag for gum. "And when did you become a Bible scholar?"

"After Daddy and I started taking classes with the rabbi. Such an interesting man."

"Ever take an ethics course?"

Aunt Roz flinched. "What for? We don't even cheat on our taxes. Now your uncle Marty. He should take a class like that."

"Anyway." Lauren waved. "As I was saying, a lot of women use friends or family as their surrogate, rather than paying a complete stranger."

"Friends are good." Shelby nodded. "You have a lot of those. What about Elise Finklestein? I remember her as the real mother earth type."

"No. She had two tough pregnancies, and Mitch and her are sort of on the rocks."

"What about Sari Wishnick? She's a very pretty girl."

"She's diabetic." Lauren drummed on the table. "Too high-risk."

"Okay, then. What about that girl who you worked with at Macy's? The one who was built like a Mack truck? She could probably carry triplets."

"Who? Robyn Nagel? She'd never do it. She's single and totally into her career."

"Well so am I. Why doesn't that disqualify me?"

"Because, Shel," Lauren whispered, "if I can't use my own eggs, I'd at least want my baby to have some of our genetic material."

"If you ask me, you should at least think about it," Aunt Roz stuck her nose in.

"We didn't ask you," Shelby said firmly.

"All I'm saying is, every once in a while it wouldn't hurt you to do something nice for your sister. That's all."

"Excuse me." Shelby bit her lip. "But, I believe the definition of being nice to a sister is lending her your Manolo Blahniks for the night, or treating her to a facial. It does not generally include screwing her husband." She caught Aunt Roz's good eye. "That, I believe, is called adultery."

"Oh! Is that the problem?" Lauren's face lit up. "You think you have to . . . with Avi?"

"There is no problem, Lauren. All you need to do is go buy a dozen eggs at your nearest infertility clinic, mingle them in a nice,

Mikasa dish with Avi's sperm, then stick the ones that take into a nineteen-year-old who needs the money!"

"What kind of way is that to talk to a sister?" Aunt Roz tried pointing her cast in Shelby's face. "If my sister was alive, may she rest in peace, I would never turn my back on her."

Shelby buried her face in her hands, then looked up. "Give me a fucking break, Aunt Roz. I don't ever recall you being nominated for Sister of the Year."

"How dare you? No one was more devoted to your mother than I was."

"Some devotion," Shelby mumbled. "You slept with her husband, for God's sake."

"Shelby!" Lauren covered Aunt Roz's ears. "Don't be mean. They were already married."

"Like hell!"

"Oh, my God. Stop it!" Lauren cried. "You don't know what you're saying."

Shelby closed her eyes and took a deep breath. "I know exactly what I'm saying. Ask her yourself. Go on. Ask her if while Mommy was dying, she was sleeping with Daddy, got pregnant with Eric, then passed him off as our first cousin."

"Shelby, what is wrong with you?" Lauren gasped. "It's like you've got that thing I saw on *20/20*. Tourette's Syndrome. You say the most outrageous things for no good reason."

"I wish I was making this up," Shelby's hands shook. "But I'm not. Am I, Aunt Roz?"

"I have no idea what you're talking about." She looked down. "Lauren's right. You just say whatever the hell you want. Big deal if you hurt someone's feelings."

"Is that what you think? That I entertain myself by dreaming up these outrageous tales? Believe me. I know what I'm saying. Every word. Lauren, look at me. Ever wonder why Eric has Daddy's build and Daddy's nose?"

"Sheer coincidence!" Aunt Roz cried. "You know my cousin Abe? He's a clone of his mother's stepbrother. No relation. How dare you make such an accusation? You were a child."

"Ten, actually, and excellent in math. So let's review, class. My mother got sick in June of 1969. You moved in to help take care of us in July. By Thanksgiving your stomach was so big Lauren asked if you ate the turkey and you said no, you were having a baby. I asked if you had a husband and you said, maybe one day. Mommy died in late December, Eric was born in May, and before Daddy had a chance to pick out the headstone, you were the new Mrs. Larry Lazarus."

"That proves nothing." Aunt Roz waved her arm cast. "It was no secret I was single when I got pregnant. The relationship just didn't work out. That's all."

"Sure it did. The man you were in a relationship with was Daddy. While he was still married to your sister."

Lauren looked from Aunt Roz to Shelby and back, her bottom lip trembling. "Are you saying . . . they had an affair? That Eric really is related to us?"

"That's my story, and I'm sticking to it." Shelby folded her arms.

"Oh, God. That means he's our first cousin, our stepbrother, *and* our half-brother!"

"Bingo! Woody Allen's got nothing on us!"

Aunt Roz gazed out the window. "It wasn't anything like you said."

"Yes it was." Shelby pounded the table. "I saw how you looked at him all googly-eyed. I saw how you trapped him so you could have the big house and the fancy car . . ."

"For your information, your mother thought she was settling when she married your father. I loved him the minute I met him." Aunt Roz cried softly.

Lauren looked on in disbelief. She didn't know whom to hate more. Shelby for the truth, or Aunt Roz for the deceit. "How come you never told me, Shel?"

"Because you love Aunt Roz. You never would have believed me."

Lauren's eyes welled up in response. "How long . . . have you known?"

"I don't know. Forever. I mean to me it was so obvious. When Eric was born, all of a sudden the guest room became the nursery. And when I asked Daddy where Aunt Roz was going to sleep now, he said the living room. But once I left my library book on the couch to see if it got moved, and the next morning it was exactly where I'd left it."

Lauren wept into a tissue.

"Then, once I was helping Aunt Roz change Eric's diaper and I asked where Eric's daddy was and she looked at me like how did I know there had to be a daddy to get a baby? Like I was an idiot. But when she wouldn't answer me, that's when I knew."

"Wow. Even then you had these great instincts."

"Thank you." Shelby blushed. She'd never really thought about how or when she'd first realized she had the inbred ability to be a reporter, but Lauren was right. It was in her blood.

Lauren looked over at a dazed Aunt Roz. "How dumb do I feel? I had no idea."

"This is the thanks I get for keeping the family together," Aunt Roz muttered.

"But let me ask you something, and don't be insulted," Lauren said wistfully. "You don't actually know for sure that you're right? I mean you don't have proof, proof."

Shelby nodded. "You want to know what it is?"

"Only if it's not, you know, gross."

"Remember two years ago when my apartment got robbed, and my passport and credit cards were stolen?"

"Not really," Lauren shrugged.

"Yes, you do. It was around the time I was going to Rome and needed my passport. Which I couldn't replace without my birth certificate, which was also stolen. So when I flew home for the High Holidays, I went searching in the attic for the original. But when I found the envelope with the birth certificates, there were four of them. One for me, one for you, and two for Eric."

"Why two?" Lauren nibbled at a hang nail.

"The first one listed Lawrence Joseph Lazarus as his father," she paused. "And the other one said, 'Father Unknown.' "

"Oh my God. I always thought he was a Lazarus because Daddy adopted him."

"Nope."

"And two years ago . . . that's when you stopped speaking to us . . ." Lauren looked away, trying not to hyperventilate.

"Yep."

"I think I'm going to puke."

"See? See what you've done?" Aunt Roz suddenly tried inching closer to Shelby to smack her with her cast. "You made your sister sick, and you spoiled my big day out. I always said you were the bad seed."

"Me?" Shelby cried out. "Why am I the bad seed? You betrayed my mother, lied to her children, then covered it up for thirty years. All I did was tell the truth."

"Take me upstairs, Lauren. I never want to see my niece again as long as I live."

"In a minute." Lauren's back stiffened. "I'm sorry, Shel," she said, hugging her. "I feel terrible that you've been carrying this burden all alone. But at least it all makes sense now. I mean why you're so mad at the world and everything."

"I'm not mad at the world, Lauren. Just my family, the entire medical establishment, the Republican Party, men, people who insist on bringing cranky babies into fine restaurants—"

"I want to go now," Aunt Roz interrupted. "I'm suddenly feeling sick to my stomach."

"Join the crowd." Lauren wheeled her away. "Join the crowd."

Chapter Thirteen

It seemed only fitting, if not ironic, that for the next three days, Long Island got socked with rain. Not the on again, off again showers that annoyed hairdressers and crossing guards, but the windy, street-flooding downpours that made Shelby feel like Noah. Especially as she felt too immobilized to do anything other than hole up in the guesthouse ark and lick her wounds.

She wondered how long it took Noah to decide he didn't give a rat's ass if the sun ever came out again. Self-pity could have that effect. As could having a grandmother who'd filled a young, innocent head with the *mishegas* that whenever it rained this heavily, it meant God was crying because the children were bad.

Maybe Granny Bea Good was right, Shelby thought as she tried peering out the window through the obliterated view. She had behaved badly. And although she wasn't totally sorry she spilled the family's secret beans, she had to admit her timing sucked.

In her defense, however, surely a jury of her peers would have found her innocent of all charges, based on the fact she was provoked and the act was by no means premeditated. But when word came through Avi that the doctors were as puzzled by Aunt Roz's sudden decline as they had been the other day by her miraculous recovery, Shelby knew she was to blame.

And, too, there was the matter of Lauren's onset of depression. Once again, Avi, the host of Bad Headline News, told Shelby he had never seen his wife so blue. Given Lauren's strong affinity for family, it was of no help for her to learn that her odd but otherwise stable childhood had been based on a fraud. This on top of the fact she

But wa
practical
must
ou

might never have her own family was sin
bear. Lauren, too, had gone home to hole

Shelby left several messages for Laure
Then for reasons even Shelby did not und
Roz's hospital room. Also to no avail, for
hang up the phone the instant she heard
though Aunt Roz did manage to relay to *M*
out of the guesthouse, and out of her life. F̶ ̶, ̶s̶h̶e̶ ̶w̶a̶n̶t̶e̶d̶
Maria to remind Shelby to look in the kitchen drawer for the invitation to her nursery school reunion, which in Aunt Roz's opinion, she
should definitely attend.

No way was Shelby going to look for that stupid invitation. But
on day two of solitary confinement, she was bored enough to venture
into the kitchen to look for a little company. Even a chat with Avi
would suffice. Pity he had cut back on his visits after the spigot of
neighbors' CARE packages was turned off. Why stop by if the fridge
wasn't filled with tuna casseroles and knishes?

Maria wasn't much company either, as she was ignoring the
malevolent daughter rather than engaging her in small talk. Apparently she knew enough to hold Shelby accountable for Lauren's sadness and the fact Mrs. L's recovery had mysteriously taken a turn for
the worse.

"Oh, what the hell." Shelby opened the drawer and started rifling
the contents in search of a mailing from Temple Judea. But she found
no sign of the invitation in there. No luck in the duck, either. She
stared at the ugly ceramic relic. Good God. Who spent fifty grand
renovating a kitchen, then kept a cheap, made-in-Taiwan *tchachke*
from A&S, circa 1972, on the counter? Aunt Roz. That's who.

Shelby threw the miscellany back in the duck's bill. This whole
thing was absurd. Even if she found the invitation, there was no
guarantee the committee had located Matty. Or even if they had, that
he still had feelings for her. It was time to face the facts. Matty
Lieberman represented her past, not her future. As did the desire to
have children.

Damn Stacy Rothstein for mentioning those essays on motherhood she swore Shelby penned in third grade. Now she would always
have to wonder if as captain of her ship, she'd steered her life so dras-
tically off course, she'd lost sight of her own childhood dreams. Or,
if Stacy's memory was simply as bad as her method of birth control.

t. Maybe Shelby could solve this mystery. Her room was
y archive heaven, and the truth could be as close as those
boxes lying dormant for who knows how long. Shelby bolted
of the kitchen and up the stairs two at a time, then cringed when
she flicked on the bedroom light.

Even with the bright sunlight pouring through the darkened
shades, the room looked shabby and abandoned. A pyramid of clutter here, a scrap heap of memories there. She hoped her mother
wasn't gazing down now, only to see her once meticulous decor
awaiting a bulldozer and a broom.

And yet it wasn't the disarray that kept Shelby at bay. It was the
realization she was about to enter a danger zone. A room filled with
mementoes that appeared innocuous in nature yet were powerful
enough to graze open wounds. Mementos that would surely remind
her how her young life had been blindsided by death and deception.

But five cartons and one hour later, she was breathing easier.
There were no ticking time bombs for one very good reason. Sandy
Lazarus was not a saver. Hell, she couldn't even save herself. Her
greatest priority had been keeping an immaculate home, not the
dreamy-eyed writings of an eight-year-old.

Aunt Roz, on the other hand, seemed to have saved everything,
for there in the bottom of one of the boxes were Shelby's diaries. She
knew instantly they were the ones she'd kept in junior high, perhaps
the most prolific time of her life, naturally because of the tragic loss
of her mother.

And yet to Shelby's amazement, there was virtually no reference
to her mother's death. Only to her anger and sadness that Matty had
never written her back or bothered to visit since his family moved to
California two years earlier. *Why won't he write me?* she'd scribbled in
green ink in large, loopy letters. *He promised he'd write EVERY week.
I hate his guts. MATTHEW JAY LIEBERMAN IS A RAT FINK!!!!!!*

But in her very next entry, Shelby envisioned their life together.
Naturally they would reunite to attend the same college, get engaged, get really good jobs that paid at least five thousand dollars a
year, get married, and voilà, the smoking gun. She and Matty would
have seven children, one for each day of the week. Unbelievable!
Stacy had been right.

She wondered what had ever possessed her to want a family
large enough to form a baseball team? And how could that ridiculous

fantasy have been more important than expressing her immense grief over the loss of her mother? Looks like good old Dr. Israel, may have been right about her. Maybe she was Da Queen of Da Nile.

"Miss Shelly, Miss Shelly," Maria called out from the master bedroom. "What in the bejesus are you doing in there?"

"Research," Shelby called out. "Not that it's any of your business."

"That rat! That rat!" Maria ran in, yanked Shelby out, and quickly shut the door.

"How dare you?" Shelby screamed. "I don't care how long you've worked here, I will not tolerate name-calling by the hired help . . ."

"Take the cotton out of your ears, Missy." Maria rolled her eyes. "I'm sayin' there's a big old rat in there that comes down from the attic."

"Ewwwww," Shelby bit her fingers and winced. "A real rat? In my room?"

"Now that you mention it there were two." Maria snickered. "The big gray one and you."

"Very funny." Shelby flew down the stairs. "Thousands of comedians out of work, and they're all housekeepers. What's the name of the exterminator they use?"

"Beats me. All I know is a bunch have been here already," she shouted over the banister.

"Then we'll call in the goddamn National Guard," Shelby shouted back. "The last thing we need around here is a dirty rat!"

"You said it, sister," Maria answered. "And I'm hopin' she leaves real soon . . ."

Pity for Maria the pest control company could only set a trap to catch the rat in the attic, not the one from Chicago.

In the meantime, Shelby quietly went about her business, jogging on the treadmill, then closeting herself in the office to work at the computer, all the while listening for scratching sounds on the walls. Soon she forgot about what was lurking in the attic as she was more engrossed in what was lurking on the Internet. Particularly the *Tribune's* website.

Just because she was no longer employed by the paper didn't mean she wasn't curious as to the status of their on-line editions. Admittedly, the writing was crisp, even irreverent, but no matter how much Irving Davidoff insisted this was the wave of the future, she knew this year's Pulitzer Prize Review Board wasn't scouring the country's digital editions looking for nominees.

Shelby's next stop on the Internet was her now voluminous file on DES, and today's findings were especially disheartening. According to a report she downloaded, DES wasn't just a case of drug companies introducing a pill they would later determine to be ineffective. DES was a case of broad-based negligence and total indifference to humanity. It was a case of major pharmaceutical companies marketing dozens of forms of a synthetic estrogen time bomb over a thirty-year period. Then running like hell when the nearly five million pregnant women who downed them on a daily basis discovered that not only didn't the pills prevent miscarriages, the damn things hampered the normal development of their fetuses.

Mounds of evidence also pointed to the fact daughters were at greater risk than sons as the DES exposure wreaked havoc on the female's reproductive tract. DES daughters suffered extremely high incidences of miscarriages, ectopic pregnancies, premature labor, autoimmune diseases like lupus and MS, rare forms of vaginal and cervical cancers and structural abnormalities such as T-shaped uteruses and deviated cervixes. All because in 1947, the government approved the use of a drug for pregnant women without first testing it on pregnant women.

Finally in 1971, the FDA confirmed a link between DES daughters and vaginal cancer and pulled it off the market. Sorry about that, Shelby guessed the press releases said. Please forgive this little intergenerational tragedy we brought upon millions of families. Who knew?

Shelby was grateful Lauren's research skills were not as well honed as hers, as her sister might never recover if she understood the real ramifications of being a DES daughter. Lauren was already feeling desperate enough without having to be further victimized by the gory details.

Question was, did this information change Shelby's mind about becoming Lauren's surrogate? Nothing doing! She was sympathetic, not insane. She didn't even care about rediscovering there was a time in her youth she wanted children. That time had long since passed.

Current reality was she was thirty-eight years old, fastidious about her body weight, terrified of doctors, self-centered, and not even remotely maternal. No way would she ever want some alien being growing inside her, depleting her of her much-needed sleep and vitamins.

And yet these feelings didn't get in the way of continuing her search for Matty. Knowing full well if she actually was to find him and live out her deepest fantasy, it would be to fall in love with him, get married, and have a family.

On the other hand, there was one thing she couldn't deny. She was probably the last person on the mind of a man she hadn't seen in nearly thirty years. All the proof she needed was the fact Matty had never tracked her down. For surely if he'd tried he would have found her. Who was easier to locate than a high-profile journalist with a column in a large metropolitan newspaper?

Maybe it was just as well there was no sign of Matty. By now he was probably happily married, the father of at least two, and owner of that many dogs, if not more. Oh, how Matty loved his dogs. Shelby's only hope was that he hadn't sold out to law or medicine, and was instead, teaching comparative literature at a small college in Vermont.

On day three of confinement, out came the sun and dried up all the rain, so the eentsy beentsy spider girl, who was positively ecstatic about the change in weather, crawled out of her hut in running gear and embarked on what she hoped would be a pleasant, three-mile jog.

In spite of her recent hiatus from running, Shelby was on course to beat her best time. It was amazing what pent-up adrenaline could do for you. Until one hit a major roadblock, such as the scene of an accident. Like the one at the corner of Royal Lane and Prince Drive.

Shelby noticed traces of blood on the curb and a man's sneaker off to the side. Brand-new it seemed. Could it be her father's? Why else would there be a stranded shoe at the very intersection where the accident occurred unless it belonged to the victim of the accident? She walked up the grassy incline to fetch the size 11½ man's Nike, collapsed on the still wet ground, and cried.

Her poor, innocent father. What a high price he'd paid just to keep his aging body from further deterioration after years of neglect and gluttony. Now his body was shattered, his future instantly redefined. The pain must be indescribable, she thought. How could she not be there to comfort him? She was his daughter, his firstborn, and the closest link to his beloved Sandy. She would go to see him. Soon. Or at least before Aunt Roz had a chance to tell on her.

Shelby sprinted back to the house, sneaker in hand, arriving in the driveway with sweat pouring off her head. While bent over trying to catch her breath, Maria opened the kitchen door.

"Miss Shelly, phone's for you."

"Who is it?" she huffed, no longer bothering to correct the ignorant woman.

"Askin's not my job, dearie. Only answerin." Maria let the screen door shut.

It better not be Irma Weiner, that's all I can say. Shelby wiped her forehead with her shirt and trotted into the kitchen. "Hello?"

"Shelby? I don't know if you remember me. This is Abby Cohen. Well, now it's Rosenthal. Scott's . . . wife?"

"Sure. Hi. That's so funny. I was going to call you."

"Yes, I heard. I ran into Stacy Alter at the dentist."

God, that woman was everywhere. "So she told you I was looking for . . ."

"Yes. Are you seeing my husband?"

"Excuse me?"

"Please don't take me for stupid. Things aren't exactly great right now. I need to know."

"Yes, I'm seeing your husband. At the hospital. My father and aunt were in a serious accident, and he's one of their surgeons."

"Look, I know about the accident and you have my deepest sympathies, but I also heard you're single and gorgeous, so just lay it on the line. Did he proposition you?"

"No, of course not. Why would you think that?" Of course he did. They always do.

"Because he hasn't stopped talking about you. It's Shelby this, and Shelby that. And Stacy said you're like this big-shot journalist who looks like a Jewish Christie Brinkley and . . ."

"I'm sorry. I did nothing to encourage your husband."

"Ah-ha! So he did come on to you."

"Okay. You want the truth, seeing as how that seems to be my speciality?" Shelby's voice grew louder. "The truth, Abby, is you've made your husband's life a living hell with your outrageous demands and unending quest for more and better. Frankly, you sound like a castrating bitch who puts his balls in a vise every time you don't get your way. And yet I get the sense Scott really loves you and misses you. He needs you. So if you want my advice, here it is. When he comes home tonight, fuck his little brains out, chop up a few of your credit cards, tell him you want to start over, and I guarantee your worries will be a thing of the past."

Had they been on a radio show, the silence that followed would have been called dead air.

"So, you're not . . ." Abby didn't finish.

"God no. The last thing I want in my life right now is another man who thinks nothing of burping, farting, and picking his nose, then crawling into bed looking for oral gratification!"

Abby laughed.

"Now how about returning the favor and telling me something I want to hear."

"You want to know about Matthew Lieberman?"

"Exactly. Any clue where he might be?"

"I did ask around." Abby cleared her throat, still embarrassed by her accusation. "The problem is no one seems to remember him. Didn't he move away a long time ago?"

"Yes. In December 1969."

"Wow. How could you remember that far back?"

"Because it was a week after my mother died."

"Oh. I suppose that's not a date you would forget."

"No. So did anyone know anything at all?"

"Well I do have one possible lead," Abby hesitated.

"Really?" Shelby loved a lead.

"Yes. This morning I was talking to my mother, and she thought her sister's friend used to play mah-jongg with Matthew's grandmother's neighbor."

"Oh," Shelby's heart sunk. "In my business that's not a lead. That's a dead end."

"Maybe not. I took a shot and called my aunt, who called her friend, and the friend called the neighbor, even though they hadn't spoken in twenty years, but it turns out she'd died last year. But her husband answered and he thought he remembered Matthew's grandmother. Her name was Ruth, I think."

Amazing, Shelby thought. With all the sophisticated technology available to hunt people down, nothing compared to the precision of Jewish Geography. "What did he say about her?"

"Unfortunately, not much. He's close to ninety now and said he was just happy to remember where he left his teeth. But he did seem to recall something about his wife's friend's daughter, which would be Matthew's mother, moving to California, then getting a divorce."

"Yes. I knew about the move to California, but not about the divorce."

"It's probably why you can't find him."

"What do you mean?" Shelby loved when someone else had the insights for a change.

"Well if she got a divorce, it's possible she remarried. And if her kids were still young at the time, and it was a messy divorce, maybe she let the man adopt them and they took his last name."

It was the most sensible thing Abby had said yet. "You could be right. Thanks, Abby. I really appreciate your trying to help me. In spite of, you know . . ."

"I'm sorry about accusing you," Abby said quietly.

"It's okay. It happens all the time. Women just automatically assume . . ."

"Do you . . . this is a little awkward . . ." Abby stammered.

"It's okay. What is it?" Shelby asked.

"Have you . . . Scott would love . . . By any chance, would you be interested in a threesome?"

Chapter Fourteen

Shelby carefully spread out the plush towel, coated her skin with sunscreen, sipped from the frosty glass of water, and slowly eased her lithe body onto the oversize chaise lounge Papa Bear probably ordered from some rich-boy catalog. Was there any better way to ponder her future than to bask in solitude, comfort, and seventy-eight-degree sunshine?

As she saw it, she had two choices. Plan A called for catching the next flight to anywhere that frowned on women who invited other women into their marriage bed for a little ménage à trois pick-me-up. Perhaps that leper colony in Maui she'd once read about was just such a place.

Plan B would be much trickier. It required taking the high road, rather than the heavily traveled low road. It required staying in Manhasset so she could convince Lauren to return to this house and make peace with it, in spite of the deception that occurred here. Plan B also involved visiting her father, preferably while he was in a semiconscious state so he wasn't fully cognizant of the havoc his eldest had created in the short time she'd been home.

Which would it be? Thankfully she was free to explore her options in seclusion, as all the people she knew in the area were no longer speaking to her. Not even Pucci cared when she'd whistled for him to come over. Apparently word traveled fast in the canine community, too. Shelby Lazarus didn't just report on bad news, she was bad news.

Yet even with all the turmoil in Shelby's life, the warmth of the sunlight penetrated her body, filling her with rays of contentedness.

Within minutes her breathing slowed and she was in a dreamlike state, imagining a life where she was not only understood, but revered. Where her beliefs were not viewed as strange, but conventional. Where people came to her for guidance and direction. Where she could remove the top to her bathing suit without fear of exposing herself.

At least she could live out that part of the fantasy, she thought. It was just her and the birds. She quickly untied her straps and tossed her top on the other chair. Or so she thought. It was hard to say how long Shelby had been baking when she was suddenly startled by the feel of ice-cold water dripping down her back. In a dazed state she jumped up so fast, she forgot her cupboard was bare.

"Hi," said Avi, the culprit, as he gaped at her firm, moist breasts, panting like Pucci.

"What the hell are you doing?" Shelby tried covering up with her hands.

"Sorree, yure highness." He bowed, without taking his eyes off her. "I thought the fair maiden would like to be cooled off."

"My God! Are you always such a jackass?" Shelby pushed him out of the way to reach for her silk, man-tailored shirt hanging on the other chair. "You're a married man for Christ's sake. Have you not a shred of decency?"

"Of course. Do you see me sitting outside with nothink on?"

Shelby gulped the rest of her water. "You know what I like best about you, Avi?"

"What?" he waited breathlessly.

"Nothing." She grabbed her towel and took off for the guesthouse.

"No wait." Avi followed. "I came to see you."

"And see me you did." Shelby kept walking.

"Don't go," Avi pleaded. "You have to help me. Lauren is getting so crazy I kent even talk to her. She's a mess."

"Well no wonder." Shelby turned around. "She married the world's biggest buffoon."

"What ken I say?" He shrugged. "She loves me. But yure the only one she listens to."

"Fine. I'll go over to your place and speak to her."

"Miss Shelly, Miss Shelly." Maria opened the kitchen sliders and stepped on to the deck.

It's a simple concept, Shelby winced. Just say Shelly with a B. "Yes?"

"A man is here to see you."

"You're kidding?" she looked down at her bare legs and wet shirt. "Who is it?"

"Askin's not my job, only answerin'," Maria threw back her head. "Hey, hon." She waved to Avi. "I didn't hear you come in. Will you be wantin' lunch?"

"No time." He made sad eyes. "You didn't expect company?" Avi asked Shelby.

"No." She panicked, assuming it was Scott Rosenthal. God help her if Abby had repeated their phone conversation.

"Greetings and salutations," a tall, friendly-sounding man ushered himself into the backyard from the side of the house. "Shelby, darling. I hope I'm not interrupting your little soirée."

The glare from the sunlight made it difficult to make out the face, but she certainly knew the voice. "Ian?"

"The one and only." He took giant steps to reach her in haste, leaning over for a hug.

"What are you doing here? How did you find me?"

Ian waved his naughty-naughty finger. "In spite of what you think, I do manage to pick up a paper now and again. And when I read that dreadful story about the Lazarus couple getting whacked by a gardener I thought, that's what must have brought Shelby to New York."

"Uh-huh," Shelby eyed him suspiciously. Ian didn't so much as pee without an agenda.

"Care for a cool drink?" Maria asked the handsome guest.

"That would be lovely, thank you. Do you have iced tea?"

"Raspberry, peach, or ginseng?"

"Oh dear. A choice. Peach sounds peachy, thank you."

Shelby groaned at Ian's impersonation of a charming man.

"Avi Streiffler." Avi vigorously shook Ian's hand. "We're femily." He pointed to Shelby.

"Pleased to meet you, Avi. Ian McNierney here. Sorry to hear about the folks. This must be a difficult time." He eyed Shelby's near-barren body and practically smacked his lips.

Shelby looked down to see the outline of her perspired breasts peering through the shirt and was mortified. The two most vile men she knew were getting a free show, and the more she squirmed, the more they lapped it up. "Your concern is appreciated." She crossed her arms. "But most people sent cards."

"And I thought you deserved better. I've come to take you to dinner."

"It's three o'clock," Shelby cried.

"Then we shall start with drinks." He winked, refusing to budge.

After showering and changing, Shelby peeked into the backyard from her bathroom window and cringed. It was like an international bazaar out there with a snippy, Jamaican housekeeper, a morally vacant Israeli, and an egotistical, self-centered, British editor somehow managing to find common ground. Or at least a topic that tickled their funny bones.

Upon edging closer to the conversation, Shelby knew instinctively the source of their mutual interest was her. It was a no-brainer. The party ended the moment she was spotted.

"What's so amusing?" Shelby eyed each of the suspects.

"Oooh. That dryer buzzes before you know it." Maria took off.

"Look at the time." Avi tapped his watch. "I hef to be at JFK for a three-thirty pickup."

"We were just chatting about this and that." Ian cleared his throat as he eyed her denim shorts. "You look lovely, of course, but I was hoping you'd dress a bit more formally for dinner."

"Sorry," Shelby shrugged. "Dinner's out. I have to go meet my sister, then we'll probably run over to the hospital."

"Oh dear," Ian pouted. "I made us a reservation at the Garden City Hotel."

"Take Avi and Maria." Shelby smirked. "Then you'll have company and a song."

"Such a clever girl." Ian winked. "How I miss your tongue in my cheek."

"My tongue was never in your cheek, asshole."

"Pity. I would have made it so worth your while." He rubbed her arm.

Ian immediately regretted the boorish remark as he nearly had to apologize on bended knee to salvage the remains of the day. Finally, upon assuring Shelby he wanted to discuss an exciting freelance writing assignment he had in mind for her, she agreed to join him for coffee at a diner.

How could she refuse? A freelance assignment would jump-start her career without having to get all chummy with the kids in the newsroom. Her hours would be her own, as would be her outrageous fee. She would make sure of that. But upon hearing the gory details, Shelby balked.

"So let me get this straight," she said, wondering if she'd ever be able to drop her trademark line from her personal lexicon. "You want me to do a 'whatever happened to' piece on the socialite couples whose wedding announcements appeared in the *New York Times* on the same weekend ten years ago."

"Quite right. Aren't you the quick study?"

"Why the hell would I even want to read that crap, let alone write it? What do you *think* all the Muffies and Chippers of the world are doing? They're living in million-dollar homes in Greenwich with their 2.2 kids, their 3.2 dogs and 4.1 cars. They never winter where they summer, oh, and Chipper has new golf clubs and a twenty-two-year-old playmate on the side."

"Interesting analysis." Ian sipped his imitation cappuccino. "But let's not be too hasty pointing a finger at Chipper's extramarital relations." He winked. "Muffy has them, too."

"So what's your point? That the institution of marriage is dead?"

"That's totally daft, darling. Of course not. I just want to poke a little fun at the Old Gray Lady by showing the institution of the *New York Times* wedding section is dead."

"Uh-huh." Shelby downed the last of her coffee. "And it's your contention by dredging up a bunch of preppies whose marriages were more like mergers, you'll be able to prove their genetically disposed tendency to drink, philander, and squander Daddy's money made it impossible to keep their vows, forcing the folks from WASPYville to skulk back to their debutante balls in shame?"

"Precisely." Ian rubbed his hands. "It's an utterly delicious story, don't you think?"

"No, it's moronic," Shelby replied. "Furthermore, why would I want to personally go after the *Times*? After a piece like that ran with my byline, they wouldn't hire me to clean the toilets."

"You say that as if it's a bad thing, darling."

"Sorry. I have enough problems without committing professional suicide. I pass."

"Would this change your mind?" Ian scribbled a figure on his napkin and pushed it over.

Shelby's eyes widened. "Are you crazy? For a lousy freelance job?"

"It means a lot to me." Ian shrugged. "Think of it as a personal vendetta piece."

"I see." Shelby drummed on the table. "And would this vendetta have anything to do with the very rich and famous Alexandra Simonson Wellbourge IV?"

Ian squirmed. "What made you go down that road?"

"Because if memory serves me, after being presented at the Debutante Cotillion Ball, Ms. Simonson was to become the first Mrs. Ian James McNierney until she decided to stand you up at the altar and marry for money. I believe the heir to the Preston Hufstadt banking fortune."

"Were you also aware the man was nothing more than a depraved, suicidal, bisexual Nazi?"

"Which could explain why she's on husband number three, and face-lift number two."

"Bravo, bravo." Ian clapped. "An excellent summary of the facts."

"What I don't get is why the hell you care? You're a happily married man now."

"Yes I am. Maureen's a lovely girl. Lovely. Very lovely . . ."

"But you never got over the humiliation of being dumped on your wedding day, and now that you're in a position of power, why not expose the Mayflower sisters for what they really are?"

"If not for the press, who would these self-absorbed parasites be accountable to?"

"Okay, so let's say we prove unequivocally that after you strip away the pearls and the pedigrees, debutantes make lousy spouses. And that the deal with the Roman numeral guys is, the higher the number after their name, the lousier the sex. You really think publicizing these well-known facts will vindicate you?"

"You are sharper than a beaver quill in the ass," Ian cried. "How did I ever let you go?"

Shelby signaled the waitress to refill her cup, which pleased Ian. "So what do you think?" He leaned forward. "Have I piqued your interest?"

"Maybe. But only because it occurs to me I may have a counteroffer for you."

"Excellent." He rubbed his hands. "I love when you proposition me."

"I might be willing to write your crappy story, if you approve one I want to write."

"Go on."

"The topic is DES."

"Surely you jest." Ian groaned. "We're a newspaper." He emphasized the word new. "The DES story is so old it predates my Pulitzer."

"So does the Lindbergh kidnapping, but hear me out. Yes, the FDA finally issued a warning not to dispense it to pregnant women, but it took twenty-five years to act. By then nearly five million women had already taken megadoses of the fake hormone, and the barn door was swinging. Not only did it turn out DES significantly increased their risk of breast cancer, but they unknowingly passed on catastrophic medical and reproductive problems to their children. Now you've got millions of daughters and granddaughters walking around feeling deformed because they can't bear children or even get a clean bill of health. I'm telling you the ramifications are so widespread and injurious to families, DES makes Thalidomide look like a little mix-up at the pharmacy."

"You sound rather impassioned about this. Are you, by chance, among the victims?"

"Indirectly, yes." Shelby bowed her head. It was the first time she'd considered herself a victim of circumstances, but the association was valid. "I actually did a story on DES a few years ago, before I was aware there was a family connection. But last week when my sister, Lauren, discovered she was a DES daughter, it suddenly wasn't old news anymore."

"Of course you've spoken to your mother about this I presume."

"I can't. She died from ovarian cancer in 1969."

"Oh, dear, dear, dear." Ian actually appeared saddened. "How old was she?"

"My age," Shelby whispered. "Thirty-eight."

"I see. I never realized . . . so this woman in the hospital now? She's not your mummy?"

"No, my aunt."

"Your father married his aunt?"

Shelby groaned. Maybe she should just tattoo her forehead with the phrase, *She's my aunt, not his*. "No, a year after my mother died he married *my* aunt. My mother's younger sister."

"Likes to keep it in the family, hey?" Ian winked. "I once dated two sisters at the same time, unbeknownst to them, of course. That was quite a row when they found out . . ."

"Ian, I'm begging you . . ."

"Right. Of course." He cleared his throat. "Go on. Tell me about your sister. Lauren is it?"

"She's thirty-two and desperate to have a baby. So far she's had two miscarriages, the last of which was an ectopic pregnancy. Now her doctor says she's damaged goods and has to consider alternatives like surrogacy or adoption. But that's not all. Because of her DES exposure, she has a slew of medical problems, to say nothing of her emotional state."

Ian licked his spoon. "So you might call your story a personal vendetta piece as well."

"That's fair."

"I like it actually," a sobered Ian said. "I do. It's juicier than I expected. How would you feel about working on both stories at the same time?"

"It might cut into my suntan hour, but I should be able to manage."

"What about the money? It wasn't in the third quarter budget to do two revenge pieces."

"I'd be willing to reduce my normal and customary fee, seeing as how you're paying so generously on the first one."

"Excellent then." Ian pumped his fist. "Look out high-society debs and makers of DES. The great Shelby Lazarus is back in the saddle again."

"So I am." A nervous Shelby started shredding her napkin. God, I hope I'm not making a big mistake.

Believe me, Shelby's not making a mistake. There's no such thing. There's also no such thing as a coincidence or an accident. Everything that happens, happens for a reason. We may not understand why at the time. Or ever, because the mysteries of life are only divulged to us on a need-to-know basis. Which explains all the universal head scratching.

I know. The very notion that some greater force is calling the shots is disturbing. Frankly, if you'd asked me about karma and destiny when I was Sandy Lazarus, I would have blown cigarette smoke in your face and told you to lay off the hard stuff. No way would I have accepted the idea my life had been mapped out with all the precision of a Hadassah dinner dance. Hors d'oeuvres at 7:00 P.M., dinner, dancing at 9:00 P.M. . . .

Who wants to believe their existence is part of some master plan? Or that the good and bad in life are simply the result of a legal, binding agreement, according to God's will? To whom you're born, where and how you live, the people you meet, the work you do, the person you marry, the children you have, the circumstances of your death . . . But it's true. Nothing happens in life that isn't already in the blueprints.

Take Shelby's career, for instance. You think her desire to be a reporter was a random choice? That she just woke up one day and said I think I'll go to the Columbia School of Journalism and shoot for a Pulitzer? No, it was her destiny.

The first clue was she was born at 12:01 A.M., on January 1, 1960. That's right. Shelby was not only the first birth of the decade at Mt. Sinai Hospital, but in all five boroughs of New York. What a media frenzy that caused! Reporters and photographers scrambled over to the maternity ward to capture her face, the symbol of the bold, new era.

As it turned out, the photo of Larry and me holding Shelby in our arms was such a great shot, it made the front pages of dozens of papers. From then on, every New Year's we'd get calls from papers asking if they could interview Shelby for the morning edition. Apparently, readers associated her beautiful, angelic image with the start of another year and were clamoring to see her transformation from infant to child.

Every year we were amazed by Shelby's cooperative spirit. Normally she was so dour and stern, but the instant the newspaper people arrived, different child. She'd primp and pose, answering silly questions with a smile, understanding even at four years old the power of the press. Talk about early influences. When she got older she'd be damned if she didn't somehow find a way to stay on the front page!

But what, you may ask, was the real purpose of directing Shelby into the field of journalism? I'm thinking she returned to the physical world to learn the meaning of caring and compassion. And what better way to elicit the sympathy vote from someone than to expose them to the underbelly of the human condition?

Nice concept if you can get it, of course. Shelby's been working in the paper trade long enough to have had the compassion bug bite her by now. So what's the holdup? All I know is timing is left to the wisdom of the universe, and I have faith in the system.

Here's why. Remember when Shelby bumped into Ian at the airport and thought it was a horrible coincidence he was on the same flight? It was no coincidence. I found out from my great-grandmother Yetta, who has been on this side for what seems like forever, that it was all in the cards. That once Shelby got reacquainted with Ian, she'd end up getting a chance to write two articles that would be the catalyst for major changes in her life.

Ditto for Roz and Larry getting hit by a truck. You think that was a random accident? Have I taught you nothing?

Chapter Fifteen

Shelby wondered what planet she was on when she decided to go ahead with Plan B. If Lauren's own husband couldn't convince her to come out of their house, did she really think she'd fare any better? She had neither the patience, experience, nor cunning to know which magic key was going to unlock her sister's mental health door.

Irma Weiner would know which key. Several times Shelby picked up the phone to ask for a little assistance, but stubborn pride kept her from dialing. The last thing Shelby wanted was to have Mrs. Know-It-All portraying herself as the hero to Shelby's villain, simply because Shelby wounded Dr. Weiner, Aunt Roz, and Lauren. Unintentionally, of course.

Not that Mrs. Weiner's anger wasn't justified. All three people on the receiving end of Shelby's wrath were still reeling. All three were a question mark as to their interest in surviving.

What happened to the truth shall set you free? Shelby asked herself as she double-checked the address, then pulled into Lauren's driveway, nearly pummeling the mailbox in the process. Hopefully she'd get used to the power of the V-6 engine on Aunt Roz's car before she hurt someone.

Cute house, Shelby yawned as she rang the doorbell. If you like small, old, two-story capes. What? No white picket fence or rhododendrons in the yard?

"Hi." Lauren answered the door in pajamas. "I thought you said you were coming by later."

"I know. But I was thinking maybe you'd come with me to the hospital, and visiting hours are over at eight."

"No thanks. Maybe another time." Lauren led Shelby into the tiny kitchen, clearly anticipating Shelby's smug reaction. "I know it's small," she apologized.

"No kidding. Aren't you afraid if you put your key in the door you'll break the window?"

Lauren's shoulders fell and her eyes misted. "What do you get out of being like this?"

"Like what? Sarcastic?"

"No, like angry and mean-spirited. If you hadn't noticed, I'm not exactly in great shape at the moment. Can't you ever take it down a notch?"

"Sorry," Shelby shrugged. "But I did come bearing great news that is sure to cheer you up."

"I can hardly wait." Lauren sank into a chair.

"Now look who's being sarcastic. You're beginning to sound like me."

"Not a pretty picture, is it?" Lauren looked out the window.

"I get the point, okay?" Shelby joined her at the table. "But listen to my news. I just had a meeting with a guy I used to work for at the *Detroit Free Press*. He's over at the *New York Informer* now. Anyway, he's agreed to let me do a full-length feature about DES daughters. Isn't that great?"

"Yippee." Lauren twirled her index finger. "It's my lucky day."

"How many antidepressants did you take today?" Shelby studied Lauren's pupils.

"Not enough." She sniffed.

"I'm really sorry. I thought you'd be happy to hear I'm getting publicity for your cause."

"My cause?" Lauren jumped up. "I don't have a cause, Shelby. I have heartache. I have fear. I have aggravation. And worst of all, my body is so deformed I can't have a baby, okay? So excuse me if I don't appreciate an insensitive, publicity hound like you exploiting my problems for the sake of a friggin' byline."

Shelby was floored by Lauren's abrasiveness. For years she'd tried getting her sister to toughen up, never thinking the harsh treatment might be directed at her. Oh, for the good old days when Lauren trailed her around the house hoping to get her idol to play Barbies.

"I'm shocked." Shelby got up to take a drink of water. "I thought you'd be happy to have attention called to your problem so people would be more sensitive to you."

"The only one I need to be more sensitive to me is you." Lauren took a package of salami out of the refrigerator and sat down. "And if you say one word to me about eating this, I swear I'll shove a piece down your throat."

"Okay. No problem." Shelby jumped up. "Where's your bathroom?"

"Down the hall on the right." Lauren didn't bother getting up to lead the way.

Shelby didn't actually need to use the bathroom, she needed to go on a little fishing expedition in the medicine chest. Clearly whatever Lauren was taking was not only not helping her, it was turning her into a sardonic bitch. Even she had to admit one per family was enough.

Shelby slid open the cabinet to find at least a dozen prescription painkillers and sedatives lined up like an arsenal of weapons. Holy shit. When they remade *Valley of the Dolls*, they could have shot on location right here.

She gathered the pill bottles in her arms and returned to the kitchen. "Why do you need all this crap? You know how easy it would be to overdose?"

"Sounds like a plan." Lauren sniffed. "And what right do you have to go through my medicine chest?"

"Hey, you went through my kitchen cabinets looking for food. That's what sisters do."

"What do you know about being a sister? You're a lousy sister. You're selfish and mean and insensitive, and you won't have a baby for me."

Shelby closed her eyes in exasperation. Was every conversation going to come down to this? "I need you to understand something. It's not that I don't feel for you. It's not that I don't want you to have a baby and live happily ever after with Avi. It's that I can't help you fulfill that dream. You're right about me. I'm selfish and insensitive . . . oh, and what about my diet? You said yourself. I don't eat enough for one, let alone two."

"Yes, but you could change . . ."

"The point is I don't want to," Shelby said, raising her voice. "Besides, if anyone should be changing something about herself, it's you."

"Me?" Lauren sniffed. "What's wrong with me?"

"You're fickle, that's what's wrong. You had three different majors at four different colleges, one month you're a vegetarian, the next month you're living on Burger King . . ."

"This isn't the same thing. This is something I've always wanted."

"So was red hair, a sailboat, and a chance to be on *Jeopardy!* But then you chickened out."

"I'm not going to chicken out, Shel." Lauren reached for her hand. "I would give up my right arm to have a baby, and you know it."

"Then ask someone in Avi's family. Maybe he has a sister or a cousin . . ."

". . . Who all live in Israel. What should I tell them to do? FedEx the baby when it's born?"

"It's no less preposterous then asking a thirty-eight-year-old woman to donate her eggs, spread her legs, then put her career on hold for God knows how long. Besides, you don't even know for sure that I can get pregnant. Maybe I have fertility problems, too."

"I know." Lauren sniffed. "That's why I want you to see my doctor. If he examines you and says you're not a good candidate, then I'd have to accept it and hire someone else."

"Why wait? Let's hire someone else right now. My treat."

Lauren nodded no. "I want you."

Shelby opened her mouth, then decided against fueling the fire. Maybe Lauren was right. If a doctor examined her, there was a good chance he'd disqualify her based on age, size, or some other technicality. It didn't matter what eliminated her, as long as she proved unfit for the job.

Out of desperation to get Lauren to move on, Shelby heard herself agree. "I'm not saying I'm willing to be your surrogate," she warned. "But I guess it wouldn't hurt to get checked out."

Suddenly Lauren's whole demeanor transformed from victim to grand inquisitor. "Thank you." She threw away her tissues, like the invalid at a revival meeting tossing her crutches. "It would mean so much to me and Avi. By the way, when's the last time you saw a gynecologist?"

Shelby hemmed. "Socially . . . or by appointment?"

"By appointment."

"That would be . . . once in college. When I went on the pill."

"Are you serious?" Lauren cried. "That's the last time you had a Pap smear?"

"Actually, I've never had a Pap smear." She shivered at the very idea.

"That's crazy, Shel. Mommy died of ovarian cancer. We're at tremendous risk!"

"Uh-huh."

"I swear to God, Shel. For an intelligent woman you're an idiot. I mean I know you hate hospitals, but what do you have against going to the doctor?"

"Nothing. It's not like I made a deliberate attempt to avoid going. I just never had anything wrong with me. I take care of my body, I eat right . . ."

"I'm taking you to see my doctor, and that's that. One day you'll thank me."

"Right." Shelby stood soldier-still as Lauren hugged her tightly.

But what Shelby was really thinking was she should have realized Plan B had no upsides. Lauren was as stable as a three-legged chair, so taking responsibility for getting her back on her feet was a lose-lose situation. Even if Shelby managed to help her have a good day, it guaranteed nothing. Between the mood swings and anxiety attacks, one wrong move could send Lauren back into a tailspin. She would just have to take one day at a time.

"Okay, here's the deal." Shelby released Lauren's clutch. "I go see your doctor, you come with me to the hospital."

Lauren shook her head no.

"Why not?"

"Because I need more time."

"It's okay. I'll wait. How long do you need to shower and change?"

"No. I mean I need months. Or years. Like you had. I just can't look at them right now, and no way am I walking back into that house."

What a nightmare, Shelby thought. The shoe is on the other foot. "Look, I understand where you're coming from probably better than anyone, so be my guest. Be angry at them. But don't direct your anger at the house. It's like me with North Shore," she blurted. "All those years I avoided going back there solved absolutely nothing. The hurt and betrayal were inside me, not the building."

"What are you saying?" Lauren sulked. "That I have no right to be upset by this? I've been betrayed as much as you."

"I know that. I just want you to learn from my experience and channel your anger. It's a waste of time being so mad at the house you can't walk back in there."

"Oh my God. You hypocrite!" Lauren cried. "You've had years to deal with all of this and you're still not over it. I just found out a few days ago, okay? So don't tell me to channel my anger."

"Fine." Shelby backed off. "I'm just trying to help."

"Fine." Lauren sighed. "Are you going over to see Daddy?"

"Yes."

"I don't know, Shel. It may not be the best thing right now. He . . ."

"What?"

"He said he didn't want to see you ever again."

Shelby's face felt flush. "He told you that?"

"No, he told Avi that."

"I don't believe it. I don't care how angry Daddy is at me, he would never say that."

"Don't shoot the messenger." Lauren shrugged. "And don't blame me if he refuses to talk to you when you get there. You really crossed the line this time."

"Fine. I heard you, but I know how to talk to Daddy. Believe me, if I show up at his bedside, he's not going to kick me out. You know how long he's waited for me to spill my guts?"

"What are you going to say to him?"

"I have no idea. Now do me a favor in exchange for my very magnanimous offer. Promise me you'll throw this shit away." She pointed to the rows of pill bottles. "You don't need them. You're the sanest person I know. A little emotional at times, very high-strung, and you know nothing about nutrition. But considering everything you've been through, you're really okay. And the last thing you need right now is to get hooked on painkillers, because what surrogate is going to have a baby for a drug abuser? Besides, I heard Betty Ford no longer has a family plan."

Lauren could not contain her laughter. "Okay, but this was the most fun I've had in years."

"What? Being so stoned you couldn't match up the tops and bottoms of your pajamas?"

"No. Getting to act like you."

"What do you mean act?" Shelby narrowed her eyes. "You're not flung out on Prozac?"

"Are you joking? Me? The prude? I'm not on anything."

"Then where did all the pills come from?"

"From friends. I just had to hope you didn't read the names on the prescriptions."

"You little shit, you! You mean to tell me this whole display . . ."

"You gotta do what ya gotta do." Lauren gently tapped Shelby's cheek. "I'll call you as soon as I set up the doctor appointment. Oh, and good luck with Daddy."

"Did you also make up the part about him never wanting to see me?"

"No, unfortunately. That's the real deal."

I knew Plan B was a big mistake, Shelby thought as she backed out of the driveway, narrowly missing the mailbox again. I've been duped by my own sister, and now I'm going to get stuck answering some idiot doctor's questions about my sexual history while he secretly delights in examining my breasts. How did I not see through her ruse?

More importantly, if her father was so angry with her, why subject herself to even more angst by visiting him? She'd waited this long. What was a few more weeks to let him cool off?

But in her heart Shelby knew she didn't want to wait. Possibly she didn't even have time to wait. Scott had repeatedly said given the extensive nature of her father's injuries, they had to expect the unexpected, particularly in this early phase of recovery. Several good, productive days in a row would mean squat if he suddenly developed an infection or reacted to a strong, new drug. Then they'd have to start from ground zero, if they got another chance to start at all.

Shelby didn't even want to contemplate the prospect of never getting the opportunity to reconcile. Not because she'd decided to forgive him, but because she'd grown weary of the unresolved anger that had glued her to a shrink's chair.

She remembered the session with Dr. Kahn when he talked about how much energy was expended distancing oneself from a loved one. Shelby had vehemently disagreed, arguing she'd never felt more liberated. But, of course, he'd been right. When she had been on speaking terms with her father, she barely thought of him. Once she cut him off, however, all she did was obsess. Was he thinking about her? Was he feeling remorse? Was he ever planning to explain himself?

Shelby also had to admit that as much as she'd been devastated by his lies and deception, she still needed his assurance that he loved her and his promise that everything would be all right. But mostly what she longed for was to feel safe again. As a child, one bear hug and a kiss atop her head was all she needed to go forth and conquer. Since then, no paycheck, billboard, or man had ever come close to giving her that same sense of security.

Maybe that's what she would say to him. Being the sentimental fool he was, it's exactly what he'd want to hear. No sappy apologies, no hysteria. Just a few, choice words straight from the heart. She hoped. For now that she'd decided she wanted her father back in her life, it would be devastating if he played tit for tat.

Chapter Sixteen

To Shelby's credit, she successfully made it through the hospital parking lot, the lobby, and the elevator without losing her nerve. Of all things, it was the antiseptic smell in the hallways that made her want to bolt, for the rancid association with illness was overpowering. Yet something propelled her to hold her breath and keep moving through the corridors. Perhaps it was the words she'd uttered to Lauren only moments earlier. It was pointless to harbor anger at a building.

Anger at people was another matter completely. She tried not to think about what she would do if she so happened to bump into Dr. Glavin, Scott Rosenthal, Irma or Bernie Weiner, and especially Aunt Roz. In her sensitive state, any encounter with the enemy would surely destroy what little nerve was left in her emotional tank.

To her relief, Shelby found her way to her father's room without incident. But relief was overtaken by dread when she peeked inside. The Larry Lazarus she knew was a large, strapping fellow with vast hands and a booming voice. He could not possibly be the lump of gray clay who lay bruised and broken, almost beyond recognition, with tubes, wires, and hoses camouflaging his body. He could not be the patient idling in bed, pale and unshaven, teasing the angel of death.

"It's okay to go in." A nurse brushed past Shelby at the door. "He's all cleaned up after his little accident this morning . . . How you doing, Mr. L?" She parted the blinds to let the sunlight in. "You about ready for your dinner?"

He grumbled something about not caring one way or another.

"Looks like you have some company now. How about I bring it later?"

Shelby flinched. This wasn't how she wanted to make her entrance.

Larry looked over, then immediately turned away. "It's no one. Bring my dinner."

"She doesn't look like no one to me." The nurse checked his vital signs. "A little company is good for the spirits."

"Hello, Daddy," Shelby waved.

"Oh joy. The great Shelby has descended from the mountain. Go away. I need my rest."

"How are you feeling?" Dumbest question of the century.

"How should I be feeling?" He stared out the window. "First I was hit by a truck. Then my daughter, my flesh and blood, opens her big trap and sticks a knife in her mother's heart!"

"I'll leave you two alone." The nurse rushed out so quickly she created a breeze.

"It's not like you think," Shelby stammered at the door, taken aback by his harsh tone.

"Don't tell a dying man what to think!" he bellowed. "No matter how you slice it, you did a rotten, disgraceful thing. Go figure, I said to myself. My wife survives a terrible accident, then our daughter decides it's a good time to waltz in and finish the job."

Shelby looked down, bristling at the reference to her being Roz's daughter. But obviously this wasn't the time to fight that battle. Or any battle. Lauren was right. He didn't want to see her, so what was the point of trying to make conversation? At that she turned around and walked out the door. Plan B was over.

"Get back in here, young lady!" her father cried out, his vocal cords miraculously as strong as she remembered.

Shelby froze. What was it about a man's loud voice that stopped women in their tracks? She had smirked at Irma for coming to the same dead halt when her ex-husband yelled out her name. Now here she was, equally intimidated, standing in the doorway.

"Come over here and sit down where I can see you." He pointed to the chair next to his bed.

A little girl named Shelby followed orders. Clearly he'd come out of the coma intact.

"Why now, Shelby?" He shook his fist. "After all these years, you couldn't just let it rest?"

"I . . . It wasn't my intention, believe me. She provoked me."

"Oh, bullshit! You've never been provoked a day in your life. You did it because you saw she was too weak to defend herself."

"That's not true," Shelby protested. "Bringing it up was the last thing on my mind."

"So? What? You were in the middle of polite chitchat when all of a sudden it occurred to you, hey, now would be a good time to turn the knife?"

"That's not how it was, okay? She accused me of being a lousy sister because I won't buy into this whole stupid surrogate mother thing. Then when she said it was a shame I wasn't loyal and devoted like she was to Mommy, I guess I just lost it."

"And what did you think Lauren would do after she found out? Go out and celebrate?"

"I don't know. I wasn't thinking about her . . ."

"No, of course you didn't think about her," he yelled in spite of excruciating pain. "Why would you think of her? You're always so wrapped up in yourself and your goddamn career. But if you knew what we'd been through with her . . . Believe me. It's been one heartache after the next."

"I know."

"You know nothing!" Saliva sprayed from his mouth.

"Fine." Shelby jumped. "I know nothing."

"Don't pacify me!" He bellowed. "Lauren's been through hell, and who do you think has been there to pick up the pieces? Your mother and me! Poor kid goes and marries two different guys without a pot to piss in, and every month we're putting money in the bank so they have something to live on. And when we're not covering her expenses, we're there for her to lean on when she gets depressed because she's not pregnant. Or, because the medication to help her get pregnant is making her sick. Then finally the Great Shelby shows up, not to be a big sister to her, oh no, that would be too much to ask. No, she has to make even more trouble by telling her that her father had an affair."

Shelby was dizzy. To what did she respond first? The accusation she was a horrible person, a horrible sister, a horrible daughter? "But it's true, Daddy. You did have an affair."

"How dare you be so disrespectful!"

"I'm disrespectful?" Shelby raised her voice. "You're the one who slept with your sister-in-law while your wife was in this hospital dying of cancer. What were *you* thinking when you betrayed Mommy? That it was okay because she was too sick to find out?"

"Thinking? Who was thinking? I was in pain. An agony I hope to God you never know."

"I'm sorry." Shelby wiped her wet nose with the back of her hand. "What you did was unconscionable, inexcusable, and . . . downright shitty."

"Well how's this? I don't have one single regret. Roz saved my life."

"Yes, but she ruined mine!"

"You don't know what you're saying." He turned to her with tears in his eyes. "Roz took you into her life as if you were her own. She cared for you, she loved you, she did everything she could to help you forget your pain."

"I didn't want to forget!" Shelby cried. "I wanted to remember everything about Mommy. How she smelled so nice in the morning, how she always combed my hair and kissed my head, how she loved to pick out my clothes for the next day of school. Roz was nothing like her. She was a fat pig. I don't even know how you looked at her naked. She was nothing like Mommy."

Larry tried to prop himself up on his elbows, but had neither the strength nor the maneuverability. Even the slightest movement inflicted pain. "Come over here," he signaled.

Shelby moved closer, not expecting that in one swift motion her father would extend his arm and slap her face. He fell back in agony, as did she. He had never raised a hand to her before.

"I should have done that years ago," he huffed. "How dare you speak that way. You looked at Roz and saw someone who chose not to starve herself for the sake of being stylish. I looked at Roz and saw a loving woman who was healthy as a horse. A good woman who could move a roomful of furniture, do the shopping and cooking, and still have the strength to hold me at night.

"I tell you, watching your mother wither away to a bag of bones was a horror, and I didn't care if I lived or died, kids or no kids. But your aunt Roz. She gave me the will to carry on. She made me survive, so I was there for you and Lauren. I'm telling you right now. Without her you would have lost me, too."

Shelby was still holding her hand over the cheek her father had struck, shocked not by the soreness of her jaw, but by his words. She had never allowed herself to believe he might love another woman after her mother, let alone a woman who stole him out from under her nose. Yet he was truly speaking from the heart. He loved Roz.

"I'm sorry," she spoke softly, suddenly feeling a chill from the frosty air-conditioning. "I guess until now I never considered your needs."

"No kidding." His voice softened. "That's why I'm going to tell you a story. An unbelievable story. Like the fairy tales I used to read to you at night. Only this one is true. Every last word."

"It's okay. I don't need to hear this." Shelby stood.

"Sit down!" he barked. "You *do* need to hear this."

Shelby, the newly obedient one, sat back down.

"First of all, you have to understand this wasn't planned. It just happened."

"Men always say that. 'I swear, honey, I had no idea it was going to happen.' "

"Be quiet, or I'll slap you again. And stop with the sarcasm. You think this is easy for me?"

Shelby folded her hands in her lap.

"One morning I'm on the way home from the hospital after another sleepless night on a cot in your mother's room, and I'm depressed as hell. Scared. Shaken. Miserable. You name it. And I'm thinking, I'm not strong enough to go on. Maybe I should just drive off the side of the road.

"I knew the doctors were bullshitting me. They'd tell me about this new drug, or that new experiment so I'd keep my hopes up. But a husband knows when his wife is dying. She'd just been through another round of radiation and was weak from nausea. She couldn't go on much longer.

"Anyway, I walk in the door and there's Roz, looking like an angel, I swear. She had just moved in with us to take care of you and Lauren, and she'd been running around trying to fill your mother's shoes. She was baking, and cleaning and carpooling, the works. And remember, she was a single girl then, totally unaccustomed to our lifestyle.

"So she greets me at the door, a basket of laundry in her hand, and I say, 'Why are you doing the laundry? I'll bring it over to the plant.' And she says, 'I have to keep busy, or I'll die.' And, of course, I understand.

"Then she tells me she just made coffee and baked a fresh banana bread, and I should sit down and join her. Well, you know me. I hate banana bread, but the house smelled so wonderful, and I was just happy not to be at the hospital. So we sit at the dining room table and we talk. And the house is so nice and quiet because you girls were at school. And the phone wasn't ringing for a change, and Tony Bennett's on the radio . . .

"And I see that Roz has been crying, too, and we talk about Sandy, and how much we love her, and I take her hand because I realize I'm not the only one who's suffering. Then she kisses my hand, and I feel her tears on my skin, and I want to comfort her. So I get up, and we hug. And there we are, holding on to each other for dear life, and suddenly I go to kiss her cheek, but she turns, and our lips touch, and I'm feeling dread and shame and love all at once, and I kiss her back with more passion than I can believe, and I'm feeling her warmth, and we began to undress each other. Right there in the dining room."

"Please. Daddy. I really don't want to hear this."

"Yes. Yes you do. Because you need to understand the moment. Understand how two frightened, tired people can seek solace from one another without the *National Enquirer* passing judgment on them.

"So we go from the dining room into the living room, and there's piles of clean clothes on the couch, on the chairs, towels folded on the rugs, so much laundry I'm thinking to myself, She's trying to compete with me. She's taking in the neighbor's laundry. Anyway, I guess you could say we fell into the softness of it all, and we made love. Beautiful love. I tell you the moment still brings tears to my eyes."

And to mine, Shelby thought.

"I tell you, Shelby, it was innocent and passionate, and when it was over we didn't feel shame or dread. We felt alive. We weren't giving in to death, we were reminding ourselves we were whole and healthy. Then, of course, reality hit, and we were so embarrassed we avoided each other altogether. And that was that. No one had to know. It was our little secret."

"Until she found out she was pregnant."

"Exactly. That's when everything changed. I hoped she might tell me there was someone else, but Roz wasn't the kind to sleep around. In fact, if you want to know a little secret, she had quite a crush on me when I first met your mother. She was a little girl then. A baby. Anyway, she was heartbroken when Mommy and I got married, and I guess I knew when Roz and I made love that she still had strong feelings for me. So what was I supposed to do? She was pregnant with my child. Break her heart? Tell her to get an abortion?

"Then I began to think. Maybe this was God's plan. He was taking my wife away, but he was bringing me someone else who really loved me, and you, and Lauren. Roz is not like your mother, I know, but she's a wonderful woman. Very strong and vivacious and caring. And a helluva good bowler. A one-sixty handicap, and I don't have to tell you how that's helped our league.

"Anyway, your mother died a few months later, and now Roz is as big as a house, and of course everyone is asking questions. Who's the father? Are you getting married? So she makes up this story about a fella from Philly that didn't work out, but she was keeping the baby and living with us until she could get her own place.

"I tell you, Granny Bea was beside herself. She just lost one daughter to cancer, and now the other one is going to have an illegitimate child. She'd walk around saying, 'Thank God my Sheldon didn't live to see this day.'

"Then before we knew it, Eric was born, and I tell you now, it was the best thing that could have happened to me. Instead of living in a deep depression, I had a reason to live. I had my son to raise, and two beautiful daughters. We were a family again. A strong, healthy family. No more hospitals, and doctors, and ambulance calls in the middle of the night. We had love and stability, and I admit it was a little cockamamy how the whole thing came to be, but somehow it just seemed right. Not sinful. Not dirty."

"But it was so unfair," Shelby cried. "You never let us mourn. You swept our whole life with Mommy under the rug like she never existed. Every time I mentioned her, you'd pat my head and tell me not to be sad. You'd say, 'Let's be happy with our new mom and our new baby brother.' But I needed to keep *my* mother's memory alive. How she walked and talked, how she'd roll her eyes when you made a corny joke . . ."

"You're one hundred percent right." He shrugged. "But at the time, it was too hard for me to watch you suffer. Every time you had a bad spell, it would just remind me of how much pain I was in. The only way I could get out of bed in the morning was to think about our new life."

"I understand," Shelby cried. "But how could you have kept the truth from us? How could you have let us grow up never telling us Eric was your son?"

"Believe me, I wanted to tell you. I just couldn't seem to find the right words. Then the years went by, and everything was going along, and I said to myself, why mess things up now? Maybe it's not so bad to keep this under wraps. Then nobody gets hurt."

"Yes, but we had a right to know!" Shelby folded her arms. "I would never keep something as important as that from my children."

"Shelby, believe me. Nothing would make me happier than for you to one day know the joy of having children. And to have the chance to raise them the best you can. But eventually you'd find out, no matter hard you try, you can't always do right by them."

"I'll have to take your word for it." She sighed. "I don't think kids are in the cards for me."

"Never say never." He patted her hand. "Life is full of surprises."

"Maybe." Shelby nodded.

"You used to want kids you know." He smiled. "Lots of them. Seven I think. One for every day of the week."

"Oh my God. Not you, too." Shelby's eyes grew big. "The other day I ran into this girl I went to school with who remembered me saying the same thing, and then I found my old diary and it was in there, too. But it's so weird. I have no recollection of ever thinking anything like that."

"Are you kidding?" Daddy's eyes twinkled. "You had all kinds of great ideas. First you were going to save the world by giving away all my money. Then you were going to take a train to Alabama to beat up the people who didn't let the colored children ride the bus . . ."

"That I remember." She smiled, praying he didn't also remember that she wanted to be called Super Shelby. "But seven kids? What would I do with seven kids?"

"That's what Matty wanted to know." He laughed. "I'll never forget the look on his face when you told him the grand plan. You were just sitting there at the kitchen table eating Oreos and milk. You must have been eight or nine at the time. And you said, 'Matty, when we're in college you're going to ask me to marry you, then we'll live here, and we'll have seven children, and Granny Bea Good will be so happy because she was the youngest of seven, and then she could say there was one for every day of the week, just like her father said to her.' And he's looking at you, like okay, Shelby. Anything you say, Shelby. Your mother and I had quite a laugh over that one . . ."

"Glad I kept you all entertained." She blushed, wondering what other intimate details of her life her father remembered. But at least the mystery was solved. And now that she thought about it, the details were suddenly coming into focus. Matty splitting open his Oreos and dunking them in milk. Matty hanging on her every word. Matty's bright green eyes when he looked at her.

"You know, Shelby. We knew you knew." Her father interrupted her thoughts.

"Then why you didn't come right out and tell me?"

"Roz wanted to. It was me . . . I was afraid. . . . You were already so hostile to her . . ."

Shelby took a deep breath, knowing she might be upsetting the whole nice apple cart. "I was hostile to her because you kept insisting she was my mother, but my mother was gone. In fact, I still hate it when you call her Mommy. She's my aunt Roz."

Her father closed his eyes. "Give it a rest, Shelby. I know the facts inside and out, but she's been like a mother to you for almost thirty years. Do you mean to tell me with all she did for you, with everything she's been through, you can't give her a goddamn break?"

Give her a break? Shelby wondered. What would it be like to live without anger? Would she lose her powers, like Samson when his hair was shorn? Or would she suddenly feel empowered? The only thing she knew for certain was she was tired of this embittered journey. Maybe the truth could set you free.

"I suppose after what she's put up with she deserves better." Shelby hesitated. "But please don't expect me to call her Mom. That I simply can't do."

Her father shrugged. "The funny thing is, she always said she didn't care what you called her, as long you called her. All she ever wanted was for you to accept her. To understand she had something to offer you. A loving home. A shoulder to cry on . . ."

Just as Shelby nodded she understood, a heavyset nurse breezed in to do her scheduled chores. "How you doin', Mr. L? I see they've scheduled you for surgery tomorrow . . . Oh, hi," she acknowledged Shelby. "Well now, you must be the other daughter."

"Yes. I'm Shelby."

"Pleased to meet you, Shelby," she huffed and puffed. "Your daddy's a special man, and we're takin' excellent care of him. Now let me see who you look like." She studied Shelby's face, then looked over to Mr. Lazarus. "For sure you ain't lookin' like him. Good thing, too." She chucked Shelby's shoulder. "Seems to me you resemble your mama. Especially around the eyes. Course that's about all I can see a her right now."

Larry Lazarus held his breath. Would Shelby carry on, as she always did, about the biological implausibility of her and Aunt Roz resembling one another?

"Thank you." Shelby smiled. "Everyone says that."

Larry beamed, then blew her a kiss.

This is the great thing about eternity. You get to be around long enough to see everything!

Chapter Seventeen

Never underestimate the ability of hired help to make life bliss-ful. Within days of Shelby's reconciliation with her father, the formerly hostile Maria was not only pleasant to Shelby, she was completely at her service. Suddenly she was available to do Shelby's laundry, take her phone messages, and as a licensed driver herself, take over the Wald-baum's runs. At least *she* would remember to bring the coupons.

But when Maria also learned Shelby had apologized to Aunt Roz, as well as agreed to see a gynecologist on Lauren's behalf, she unrolled the rest of the red carpet. She stocked the refrigerator with Shelby's favorite-flavored yogurt, placed fresh flowers by her bed, and miraculously managed to pronounce her name correctly. No more Miss Shelly. It was Shelby Dear.

Shelby thanked Maria for her attentiveness, then was struck by an odd thought. Had anyone paid her since the accident? She'd never seen Lauren write out a check, or even mention an arrange-ment. Sure enough when Shelby inquired, Maria shrugged and said she was certain Mrs. L would settle up with her as soon as she was well enough. "In the meanwhile the good Lord will provide for me."

"And I'm sure Visa will be happy to wait," Shelby replied. Then she promptly asked her father for his ATM card and pin number. Upon handing the devoted woman a month's pay, plus reimburse-ments for groceries, train fare, and what Shelby wryly called "com-bat pay," a teary-eyed Maria clutched the wad of cash to her chest and thanked Shelby for her kindness and generosity.

"I don't care what anybody says about you, Shelby Dear. You've got a big heart."

It was a historic moment in Shelby's life, as it had been ages since the words *Shelby* and *big heart* had been uttered in the same sentence. But, sadly, the lovefest was about to end. In spite of her great strides on the humanitarian front, she had made an executive decision. It was time to return to Chicago, where she was free to pursue her single, selfish existence. Not that life was nirvana there, either. It was just safer than living under the constant threat of being needed.

So although she felt relieved to be on speaking terms with her father and Aunt Roz, she was not interested in suddenly becoming the long-lost, dutiful daughter who sacrificed herself for their lengthy rehabilitation. Nor did she see herself playing the role of devoted sister, procreating from her loins, just for the sake of immortalizing the Lazarus family genes.

But there was something more. Being back on Majestic Drive was harder than she imagined, with each passing day turning her youthful, bittersweet memories into an obsession. She simply could not stop wondering what her life would have been like had it gone according to plan. If Dr. Weiner had done his job and her mother was alive to nurture her. If she and Matty remained in New York and in love. It would just be easier if images of her past weren't constantly haunting her.

And, too, it would only be a matter of time before the novelty of family togetherness wore thin. Which would presumably happen upon her declaration she would not, could not, play Surrogate Barbie.

There were numerous reasons, of course, but the most compelling argument, the one she need not apologize for, had to do with the stability of Lauren and Avi's relationship. With its tenuous, flimsy backbone, it was hardly the altar on which to build a family. Shelby simply couldn't bring a life into this world that was dependent on those two cornflakes for sustenance.

Lauren, naturally, insisted that Shelby was dead wrong about her and Avi. That she simply didn't understand what made them tick. To which Shelby replied, "Fine. I'm wrong. Come to think of it, you two remind me of Tracy and Hepburn. What I don't get is how you expect me to go through with this surrogacy business after bringing me to see Dr. Dickhead."

"I'm sorry, Shel." Lauren ran after her in the office parking lot.

"How did I know Dr. Kessler would be at the hospital doing an emergency C-section, and you'd have to see his partner?"

"One little call, that's how!" Shelby cried out. "Good morning. I'm bringing over my very paranoid, terrified sister for her first pelvic exam in twenty years, and I just wanted to make sure she'll be seeing Dr. Kessler, and not his arrogant, son of a bitch associate who has about as much bedside manner as a rottweiler in heat."

"Fine. I should have called. But it's not my fault you didn't come here with an open mind."

"Damn right! It was bad enough I had to come here with open legs," Shelby yelled. "Why didn't you warn me I was going to have to slide my ass down a hard table while Dr. I-Hate-Women shoved a duckmouth and a giant Q-tip inside me?"

"How did you think they did a pelvic exam, Shel? With a psychic and a wand?"

"Whatever. I still can't believe you go to a male gynecologist. Would you use an auto mechanic who never drove a car?" Shelby slammed the car door to make her point.

She had so come with an open mind, thanks to a leftover Valium from Lauren's designer medicine collection. And it wasn't as if she was so naive she didn't expect the doctor to go where no doctor had gone before. But certain bodily explorations aside, she never imagined the whole experience would be so primitive.

Even the questionnaire she filled out prior to getting that lovely paper gown was downright insulting. *Was she sexually active?* Lord knows she gave it her best shot, but she sure as hell wasn't going to titillate the staff with Candace Bushnell-like details.

"I'm sorry this wasn't what you expected, but I still can't believe you." Lauren started the car. "I haven't heard that much swearing since I saw Eddie Murphy live at Westbury Music Fair."

"What did you think? That I'd smile for the nice man while he sexually abused me?"

"He did not abuse you. I was there the whole time. If anybody was abused, it was him."

"Oh, yeah. Let's have a sympathy party for poor Dr. Rubber Gloves. He gets to spend his whole day fondling women's breasts and staring at their asses."

"You're crazy! He's a medical doctor, not a porn star!"

"Bullshit," Shelby sulked. "Once men take off their costumes, they're all alike."

"That's not true, Shel. Dr. Kessler is a sweetheart. He would have made you feel completely comfortable before he examined you."

Shelby shook her head. "You just don't understand."

"Yes, I do. You think the whole thing is embarrassing and degrading."

"It's nothing like that!" Shelby snapped. "Nothing whatsoever!"

"Then what is it?" Lauren flinched. "Why did you get so worked up in there?"

Shelby rolled down the window and leaned back.

"Are you afraid they're going to hurt you?" Lauren persisted. "I have this friend, Denise, who gets these panic attacks whenever she goes to the doctor, and . . ."

"Stop!" Shelby yelled. "Stop right now. You want to know the problem?" She took a deep breath. "I'll tell you the problem. I'm afraid some asshole doctor will discover something terribly wrong with me, and I'll end up spending what little time I have left in tremendous pain, while he consults with someone on the golf course and drives away in his Range Rover. I'm afraid I'll never win a Pulitzer prize, or see Matty again, all because I'll be dead at thirty-eight. Just like Mommy!"

"Oh my God," Lauren gasped. "I had no idea you were even thinking anything like that. You never said a word. But of course it makes sense that that's why you're so paranoid. You poor thing."

Shelby blew into a tissue and begged Lauren to dispense with the Psych 101 chatter. The only thing she hated worse than attracting sympathy was feeling abject humiliation for having opened her emotional crypt, with its raw, dark center. For now that it was revealed, surely Lauren would seize the moment and pry even further under the pretense of helping Shelby find a cure for what ailed her.

Except that Shelby didn't want to be cured. She was happy with her fears. They were comfortable and familiar to her, and she was the consummate expert on avoiding them completely. The same way she'd learned how to preserve her safety by bypassing questionable neighborhoods when covering a story.

On the other hand, this breakdown in the car was a defining moment, for it was then Shelby knew her only choice was to leave. She thanked Lauren for not dwelling on her little outburst and insisted she'd be fine after she showered and rested. But no sooner did Lauren drop her home than Shelby packed, called United, then paged Avi.

"You're picking me up at one o'clock and taking me to La Guardia. And if you so much as breathe a word of this to Lauren, I swear I'll tell her you've been hitting on me since the minute we met. And then you can damn well kiss my daddy's money good-bye. Got it?"

Avi got it. At exactly one o'clock, he honked his horn, and Shelby was on her way, confident Lauren could not intervene. After she arrived in Chicago she would call and explain herself. And, naturally, she would promise to return on a regular basis. She just needed her permanent address to have a different zip code than her family's. They would simply have to understand, as she was not going to give them a choice.

Some things never change. Shelby was always good at running away. In fact, as a child, escape and denial were pretty much her two best friends. The minute things didn't go her way she'd head for Matty's house, or ride her bike around until her legs gave out. "Give her time," I'd tell Larry, whose first reaction was to follow her in the car. "She'll be back." Sure enough, like the swallows of Capistrano, she always returned home in time for dinner.

I do hope Lauren remembers that about her sister. Because she's certainly not going to be happy when she discovers Shelby has flown the coop. First-class, no less.

Avi promised Shelby that he would give her a head start, but he never specified how much of one. Immediately after dropping Shelby at the United terminal, he phoned Lauren.

"What do you mean she's on her way home?" Lauren screamed into her cell phone.

"What ken we do? She changed her mind about helping us."

"Well, for starters, we didn't have to provide the getaway car!"

I hate when Lauren drives like a speed demon. It puts a lot of pressure on me to keep her out of harm's way, and lately her mind has been so preoccupied, it's practically become a full-time job. Right now she's on the

Grand Central Parkway, but the way she's flying by, you'd think she was in the cockpit of a small plane.

It's because she's on a mission. As soon as she realized that her ticket to motherhood was ticketed for a flight home to Chicago, she knew she had to think of a way to stop her. Once Shelby set foot on that plane, she'd be focused on getting a new job, a new boyfriend, a new life. All hope of her saying yes to being a surrogate would disappear into the clouds. Not that Shelby had budged on the issue since the last three times Lauren brought it up.

Unfortunately, Shelby isn't the only one Lauren has to convince to play the surrogate sweepstakes. Avi, too, is less enthusiastic these days now that he's discovered the process of fathering a baby with a woman other than his wife has nothing to do with having sex. It's all lab and no love.

But first things first. Lauren needs to find Shelby, then find the right words to get her to at least think about bearing her a child. Oh look. There's Shelby getting coffee. And there's Lauren, driving round and round, looking for a parking spot. What if I try to find her a spot, and you try to delay Shelby's flight? Oh, right. This is my story. I'm on my own here.

Avi had guessed Shelby was on United's flight # 27 based on the time she arrived at the airport, but Lauren couldn't be bothered with details. She'd find her sister if she had to scour every inch of the terminal. Or not. Almost immediately she found Shelby sitting quietly in the gate area, sipping coffee, and reading what looked like a diary.

Lauren knew she would have to approach gingerly. So before walking the plank, she checked the flight's departure time, looked at her watch, and calculated she had fifteen minutes to say what she was going to say. Whatever that was.

Lauren cleared her throat. "Hey, Shel."

"Oh God." Shelby jumped. "I swear I'm going to kill Avi. He promised to give me a big lead!"

"C'mon, Shel. He's my husband. He loves me."

"Whatever . . . How did you get here so fast? He dropped me off not twenty minutes ago."

"What ken I say?" she mimicked her husband. "He taught me lots of shortcuts."

Shelby nodded, sipping the last drip of coffee. "It's not going to help, you know. There's nothing you can say to make me change my mind."

"I know. I just wanted to make sure I saw you before you left, so I could at least say thank you for everything you did."

"You don't really expect me to believe that?" Shelby searched her bag for a mint.

"No, really. I mean it. I want you to know how much it meant to me that you saw the doctor, even though it totally freaked you out. I mean, everyone said you were too selfish to do it, but I disagreed. I said deep down you were a very kind, loving person."

"Who's everyone?" Shelby stuck out her chin.

"Doesn't matter. My point is I wanted you to know that even though this isn't working out the way I hoped, I really appreciate that you tried."

"Uh-huh," Shelby said. "You do know your ruse is about as see-through as Saran Wrap."

Lauren shrugged. "So watcha reading?"

"An old diary." Shelby looked down at the faded yellow book with the legendary seventies daisy on the cover. "The one I kept in seventh grade."

"Oh, God. I would hate to read mine. That was the year I got my period and my boobs grew like crazy. I was miserable."

"I actually remember that." Shelby started to laugh. "Aunt Roz took you to A&S to buy your first bra, and you came home with this monster-sized thing that would have fit Granny Bea Good."

"Yeah, and then you yelled at her for being such an idiot, and drove me back over there so you could help me pick out something pretty."

"But she needs SUPPORT," Shelby mimicked Aunt Roz.

Lauren laughed and wiped her eye. "I'm not sure, but that might have been the nicest thing you ever did for me."

"Oh come on. I used to do lots of nice things for you."

"Like what?" Lauren began to breathe easier.

"Are you kidding? Don't you remember how I used to shlep you and your friends all over the place? Oh and how about that time I drove you and what's his name into the city so you could have a real date? And then . . ."

"Okay, okay." Lauren laughed. "You were a good sister. Now what I need . . . is for you to be the best sister in the whole world."

"Whoa." Shelby held up her hand. "I thought you came here to say thanks. No pressure."

"I lied?" Lauren bit her lip.

"Forget it." Shelby looked down. "All I said was I'd get examined. That's it."

"What if we find a different doctor?" Lauren pleaded. "I spoke to my friend Elise, and she uses Murray Hill OB/GYN in the city. All the doctors are women, and she loves them . . ."

"It has nothing to do with who the doctor is, Lauren. It has to do with the personal decision I've made. I do not want to lie on a table getting sperm shot up me so I can spend the next nine months peeing and puking, until finally I get the privilege of dying during childbirth."

Lauren picked at a hangnail. It didn't take General Patton to see she was not only going to lose the battle, but the war. Time to resort to her final option. She suddenly threw herself onto the floor and begged. "Please, please, please have my baby," she wailed so loud all the passengers within earshot looked over, trying to guess who these women were to each other.

"Stop it!" Shelby gritted. "You're creating a scene. They're going to think we're gay."

"I don't care." Lauren bawled. "I just wish Mommy was alive so she could see what a selfish person you turned into."

"I resent that!"

"Well, I resent you, Shel. You got Mommy's skinny body, her pretty face, her brains. All I inherited was her widow's peak and DES!" She buried her face and sobbed.

Shelby wanted to pummel Lauren for acting out in public. "Look, I'm sorry you got gypped. But that still doesn't give you the right to impose your dreams on me without any consideration of how it will affect my life."

"I have no choice." Lauren wiped her tears on her sleeve. "You're the only one who can help me. And what about considering how your selfish decision will affect my life?"

"Why am I being selfish? Just because things didn't turn out the way you wanted doesn't mean I have to turn my whole life upside down and make everything better. If you and Avi are so gung ho about having a baby, then talk to an attorney about adoption."

Suddenly the gate area was buzzing. Shelby wasn't sure exactly how or when she lost control of their conversation. She only knew from the din of debate, fellow passengers had taken it upon themselves to argue about which of the sisters was right.

In fact, opinions were flying, which was more than could be said for their flight. An unexpected delay was announced due to a surprise storm that had hit the Midwest, stranding dozens of planes in the air. But many of the passengers didn't seem to care, as they were otherwise engaged.

"Sounds to me like you owe her." A grandmother wagged her finger at Shelby.

"I loved being pregnant," a young mother offered. "You get to eat whatever you want."

"We would do it for each other." Two older women, presumably sisters, clutched hands.

Shelby looked at the circle of strangers who felt within their rights to share their position on the matter. Had the world gone mad? Didn't they realize that conceiving and carrying a baby was a life-altering decision that would have repercussions long after her uterus was vacated?

She would be linked biologically to this child forever, say nothing of the connection if they actually looked alike. People would presume they were mother and child, requiring an explanation of the relationship. But hadn't she done enough explaining after Aunt Roz became her stepmother? The last thing she wanted was to spend the rest of her life clarifying yet another unusual familial arrangement.

And yet looking into Lauren's desperate eyes, Shelby couldn't ignore their bond. In spite of their major differences, Lauren was still her baby sister. The one who climbed on her lap and begged to be read to. The one who followed her around the house pleading with Shelby to play. The one who drove out to the Hamptons to fetch Shelby when she was too stoned to get herself home. The one who sent flowers every time Shelby got a new job. The one who had really never asked anything of her, other than love and friendship.

Then again, she'd be crazy to make a decision of this magnitude with a gun to her head. If she said yes on impulse, she'd be committing herself to taking endless tests that involved needles. She'd be subjecting herself to humiliating, spread-eagle indignities at the doctor's office. She'd have to take those awful iron pills, which she'd heard from friends made doodies come out hard as rocks. Her wardrobe would consist of polyester jumpers. She'd have to eat.

But the greatest sacrifice, clearly, would be her own sex life. No doubt Lauren hadn't considered that for a second. Why should she? She could still be getting it on with her husband while Shelby's ankles swelled, her back went into spasms, and she had to pee every fifteen minutes. Oh, sure. She'd be real desirable then. Men would come running.

She could just imagine trying to get intimate with a man when she was, say, six months gone. "Don't worry." She'd smile at her protruding belly. "It's not mine."

On the other hand, nine months wasn't that long of a commitment. Hell, she'd done investigative reports that took longer than that. And other than her commitments to Ian, it wasn't as if she was actually busy at the moment, given she was neither employed nor in a relationship. Plus, what did she really expect to do when she got back to Chicago? Look for more freelance work? Become a consultant? She hated the idea of constantly having to solicit assignments.

It also occurred to her that the surrogacy idea no longer seemed as creepy and outlandish as it had when Lauren first mentioned it. In fact, now that the shock value wore off, it seemed fairly noble. No wonder women were offering their bodies in record numbers. To them, bringing life into the world for another was a true blessing. A once-in-a-lifetime chance to play God's little helper.

Shelby cleared her throat. "If I did this would you think I was noble?"

Lauren's eyes beamed. "I wouldn't say noble exactly, but definitely gutsy. Oh, and moral."

"Moral?"

"Yeah. I mean think about Daddy and Aunt Roz." Lauren seized the possible breakthrough moment. "The reason you resented them so much was not only because they did something dishonest and impure, but because they took away your ability ever to trust them again. And in your mind, trust was the most sacred thing there was. Which is the same with me. I mean even though you like to come off tough as nails, we're really the same. We're not comfortable unless we know the people in our lives can be trusted implicitly."

"Lauren, that may very well be the most intelligent thing you've ever said."

"Well, I'm glad you understand where I'm coming from because it's the same reason I keep telling you my surrogate can't be a total stranger. If I pay a woman I don't know to carry my baby, how can I be sure she won't run out on me? Or change her mind and get an abortion? I've even heard stories where some of these women get pregnant and sell the baby to the highest bidder."

"No way."

"It's true. I swear to God." Lauren talked faster and faster. "That's why if you were in my shoes, wouldn't you want your surrogate to be someone who knew and loved you? Someone like your sister?"

Shelby closed her eyes. God help her. What should she do? What would her mother want her to do? Scratch that. She knew exactly what her mother would want her to do.

Call it serendipity, divine intervention, or even pregnancy poltergeist. But at that very moment, a young woman pushing a baby stroller entered the gate area and planted herself in the empty seat beside Shelby. Had some busybody passenger put her up to it?

None of the casual observers moved a muscle as they studied Shelby's face, watching her watch the contented-looking woman and her smiling baby boy. When the mommy tickled his little foot, he chuckled. When she kissed his tiny hand, he kicked happily while downing his bottle.

Then he turned toward Shelby and cooed. If it was supposed to be a sign, it was working.

"You think we could have a baby this cute?" Shelby whispered.

"Are you kidding? With your genes?" Lauren squeezed her arm. "Even cuter."

"I have to admit he is sort of precious." Shelby's heart pounded. "Excuse me?" she tapped the woman's shoulder. "Did you like being pregnant?"

The woman stared at her. "I'm sorry?"

"My sister wants me to have her baby, and I was just wondering if pregnancy sucks."

"Oh. Well, I may not be the best person to ask. I was considered high-risk and spent the last trimester confined to bed. But he was worth it. Weren't you, Roger Rabbit?" She wiggled his nose.

Shelby nodded. Lauren would be just like this woman. Affectionate. Doting. Totally out of control with the goo-gooing and ga-gaaing. Actually, she'd make a great mother.

After a moment of silence, Lauren leaned over. "What are you thinking, Shel?"

Shelby hesitated. "Did you know I once thought I'd have seven kids?"

"You?" Lauren laughed. "No way."

"Diaries don't lie." Shelby tossed the book in her bag. "But that was a lifetime ago. Right now I don't even have seven friends . . . Anyway, I was also thinking about Daddy and Aunt Roz."

"Why?" Lauren could not hide her disappointment that Shelby changed the subject.

"I don't know. I guess I was thinking about the bizarre circumstances that brought them together. How none of it was planned. It just happened, and then somehow it all worked out fine."

"Uh-huh," Lauren held her breath. "Anything else?"

"No, that's really about it." Shelby shrugged. "Life doesn't always go according to plan, but it's possible to still get the happy ending."

"So . . . does that mean you'll think about it some more?" she gripped the arm of her seat.

"No. I can't think about this for another second or I'll take a bullet to my head. Let's just say I might be willing to do this under two conditions." She could hardly believe these words were spewing forth from her mouth.

"You name it!" the grandmother in the seat behind her yelled.

"It's about time!" another interloper shouted.

"Anything." Lauren nodded.

"You'd have to promise to stick to me like glue through the whole thing. And . . . you'd have to get Prada to make my maternity clothes, because I am highly allergic to polyester."

Lauren leapt to her feet, mauling Shelby with hugs and kisses while bystanders cheered wildly. This was the decision they'd all hoped for. Shelby looked around at the jubilant crowd and shook her head. Indeed, the world had gone mad.

Did you guess it was me who created the wicked rainstorm in Chicago that brought O'Hare to its knees? It was pretty cool actually, delaying hundreds of westbound flights in midair, just so Lauren and Shelby had time to talk. Who would have thought that would be the easy part, compared to finding parking at La Guardia? When did they build those ridiculously small lots? Before the advent of cars?

Anyway, I am absolutely beside myself with joy. The very idea that Shelby could have a baby for Lauren was such a crazy notion when it first came to me. Although even after I planted the seed of the idea in Lauren's head, I never really believed she'd get Shelby to say yes.

But now that she did, wouldn't a little girl be so nice? Then Lauren could get a chance to experience that whole mother-daughter bonding thing she missed out on. Of course a little boy would be great, too. Is anything sweeter than a son holding his mother's hand?

Maybe Lauren shall have both. Just not at the same time, of course. Oh, God. Could you imagine Shelby carrying twins? Forget I even said that.

Chapter Eighteen

From the moment Shelby agreed to act as the Streiffler surrogate, every word out of Lauren's mouth was about THE BABY; every medical, legal, emotional, and financial issue they'd have to address to prepare for THE BABY. The regularity of Shelby's menstrual cycle, so they could time the first insemination to make THE BABY.

Lauren mistakenly assumed because this was a partnership agreement in the full nine months of the word, Shelby would be anxious to be part of the planning. To the contrary, all Shelby cared about was not feeling slimed when Avi's sperm invaded her cervix. Never was it her intent to become a walking biology dictionary or an expert on artificial reproductive technologies.

Which is why she had no problem boarding her flight to Chicago the fateful afternoon she agreed to the surrogate scenario. "It's really simple," Shelby explained when Lauren grabbed her leg, just as she would to Aunt Roz when a baby-sitter showed up. "If I'm staying in New York for a while, I need my clothes, I need to have my mail forwarded, I have to decide what to do with my condo and my car. And, you may not believe this, but I'm very concerned about my plant."

Lauren pleaded with her to take care of these things later, certain if Shelby stepped foot on that plane, she'd become a fugitive. Then Lauren would have to pay a private detective to set up an international manhunt, and that would be so time-consuming and expensive, Daddy might change his mind about paying for everything, and then she'd never have THE BABY.

"I promise I'll be back in three or four days. You have my word."

"Give me Mommy's locket." Lauren sniffed. "Then I'll know you're not lying."

"Hell no." Shelby clutched the tiny heart of diamonds her father gave her the day of her mother's funeral. She'd never removed it, not even on her mountain-climbing trip to the Andes.

"Yes!" Lauren stamped. "It's the only way you can prove to me you're coming back."

"I'm not taking it off just so you don't go off into some paranoid, schizophrenic zone. You know that thing we just discussed called trust? I gave you my word. That should be good enough."

"Don't worry, dear. I'll keep my eye on her," the nice grandmother whispered to Lauren as she boarded the plane.

But surveillance wasn't necessary, as Shelby not only made good on her promise, she returned a day earlier than expected, with blessings of approval from David, Dr. Kahn, and even Walter Sipowicz, whose home she would not leave until he agreed to listen to her bizarre tale.

She confided to all of them that in spite of the cataclysmic upheaval that had catapulted her back home, she couldn't ever remember being more at peace. Not bad considering she was unemployed, single, and about to become impregnated with the aid of her brother-in-law's semen from a catheter disguised as a high-tech turkey baster. Thanksgiving would never be the same.

Shelby would never have guessed that after she lost her job, her dance card would still be filled from morning to night. Some days were veritable juggling acts, getting to meetings, appointments, and the hospital without running into major scheduling conflicts.

"I need a secretary," she winced, looking at her date book, then the clock. It was only 7 A.M., but if she was going to get in her three-mile jog, shower and dress and be at the hospital by eight, she was already running late. And late was not an option, as she would be seeing the reproductive endocrinologist at nine, the adoption attorney at eleven, and Ian at two. Oh, for the good old days when she could enlist the aid of underlings to, on a moment's notice, move her meetings up, back, or cancel them entirely if they no longer served her purpose.

As an independent operator, however, she alone had to do the

juggling. And the people to whom she now reported, her father and
Aunt Roz, were not exactly flexible. They insisted Shelby visit first
thing in the morning before they were whisked off to their own hec-
tic schedule of X-rays, physical therapy, and surgery.

Dr. Weiner, on the other hand, was weak and incoherent in the
morning, particularly if he'd gone through chemo the previous day.
He preferred Shelby to visit in the afternoon, when he felt strong
enough to sit up or be wheeled to the solarium.

No one was more taken aback than Shelby when she forged a
bond with her nemesis, as their friendship began unexpectedly. Instead of whizzing past his room as she normally did, one morning it
dawned on her he might be a good source for her DES article. She'd
hit a brick wall trying to get doctors to openly admit to having prescribed the drug, and who better than a dying man to fess up?
Turned out Dr. Weiner not only had excellent recall of the DES
days, he remembered the dozens of patients to whom he'd given it.
Once again she was off and running.

In gratitude, the next day she stopped by to chat, and the day
after that, only to discover Dr. Weiner was not only well versed on a
variety of subjects, but had a wicked sense of humor. From then on,
it wasn't unusual for Irma to walk in and find the two of them howl-
ing with laughter over something silly, oblivious to his imminent
death.

On one occasion, however, there were tears. Dr. Weiner happened to comment on the remarkable similarities between Shelby
and her mother, and although Shelby was delighted with the comparison, she choked up at the realization she was hearing these words
in a place she previously refused to go, from a man she previously refused to acknowledge.

Dr. Kahn would never believe that his most obstreperous patient
had made such enormous strides without his assistance. But Shelby
was not only marching through the halls of North Shore every day,
she knew the shortcuts connecting the wings. She could also greet
many of the doctors and nurses by name, even those whose names
had six consecutive consonants.

*As much as I prayed Shelby would come to grips with her unhappy
childhood and finally move on, I was beginning to think she was a hopeless
cause. But I was wrong. She not only laid to rest her battles with her father*

and Roz, she took the single most courageous step of her selfish life by agree-
ing to carry Lauren's child. Frankly, this is the kind of magic moment a
parent waits for. The sign that their self-centered, wicked-tongued child
does in fact have a conscience and a heart. Sure, I waited longer than most
to get this kind of validation. Then again, is there ever a bad time to get
good news?

"Technically, this is a very simple process," Dr. Vincent Grasso explained to the group. "All we need is one sperm, one egg, and one uterus."

"Yeah, and thirty thousand dollars," Avi whispered.

"Shhh!" Lauren's ears reddened. "We've been through this. Daddy's taking care of it."

Dr. Grasso smiled; the warm-up to his canned speech. "I assure you, whatever your concerns, we do everything possible to make this a positive experience for everyone involved. But before we get to the nitty-gritty of how things work at the Family Reproductive Institute, I'd like to take a few minutes to make sure we're all on the same page."

Three heads nodded in unison, like the bobbing dolls sold at Thruway gift shops.

"Shelby, let's start with you, dear. I understand your sister and brother-in-law have discussed their situation with you at great length, and have also discussed the psychological, financial, and legal ramifications of your decision to act as their surrogate."

"In our family we don't discuss, we ramrod." Shelby tried smiling. "But yes, I'm aware this is the biggest decision of my life. I just hope when it's all over, I have no regrets."

"Very understandable, which is why I can't stress enough the importance of working out any conflicts or concerns in advance through psychological evaluations."

"No need." Shelby smirked. "When I said yes to this, I already knew I was crazy."

"What she means," Lauren interrupted, "is that she'd be crazy not to help us because she loves us so much."

"I still kent understand what is the need for laboratories and fertility drugs," Avi said.

"Fertility drugs?" Shelby was finally paying attention. "What fertility drugs?"

"We're getting a little ahead of ourselves here"—Dr. Grasso blew his nose—"but I'll be happy to explain. When the maternal age of the surrogate is over thirty-five, we generally do two consecutive intrauterine inseminations each menstrual cycle, using Clomid for five days prior to ovulation to stimulate the ovaries and, hopefully, increase the number of eggs that mature."

"Clomid's not a shot," Lauren assured Shelby. "I've taken it. They're these tiny little pills."

"Yeah, like the tiny little pills Mommy took," Shelby gritted. 'Good news, Mrs. Lazarus. Forget any more of those nasty miscarriages. The bad news is, you might get cancer.' Now it's, 'Good news, Shelby. You might be having a litter. The bad news is, you might get cancer.' "

"If I could interject here"—Dr. Grasso coughed—"I understand your concerns, but according to the family's medical history, your mother received eleven thousand milligrams of DES over a one-year period, with devastating results. But Clomid is not in the same class of drugs, nor has it been proven harmful to either the mother or the fetus. Besides, we're talking about such a limited exposure, the only possible side effects might be headaches and bloating. Maybe some cramping."

"What about weight gain?" Shelby's heart raced.

"It's possible, but we don't consider that a serious problem."

"Easy for you to say." Shelby folded her arms.

"My sister's a fanatic about her weight." Lauren smiled. "But I'm sure she'll get over it once she actually gets pregnant."

"Yes, of course." Dr. Grasso nodded, quite familiar with vain women who wanted to experience the joys of pregnancy without deforming their gym-hard bodies. "Now insofar as Clomid increasing the odds of multiple births, again, there's a slightly elevated chance, but in your case, by virtue of your age, the risk is already present. As is the risk of miscarriage. A maternal age of thirty-eight carries the possibility of a one-third chance of loss within the first trimester."

"Uh-huh." Shelby hated bad odds worse than she hated fear of failing.

"Now the one risk that greatly concerns us, of course," Dr. Grasso continued, "is the spread of infection through insemination of contaminated sperm."

"You mean AIDS?" Shelby shuddered. Dr. Grasso had no idea

how real that risk was. Lord knows if even Avi had kept count of the number of women he'd had sex with.

"AIDS, gonorrhea, any sexually transmitted disease . . ."

"Avi's clean," Lauren jumped in. "He's been tested."

"Yes, I'm sure he was," Dr. Grasso replied. "Nevertheless, prior to any insemination, we do extensive screening of the donor's blood, then wash and process the sperm catch to make sure nothing infectious is transmitted to the surrogate. It's standard operating procedure."

"Thank God," Shelby mumbled.

"As for your suggestion, Mr. Streiffler, that all of this effort could be avoided by opting for copulation, I understand your thinking." He winked. "But we don't go down that road for the simple reason the divorce rate would surely exceed the birth rate. We've found it's best to reduce this matter to a painless medical procedure that hopefully ends with the same happy results."

Avi shrugged. "I still think the odds are better if we go the natural way."

"No"—Shelby glared—"because the odds of my letting you touch me are slim to none."

"Cut it out," Lauren whispered to Shelby. "He's going to think we don't have any team spirit . . . Doctor, could you tell us how many months it usually takes for the surrogate to get pregnant?"

"Of course," Dr. Grasso replied while looking through some paperwork. "We have a 75 percent to 85 percent success rate with intrauterine inseminations using fresh donor semen when the procedure is repeated for an average of three consecutive months."

"And what about the 25 percent who fail?" Shelby asked. "You probably tell the prospective parents to find themselves another surrogate. Right?"

"Not necessarily." Dr. Grasso looked up. "If after three months there hasn't been a conception, we simply move on to the next phase, which is a bit more aggressive."

"You mean in vitro fertilization." Lauren wanted to show she was in familiar territory.

"In vitro and/or the use of different types of fertility drugs."

"Nothing doing." Shelby grabbed Lauren's hand. "Three strikes and I'm out. Game over."

"Perhaps it's best not to cross that bridge unless we have to." Dr.

Grasso was growing impatient. "Naturally, we do everything possible to ensure success, and if the surrogate is in good physical health, and of a cooperative nature, we're better than halfway there."

"Oh, don't worry about Shelby." Lauren patted her hand. "She's the most cooperative person the world."

"Yes, I see that." Dr. Grasso smirked.

Team BABY's next stop was the attorney's office, where Shelby's only question after meeting the lawyer was how smart this woman could be if she chose to hyphenate her name. "I'm telling you, if I was born Nancy Less, and was dumb enough to marry a Thomas Moore, the least I would have done was pick one of their surnames. Not both."

"That's what bothers you?" Lauren cried, after dropping Avi off at the house to get his car. "That her name is Mrs. Less-Moore?"

"Damn right. Don't you see? If her personal judgment is so bad, how good could her legal judgment be? It's like being introduced to a hairdresser and wondering, if she's so great at styling hair, what's that rat's nest on top of her head? . . . I'm never going to make the train."

"Yes, you will. You've got seven minutes, and I know all the shortcuts to the station."

"At least Avi is good for something." Shelby yawned.

"Don't pick on him, Shel. This is never going to work if you two don't stop fighting."

"I'm sorry. I'm just not crazy about the guy, especially since he won't shut up about screwing me, rather than jerking off into a Dixie cup. I thought you worked all this out already."

"We did. You just don't understand him. That's all."

"Oh, I understand him fine." Shelby looked at her watch again.

"You'll make it. I promise." Lauren ran a red light.

"Preferably alive." Shelby clutched the door handle as Lauren floored the gas pedal.

"You see, Avi comes from this very traditional, Israeli, male-macho background. He may look hip, but he's really old-fashioned. So, it's not that he doesn't want to be faithful to me, he has this need to prove his virility. I mean, even though none of the fertility problems are his, inside I know he feels shame. Like there's something he should be able to do to make things right."

"You really believe that?"

"Yes. Otherwise, I'd have to kill him and leave his body in the trunk of his car. Now tell me what you thought about what Mrs. More or Less said."

"See what I mean? You're already goofing on her name." Shelby jabbed Lauren's shoulder. "Anyway, there's nothing to think about. It's all pretty straightforward. I'm considered the biological and legal mother of the baby until the baby is born. Immediately afterward we do the stepparent adoption, then you get all the parental rights, and Daddy gets all the bills."

"What about the . . . control issues?" Lauren hesitated. "During the pregnancy."

"What control issues?"

"You know. Like how you take care of yourself."

"What's wrong with the way I take care of myself? I'm the most vain person I know."

"I don't mean that." Lauren hesitated. "I mean, what about my legal rights if, let's say, you don't take your prenatal vitamins? Or, you decide to drink with dinner? Or, the thing I'm really worried about is you starving yourself like you always do."

"So let me get this straight. You want it in a contract I have to take iron pills, lay off wine, and eat three meals a day?"

"It's not just that. It's a lot of things. Who gets to choose the doctor? Or, who decides how much anesthesia you get during labor? Or, what if you don't cooperate when it's time to do certain tests? There are ultrasounds and an amnio to rule out birth defects, a blood test for spina bifida . . ."

"Didn't I hear you say I was the most cooperative person in the world?"

"Yes." Lauren shrugged. "But I was just trying to show Dr. Grasso we're a good team."

"Yeah, like the Three Stooges . . . Look. Believe me. I've thought long and hard about this decision by now, and I know what I'm in for. A year of hell. But when I said I'd do it, it was with the implicit understanding I was buying in to the whole program."

"You mean that?" Lauren cried. "You'll even take the blood tests?"

"I don't know how." Shelby shivered. "But yes."

"Why are you being so nice to me?"

"Hell if I know. Maybe because you got me to the train on time. I'll call you from the office to let you know what time to pick me up."

"Okay. And, Shel? Thank you from the bottom of my heart." She patted her chest.

"No problem . . . Oh, yeah. If my pimp calls? Tell him I'm taking a short leave of absence to have a baby, but not to cut off my cocaine supply because I still need my fix."

"Oh, go screw yourself." Lauren gently clinked Shelby with a water bottle.

"I believe that's precisely what surrogates do." Shelby shut the car door.

Chapter Nineteen

When Shelby asked Ian to arrange for her to have an office at the *Informer*, he said he would personally tend to the matter himself. He even promised to secure one with a great view. So imagine her shock when she arrived her first day on the job and was escorted to her new home. May it ever be so humble.

"This is where you expect me to work?" she grabbed Ian by his tie. "It's a cubicle."

"The better to see you with, my dear."

"But you promised me a nice view." Shelby threw down her box of important possessions.

"This is a nice view." Ian flung open his arms. "Of the greatest newsroom in the world. And as an added bonus, you get to be situated right next to Warner Lamm."

"Who?"

"Why, Shelby. Have you been dwelling in a cave? He's the world famous astrologer who writes our daily horoscope column. Surely you're a big fan."

"Only if he tells me it's a good day to kill an editor."

A week later, the famous astrological jack-in-the-box popped his head up over their shared cubicle wall. "Hi, Shelby," he sang. "How are *you* today?"

"I don't know, Warner. Why don't you tell me?" Shelby kept on working. "You're the resident psycho." Why had she agreed to let Ian help her find a place to set up shop? She should have known he'd pull an immature prank like putting her next to a gay voodoo doll.

"Actually, I do know how you are." He winked. "Because I did your chart like you asked."

"I didn't ask." Shelby finally looked up. "You begged, remember?"

"Yes, but you were most cooperative when I said I needed your date and time of birth."

Cooperative. There was that word again. She hadn't heard it this much since kindergarten. "That's because I figured it would be a hell of a lot easier to fork over the information than have you hound me every time I walked in here. Have you seen Ian?"

"How do you mean, seen?" Warner winked.

"Jeez! How much fruit did you eat today? I mean do you know if he's back from lunch?"

"I'm not my brother's keeper." Warner pouted. "Ask Ann. She always knows where he is."

Shelby stood up, peered over the sea of cubicles, and watched the throngs of reporters and editors scurrying through the maze. How she loved the electricity of a newsroom, with all its ringing phones, urgent chatter, and speedy fingers pounding computer keyboards. Yes, every newsroom was the same shit, different zip code. But that's why it felt like home.

"See her? She's over at Ziggy's desk." Warner stood on his chair and used his two middle fingers to whistle. "Annie Bananie! Where's Ian?"

"Not back from lunch yet," she yelled back.

"Thank you." Warner blew her a kiss, then stepped down. "He's not back yet."

"Proving once again, news travels fast. Thanks."

Shelby sat down and sighed. She never learned. Every time she rushed to arrive somewhere promptly, it was always a wasted effort. Why did people spend thousands of dollars on fancy watches if they never bothered to look at them? But at least now she'd have time to go over her notes for the meeting and check her voice mail. Which, to her disappointment, took a total of five seconds, as none of the wedding couples she'd located had returned her calls.

At least the DES piece was going well. She'd completed three solid interviews, and each story was so compelling and tragic, it made Lauren's experience look like a cakewalk.

Her most extensive notes came from a young woman in upstate New York who had been through five years of infertility workups, abnormal Pap smears, painful tests to check her fallopian tubes, four unsuccessful inseminations, one laparoscopy to remove recurring endometriosis, and two miscarriages. The last one was at sixteen weeks, in spite of her double cerclage stitch to keep her cervix closed. She and her husband were in the process of looking for a surrogate when she discovered her husband was seeing someone. DES had taken its toll in more ways than one.

In the other two cases, the women had miraculously managed to cross the motherhood finish line, albeit through extreme measures. But at least they were fortunate enough to be discussing their situations while bouncing babies on their knees. On the other hand, their DES troubles were hardly over. One had a breast cancer scare, the other a test to rule out cervical cancer. And, too, they were plagued with worry and guilt, not knowing if they'd passed on the DES curse to their children. Evidence was mounting that the next generation would not be spared.

Shelby reviewed her notes and sighed. This story had certainly been more of an eye-opener than she'd expected. Over the years she'd known plenty of couples with infertility issues, and of course Lauren's medical problems were deeply embedded in her personal landscape. But until now, she'd never understood the mental anguish women felt when denied the privilege of motherhood.

The trouble with the story, however, was that in comparison, it made the *Times* wedding piece seem so trite and shallow. Rich debutantes didn't have real problems. Their biggest source of angst was worrying if their trust fund could cover summers in the south of France, with enough cash left over to shop at the couture shows in Paris.

Not that Shelby felt every story had to be gripping to be good. As a former assignment editor, she understood the importance of having filler in the can for the inescapable slow news day. Question was, did she want to contribute to the soft side anymore? The answer was Ian wouldn't give a damn about her conflict. The only way he'd run her piece was if it was turned in with his.

Unfortunately, the research for the revenge story wasn't going well. She'd tracked down two of the couples whose wedding announcements appeared in the *Times* the weekend of May 25, 1988, only to discover they'd already split up. Alexandra Simonson Wellbourge IV, not surprisingly, hung up the minute Shelby identified herself as an *Informer* reporter. The next three couples she'd located had yet to return her calls. And the remaining eight couples she had yet to locate at all.

Maybe she could convince Ian to change the focus of the story. Instead of examining the staying power of debutante marriages, it might be interesting to explore the evolution of the *New York Times* wedding announcements.

For decades, this was considered the penultimate sports page for women. The only game in town when the mink and manure set had a betrothal to announce. To flip through the hallowed Sunday section, an outsider might never suspect there were people of color living in the New York area. Or that there were any other religious affiliations than Episcopalian or Roman Catholic. The *New York Times* weddings weren't just restricted, they were vaulted shut, lest some pedestrian, middle-class couple might presume to be worthy of a column inch.

Over the years, however, under the guise of political correctness, the *Times* had relaxed their tough stance on intruders, much to the chagrin of the Cotillion debs. At Shelby's count, yesterday's wedding section included two African-American couples, one Asian couple, several Jewish couples, and even, get the smelling salts, a racially mixed couple.

No doubt this explained the undercurrent of dissatisfaction among the ladies who lunched. Clearly the *Times* had lost its luster and cachet if, good God, an Italian bride from Staten Island could be featured. What was next? Homosexual couples? Thank heavens for *Town and Country* magazine. At least their editors still understood the important role of wealth and prominence, and would never be caught dead slumming for wedding coverage.

"Yoo-hoo." Warner wheeled himself over on his task chair. "So, how's it going today?"

Shelby jumped. "Why do you keep asking me that? You already know."

"True." He clasped his hands. "I was just looking for confirmation."

"Maybe you should get a real job, Warner. This one doesn't take up enough of your time."

"Oh, contraire, my dear. I start my day at five, so by midafternoon, I'm completely *ferklempt*. You know what I mean?"

Shelby laughed. "Yes, I do. But tell me. Is there a reason for your visit?"

"Yes!" Warner clapped. "I want to tell you all about yourself. The stars know all."

"Oh God," Shelby groaned. "Look, I know your column has a huge following, and I'm all for anything that sells papers. I'm just never going to be one of your readers who gets snookered into believing any of that voodoo bullshit you write."

"Snookered? Voodoo? Oh I love it. It's so . . . deliciously fifties. But let me ask you this. Have you ever had a professional astrologer do your natal chart?"

"No, but at a state fair I once had my palm read, and learned my true calling was to be a minister. Then I went and washed my hands and the same guy told me I should be a pilot."

"A minister or a pilot." Warner slapped his knee. "That's hilarious. I hope you didn't pay."

"Of course I paid. He was my date."

Warner laughed. "You are a true Capricorn, my dear."

"Which means what?' "

"Well, you've got this marvelously, dry sense of humor, and you're so witty and outspoken. But that has more to do with your third house cusp being a six Sagittarius."

"You see? That's the problem with all of you guys. You need interpreters."

"If I promise to explain everything, do you promise to pay close attention?"

"If I promise to pay close attention, do you promise to go away?"

"Shelby, dear, is that any way to speak to someone who is going to illuminate your life with profound insights?"

"To hell with insights. Just tell me if my parents will be all right, if I'll actually get pregnant, and if I'll ever be nominated for a Pulitzer?"

"Yes, yes, and yes!" Warner applauded wildly.

"Really?" Shelby leaned in. "How do you know that?"

"Because I'm the great and masterful Warner, and when I did your natal chart I was just bursting with excitement. I could see you had a really crappy childhood. Full of lies and deception, loneliness and loss, nobody cared about you, nobody understood you . . . uch, you poor thing, I don't know how you survived. But according to your planetary aspects and transits, over the next twelve months, we're talking major turnaround time, baby. Finally, your Venus will be in

Scorpio, your Jupiter in Sagittarius, and your Moon in Aquarius. I'm telling you the alignments of the planets will be so fantastico"— Warner patted her hand—"you can kiss those blue days good-bye."

"Yeah, but how do you know specifically the three things I asked you about will actually happen?"

"Because the planets never lie, and Warner knows what he's talking about."

"Okay, that's it. Spill the beans, or I tape your dancing feet to the floor."

"My, my. Aren't we testy? Tell you what. Come to my place in the Village, and I'll tell you the whole damn story. But here's a sneak preview. Healing and recovery will surround you, career rewards are in the air, and you are most definitely going to end up in a family way!"

"Anything else?"

"Why, Shelby. I thought you couldn't be snookered?"

"Anything else?" her voice quivered.

"There *was* one other little aspect I found quite interesting. It had to do with reuniting with loved ones."

"Really? That is interesting. I recently reconciled with my father and stepmother. Oh, and when I first got to New York, I saw my dead mother's face in the rearview mirror of a car."

"No, that's not it. I'm seeing an event that's still on the horizon."

"Hmm . . . I can't think of anyone else . . . Unless . . . Oh, my God."

"What?"

"I've been searching for a childhood friend for a really long time. Do you think . . ."

"It's possible. What I do know is the timing is around a Venus retrograde, which means when it happens, it's going to be under very strange circumstances. There will be lots of confusion and misunderstandings. And then boom, major fireworks and love is in the air!"

"What's your address?" Shelby whipped out her Palm Pilot. "I can be at your place anytime. Name the day."

I know exactly why that Ian fellow put Shelby next to the little fageleh who does the paper's horoscopes. He's hoping to finally arouse her curiosity, and help her understand that all the energy of the universe, the planets, the oceans, and the beings is truly interconnected. That those who work with the natural ebb and flow of life forces are at peace, and the rest are left to fight the mighty tide of adversity and misfortune.

That's the basis of astrology you know. That the planetary cycles are directly related to the events on earth. And the reason why for centuries, people who paid close attention to the rhythmic signs of the time were so accomplished. I'm not kidding. You think the three wise men (aptly named), Pythagoras, Nostradamus, and Isaac Newton just got lucky? No. They studied the stars. Even the world's first shrink, Carl Jung, understood the link between the man and the moon, so to speak. He said, and I quote, "We are born at a given moment, in a given place, and like vintage years of wine, we have the qualities of the year and of the season in which we are born."

Do I think Shelby will ever understand any of this? No. But then I also never expected to look down and see her eating Krispy Kreme donuts, either.

The familiar route to the Family Reproductive Institute in Garden City was quickly becoming the all-too-familiar route. In spite of the fact Shelby diligently took a daily regimen of prenatal vitamins to build up her folic acids, carefully monitored her cycles with her handy home ovulation detection kit, and took the prescribed amount of Clomid, the first two months of inseminations were a bust. And the natives were growing restless.

Avi was not happy having to drop everything in the middle of his busy day to run over to the Center and masturbate on demand when Shelby phoned, and said, "It's me. Get over there." Nor was he pleased Lauren was unsympathetic to his plight. She should try reaching orgasm in a small room with no one around to help out, he thought.

A very understanding technician at the Institute suggested he bring in a few issues of *Penthouse* and some silk undies from his wife's drawer. But Avi had a better solution.

"Maybe Shelby ken be naked in the room with me?" he suggested to Lauren.

"Are you out of your mind?" she replied.

"How about a picture of her naked? She doesn't have to smile."

A quick-reacting Avi ducked, just before an airborne object sailed past his head.

Shelby wasn't exactly having the best time either. There was no joy in getting completely undressed in an air-conditioned examining room, putting on a stiff paper gown, and lying with her feet propped in cold metal stirrups.

Nor was it pleasant waiting for the technician to come in with Avi's hot-off-the-press sperm catch. Or having to lie still while the slim catheter was carefully inserted transvaginally.

Not that she'd actually succeeded on that front. During the first insemination, they needed two medical assistants to hold her down and one doctor to revive her.

The second insemination went a little more smoothly. Shelby actually remained on the table for the entire procedure, and never passed out. She did, however, vomit all over herself, after discovering her stomach didn't agree with the yogurt that must have gone bad.

"I hope you're not disappointed if we don't make you this year's poster child," Gabe, the kindly technician, chuckled afterward. "But at least this time you didn't try to choke me."

"Don't remind me." Shelby tugged at his tie.

"Did you mean what you said at Dr. Grasso's office?" Lauren asked Shelby on the drive over to the Family Reproductive Institute for the third series of inseminations. "It's three strikes and you're out?"

"I don't know." Shelby shrugged. "If it doesn't take this time, maybe you should just take it as a sign you need to find someone else."

"No."

"Lauren, don't be delusional! You know as well as I, the odds are a hundred times better with a younger woman. Twenty-year-olds can get pregnant at the scent of sperm in the room."

"Is this your way of saying you're giving up?"

"I didn't say that. I just don't think you should be putting all my eggs in one basket."

Lauren laughed. No matter how bad she felt, Shelby could always cheer her up.

"On the other hand"—Shelby coughed—"there is something about this I didn't tell you."

"Oh my God. Is it something bad?" Lauren nearly careened off the road.

"No, it's something good. Would you please watch what you're doing? In this country we drive on the right."

"Sorry. You've got me so nervous. What didn't you tell me?"

"Well . . . the *Informer* has this supposedly well-known astrologer who writes the daily horoscopes and then does these private charts on the side. Anyway, he did a reading for me."

"Oh my God. You got a reading from Warner Lamm?"

"Yes. You've heard of him?"

"Are you serious? He's so amazing, people wait a whole year to get a reading with him. I can't believe you actually know him and didn't tell me. You have to get me in."

"Okay, okay. But I'm telling you he's a fruitcake. On the other hand, I have to admit the things he told me blew me away."

"Like what?"

"Well for starters, he pegged my personality to a tee."

"Sorry." Lauren snickered. "But that doesn't take a psychic to figure out."

"Very funny. No, I'm serious. I have the whole thing on tape, and although a lot of it was gobbledygook, you'll be happy to know he told me why I'm so cynical, distant, and mean-spirited. It has something to do with my ascendant being squared to my Saturn . . ."

"Ah-hah! I knew it wasn't my imagination." Lauren nodded. "What else?"

"He said my Moon was in Aquarius, so I'll always have lots of friends and acquaintances, but no real attachments because my privacy and freedom are more important. But this was the really cool part. He also said I have Mercury in Sagittarius, which explains why I'm always looking for the hidden patterns in things. In other words, I don't care about the facts as much as I care about what they mean."

"I'd say that's true. That's why you're such a good reporter."

"Exactly."

"But what does any of this have to do with THE BABY?"

"I'm getting there. One of the other things he said was he saw me being in the family way."

"Really?" This time Lauren did career off the road onto the shoulder. "Are you serious? The great Warner Lamm told you you'd get pregnant?"

"That's what I'm saying."

"Oh my God." Lauren hugged Shelby. "That's the best news I think I've ever heard. When?"

"Sometime this year. It's on the horizon, he said."

"I have to call Avi!" Lauren screamed. "This is so unbelievable. I'm shaking, Shel. I knew this would all work out if I just kept the faith."

While waiting for the third insemination to begin, Shelby lay quietly, feeling surprisingly calm. Maybe it was the positive reading she'd gotten from Warner, or the fact she'd simply grown accustomed to the drill. But in all likelihood, the reason she felt relaxed was because she'd remanded Lauren to the waiting room. "Then I won't have to listen to your stupid old Indian chants while you wave a dream catcher and peppermint incense in my face."

"You seem so relaxed," Gabe, the technician, said. "Did you meditate like I told you to?"

"No. I got rid of Lauren like you told me to."

"Good thinking. I couldn't take any more of that peppermint incense. Now just promise me I won't have to play middle linebacker and tackle you today."

"I'll be good, I promise."

"Okay then." He carefully inserted the catheter. "Let's take a deep breath and think only good thoughts."

Chapter Twenty

Perhaps the only ritual reminiscent of Shelby's former life was that she still got up every morning at seven to do a three-mile jog. Even after Lauren begged her not to, citing the near tragedy with their father and Aunt Roz as reason enough to stop. "It's so risky," she cried.

Of course, Shelby knew the real reason Lauren kept nagging her was she feared Shelby's rigorous run might jostle Avi's sperm to a point where they'd get so mixed up they'd never find an egg. But even after Dr. Grasso assured Lauren that exercise had no bearing on conception, she still trailed Shelby by car, just in case she was suddenly felled by the heat, or stumbled on a pebble and twisted her ankle.

But now that a chill was in the early-November air, Shelby begged Lauren to stay home. With no humidity, she was in runner's paradise, and the invigorating outing was the one thing keeping her sane. "The only sex I've had in the past three months has been with a goddamn turkey baster!" she complained. "So get off my case."

The next morning, however, Shelby returned from her run feeling nauseous and weak, and collapsed. Maybe she had been pushing herself too hard, especially now that the flu was going around the office. Tomorrow she'd take it easy and build up her strength. Then she'd be fine again.

Or not. For at that moment, vomit was erupting from the pit of her stomach. Down on her knees she fell, retching into the toilet bowl, holding on to the cool porcelain for dear life as the room spun.

Was anything worse than the dry heaves and the head-banger that followed?

Finally, Shelby slumped in a heap on the floor. This was the damn flu, all right. She probably caught it from Warner. Hadn't he come in last week looking white as a ghost? And then had the nerve to use her phone because the cord on his had too much static? Shit!

Just as she crawled into bed, the phone rang. "Oh, God! Not now!" she yelled before picking up. "What do you want?"

"Good morning to you, too," Lauren said. "What's with you?"

"I'm sick, okay?" Shelby groaned. "I think I have the flu. Call me back later."

"No! Wait," Lauren screamed. "How do you know you're sick?"

"Because I just puked all over myself, and half the office is out with the flu."

"But that doesn't mean you have it," she squealed. "Maybe it's morning sickness."

A stunned Shelby bolted upright. Morning sickness? "What's today?" The question nearly made her puke again.

"The seventh. November 7. Look at the chart I gave you. You'll see. Your last period was October 3. I remember because it was the day before Avi's birthday. Then you got inseminated two weeks later. So count. It's almost three weeks later. You should have gotten your period by now. Right?"

"Uh-huh." Shelby started to feel faint.

"Well. Did you get it?" Lauren, the prosecutor, asked.

"No. And come to think of it, my boobs are killing me."

"Oh, my God!" Lauren screamed. "This might be it. Go get the home pregnancy kit I bought. It's on the top shelf of the linen closet. No wait. I'm coming over. Promise me you won't do anything until I get there. Don't even pee."

Shelby hung up, just in time to race back to the toilet. Did Lauren know what she was talking about? God help her if she was wrong. God help them both if she was right.

"What took you so long?" Shelby flung open the door to the guesthouse. "I have to pee so bad it's going to come through my nose."

"Sorry." Lauren ran in holding a plastic sack. "I decided to stop at the drugstore to get another test kit. In case the first one isn't conclusive."

"You mean in case it doesn't test positive." Shelby grabbed the bag. "I wouldn't get my hopes up. This couldn't possibly be pregnancy. I feel like death. What do I have to do?" She held her crotch.

"Nothing. Just pee on the end of the stick."

"Which end?"

"Which end?" Lauren laughed. "Are you serious? Don't you keep a case of these at home?"

"What kind of girl do you think I am?" Shelby wiggled.

"Here. Give me that." Lauren pulled the kit out of the bag and tore open a tester. "See these two bars. Pee on those."

"Okay. Wish me luck," Shelby grabbed it. "I'm not used to having a target."

Lauren stood by the door, never more anxious to hear the beautiful sounds of tinkling. "How many times did you throw up?" she asked.

"I lost count."

"Did you eat anything this morning?" Lauren put her ear to the door.

"I didn't have time."

"Shel-bee," Lauren whined. "You promised you wouldn't starve yourself."

"I haven't, okay? I did my run, came back to shower, and then I was going to have breakfast when the attack of the killer bug hit me. Are you standing right by the door?"

"Yes."

"Well don't. I can't pee if there's an audience."

"Sorry." Lauren started to pace over by the bed.

She, too, felt suddenly nauseous. Was it possible to be experiencing sympathy pains already? Or, God forbid, the flu? Finally, at the sound of the toilet flushing, Lauren ran back to the door, tripped over Shelby's running shoes, lost her balance, and collided with Shelby, just as Shelby was opening the door with the cup of urine in her hand.

They watched the warm, yellow liquid spill over the top of the cup onto Shelby's shirt.

"You idiot!" Shelby shouted. "Look what you did!"

"I'm sorry," Lauren yelled back. "I tripped over your stupid shoes. And why did you pee in a cup? I told you to pee on the stick. You're the idiot . . ."

"I did pee on the stick, but then I figured since I had plenty of extra, I'd put it in here. In case we needed more."

"It's not a recipe, Shel." Lauren laughed. "So where is it?"

"It's in there. I figure I'll take a shower and when I'm out . . . we'll look at it I guess."

"Are you serious? You're going to take a shower now? You're not even going to wait to see if the two lines turn pink?"

"What difference does it make? A few minutes either way won't matter."

"Shel-bee," Lauren whined. "Don't be negative. This is the moment we've waited for."

"I'm not being negative. But I've got vomit on my arm and piss on my shirt."

"Fine. Then give me the stick. I'll watch it out here."

Lauren sat at the desk by the window, and reread the directions to make sure she knew how this test kit worked. She hadn't used this brand before, but her friend Elise thought it was the most accurate. At least the instructions were clear. Wait three minutes before examining the tester. If both test bars turned pink, it was positive for pregnancy. If one stayed blue, the result was negative.

"Please be pink. Please be pink."

At two minutes and counting, the phone rang, startling Lauren. Should she get it? There was no answering machine on this line, and Shelby would be pissed if she missed a call from the office. But Lauren was too nervous to move. Oh, what the hell. She picked up the cup and slowly carried it over to the phone on the nightstand. "Hello?"

"Shelby, is that you, dear?"

"No, it's Lauren. Who's this?"

"It's Irma," she said quietly. "Irma Weiner. Is Shelby there?"

"She's busy at the moment. Can I take a message?" One minute and counting.

"Well actually . . . no. I think it's best if I speak to her myself. Could you have her call me back as soon as possible? I'm at home."

"Does she have your number?"

"Yes."

"Is everything all right, Irma?" Lauren couldn't believe she was actually carrying on a phone conversation while her heart was pounding so fast it felt as if it would burst.

Irma hesitated again. "Actually, no dear. I have some rather unfortunate news to share. I . . . oh boy, I didn't want to have to leave her a message. But please tell her . . . Dr. Weiner passed away early this morning."

"Uh-huh," Lauren held up the test strip to the light. "Yes! Yes! Yes!" It was the most beautiful shade of pink she'd ever seen.

"What did you say?" Irma gasped.

"It turned pink." She jumped up and down. "The stick turned pink!"

"Excuse me?"

Lauren heard Irma's voice and panicked. "I'm sorry. Did you just say Dr. Weiner died?"

"Yes. What's going on over there?"

"I am so, so sorry. But the most incredible thing just happened. Shelby took a home pregnancy test a few minutes ago, and it came out positive!"

"That's wonderful," Irma let out a joyous cry. "I'm so happy for you. Can I speak to her?"

"No, because she doesn't even know yet. She's still in the shower."

"Oh, dear. Well, look. This is going to be a very exciting time for you two, and I don't want to spoil it. Please don't say anything to her yet."

"Are you sure? I know Shelby's going to want to know."

"I think it's best, dear. He's gone, and there's nothing we can do for him. Your news is about life. About the future. It's just so ironic though, don't you think? One soul moves on, another one moves in. So goes the circle of life . . . We'll be doing something graveside. I'll call back after I've finalized the arrangements."

"Okay, and I'm really sorry for your loss." Lauren was proud to be mindful of her manners at such an auspicious time. Then she raced to the bathroom. "Shelby!" she pounded. "Open up."

Shelby opened the door, took one look at Lauren's jubilant face, and didn't need a reporter's instincts to know the outcome. "I'm pregnant." She grabbed hold of the door handle.

Lauren nodded, covering her mouth as if she'd just been declared the new Miss America.

"Are you absolutely sure?" Shelby's voice quivered.

"It doesn't get any pinker than this!" Lauren held up the stick, hugging Shelby tightly.

Then they broke down in tears, for different reasons, of course. But the relief on Lauren's face was no match for the fear on Shelby's. "Are you absolutely sure it's not a false positive because the sample was so small?"

"No, it's not a false positive. You've got all the symptoms, Shel. And I followed the directions perfectly. This is for real. You're having my baby," Lauren sang. "What a wonderful way to say how much I love you . . ."

"Oh, shut up." Shelby threw a pillow at her face.

"Let's call Avi," Lauren ran for the phone. "Then we'll go see Mommy and Daddy and tell them in person. They are absolutely going to freak. What an incredible week this will be. They're finally both up and around, now they're going to have a grandchild. . . ."

"I want to stop by and see Dr. Weiner, too. This will pretty much make his day."

"Maybe not," Lauren mumbled. What should she do? Irma made her promise not to tell.

"What do you mean?" the intuitive Shelby never misread a facial cue. "What's wrong?"

Lauren bowed her head. "Shelby, Irma called while you were in the shower. Dr. Weiner . . ."

Shelby went ashen. "Oh no. When?"

"Early this morning. I am so sorry. She told me not to tell you. She knew you'd be upset."

Shelby sank into a chair. "I can't believe it. I can't fucking believe it!"

"I know," Lauren gently stroked Shelby's hair. "It's so unfair he had to die now. "

"It's not that," Shelby cried. "We all knew he was terminal. It was only a matter of time. I'm just pissed I finally did something totally unselfish, and now I can't tell him my good news."

Lauren cleared her throat. "You mean our good news."

"Whatever," Shelby corrected herself. "Our good news."

"That's what bothers you, Shel? That he died before he could give you a pat on the back?"

"No." Shelby blew her nose. "I don't know. I just can't believe all of this is happening at once. What a freaking joke. Someone checks out, someone else checks in."

"That's what Irma said." Lauren smiled.

Shelby looked up. "You told her I was pregnant before you told me? That was pretty tacky, don't you think?"

"I'm sorry. I had no choice. Here she is, telling me her husband just died, and I'm screaming that the stick turned pink! I sounded like a total moron."

"Oh," Shelby said. Then she burst out laughing.

"What?"

"That's the funniest thing I've ever heard." Shelby started to howl.

"No it's not."

"Yes it is. A woman calls to say her husband's dead, and you act like it's the greatest news in the world." Shelby snorted. "And guess who else would have thought that was hysterical?"

"Dr. Weiner?" Lauren smiled.

"Exactly. Good old Dr. Weiner. Shit . . . When's the funeral?"

"Irma said she'd call back after she made all the arrangements. But you're not thinking of going, are you?"

"Of course I'll go. She'd be really hurt if I didn't."

"But she said it was going to be graveside."

"So?"

"So, don't you know it's bad luck to go to a cemetery when you're pregnant?"

"Oh, please. Don't get started with all the *mishegas*. What do you think will happen? I'll be struck by lightning?"

Lauren nodded. "Please, Shel. I'm begging you. Pay a *shiva* call. Send flowers. Make a donation. Don't go to his grave. I've waited so long . . . We can't take chances . . ."

"You're being ridiculous. And besides, as far as I'm concerned, this isn't your decision. It's my baby until it's born."

Her baby? Lauren's eyes opened wide, terror ripping through her veins.

PART III

Oh Mama

Chapter Twenty-one

Shelby vowed never again to speak ill of the flu. At least the flu eventually went away, unlike morning sickness, which continued day and night. And although Lauren was at her side feeding her saltines and stroking her hair, it was to no avail. Suffering would be Shelby's exclusive domain, as long as life was growing inside her.

Lauren was secretly relieved Shelby was having such a rough time. All her experienced friends said the worse the morning sickness, the healthier the baby. She had no idea if there was any medical merit to their findings, she was just happy to hear it was a good sign. But the other reason she wasn't bothered was that Shelby was too nauseous to attend Dr. Weiner's funeral.

In fact for the first several weeks after the home pregnancy test confirmed the news, Shelby didn't go much of anywhere. She'd lie by the pool while Pucci and Maria doted on her. Occasionally she'd venture upstairs to the office to do some work, but her attention span was limited owing to the fact she was frequently interrupted by waves of nausea.

When Dr. Kessler insisted on examining Shelby to confirm either a pregnancy, or a virus, she didn't argue until she learned he couldn't make a definitive diagnosis without first drawing a small amount of blood. Fortunately she passed out *after* he got his sample.

Eventually the nausea subsided, and Shelby returned to her writing assignments. Or at least the DES piece, as the wedding article was now a huge bore, what with so many brides and grooms confessing they'd married for many reasons, with love being at the bottom of the list.

Conversely, the DES story continued to fascinate her, mainly because three generations of victims had inundated her with case histories, medical records, legal briefs, insurance claims, government reports and a wealth of other source material unlike anything she'd ever seen.

After poring over the documents night after night, it truly puzzled Shelby that none of the network news magazines had jumped on the story. Lord knows if the world's largest drug companies had marketed a pill to five million people that resulted in deformed limbs, the condemnation and demands for retribution would be relentless. But as a silent and invisible tragedy, one that was perceived as old news, it was growing increasingly difficult for DES to cause a stir.

And, too, Shelby sensed that without benefit of a three-hankie, made-for-TV weeper, or a celebrity victim/spokesperson, this cause was nowhere on the sympathy radar screen. So it came as no surprise when even Ian indicated he was growing out of love with the story.

"Must we dwell so much on the negatives?" he asked upon beckoning her into his office one afternoon. "Surely there must be a happy ending now and again?"

"Get real!" Shelby threw down the reporter's gauntlet. "I can't even find one lousy happy ending for the stupid wedding story, and that was supposed to have nothing but happy endings.

"Besides, what sort of happy ending did you have in mind for young women whose patience, courage, and faith are put to the test every day? Whose reproductive systems are permanently deformed? Who live in fear of getting breast cancer, knowing that after forty, their risk is 2.5 times higher than non-exposed women? Who worry about other forms of cancer, early menopause, hormone replacement therapy, the ill effects of DES on their sons and grandsons . . ."

"Yes, yes." Ian juggled rubber balls. "I read through all your research, exhaustive as it was, but I must share with you this little teensy weensy problem I'm having."

"What?" Shelby stood with hands on hips. "Not enough deaths to satisfy the Gladiators who double as our readers?"

"No, it's just, how shall I put this? Where's the scandalous aspect? Who are we indicting exactly? Can't we at least out a celebrity or two who have been keeping this terrible secret under their gynecologists' rug?"

Shelby's jaw dropped. "Are you suggesting the story isn't newsworthy enough for you unless I uncover a star's DES exposure?"

"Ah. There you go." Ian clapped. "Smart as a whip, as usual."

"I can't believe what you're saying," she cried. "You're not going to run this unless I dumb it down to the category of a Hollywood sob story, are you?"

"Let's just say in its current form, the piece is such a downer it reads like a Brontë sisters reunion. Perhaps you're just too close to the facts."

"Damn right I'm too close. If it wasn't for DES, I wouldn't be pregnant right now."

"I beg your pardon?" Ian dropped the balls. "Did you say pregnant, as in, with child?"

"Ah. There you go," Shelby clapped. "Smart as a whip, as usual."

"Really," Ian stroked his chin. "And who's the lucky papa?"

"Remember Avi?"

"Your brother-in-law?"

"Bingo!"

"Why, Shelby." Ian found the news titillating. "You naughty girl. And you accuse me of being depraved? Does your sister know?"

"Of course she knows." Shelby winked. "She was there!"

The ashen look on Ian's face kept Shelby afloat the rest of the day. Then again, although she was loath to admit it, there might be some validity to his criticism. The tone in her draft copy was both ominous and heavy-handed, unlike the brash writing that was the paper's signature style. Maybe tonight she would review her notes to see how the copy could be spiced up, *Informer* style.

In the meantime, she would force herself to go back to work on Ian's pet project, just in case she needed a bargaining chip. No way was he getting his little wedding piece if he killed her DES story, as it was turning into the finest investigative report of her career. If she did say so herself.

Later that day, Shelby peeked over her cubicle. "What do you make of this, Warner?" She handed him a stack of old *New York Times* wedding announcements. "I'm working on a piece about couples who got married on the same weekend ten years ago, and of the eight couples I've tracked down so far, only one is still together. Any chance there was some sort of full moon thing going on that made all this wedded bliss blow up like a shaken can of Coke?"

Warner pushed his glasses up his nose to study the clippings. "The naysayers always make the best students," he said.

"Excuse me?"

"I'm saying it's always people like you who jump up and down that there's no validity to astrology, then become my prize pupils. So in answer to your question, yes, you could be correct in assuming there was some sort of planetary configuration that caused those marriages to be doomed from the start. But I'd have to look it up in my ephemeris to be sure."

"Your what?"

"An ephemeris. It's a special book showing precisely where each planet was at noon and midnight, relative to the others, for every day of the year, according to Greenwich Mean Time."

"Ha! I'll tell you about Greenwich Mean Time." Shelby laughed. "That's when the snooty town fathers of Greenwich, Connecticut, close their borders to the riffraff from the Bronx so they can't drive over to buy their Powerball lottery tickets."

"You Capricorns are such a riot." Warner hee-hawed, then regained his dignity. "But tell me. What do you know about these couples? Do they seem to have any common bonds?"

"You mean aside from the fact that as kids, even their piggy banks had vice presidents?"

"No, silly. What busted their marriages? Was it cheating, alcohol, cross-dressing, all of the above perhaps?"

"Let me think." Shelby took the clippings back. "Well, in the case of Leigh Seton McDonnell, who wed Henry Preston Jennings, I interviewed Mrs. Jennings, and she talked a lot about the difficulty her husband faced as a third-generation lawyer at the prestigious firm his grandfather founded. Oh, and something about his fetish for baby-sitters.

"Then in the case of Elizabeth Drake Brown and Douglas Colin Wigglesworth . . ."

"Wigglesworth?" Warner snorted. "Where do they get these ridiculous-sounding names?"

"On the *Mayflower*, of course. Who wants Higginbottom?" she yelled. "Who wants Drinkwater? Anyway, in their case, according to the husband, things got off to a rocky start because his wife never got over her first fiancé, a Mr. James Woodrow Easterbrook. Apparently while good old Doug was slaving away at his trading desk down on Wall Street, Mrs. Wigglesworth was getting her wiggles' worth at the Plaza Hotel. He said the marriage broke up before their third anniversary, when his wife announced she was carrying Mr. Easterbrook's child."

"I'd have to check, but it could have been a void-of-course moon." Warner sighed.

"Never heard of it." Shelby stretched. "Is it like a full moon? Crime jumps, pregnant women go into labor? That sort of thing?"

"No, but you get an 'A' for being so abso-fucking-lutely close. A void-of-course is a much rarer planetary occurrence. It's when the moon is in conjunction with Venus retrograde."

"In English, please?"

"Let's just say it would be a fairly crappy time to get married."

"Why?"

"Because Venus is the planet ruling love, trust, and relationships, and during a void-of-course, it loses most of its positive energy. It would be like trying to launch a hot-air balloon without the gas. Much as you want to fly, you can forget about the liftoff."

"And you think it's possible that on May 25, 1988, the moon was void-of-whatever?"

"Warner is not a betting man. But if what you say is true, that every couple you've interviewed so far has a rocky marriage, then yes, I'd be willing to put my money on it."

"Would you be a sweetheart and check for me?"

"Nothing would give me greater pleasure. When do you need to know?"

"By the end of the week. I'm driving up to Chappaqua on Saturday to interview the M.J. McCreighs, the only anniversary couple I've found so far who hasn't split up."

"Aye, aye, Captain Shelby," he saluted. "Oh, how I love converts."

Shelby studied the directions Mrs. McCreigh gave her, checked her cell phone to make sure it was fully charged and took a deep breath. It was a splendid day for a drive to beautiful Westchester County, and she was actually feeling strong. Although she was somewhat bewildered to be experiencing hot flashes at the same time she

was experiencing nausea. What if she turned out to be the first pregnant woman to experience signs of menopause?

At least she was getting away from her near-claustrophobic life at
home, where well meaning people were constantly hovering, as if one
wrong move on her part might end the whole damn fairy tale. But
when Lauren insisted she drive Shelby to her appointment, Shelby
put her foot down. "Lay off, okay? I'm pregnant, not a cripple."

"Fine. I was just trying to be helpful." Lauren shrugged. "Anyway, Avi and I are going house hunting today. There's a three-
bedroom colonial in Roslyn that sounds perfect for us."

"Good," Shelby said. "Spend some time with your husband for
a change. I need the break."

So when her cell phone rang, just as she was heading onto the
Whitestone Bridge, she jumped. She hadn't intended to receive calls,
only to make them if she got lost. As she fumbled to reach for the
phone, she hoped it wasn't the McCreighs calling to cancel on her.

"Oh my God, oh my God, oh my God," the shaky voice cried.

It was déjà vu all over again. "Lauren?" Of course it was Lauren.

"He did it. He really did it. I can't believe he did it."

"Who, what, where . . ." Shelby repeated her old mantra.

"Avi. He left us. He left for Israel, the son of a bitch."

"What?" Shelby swerved into the right lane, lucky to apply the
brakes before crashing into the fence that separated the bridge from
Flushing Bay.

"He just called me from the airport," Lauren sobbed. "He told
me he had one run to do this morning, and then he'd pick me up so
we could go meet that realtor. But it was a lie . . ."

Shelby's head spun. She couldn't drive while under the influence
of hysteria, as confirmed by the driver behind her who furiously
waved his middle finger at her. But there was no place to pull over,
and no way to get Lauren to stop talking.

"Things haven't been great. You were right. But I never thought
he'd pick up and leave. What are we going to do?"

"What do you mean we?" Shelby tried to steer while holding the
phone in the cradle of her neck. "He'd didn't leave me, he left you."

"No, he left both of us, Shel. You're carrying his child."

"So what?" Shelby shouted over traffic. "We had a deal, remember? This Bud's for you."

"I know. I know," Lauren whimpered. "Where are you?"

"The Whitestone Bridge."

"Are you serious? Be careful. You could have an accident!"

"The odds are good," Shelby looked in her rearview mirror to see if the hostile man behind her was still on her tail. Fortunately, he was busy picking his nose. "Hold on. Traffic is slowing down. We're getting close to the bridge."

Shelby scrambled for change in the ashtray, then tried focusing on Lauren, all the while trying to avoid ramming into the limo in front of her. "Tell me exactly what happened."

Lauren tried to control her sobbing. "He . . . We found out yesterday . . . Oh, my God. You're going to kill me."

"What?" Shelby screamed. "I can't hear you that great."

"He said he couldn't go through with it," she shouted. "That the whole thing was too crazy."

"But he was the one who came up with the idea in the first place."

"Yes, but that was before . . . that was before we knew . . . Dr. Kessler's office called yesterday. They got your test results back."

"Oh my God. Is there a problem?" Shelby started to feel light headed. "Are we talking Down's syndrome? Missing fingers and toes?"

"No, nothing like that."

"Well, okay then. What could be so terrible?"

"Um . . . you see . . . they think it's more than one," Lauren blurted.

"Come again," Shelby screamed. "Did you say more than one?"

"Yes." Lauren started to bawl.

"Are you freakin' kidding me?" Shelby slammed on the brakes, screeching so loud the sound probably reverberated for miles. Miraculously, the alert driver behind her avoided a collision.

Shelby put on her flashers, causing drivers to have to merge into one lane. As they honked and cursed, she heard Lauren say something about two fetal sacs showing up in the sonogram.

"OH. MY. GOD." Shelby could barely breathe.

"Pull over, Shelby," Lauren cried. "Please!"

"No that's okay. Don't worry about it. I'm fine. Really. This is perfect timing. I can drive right into Flushing Bay and end it all right here."

"Shelby, please." Lauren was pleading now. "You're scaring me."

"I'm scaring you?" Shelby shook in disbelief. "Hold on." She managed to put the car in drive, cross the bridge, and pull over onto the shoulder. "Okay," she finally said, sliding down into the seat. "Tell me everything and take it from the top."

It didn't take long to get the gist of the story. Avi had been acting even stranger than normal upon learning Shelby was pregnant. Turns out, although he and Lauren had discussed the idea at great length, when reality hit, he was simply too much of a traditionalist to accept the idea of a woman other than his wife bearing his child. Then when they learned Shelby was possibly carrying twins, he freaked. Adding to the frenzy, that same day, his cousin called from Israel to talk about his new rock band, which was in dire need of a lead guitarist. That was all the coaxing Avi needed. Seemed he wanted a big break more than he wanted a baby. So he stuck his suitcase in his trunk, drove to JFK, and boarded the next flight to Tel Aviv. Courtesy of Lauren's Visa card.

"That little shit!" Shelby seethed. "I told you he was a putz."

"I know," Lauren cried, her voice hoarse from hysteria. "What should I do?"

"Hell if I know." Shelby closed her eyes. "Oh, my God! Twins! Are you sure?"

"They want to confirm it with other tests, but yes, they're pretty sure."

"I can't friggin' believe this. No wonder I've been so sick. When did you plan to tell me? When I was in labor?"

"Believe me, I wanted to tell you," Lauren cried. "But Avi said we should wait."

"For what? For him to get the hell out of the country?"

Lauren wailed even louder.

"This is a goddamn nightmare." Shelby started to sweat. "Do you have any idea how much weight I'm going to gain now?"

"I heard that's nothing compared to the swelling and the hemorrhoids," she blurted.

"Oh great!" Shelby yelled. "I swear I'm going to kill you!"

"Not if I kill myself first," Lauren wailed.

After hanging up, Shelby's mind went into high gear. She could go right home to start looking for reputable abortion clinics. Or, she could pack a bag as fast as Avi, fly to Tel Aviv, and track his sorry ass down. Or, she could just continue on her way to meet the McCreighs as planned. She chose door number three, as it was the only option that did not involve premeditated murder.

I know things don't look great at the moment, but I hope the girls don't panic. You know me. I think there's a logical explanation for everything that happens. Even something as pathetic as Avi jumping ship. It reminds me of 1966, when my own little world was falling apart.

Larry was so busy building the business, he was never home. My father died in June, and my chain-smoking mother became attached to my hip. I was pregnant with Lauren, and Shelby was going through a difficult stage. Again. Oh, and my girlfriends had all but abandoned me in favor of playing tennis, going out to lunch, and shopping.

Not that I was passing judgment. I liked having nice things, too, and was crazy about my canary yellow Cadillac convertible, and the three-carat diamond Larry surprised me with on our tenth anniversary. I just couldn't help but wonder what purpose was being served by my being a bored little housewife whose highlight of the week was driving into the city to have lunch at Saks, and see the Wednesday matinee of Mame?

I remember chatting about this with Matty's mom, Carol, a rare event in those days in spite of our children being inseparable. Truthfully, the fact we weren't close was my doing. I guess I assumed since her husband struggled financially, we'd never be able to travel in the same social circles. My closest friends were of the country club variety, hers of the mah-jongg-at-my-house crowd. She shopped at Korvettes; I frequented the better department stores. While we were busy planning our next cruise, she was hoping to swing a week at a bungalow colony in the Catskills.

This all sounds rather shallow and pathetic, I know. And I could kick myself now, for it turns out this very smart, outspoken lady gave me the best advice of my life.

Turns out she had just read The Feminine Mystique *cover to cover and liked it. Yet, with all due respect to Betty Friedan, she said to hell with my own little identity crisis. I should get off my skinny little rump and devote all my energy to being a good mother.*

At the time, I didn't take kindly to her blunt message, even though I suspected she was right. Perhaps Shelby's somber moods and ornery behavior could be tempered by my spending more time with her. Still, I insisted Carol was wrong; that the problem was simple. Shelby was acting out because of the new baby coming. But it was I who was wrong. For even at six, Shelby was too selfish to consider how a new family addition would have any bearing on her life. What bothered her more was that things with her and Matty were changing.

Up until then, they'd simply done everything together. Slept in each other's beds. Taken baths. Read comic books. Shared glorious summer days in the pool. Gone to the movies. Made Jiffy Pop on the stove to bring to the movies. Carried on so, until one of the grown-ups drove them over to Baskin-Robbins for double dips of Rocky Road and Peppermint . . .

But by first grade, different ball game. Suddenly Matty preferred playing football than making Tollhouse cookies with Shelby. He preferred running around in his Batman costume to sitting with her through another of Miss Elaine's story hours at the library. And in school, Matty made lots of new friends while Shelby made no attempt to mingle.

Every day at three o'clock, she'd wait to see if he had plans, and even if he did, she'd ring his doorbell anyhow. Of course she was always invited to stay, but with her flawless instincts, she knew three was a crowd.

Thanks to Carol's incessant prodding, I picked up the slack and spent inordinate amounts of time with Shelby. We began to do everything together and forged a bond that never would have happened if I'd relegated the task of raising her to my mother, or the maid.

Only now can I see how circumstances conspired, giving me the opportunity to take a lead role in Shelby's life. And in fact I can safely say, it was the most important work I ever did. For little did I know then that it would not only be our best years together, it would be our last years together.

So you see? It's not time for Shelby and Lauren to jump off the deep end. Soon, I'm sure, they'll discover the reason Avi left, and realize it was all for the best.

God help me if I'm wrong.

Chapter Twenty-two

It was an amazing feat that Shelby was able to drive along the narrow Hutchinson River Parkway without incident, given she was having difficulty breathing and had a stabbing pain running down her arm. This could only mean one thing. She was having a heart attack, and the next stop for her was not the town of Chappaqua, but the village of Cardiac Arrest.

How did this happen to her? Once upon a time she was a high-paid journalist enjoying perk-filled days with no real personal obligations. Now she was living back home, visiting sick people in the hospital, carrying her sister's twins, and wondering if the babies' father was going to get his cowardly ass back to New York where it belonged.

And how would she be able to conduct a decent interview right now? Shelby was the first to admit it was difficult enough for her to act cheerful and friendly on a good day, let alone when her life was in turmoil. To say nothing of the fact that when she'd spoken to Mrs. McCreigh on the phone, she hadn't exactly heard the voice of Little Mary Sunshine, either.

Shelby recalled that the woman was not only curt and evasive, but quite indifferent about her pending tenth anniversary. God help her if the only reason that Mrs. McCreigh had agreed to meet with her was to sit there and promote all her pet charity projects. Shelby cringed at the prospect of listening to yet another woman who ignored her kids and mistreated her nanny try to pass herself off as this selfless philanthropist who worked tirelessly for underprivileged children.

On the other hand, who cared if Mrs. McCreigh was a bitch? Focusing on work would sure beat dwelling on her own seriously malfunctioning life. Besides, she would have a good laugh when the interview was over. So that was that. For the rest of the ride she would think of nothing other than the McCreighs and how their ten-year-old marital journey had begun.

Shelby remembered after reading the McCreighs' engagement announcement and looking at the bride-to-be's photo from the exclusive Bachrach studio, that Gwendolyn was the quintessential deb. The blond, well-bred trophy girl who made Mummy and Daddy proud. Known as "Gwenny," Mrs. McCreigh was the eldest daughter of William Lloyd Armonk, a prominent Manhattan attorney, and the former Evelyn Peck of Bedford Hills, an antique dealer on the Upper East Side. The Armonks resided in New York City and Martha's Vineyard, Massachusetts. Gwenny attended Mummy's alma mater, The Spence School, and graduated cum laude from Wellesley College. She was presented at the Junior League Ball in 1985 and worked as an account executive at the advertising agency, Ogilvy & Mather.

The bio of Gwenny's then fiancé, M. Jay McCreigh, known as MJ, was a bit more sketchy. There was no reference to a father, only a mother, a one Carol McCreigh, who managed a realty concern in Portland, Oregon. And although MJ's pedigree was not up to the Armonk and Peck family standards, at least the boy had gotten a respectable education. Somehow he'd graduated with honors from Brown, then completed his MBA at Wharton. Still, it didn't take the keepers of the Social Register to see Gwendolyn Peck Armonk McCreigh had married beneath her.

Another curious thing was the wedding itself. Typically Anglo-Saxon couples had elaborate church affairs officiated by a very reverend, or an Episcopal minister who was invariably related to the mother of the bride. But for some reason, the McCreighs were wed in a judge's chambers. If she remembered, she would casually mention it and see if it added some oomph to the story.

In the meantime, it was back to reality and the road. If she didn't start paying attention, she'd never find her way to their house. Thankfully, traffic lightened up and she could cruise along at 70 mph. That was until she caught up to some jerk in a Range Rover who dared to be doing the speed limit in the left lane. Why buy an expensive truck, only to drive it like your grandmother?

Naturally when Shelby passed him, she aimed her intimidating, make-my-day glare in his direction. Then she swerved back into the left lane, nearly cutting him off. Damn right it was road rage. How else could morons like him be taught to drive? But when she checked in the rearview mirror to see the man's reaction, she nearly drove off the road.

Incredibly, he looked just like Ed Lieberman, Matty's father. Only a much younger version, of course, as Mr. Lieberman would be in his late sixties by now. This guy was definitely more her age. Oh God. What was she thinking? That the man behind the wheel could be . . . Matty?

Shelby's heart raced as she veered back into the right lane to catch another glimpse. He was a handsome hunk with wavy, brown hair and broad shoulders, but surely her subconscious mind was playing tricks after getting Lauren's shocking call. No one ever actually ran into their long-lost love on the highway. Except in those cheap airport novels you left in the seat pocket of the plane.

As Shelby agonized over what to do, Mr. Range Rover appeared to be doing some agonizing of his own. Did he think she was trying to kill him or pick him up? Either way, she'd gotten his attention. But now what? Speed up to get another good look, of course.

Unfortunately that meant barreling down a crowded highway, weaving in and out of lanes, with no real justification other than wishful thinking and a hunch. All the while contemplating what to do if and when he drove off in a different direction. She was scheduled to meet the McCreighs at one, so forget having enough time to follow this man home.

Where was she going anyway? Shelby tried to read the directions while following the other car's every move. From the Hutch she had to bear north onto I-684 for approximately four and a half miles, take that to Exit 2 near the Westchester Airport, then follow the signs to Country Road 135. Damn! So many roads, so many opportunities to ditch her!

In the meantime, she realized a large dog was pacing in the back of his truck. Cool! The Rover had its own Rover, and upon closer inspection, wasn't it a collie? Matty adored collies. Growing up, he couldn't have a dog because of his father's allergies, so he'd named his goldfish Lassie.

This had to be a sign from above! Shelby gripped the steering wheel, then quickly changed lanes again so she could drive alongside him. A fine idea if not for the old woman in a Buick who'd never driven a mile over the limit and wasn't about to start now.

Miraculously, the woman turned off at the next exit, finally allowing Shelby to get close enough to make eye contact. Only to discover the man looked totally befuddled. How to telegraph that she wasn't some crazed woman on a bender, that they were possibly childhood sweethearts? No time, as she had to turn on I-684. Unbelievable! So did he.

Shelby was torn between excitement and dread. It would be an amazing coincidence if he was heading to Chappaqua, too. Then maybe she could signal him to pull over, apologize for the confusion, and ask one or two questions, like maybe where he grew up. But what if he was a family man who had been on his way to his son's Little League game until he discovered a blond vixen on his tail? Was he thinking, good-bye son, hello fantasy-filled, no-one-has-to-know nooner?

Sweat ran down Shelby's cheeks, even though the air-conditioning was cranked so high the car was as cold as a meat locker. Forget about the perils of driving drunk. She was discovering how risky it was to speed while intoxicated with terrifying thoughts. And yet she so wanted to believe in this happy-ending fairy tale, not even wild horses could stop her now.

Not true of a New York State trooper.

"Shit, shit, shit!" Shelby cried out, brilliantly deducing that the loud siren and flashing red lights were meant to get her attention. There should be a law against ambushing motorists! Now she'd have to pull over, listen to some boring lecture on aggressive driving, wait for the cop to take his sweet time writing out the damn ticket, all while losing precious minutes.

Shelby indicated she was pulling over and hoped the trooper would relax once he realized she was an otherwise law-abiding citizen. What a shame she wasn't back home, as she had great connections in virtually every police precinct. But from this guy's stern, don't-even-think-of-messing-with-me expression, it was going to take more than a get-out-of-jail-free card from the Chicago Police Department to be let off the hook.

Shelby rolled down her window and took a deep breath. She knew the drill. Don't say a word, and don't make any sudden moves or the cop might think you're reaching for a gun.

"Do you have a problem with the speed limit the state of New York has deemed safe to travel at?" he barked.

"No, sir. No, Officer . . . Donnelly." Shelby read the name on the badge and guessed from his growl he wasn't the type to take kindly to being told A, it was grammatically incorrect to end a sentence with a preposition or B, adding a little fiber to his diet would make him less irritable.

"Were you aware you were clocked doing seventy-six in a fifty-five?"

"No, sir. I'm sorry," Shelby smiled. Perhaps he would warm up to a conciliatory blonde.

"Are you also aware that drag racing and reckless endangerment are serious crimes, punishable by large fines and, if convicted, possible incarceration?"

"Really?" Shelby whispered. Not good. Not good at all. If he hauled her in to the local police station, she didn't exactly have a list of good criminal attorneys at her fingertips. Hell, she didn't even have a list of lousy criminal attorneys.

"License and registration," he ordered.

"Permission to get my pocketbook from the backseat?" she asked sweetly.

"Yeah fine." He started to write out a ticket.

Shelby could tell by the fury in his pen he was not being swayed by her spirit of cooperation. He did say, however, that he was very concerned that her Illinois driver's license was expired, as was the car registration, which was not even registered to her.

"I can explain everything, Officer," she started.

"Save it for the judge," he instructed. "And wait here while I verify this with DMV."

"Of course." Shelby buried her hands in her face. What a nightmare. Cops, judges, lawyers', lawyers bills. All because she'd followed her heart and driven a teensy bit over the limit. For that she was being treated like a savage criminal?

Shelby searched her pocketbook for her cell phone. She'd call the McCreighs, tell them she had car trouble (not an outright lie) and reschedule for another day. But before she could dial, she looked in her rearview mirror and clutched her shirt. The Range Rover and another patrol car had exited the highway and were pulling up behind Officer Donnelly's squad car.

"What the heck . . ." she heard Officer Donnelly yell over the din of trucks flying by.

"I guess he wasn't expecting company," an ecstatic Shelby cheered. She quickly opened her door and ran over. "Excuse me, Officer," she said. "Would it be possible for me to go talk to the other driver? I think he might be an old friend of mine."

Officer Donnelly removed his sunglasses, making sure he had solid eye contact with Shelby. "Ma'am, you are in serious trouble, and I suggest that you start to worry less about your social life and more about the number of moving violations you're about to be cited for. Now return to your vehicle and stay there until you receive further instructions."

"Yes, sir." Shelby looked over and spotted the driver in the Range Rover getting out of the car to speak to the other cop. It was her first close-up glimpse and now she wanted to cry. Clearly she had made an enormous mistake. Ed Lieberman was a nice-looking man, but no way could this hotty be his son. He was positively magazine-ad dashing, with a towering, muscular body, and the best backside she'd seen in years. Maybe she *should* be locked up for the stupid thing she'd done.

"It goes to state of mind." She could hear her attorney's opening statement at the hearing. "My client had just learned she was pregnant with twins and that the father had fled the country."

Oh God. The officer and the gentleman were walking over. Now she didn't care if she got cuffed and booked. No way was she budging.

"Stay right there," Officer Donnelly ordered as he met up with his fellow law enforcer.

Meanwhile, the other driver walked over to Shelby and her heart started to pound.

"Hello," Shelby said the instant he was in earshot. "You're probably wondering what the heck is going on."

"You could say that." He folded his arms.

"Okay. Well. First of all let me say how sorry I am," she began. "I swear I've never done anything like this before in my life. It was all a huge mistake. I thought you were someone I knew. An old friend."

"Uh-huh." He removed his sunglasses to get a better look at the perpetrator. "He must have been pretty special to risk life and limb like that. Especially that fancy move when you cut me off."

"You have every right to be angry . . ."

"It's okay." He started to smile. "The important thing is no one got hurt."

"Right. Of course." Shelby smiled back. How incredible was this guy that he could actually be nice to a woman who nearly killed him in a high-speed chase? "Look, we're probably going to get hit with some serious fines, and I just want you to know that since this was all my fault, I'm willing to take care of the whole thing."

"Don't worry about it." He kicked a pebble. "That won't be necessary."

"It won't?"

"No." He cleared his throat. "Let's just say I have a fairly good connection in Albany."

"Oh. Do you work in government?"

"Not exactly. My wife is Bill Armonk's daughter."

And that's supposed to mean something to me? Shelby thought. "Wait a minute. Bill Armonk . . . Where do I know that name from?"

"I take it you're not from New York."

"Used to be . . . it's been a while . . . oh hold it . . . oh my God . . . are you talking about Bill Armonk, as in William Lloyd Armonk?"

"Yes, but these days most people refer to him as Lieutenant Governor Armonk."

"Lieutenant governor?" she started to palpitate. "I'm sorry. I had no idea."

"I can see that. Anyway, I just wanted you to know your secret is safe with me."

"My secret?"

"You know. That you . . . tried to pick up his son-in-law on the Hutch."

"No, no. I wasn't doing that at all. I swear," Shelby stammered. "I thought you were this friend I grew up with . . . when I passed you . . . I don't know . . . your face looked so familiar."

"Gotcha." He nodded, staring as if he was trying to place her, too. "Sorry. I guess I wasn't who you thought."

Oh believe me. I'm sorry, too. "Actually it just dawned on me that you are sort of."

"Excuse me?"

"Who I'm looking for." Shelby took a deep breath. "I mean no, you're not who I thought at the beginning . . . I'm not sure how to ask this . . . If you're Mr. Armonk's son-in-law, does that make you M.J. McCreigh?"

"You lost me. You didn't know he was the lieutenant governor, but you know my name? Who are you?"

"A reporter for the *New York Informer*."

"Oh, you're kidding. The one doing that story about our anniversary?"

Shelby nodded.

"That's really funny. So we were both on the way to my house?"

"I guess so." Shelby laughed. "Small world."

"I'm sorry. I don't know your name. The only thing my wife said to me before I left was to be back at one to do an interview with some lady."

"I'm the lady," she extended her hand. "Shelby Lazarus. Pleased to meet you."

Mr. McCreigh's face turned ashen. "I'm sorry. I couldn't hear you." He pointed to the trucks. "Could you repeat that?"

She cupped her hands and shouted. "Shelby Lazarus."

His expression went from amused to shocked to elated. He grabbed Shelby and hugged her so hard she could barely breathe, just as Officer Donnelly returned. Shelby prayed it was not to apprehend her.

"Careful there, Mr. McCreigh." A softer, sweeter cop tried moving them away from the passing cars. "We don't generally recommend state roads for reunions. Looks like this is your lucky day, ma'am." He returned her license and registration. "Seems as if all charges against you are being dropped . . ."

M.J. McCreigh didn't hear a word being said. "After you said that you thought I was an old friend, I looked at your face and said to myself, wait a minute. Could it be her?"

"Okay, now I'm the one who's a little confused. Do you know me?"

"Did you grow up on Long Island?"

"Yes."

"In Manhasset?"

"Yes?"

"At 68 Majestic Court?"

Shelby swallowed hard.

"And did this friend of yours used to call you Shebby?" He pushed the bangs from her eyes. "And write you poems, and build you snowmen, and make you eat Campbell's chicken noodle soup in July . . ."

"So I'd be warm enough to jump into a freezing pool."

"Oh my God!" his jaw dropped.

"Matty?" she whispered.

He nodded yes, and the world on the edge of State Road 120 suddenly came to a standstill. She'd been right? Incredibly, miraculously right? She stared deep into Matty's great green eyes, located the tiny birthmark on his left earlobe, then let out a primal scream that startled the previously unflappable Officer Donnelly.

"Long time no see." Matty kissed her, doing his manly best to hold back tears.

"I don't understand." Shelby started to cry. "How can you be . . . You just said your name was M.J. McCreigh."

"Yeah, which is it?" Officer Donnelly eyed him suspiciously.

"Both, actually."

"I got a minute I can spare," he said. "Give me the short version."

"Okay." Matty took a deep breath. "The short version is I was born Matthew Jay Lieberman, we moved to California, my dad split, my mother remarried, and her new husband adopted my sister and me. After that I was Matthew Jay McCreigh. M.J. for short."

"Ah-hah," Officer Donnelly said. "And you didn't recognize the lady, she recognized you?"

"It's been almost thirty years." Matty held Shelby's hand.

"Well that's a hell of a good story to tell the grandkids." He chuckled. "Aw, don't cry, ma'am."

"You don't understand," Shelby's whole body convulsed. "I was afraid I would never see him again. And for it to happen today of all days . . ."

"It's not your birthday," Matty said.

"No," she replied, wiping her eyes with the tail of her shirt. "It's just that my life is such a mess right now. A couple of months ago my dad and stepmother, you remember Aunt Roz, were out jogging and were hit by a truck a few blocks from the house. Right on Royal

Lane. Anyway, they nearly died. Then after I flew home, I found out I lost my job, Lauren told me she'd discovered she was a DES daughter, and she needed me to be her surrogate mother, which I agreed to do, and then today on the way here, she called me in the car, hysterical crying, to say the test showed I was pregnant with twins, and that when her husband found out, he packed his bags and took off for Israel because the situation was too crazy for him . . ."

Matthew's eyes opened as wide as bagels. "Your father and Aunt Roz jog?"

"That's what I said!" Shelby burst into laughter.

"All right." Officer Donnelly looked at his watch. "Looks like you two have some catching up to do. Meanwhile, ma'am, I suggest you hightail it back to the Illinois DMV as soon as possible to apply for a new license. The one you're carrying expired in June. Of last year."

"I will," Shelby was still shaking. "I promise."

"And please give my regards to the lieutenant governor." Officer Donnelly winked to Matty. "Tell him the boys support his aggressive plans for vehicle confiscation."

"Will do, Officer . . . ?"

"Donnelly," Shelby finished his sentence, just like old times.

"Without a doubt, I'd have to say this is the most amazing thing that's ever happened to me." Matty touched his heart. "Look at you. You're gorgeous."

"No, I'm not." She blushed. "I've probably got mascara running down my face."

"Yeah, but it's definitely your color."

"Forgive me." Shelby tried to catch her breath. "I'm in shock. You have no idea how long I've been looking for you. And the last place I ever expected to run into you was on a highway."

"Almost literally." Matty chucked her shoulder. "Come. We'll go back to my car. There's someone I'd like you to meet."

Shelby couldn't move. Please God, not his kids. As thrilled as she was to see him, she wasn't ready to face reality. He was married, to the lieutenant governor's daughter no less, they probably had beautiful children, a magnificent home, health and happiness . . .

"What's the matter?" he asked.

"I'm not ready to meet your children. I need a minute to collect myself."

"Okay, but how long do you need to meet my dog?"

"Your dog?" Shelby laughed. "Oh, right. I saw him in the back of your car."

"He's a she actually, and I think you'll appreciate her name. At least I hope you will."

"Is it Lassie? After your goldfish?"

"You remembered that?" Matty sighed. "Pretty incredible, but no, it isn't her name. Her name . . . this is kind of embarrassing . . . is Laz."

"Are you serious? You named your dog after me? Why?"

"It's a very long story." He shrugged. "And the truth is, I've thought about you, too, Shelby. A lot."

Shelby looked down, barely able to see her own feet as her eyes were filling with tears again. What an incredibly, loving admission he'd just made. He'd thought of her. A lot. It could only mean one thing. She didn't care if Matty was married to the goddamn emperor's daughter. She was going to win back his heart if it was the last thing she did. What did they used to say when they were kids? Finders keepers, losers weepers?

Score one for Mom. No, not for the extraordinary circumstances that have just unfolded that finally brought Shelby and Matty back together. I'd like to take credit for that, and so would her Spirit Guides and the angels who watch over her. But we've all seen her karmic map and know the crazy circumstances of her life are unfolding exactly as they were predestined.

All I'm saying is, the little car trouble she's about to have? That's my doing. And if you're wondering what good that's going to do, let's just say it will be like chicken soup. It couldn't hurt.

From this plane it's referred to as divine intervention, or as I like to call it, a little help from above. Where Shelby is right now, she'd call it a pushy, Jewish mother butting in.

You gotta do what you gotta do.

Chapter Twenty-three

Matty naturally suggested that Shelby follow him home so she didn't get lost. Little did he know it had been her intention from the start, but what an incredible dream come true that rather than having to tail him the whole way, he was serving as her private escort. Good thing, too, for with the tidal wave of extraordinary events that had unfolded since this morning, she was feeling too light-headed and unhinged to be able to read a map.

Besides, the only navigational matters she wanted to think about were more personal. Whether to stick with the pregnancy or terminate it now that the father had gone AWOL, how she would handle meeting Matty's lucky bride and beautiful children, how she would feel seeing his presumably grand house, how to finagle seeing him again, and uh-oh, what to do now that a stupid red light on the dashboard was blinking, service engine, service engine, service engine . . .

"Nooooo." She smacked the steering wheel. "Not car trouble now. Haven't I had enough to deal with today?" What the hell did it mean anyway? She knew as much about what was lurking inside the hood of her car as she did about what was lurking inside her uterus.

Shelby thought about trying to signal Matty to pull over, but when she saw the sign, WELCOME TO CHAPPAQUA, she decided to chance it and deal with the problem when she got to the house. He had told her he had a wonderful surprise waiting for her, and although she had no idea how that was possible given that their meeting was totally accidental, she was busting to find out what he meant. If he'd named his dog after her, who knows what other ways he could prove he'd thought about her? A lot.

Shelby was practically giddy with excitement as she followed the Range Rover down a long, winding road set in a great, green forest against a backdrop of palatial, gated estates. One could only wonder the property tax rate these homeowners paid for the privilege, but it was probably like being handed a menu without prices at a fine restaurant. If you had to ask, you couldn't afford to eat there. And from the looks of the imposing homes that dotted Chappaqua's landscape, clearly these people weren't quibbling with the maître d'.

And yet in spite of the fact she was quickly growing accustomed to the grandeur, she could not believe her eyes when Matty signaled he was turning, then waited momentarily for a massive, iron gate to open electronically. For God's sake, he was pulling into what looked like the New York version of the Ewing Ranch. J.R. and Bobby eat your hearts out.

The house, if you pardoned the expression, was an exquisite red-brick Tudor with stone pillars that stood high atop a hill overlooking acres of lush, rolling lawns. The better to put the stables, tennis court, pool, and assorted guest cottages, my dear, Shelby thought. But how could you send out for pizza, then answer the door with a straight face?

Clearly this had to be the surprise Matty was talking about. Poor, Jewish boy from a broken home marries into prominent gentile, Republican family and lives happily ever after in the magic kingdom. No wonder he'd been so excited about bringing her back here. It was the best show-and-tell he ever had.

Unlike where they'd grown up, in the Formica capital of the world, Shelby imagined this place would be teeming with Georgian silver, Canton china, brass candlesticks, Chippendale secretaries, Mother's needlepoint pillows, and enough nautical *tchachkes* to make Daddy feel as though he was back on the Vineyard.

The living room, she assumed, would be a veritable tartan plaid convention boasting furniture that gleamed and ancestral portraits that hung gallery-perfect. The throw pillows, dried flowers, and coffee table books would all be flawlessly arranged, and not a single toy would be left lying around. In fact, the only thing missing would be the velvet ropes.

So no way was she getting out of the car until she'd had time to put herself back together. How could she possibly walk in looking like the hired help when she was about to meet the "other woman"?

Damn. Any chance Aunt Roz kept a strand of pearls in the glove compartment?

"Well?" A beaming Matty opened Shelby's car door. "What do you think?"

"It's not bad if you like small and charming." She sniffed. "Jesus, Matty. You could have told me you were the Crown Prince of Chappaqua."

"Oh, come on. It's not *that* big."

"True. I think Hearst Castle is slightly larger."

"Sorry. Hate to brag, but we recently measured, and we beat it by a few thousand square feet." He cupped her chin. "What do you say we go in? There's someone who will absolutely go crazy when she sees you."

"Are we talking royalty, celebrity, or high-ranking official?"

"All of the above. It's my mother."

"Oh, God, you're kidding? That's wonderful. Does she live with you?"

"God no," he cringed. "She and Gwenny don't see eye to eye on much. In fact, the only reason she came in is, remember her brother? My uncle Irving?"

"Of course," Shelby smiled. "The best part of summer was visiting him at the Jersey Shore."

"I know." Matty nodded. "Anyway, he just died of cancer, and she flew in for the funeral."

"Uncle Irving died?" Shelby clutched her heart. "I am so sorry. I loved him."

"Thank you, but he'd been sick for a long time. In the meantime, I have to take her back to La Guardia soon, and I want us all to have as much time as possible."

"Aw, can't James drive her?" Shelby pleaded.

"No, sorry. He has to clean the stables on Saturdays."

Shelby laughed so hard she snorted.

"It was so much cooler when you made Kool-Aid come out your nose." Matty winked.

"Can't say I've done that in a while." Shelby wanted to rest her head on his shoulder. Matty was everything she remembered and more. So sweet and funny and adorable and wonderful and now handsome and sexy, too. God, what she wouldn't give to be with him.

"You ready?" he took her hand.

"Would you mind very much if I tried to put myself together before I go in? I promise I'll just be a minute."

"Sure. Of course," he pushed the bangs from her eyes. "But honest, Shelby. You look great."

"Thanks." She actually blushed.

No doubt seeing him again was not at all how Shelby imagined it would be. Her daydreams about running into Matty Lieberman, and there had been hundreds, had been more in the vein of bumping into him at a restaurant when she was dressed in a little black number by Armani that cost more than her zip code. Or, crossing paths at a busy airport like O'Hare, just as they were passing a billboard on which her face appeared. But in all the scenarios, never once did she envision an encounter that also included a New York State trooper, Matty's mother, and his wife.

Interestingly, even in a worst-case scenario, she never imagined running into him when her hair was windblown, her face was dirty, and her makeup was worn off. Talk about needing emergency roadside assistance. She would have paid a king's ransom for someone to pull up with a hairblower and a washcloth. Instead, she was left to ransack her bag looking for anything resembling beauty items. Then when she concluded she'd done her best to revive herself given her limited resources, she approached the McCreighs' massive front door.

But even before she could tap the solid brass knocker, Matty was anxiously waiting. "Come on in. Can I get you a cold drink, would you like to use the bathroom, do you need to use the phone, how are you feeling. . . ."

"Wow, slow down." Shelby laughed, touched that he was trying so hard to make her feel welcome. "I'm fine. A cold drink would be great, the bathroom would be even better."

And then after turning out the bathroom light, but before getting a chance to snoop around, he was calling his mother to come downstairs.

"I can't wait to meet your wife," Shelby lied, as they waited for the former Mrs. Lieberman to descend the longest spiral staircase she had ever seen. "Is she here?"

"Actually, I don't know where she is." His brow furrowed.

"Which is very unlike her. She's always so punctual. But I'm sure she'll be back soon. She must have gone out on an errand."

"No problem," Shelby replied, wondering what possible errand a lieutenant governor's daughter needed to run? A quick stop at a Christian Lacroix trunk show?

"Mother, come down here," Matty yelled again.

"What is it, darling?" she called from upstairs. "I hope it's not time to leave yet. I still haven't finished packing."

"No, we have time. But there's someone I want you to meet. Someone really special."

"Can it wait?"

"I think she's waited long enough. Please just come down . . . Do you know where Gwen is?"

"I give up. Where?" She carefully took one step at a time.

"That's what I'm asking you? Have you seen her? Do you know where she went?"

"All I know is she took off like a bat out of hell right after you left. Who knows? Maybe she was running low on headbands."

"Mother! Stop it!"

But Shelby was loving every minute of this familiar exchange. The teasing, loose-lipped Mrs. Lieberman saying whatever came to mind, to the chagrin of her helpless son. And how wonderful she looked. Tall and slender as she remembered, with the same store-dyed red hair. But then as she looked closely, there were laugh lines around the mouth and wrinkles around the eyes.

"You're impossible!" Matty took a deep breath and reached for Shelby's hand. "Mother, I asked you to come down here because look who I found."

Carol McCreigh studied Shelby up and down with approval. "I have no idea. Miss July?"

"No." He laughed nervously. "Although I agree with you, she certainly could be. But look again. Really close. What former person in our life does she remind you of?"

Once again Mrs. McCreigh examined Shelby, checking out the eyes, the hair, the coloring. And then a strange sense of déjà vu came over her and she threw open her arms. "Oh, for heaven's sake," she cried. "Shelby?"

"Yes." Shelby embraced her, taken aback that they were approximately the same height.

"I can't believe my eyes. You're an absolute vision."

"Thank you, and you look wonderful, too," Shelby returned, her heart filled with joy.

"I can't believe how much you look like Sandy. I should have figured it out right away. Oh for heaven's sake," she repeated. "What happened? Did you two just bump into each other?"

"Just about." Matty chuckled as he ushered her and Shelby into the sitting room, or parlor, or Shelby wasn't sure what the hell to call it, with its wall of French doors, stone fireplace, and books from floor to ceiling.

"Like the Palace of Versailles, isn't it?" Mrs. McCreigh asked as she watched marvel cross Shelby's face.

"Actually, it reminds me of your house on Majestic Court." She looked around.

"It does?" Matty and his mother replied in unison.

"Sure. With the den being off the kitchen and all."

Hands down, it was the greatest one-liner of her life, and the key that opened the door to a magical conversation, where Shelby offered up the *Reader's Digest*, condensed version of her volatile life since 1969. For someone like herself who coveted privacy, it amazed her how comfortable she felt spilling her guts.

And obviously the phenomenon of sharing was so new and strange, she'd completely monopolized the conversation. She expressed her condolences to Mrs. McCreigh on the loss of her brother and recalled the fun times she had at his home on the Jersey Shore. Then suddenly darkness descended. Gwendolyn Armonk McCreigh walked in with a puss that could have killed Boots.

"Are you the reporter from the *Informer*?"

"Yes, hello . . ." Shelby stood up to shake her hand. Was it just her imagination, or had the house gone from sunny and cheerful to black and ominous the minute Gwen entered?

"Good. Because here's a late-breaking story for you." She put two Ann Taylor shopping bags down and marched over to the window. "Your car is leaking oil all over our driveway, and I'm afraid the surface is damaged. We'll have to bill you or the paper for the repaving. Right, honey?"

"I'm sure if there's a problem, the paper will do the responsible thing." An embarrassed husband ran over to peck his wife's cheek.

Don't hold your breath, Shelby thought. "I'm very sorry," she said instead. "It must be why this red whatchamacallit light kept blinking on my way over here. Let me know what the damage is, and I'll . . ."

"Gwen, please," Matty interrupted. "I'm sure this isn't going to be a problem . . . Honey, there's something important I have to tell you. This is Shelby Lazarus."

"Yes, I know." Gwen removed a cigarette from a gold case in an end table drawer. "We spoke on the phone."

"The funny thing is, you never mentioned her name. You just said a reporter was coming over, and as it turns out, we go back a long time. We grew up together."

"Is that right?" Gwen took a long drag as she eyed Shelby's legs. "Nice to meet you. How long will this take?"

"Fifteen, twenty minutes tops?" Shelby smiled. No doubt the longest fifteen, twenty minutes of her life. What had Matty seen in this woman, aside from her beauty, prominence, and vast wealth?

"Fine, but no more than that. I need to get my roast in the oven." She addressed her husband. "Mummy and Daddy will be here at six for drinks, then Missy and Bink are joining us at seven."

And will Chip and Dip be here, too? Shelby wanted to howl. Instead, she found herself coughing from smoke inhalation. Did she dare ask the lady of the house to step outside?

Thankfully Matty came to the rescue. "Gwen, honey. Shelby just found out she's pregnant. I'm sure she doesn't want to be around smoke."

"Is that right?" Gwen eyed the other blonde's flat abs. "No problem." She extinguished the offending cigarette and narrowed her eyes. "Is she the one you named your dog after?"

"Yes," the elder Mrs. McCreigh said. "But you'd think if he was naming it after a bitch . . ."

"MOTHER!" Matty hollered. "Does it ever occur to you not to speak?"

"Sorry, darling." She patted his cheek. "Sometimes I forget my place. Old age and all. I think I'll go up and finish packing. Shelby, dear. Please don't go without saying good-bye."

"Of course." Shelby hugged her.

"Isn't it time to take her to the airport?" Gwen gritted.

"Soon." Matty shook his head in disbelief.

"Not soon enough," Gwen muttered as she settled into the floral chintz couch. "Could we please get started?"

"Of course." Shelby fetched her notebook and chose a burnished, red leather chair close enough to hear, but too far to be bitten. "So," she smiled, "how did you and Matty meet?"

"Matty?" Gwen raised an eyebrow. "That's rather adorable . . ."

Shelby blushed. Nothing like calling a grown man by his baby name.

"How we met is a great story, isn't it, honey?" He laughed nervously as he plopped himself down on the couch next to his wife.

"One of your favorites." Gwen sniffed.

"We were at Lincoln Center." He ignored his wife's indifference. "Gwenny had brought her mother to the ballet, and I had just moved to New York and was dragged there by an old college buddy whose girlfriend was performing. Anyway, it's intermission, and as usual, the line to the ladies' room is a mile long. But not the men's room. All of a sudden, Gwen decides to take matters into her own hands."

"Don't tell me?" Shelby impersonated a fascinated journalist.

"That's right." Matty grinned. "She was determined not to stand on ceremony *or* on line." He laughed at his own joke. "So in she walks, while I'm relieving myself. Now as you can imagine, I was caught off guard. I mean here's this beautiful young maiden and me, not exactly ready for company." He squeezed Gwen's arm as if this private moment was something special.

"And the rest, as they say, is history." Gwen looked out the window.

Matty nodded, still smiling from the recanting of the story. And how wonderful he looked, with his impish grin that begged you to love him, like an overgrown dog who still thought he was a puppy. Trouble was, Shelby stared too long at him, causing Gwen to move in closer. The signal he had permission to touch her.

Shelby kept a steady smile going when Matty placed his arm around his wife's narrow shoulder. "That really was a great story." She looked down at her notes. Get me out of here.

With her remaining time, Shelby lobbed softball questions, with the same predictable outcome. Matty's answers were animated and sincere. Gwen's repertoire included two different type of smirks and a groan. She spoke up only once.

"Do you know that man at your newspaper who does the horoscopes?"

"You mean Warner Lamm? Yes, I do."

"I like him." She nodded. "Does he do private readings?"

"Uh-huh. Although I understand it takes forever to get an appointment . . ."

"But you could get me in if you wanted. Isn't that right?" She sniffed.

"Why, Gwenny," Matty teased, "you'd actually go to someone like that?"

"Why not? You once did."

"Not that I can recall." His face reddened.

"Well, maybe he wasn't an astrologer exactly, but he was something."

"Do you mean that healer I went to in the city?"

"Yes, him."

"They're not the same thing," he gritted. "That man put an end to my back pain."

"Which was all in your head."

"I hardly think a flare-up of the sciatic nerve is something one imagines, darling."

Oh God. We even have back problems in common, Shelby thought. Maybe it's a sign. "Okay, how about I talk to Warner first thing Monday?" she said. "I'm sure he'd be delighted to read for you, Mrs. McCreigh. . . . Is there time for one last question?"

"Ask away," Matty appeared none too anxious to be alone with his wife.

Gwen looked at her watch.

"Forgive me, but I haven't even asked about your children?" Shelby prayed the marriage had never been consummated, let alone produced offspring.

"We have a daughter, Emily." Matty looked down. "She's turning six."

"I really must be getting my roast in the oven," Gwen said, storming off to the kitchen.

"I'm sorry," Shelby stood up. "Did I say something wrong?"

"No, of course not," Matty stood, too. "It's just . . . we're having a difficult time at the moment. Emily is . . . not well . . . she's in a home now . . ."

"Matty, I'm so sorry. I didn't know . . ."

"Will you excuse me for a minute?" He didn't wait for a reply and ran after his wife. "Mother, come back down, please. Keep Shelby company."

"It's okay. I'm fine." Shelby shooed him out. Poor man was so conflicted. Besides, she wanted time to scope out the room looking for pictures of Emily. But on her way to check out what looked like family photos on the mantel, she bumped into Gwen's shopping bags and discovered they were empty.

Shelby immediately put on her reporter's hat and began considering the different reasons a woman would want to give the appearance she'd just been to the mall. Unfortunately, even a cub reporter could put two and two together. The only reason to show up with nothing in the bags was so a husband, for instance, never suspected where his wife had really been. Or with whom.

"So, darling, tell me," the elder Mrs. McCreigh asked, startling her. "What do you think of all this?"

"Oh, it's incredible all right," Shelby laughed. And getting better every minute.

"Doesn't Matthew look marvelous?" the proud mother asked.

"Yes, he does."

"I mean not bad. Considering everything. I don't know how much he's told you."

"Nothing really," Shelby thought it best to let the remark pass. "Tell me. How is Wendy doing?"

"Fantastic!" Mrs. McCreigh clapped. "She married such a great guy. A surgeon! They have four beautiful children, a gorgeous home, she writes children's books in her spare time . . ."

"Wow! She must be really busy."

"It's crazy how she runs with them, to soccer, gymnastics, dance classes, music lessons. All I can say is, thank God I didn't have to wait around for that little *pisher* to open her legs." She nodded toward the kitchen. "Otherwise, I'd still be waiting for grandchildren."

Shelby nodded, but wasn't sure what to make of the comment. Matty had just said he and Gwen had a daughter, Emily. But better let that one pass, too. The mere mention of a child had caused Gwen to flee. She didn't want the elder Mrs. McCreigh to run away as well.

"You have no idea how long I tried to find your family." Shelby smiled wistfully. "I've looked everywhere. What happened to you guys? And what's with the alias?"

Mrs. McCreigh planted a juicy kiss on Shelby's cheek. "It's a very long story, dear, and not one I can discuss now. But I'll tell you this much. I haven't seen Matthew this happy since he was ten."

Chapter Twenty-four

Say what you would about the rich. Their walls were as thin as everyone else's. Either that, or Gwen had especially strong lungs. For even from inside the guest bathroom, Shelby could hear her carrying on in the kitchen. "I don't give a damn what kind of car trouble she's having! Let her call Triple A!"

"But that's not necessary, dear," Matthew argued. "I know the owner of the Lexus dealer in White Plains."

"No you don't! We've never owned a Lexus."

"I just know him, okay? And I know he'll be happy to help Shelby out."

"Oh, go to hell!" Gwen slammed a cabinet door. "I don't care what you do for your little girlfriend. Just make sure you're back in time to help me this evening."

His little girlfriend? Shelby giggled as she snuck out the front door and ran to her car to retrieve her cell phone and sunglasses. Hopefully, Matty wouldn't realize she'd overheard their arguing. But she would definitely tell him how much she appreciated his help in arranging for her car to be towed and serviced.

Even better was his generous offer to drive her back to Long Island after they dropped off his mother. Finally, she would get the chance to probe what surely would be the most important investigative story of her life. Where Matty Lieberman had been hiding all these years, and how he ended up married to Wifey Dearest.

Unfortunately, the ride to the airport was not the gabfest Shelby expected, as once the shock of being reunited wore off, reality set in. Who among them was not thinking about the staggering implications of Matty and Shelby seeing each other again? No wonder conversation was limited to awkward small talk, lodged in between long silences.

But when Shelby realized they were driving over the Whitestone Bridge, the very place where only a few hours earlier she'd had her meltdown, she had to say something. "Would anyone like to hear about my day?"

"Love to," Matty replied immediately.

"Okay then. Let's see." She cleared her throat. "I started out the morning at the hospital where the head orthopedic surgeon told me the pins he put in my dad's hip aren't doing the trick, and now he's probably going to need a whole hip replacement. Then my aunt Roz's plastic surgeon told me her face isn't healing as well as he had hoped, and he may have no choice other than to do a procedure that's even more painful than skin grafts.

"From there I attended a workshop for surrogate mothers, which I thought would be helpful. But instead of hearing all kinds of warm and fuzzy stories about families living happily ever after thanks to their hero surrogates, all they talked about were the horror stories. Girls who took the money and ran. Parents who refused to take babies with birth defects. Lawyers who botched the adoption proceedings. Fertility clinics that botched the inseminations. All I can say is Lauren is damn lucky I didn't register for this class before I got pregnant.

"Then after the workshop, I drove into the city to pick up a file at the *Informer* that was left there for me, coincidentally, by my good friend, Warner Lamm. The file contains information on a rare planetary occurrence, something called a void-of-course moon, which may have been in a rare conjunction with Venus retrograde on the weekend of May 25, 1988."

"Whoa," Matty laughed. "I didn't understand a word of that."

"Me either."

"Well, what does it mean? Is it good or bad?"

"I'll let you know as soon as I read the file. Anyway, from the city I drove to your house, and just as I was crossing this very bridge, Lauren called to say not only had her husband left her, but the baby I'm carrying for them is probably not one, but two.

"Then a few minutes after that, I see this familiar face drive by in a Range Rover, and the rest you know."

"That's not a day, it's a miniseries." Matty turned to her. "I can't believe how well you're holding up under all this pressure."

Mrs. McCreigh piped up from the backseat. "Well, if you ask me, the thing I can't believe is that Roz and your father are still together."

"Nobody asked you," Matty snapped.

"It's okay." Shelby laughed. "I didn't give it more than a year myself, but actually they're good together. The thing is, how did you know they got married? You had already moved."

"Are you kidding? I stayed in touch with Bobbie Bernstein and didn't miss a thing. I knew the Gelfmans' split up, that Jack Stein died and left everything to his secretary, Lester Greenberg lost his shirt in the market . . ."

"We get the picture." he groaned.

"Anyway," Mrs. McCreigh continued, "after Roz moved in with you, it didn't take a genius to figure out her game plan. I had my money on her the whole time."

"Enough!" Matty glared at her through the rearview mirror. "I'd really appreciate it if you kept your opinions to yourself."

"Why should I?" She laughed. "People like to know the truth. Right, Shelby?"

"Absolutely." She looked over at Matty, who was rolling his eyes. But to Shelby the familiar banter was magical and healing. How reassuring it was to feel the same intense connection to these people, in spite of the unfortunate, thirty-year gulf that had separated them.

"Go back to the part about you and these babies." Matty looked straight ahead. "They're biologically yours, but you're giving them back to Lauren?"

"The minute they're born."

"Won't that be hard?" he asked. "It's a pretty emotional time."

"Maybe. But the way I feel at the moment, I'll probably get off the delivery table and do a little dance in the end zone."

"That's what I would do if a certain couple split up," Mrs. McCreigh mumbled.

Shelby tried hard not to snicker.

"Mother, what is wrong with you?"

"What? Your marriage is your business, dear. I stopped trying to figure it out years ago."

"Why do I even bother?" Matty gripped the steering wheel.

"So Shelby. Let's hear more about you, darling. Are you married?"

"Oh my God, Mother. I'm pulling over."

"I'm okay," Shelby whispered. "Relax . . . No, I'm still single."

"Seeing anyone seriously?"

"Not anymore."

"You're killing me, you know that? Please stop interrogating her."

"Oh please," Mrs. McCreigh waved. "You know you're dying to know, too. So where do you live, dear? I'll bet you have a great apartment in the city."

"As a matter of fact I do, only it's not in New York. Until the accident, I was living in Chicago, working for the *Tribune* as a columnist."

"That sounds marvelous. I always knew you'd be a big success. So do you plan to move back after you have the babies?"

"I can't let you do this." Matty turned around. "This is none of our business."

Shelby laughed. "You would have made a hell of a reporter, Mrs. Lieber . . . McCreigh. Sorry. It's really hard calling you by a different name."

"That's nothing! Try answering to a different name," she replied. "Tell you what. You're old enough to vote. Call me Carol."

"Okay. Carol. Anyway, the answer to your question is I have no idea what I'll do when this is over. After everything that's happened to me, I've come to the conclusion that it's pointless to worry about the future because what's supposed to happen, will, whether you want it to or not. It's like my grandmother used to say at funerals. 'Man makes plans and God laughs.' "

"I say that all the time, too." Matty nodded.

"Well it's true," Shelby said. "I mean I always imagined you'd be living in Vermont or Maine, with a sweet little wife, a bunch of kids and dogs, and a Ph.D. in comparative literature."

"And I always imagined you'd be living on Park Avenue with a Wall Street guy, beautiful children, a nanny, and a house in the Hamptons."

Carol coughed. "And I always imagined you two would be together."

By the time they arrived at La Guardia, Shelby's racing heart was overcome by two important needs. She had to pee and then speak to Lauren, as they hadn't talked since that frantic phone call this morning. She guessed their conversation would be a long one, unless Lauren had raided the designer pills in her medicine chest and was passed out on the bathroom floor.

In anticipation of a stressful call, Shelby said her good-byes to Carol, hit the ladies' room, and returned to the car to make the call. Never did she expect to hear a cheerful voice on the line.

"Hi. Where are you?" Lauren asked.

"You wouldn't believe it if I told you, so let's deal with you first. How are you doing?"

"Fine."

"No, c'mon. Really."

"I mean it. I'm okay. In fact I don't have much time to talk, because do you remember Andrea Horowitz, the girl who was on my first Israel trip?"

"Not exactly."

"Doesn't matter. Avi and I went out with her and her husband a few times, but then they split up. Anyway, she's divorced now, two kids, the whole bit, and I called her a little while ago to commiserate, and she happened to mention that she was going to a singles dance at the Temple tonight, and said I should go with her. So I said okay, and now she's picking me up in a few minutes so we can go shopping for something nice to wear, and . . ."

"Whoa! Hold on," Shelby exploded. "A few hours ago you were suicidal because your husband left you, and now you're going to Bloomingdale's so you can look hot at a singles dance?"

"Don't say it like that."

"But you're not single, Lauren! I'm sure Avi will be back once he comes to his senses."

"Maybe. But just in case . . . I mean what do you expect me to do? Sit around waiting for him to decide what he wants to do with his life?"

"Yes, actually. And correct me if I'm wrong, but in six short months, you'll be the proud mother of twins. So even if you're shopping for husband number three by then, you're going to have to inform the lucky guy you're coming to the party with Ike and Mike."

"Whatever."

"No. Not 'whatever,'" Shelby mimicked the attitude. "I'm sure Avi realized he made a huge mistake and is on his way back. How would it look if you didn't even wait a day before you started dating?"

"He's not coming back," Lauren said.

"How do you know?"

"Because I spoke to his mother in Israel, and she told me that he called her three weeks ago to say he was coming home. And that whole business with his cousin and the rock band? It was a lie, so I'd think he was leaving to follow his dream, or something like that."

"Uh-huh."

"But don't worry about the babies, Shel. I still want them. More than you could possibly know. And I already spoke to Mommy and Daddy, and they're behind us one hundred percent. And I also called the divorce attorney I used for me and Allen."

"Did he offer you a frequency discount?"

"Why are you being like this, Shel? I have to do what I have to do."

"Me too."

"What does that mean?"

"I don't know."

"You're spooking me out. You aren't thinking . . . you wouldn't go and . . . oh my God. Promise me right now you're not going to have an abortion."

"Don't be ridiculous. Things are working out exactly as I hoped. I got pregnant with twins. Avi ran away. We're both single. Now we get to divvy up the litter. I've got dibs if one's a girl."

From that point, the conversation went downhill, and Shelby found herself so incensed by Lauren's cavalier attitude, that it only occurred to her after they hung up that she'd never even told her about finding Matty Lieberman. But when she redialed, the answering machine picked up. Once again Lauren was off and running in the singles' race. Gentlemen, start your party engines.

Shelby leaned back into the headrest and was about to close her eyes when she spotted Matty sprinting to the car holding a bouquet of flowers. To hell with Lauren. She was about to be alone with her long-lost love, and the sexual attraction to him was overpowering. If she could just have an hour to lie on top of this man, she'd die happy.

"These are for you," he said, sliding into his seat and handing her the flowers.

"Thank you." She looked down at the wilted mess that had probably been laying dormant in an airport refrigerator since last week. "You shouldn't have."

"I didn't." He sighed. "They're from you-know-who. I tend to go for the arrangements that cost more than seven dollars."

Shelby laughed. "Now, now. It's the thought . . ."

"Do you want to know what she really said?" he asked.

"I'm not sure. Do I?"

"I'll tell you anyway. She said 'remember to use a condom. Who knows where she's been'?"

"Get out of here!" Shelby clapped. "She said that?"

"I swear to you those were her exact words."

"She's even more of a pisser than I remember." Shelby wiped her eye. "Why would she even think something like that? You're a married man."

"And you're a pregnant woman." He sighed. "It's amazing. I know this woman my entire life, and she still floors me with the ridiculous things that come out of her mouth."

"Yes, but her heart's in the right place." Shelby patted his warm hand.

"Do you . . . are you in a hurry to get back?" he cocked his head.

"Actually, no. I just spoke to Lauren, and she's doing much better than I expected. But isn't Gwen expecting you home to help her?"

"It's okay. My wife is the Martha Stewart of entertaining. The only job she thinks I can handle is filling the ice buckets, and by now I have it down to a science. It's all in the wrists."

Shelby giggled. Could Matty be any more adorable? "What did you have in mind?" The back of the car, or a hotel in midtown Manhattan? Please?

"How would you feel about heading into the city?"

"Sounds great." I hear Le Meridian has day rates.

"I like the Roof Garden at the Metropolitan Museum of Art. Have you been there?"

"No." Damn! His mind wasn't in the gutter like hers.

"C'mon then. The view of Central Park is great, and we can catch up on old times. Wait until you hear my life's story. I promise you'll be glued to your seat."

"Believe me. I already am."

See how a little car trouble can make a big difference when you're try-ing to jump-start a relationship? If all that oil hadn't dripped out on to the driveway, Shelby would have had to say her good-byes at the house and not had a good reason to see Matty again.

Am I getting good at this, or what?

Matty might have been right about the view from the Roof Garden at the Met being spectacular, but Shelby could have been atop Mt. Everest and not looked out. For her gaze was fixed on her subject, her thoughts focused on his heartening story. Even the cackling of mingling singles could not divert her attention.

Abby Rosenthal had been right, too. The reason Shelby was unable to locate her childhood friend was because his mother remarried, and her new husband adopted her children. From that day forward, Matthew Jay Lieberman ceased to exist by that name.

"Remember how my parents fought constantly?" he sipped his Dubonnet on the rocks.

Shelby nodded. Who could forget the constant shouting coming from the Liebermans' house? She even recalled the time her father ran over in his bathrobe in the middle of the night to beg Ed and Carol to give it a rest. Things quieted down for a while, but eventually the familiar echo of yelling and car doors slamming returned.

"Believe it or not, things got worse after we moved. My dad went to work for this Hollywood talent agency, and it was so cutthroat, they canned him after three months.

"It was pretty bad. We were totally broke from the move, my mother was homesick, Wendy was just a baby and very fussy, and I was this lost soul who didn't have a clue what had happened to my nice little world. I'd sit in my room and cry, which really got my dad crazy.

"I guess it was about a year later he split. He met some woman at a bar who had a few bucks from a lawsuit, and it was as if we never existed. That was hell. We couldn't afford to keep the house, my mother couldn't get a decent job because she had no one to watch Wendy . . . She'd just asked her parents if we could come back to live with them in New York, when a cousin of hers from Portland called to say we could stay with her until we got back on our feet.

"And that's what we did. We sold the house in like two weeks, packed up the car, and it was Portland or bust."

"Whatever happened to your dad?" Shelby asked.

"Never saw him again." he shrugged. "Although I found out

later he'd tried tracking us down. But by then my mom was already remarried, and would have told him to drop dead . . . which is exactly what he did.

"One night we got a call from his brother saying he had liver cancer, and had died in some seedy boardinghouse in a bad part of L.A. Can you believe it? My father? A drunken bum, penniless, dead at forty-six?"

"Unbelievable," Shelby said, although the news of his early demise didn't surprise her. She'd never liked Matty's dad. He was either cranky or sleeping, and way too quick with the slapping hand. How many times had Matty come over with the imprint still on his face?

"But your mom got remarried. So were things okay after that?"

"I wish . . . Husband number two was another real prize, a Mr. Philip 'Deke' McCreigh. Portland's own Donald Trump. Part confirmed bachelor, part real estate tycoon."

"His name was Deke?" Shelby raised her eyebrow.

"What can I say? It was the Wild West. His brother was Pike, and his dad was Dodger. Every one had good-old-boy names."

"Really? What was yours?" Shelby sipped her sparkling water and lime.

"Do you promise not to tell another living soul?" Matty looked around.

"Scout's honor."

"Guzzler."

"Guzzler?"

"Don't make fun. I thought it was rather distinguished compared to everyone else's."

"Was there any particular significance to the name, or did you pick it out of a hat during sing-along time on a camping trip?"

"Touché." He wagged his finger. "The name *was* given to me on a camping trip. But it was because I guzzled all the water out of everyone's canteens."

"Hey, you used to do that to me, too! You'd say, 'Look at the birdie,' then steal my cherry Kool-Aid."

"Only because my mother would never buy that stuff. She was afraid we were all going to die from red dye number two. Remember? Anyway, after we moved to Portland, my mother answered a help wanted ad, and the guy who hired her was Deke. He needed a secretary, she needed a man. He liked her dancer's legs, she liked his money. Six months later they got married, and for my thirteenth birthday, I got a stepdad and a bike."

"That sounds wonderful. I mean especially after what you'd already been through."

"Yeah, well, looks can be deceiving. I hated the son of a bitch. He drank a lot, and he was never around. But my mother didn't care. She had money, prestige, and every year he'd buy her a new car so she could pull up to garden club meetings looking prosperous."

"And I take it he eventually adopted you?" Shelby couldn't help sounding like a reporter.

Matty nodded. "About a year after they got married, she convinced him it would look more proper if he took legal responsibility for us. And he was really big on looking proper."

"And, that's when you became Matthew J. McCreigh."

"Yes."

"I can't even imagine how strange that must have been. To suddenly have this whole new identity, almost like you were in the witness protection program."

"Tell me about it. But the strangest part about it was the deal he struck with us. He would only agree to adopt us if we agreed to stop being Jewish."

"What did he expect you to do? Stop eating bagels?"

"Yes, and stop going to temple. And forget about having a Bar Mitzvah. Oh, and we also had to promise never to mention anything about the Jewish holidays or customs. Instead we became Sunday churchgoers so Deke could show us off to all the fine, upstanding, Christian neighbors who had started a whisper campaign about the money-grubbing Jew from New York who conned good old Deke into adopting her kids."

"Matty, it sounds surreal. You must have been miserable."

"If it weren't for a couple of great friends I made in high school, and their families, I don't know what would have become of me. I practically lived at their houses."

"What happened after that?"

He stirred the last of his iced-down drink and chugged it. Several times he started to speak but held back. "It's hard. This part is hard."

Shelby reached across the table and squeezed his hand.

"I got into Brown you know."

"Yes, I read that in your engagement announcement."

"I can't remember. Did it also happen to say I was class valedictorian, or that I was an all-state track and tennis star?"

"No."

"Did it say the summer I graduated high school, I found good old Deke in bed with the young man who lived in the house across the street, who was on summer break from USC?"

"No . . ."

"Did it say the following morning, my mother found Deke floating at the bottom of our pool with a self-inflicted bullet wound to his neck?"

"Oh my God!"

"I didn't think so," he gulped the rest of his drink. "That sort of thing tends to mess up perfectly nice engagement announcements."

"I can't believe what you're telling me." Shelby covered her mouth. "You poor thing."

"No, please. Don't pity me. Somehow my mom stayed strong during the whole thing and never let Wendy or me fall apart. She put us right into therapy . . . bought a house in one of the suburbs where no one knew us . . . she kept saying, 'It's not your fault, kids. You did nothing wrong.' Which was exactly what we needed to hear."

"Thank God she did all the right things."

"I know better than anyone what a royal pain in the ass my mother can be, but believe me I am grateful that she was such a tough old bird. Wendy did great in school, I graduated with honors from Brown, went on to Wharton for my MBA. Then, listen to this. At my graduation, she hands me a check for $250,000 and says it's combat pay because it came from the proceeds of Deke's life insurance. She'd been saving it so I could start my own business, which I did. And today I run a very successful educational software company that's about to go public."

"Wow!" Shelby clutched her heart. "That's quite a story."

Matty smiled. "A real movie-of-the-week, right?"

"Starring Carol Burnett as your mother."

"Perfect casting." He nodded. "Another tall redhead whose name is Carol."

After an awkward silence, Shelby was about to bring up the subject of Gwen when Matty's cell phone rang. The cold reality check they weren't in Casablanca anymore. And proof his wife had these uncanny instincts about when her husband was becoming infatuated with another woman.

He excused himself, leaving Shelby to ponder the enormity of the intimate moment they'd just shared. And pray that something would dare come of it.

"Hey." Matty returned a few minutes later, his boyish grin erased.

"Let me guess. Gwen wanted to know why you're not back yet."

"Yes," he said. "We've got company coming."

"Right. Mummy and Daddy and Chippy and Dippy and Pluto and Goofy . . ."

"Be nice. My in-laws are nice enough people."

"I'm sorry. Of course they are." Shelby sighed. Why wasn't he sitting down? She felt like a character in a twisted version of *Cinderella*. When the clock struck twelve, the dutiful prince returned to his kingdom, where sadly he lived out his life with the wrong maiden.

"It's later than I thought." He looked at his watch. "Do you think . . . I really hate to ask you this. But would it be possible for you to take the train home?"

"The train?" Shelby felt as if she'd just taken a kick in the gut. "Sure. No problem." How could he could even think of leaving her in her fragile state to fend for herself in the big, bad apple? Never mind that she grew up here, too, and knew every inch of the city.

"You sure you don't mind?" He looked at his watch again.

Of course I mind, but obviously that's not going to matter. "It's fine." Shelby tried to choke back tears. That was some Svengali-like hold Gwen had on him. One phone call, and his entire demeanor changed.

"It was great seeing you, Shelby." He bent down to embrace her. "I'll never forget this day."

"Wait. So, that's it? We'll try running into each other every thirty years, give or take?"

Matty pushed the bangs from her face. "My life is so complicated. I can't even begin to explain my commitments, my obligations . . ."

"I understand. But how can you just disappear into the sunset? Don't you want to see me again? E-mail me? Wait. At least let me write down my screen name." She scribbled that and her cellphone number on a napkin.

He reached into his breast pocket. "Good idea. Here's my card. Definitely keep in touch, and please tell your dad and Roz I wish them well. Oh and Lauren, too."

Shelby reached for Matty's hand and looked him straight in the eye. "Do you love her?"

He hesitated. "Yes."

"Okay. Then I guess that's all I need to know. It's not for me to question."

But of course it was exactly what she was doing. Questioning what kind of merciful God would have her reunite with the one person with whom she could spend the rest of her life, only to learn he was married with a sick child? And what the hell did Warner Lamm know about anything? There wasn't going to be any love in the air!

"I love her. It's living with her that's a problem." Matty sat down again. "We went through a trial separation last year, then decided to give it another try. For Emily's sake."

"I may be going out on a limb here," Shelby blurted, "but how can you be so sure she's as totally committed to the marriage as you are?"

"Excuse me?"

"The shopping bags Gwen walked in with before. They were empty. That's a sign, Matty. When women don't want their husbands to know where they've been, they make it look like they've just come from the mall." Somebody had to open his eyes, and it might as well be her.

"That's what you think?" he asked. "You spent maybe fifteen minutes with my wife and made assumptions about her based on the fact she had nothing in her shopping bags?"

"That, and the way she treats you . . ."

"Don't go there." Matty closed his eyes. "I know where Gwen was this morning. She drove out to Connecticut to visit our daughter at the home we had to place her in a few months ago. Emily was born with Down's syndrome. She's severely retarded, has limited mobility, and now a degenerative heart condition. We couldn't care for her at home anymore. Gwen always bakes muffins and cookies to bring to her and the other children, and she likes to use the big store bag because they hold a lot. That's why they were empty."

"Oh my God." Shelby's jaw dropped. "I'm sorry. I feel so stupid."

"It's okay." He patted her hand. "I know you still love me like a sister. You thought you were looking out for my best interests."

A sister? That's how he thought of her? She might as well find a razor blade and her biggest artery.

"But now . . . seeing you again," he started.

Hold the razor blade.

"This is such a confusing time in my life.."

"Matty, stop. I feel as though I've spent *my* entire life looking for you, hoping to resume where we left off. Hoping the love we felt as children would somehow endure. But you have a wife and a child, and I'm finally going to have to accept the fact that we were not meant to be together."

Matty bent over to kiss Shelby firmly on the lips, and the electrical impulses that surged through her body nearly melted what little resistance she had left. She kissed him back so passionately, the blood rushed to her face and her panties felt moist. When they finally separated, she was breathless and limp. "Why did you do that?" she cried.

"I'm sorry. I just had to know."

"Know what? That I still love you? That I've always loved you? That not a day has gone by that I didn't think of you and wonder where you were?"

"All of the above." He cupped her face in his warm hands.

"That was too good. It's just not fair!" She sobbed into his chest. "I've never found anyone else I cared for as much as you . . ."

"Shhh." He held her tightly.

"What are we going to do?" Shelby looked in his eyes.

"I don't know."

"Why not?"

"Shelby, if you're asking me would I love to run away with you and live happily ever after, the answer is yes. But if you're asking me if I will . . . the answer is no. Nothing in my life has ever worked out the way I hoped or planned, but it's still my life. I'm just playing the cards I was dealt."

"But if you stay in a bad marriage, it only makes you a martyr."

"Please don't judge me, Shelby. You have no idea what I have to endure every day just to get by. And believe me, my daughter doesn't think of me as a martyr. To her I'm a hero. I would never do anything to sacrifice her happiness or well-being."

"I can understand that. But what about Gwen?"

"Are you asking why I stay in a marriage that's not perfect?"

"I guess."

"Do you know any couple that doesn't have issues? And it's not like I haven't thought about walking out the door. But I'm not a quitter, Shelby. I mean if I learned anything from my childhood, it's that you have to tough things out. That's why I work hard every day. I try to stay focused on all the positives in my life . . . Maybe you think I'm being a fool. I think I'm doing right by my family, just like my mother did when her life was so difficult. It's called survival."

"Okay. I hear you." Shelby took a deep breath and reached under the table for her pocketbook. "But I have to be honest, too. I'm dying a thousand deaths here, and I can't pretend to be some old friend from the neighborhood who thought it would be fun to have a drink and reminisce."

"Shelby, please don't leave angry." Matty reached for her hand.

"I'm not angry. I'm grieving. And frankly, I'm sorry this ever happened today."

"Now you're breaking my heart. I'm not sorry at all. In fact I feel really lucky that we found each other again. There's no reason we can't be friends."

FRIENDS? Shelby couldn't listen to another word, and ran back into the museum to take the nearest elevator down. A torrent of tears unleashed the minute the doors closed. All he wanted was to be friends? No way. He had to have the same intense feelings for her as she did for him because that kiss could have melted a nun.

Sorry, Matty. Friends is not an option for us. You'll have to do better than that.

Chapter Twenty-five

Never before had Shelby felt a need to pour her heart out to someone. Anyone. Pity the relationship cupboard was bare. Maria was off, Lauren was busy testing her single's wings, and she dared not call the hospital. If her father and Aunt Roz knew she was home with nothing to do, they'd insist on her joining them for a game of bridge with the Markowitzes.

Instead, Shelby crawled into bed, continued her crying jag, and tried to fall sleep without the aid of a Sominex. Now that she was pregnant, every decent drug was *verboten*. Good Lord. Was there any aspect of her life that hadn't undergone a drastic change or been mired by chaos?

And yet, even she had to admit that she didn't regret the events that had unfolded since the accident. If she hadn't flown home that day, she never would have run into Ian, never gone to work for him, and certainly never gotten the assignment that ultimately delivered her to Matty's door.

Wasn't this what Warner had been telling her all along? Not only did everything happen for a reason, there was always a pre-ordained timetable. Timing was everything, indeed. But did that mean she believed in this whole void-of-course moon business?

Shelby flicked on the light to look for the file Warner had left for her at the office. With everything else that had gone on today, she'd forgotten to read his report. Now nothing was more important than finding out if Matthew and Gwen exchanged vows on a marital doomsday. Ha! They might have thought theirs was a match made in heaven, but only if Venus wasn't retrograde.

Shelby sank into the recliner and began to read Warner's notes. Talk about nearly falling off your rocker. Her initial hunch had been right. May 25, the day that the McCreighs and all those other unsuspecting couples got married, was astrologically doomed. The moon was void-of-course, making it the worst possible time to commit, buy, or start any venture. Then Saturn was squaring Venus, which meant the house of partnerships was in turmoil. Plus, 1988 was a two year for the universe, which always signified a big surge in the divorce rate.

Shelby laughed. How little of this she really understood. Sextiles, conjunctions, squares, trines, contraparallels. Warner's world sounded more like a geometry class than an explanation of the cosmos. But after reviewing his notes, there was one thing she was sure of. No matter how vehemently Matty insisted his marriage would succeed, there were much greater forces at work.

Did this mean she was starting to believe in astrology? Yes, and furthermore, when she was feeling depressed, the best therapy for her was to write. What an idea! She would turn Ian's ridiculous wedding piece into an edgy story for singles on how to pick the best day to say "I do."

"I do." The two saddest words in the world for Shelby, not counting "if only."

Well I'll be. I think that ringing I hear is the sound of Shelby's wake-up call. I just hope she doesn't confuse it with the one at the Ritz where she rolls over, then goes back to sleep.

Warner loved the idea of Shelby turning the story into an Astrology 101 crash course on how to choose the right wedding date. He was tickled by the fact she asked him to share a byline and help her rewrite the piece. He was not thrilled, however, to discuss this matter at eight o'clock on a Sunday morning.

"Good God, Shelby." He yawned. "Have you any idea what time it is?"

"Yes, but you said you were an early bird. That you start your day at five."

"On workdays, darling. On weekends little Warner parties his tushy off till five, then goes nighty-night with the lucky winner."

"Oops. Sorry." She cringed at the idea of a naked Warner in the arms of a willowy young boy from Iowa. "How about I call you back later?"

"How about we discuss this at the office tomorrow?"

"You're the expert on timing," she replied. "Warner?"

"Yes?"

"You were right, you know," Shelby blurted.

"About what?"

"Basically everything."

"You give me too much credit, dear. I don't write the script, I'm just the first to read it."

It was one thing for Warner to blow her off. It was quite another for her own father to do it. "Daddy, why aren't you answering me? Didn't you hear a word I said?" Shelby nudged his arm.

"Maybe you should come back." He turned over and winced. "Today's not a good day."

"How can you tell?" Shelby checked her watch. "It's not even nine o'clock."

"Believe me it doesn't matter. A.M., P.M. Yesterday, today, tomorrow. It's all the same to me. So excuse me if I'm not paying attention to your sad tale. At least when you're finished moaning and groaning, you can get up and walk out of this place."

Shelby nodded. The doctors had warned her about accident victims who survived the accident, but not the depression that followed. They warned her to expect difficult, moody periods, when loved ones would insist they couldn't go on another day. And she had well expected that sort of thing from Aunt Roz, the *kvetch*.

But never from her indomitable, high-spirited father. A man who never saw a tee time he didn't like. A man who wasn't happy unless he was entertaining a houseful of people. Before the accident, anyway. Now, life as he knew it was over, and his recovery slow and painful. Could she honestly blame him for wallowing in self-pity and not wanting to listen to her carry on about all the injustices in her life?

"Sorry, Daddy. I'm sure my problems seem trivial compared to yours."

"You got that right."

"But what am I going to do about the babies?"

"What's to do? Avi's leaving changes nothing. Lauren will have to do this on her own."

"Oh, please. She can't even buy bagels on her own. First she has to ask everyone in the store their opinion." Shelby mimicked, " 'Which do you think looks better? The pumpernickel rye or cinnamon raisin?' She's like a fifteen-year-old in a thirty-year-old's body! No way is she ready to be a single mom."

"Fine. You're such a big shot. You keep them."

"Oh, no, no, no. My gig is up at the end of nine months . . ."

"Enough already with the foolishness, Shelby! What do you want me to say? Go have an abortion now that Avi's gone? To hell with him! Life is precious, and you don't go spitting in God's eye, especially after what your mother and I have been through! You should be grateful you've been given a chance to create life and add to our beautiful family."

Shelby sat quietly, contemplating her father's compelling words when in walked the culprit.

"Hey, Shel. What are you doing here so early?"

"I needed to talk to Daddy about a few things."

"Me too." Lauren nodded.

"*Oy gutenu.*" Daddy grimaced when he tried turning the other way. "Another country that thinks their world is ending. Why don't you girls go bother your mother?"

"What's with him?" Lauren asked.

"He's having a bad day. Did you hear from Avi?"

"Yes."

"And?" Shelby motioned with her hands. "What did he say?"

"He said he's really sorry about everything, that it didn't work out the way he expected, and he wishes me the best of luck, and could I please send him the sheet music he left in the closet?"

"That little shit. When's the bonfire?"

"Shel-bee," Lauren whined. "I'm not going to burn his music. He didn't mean to hurt me."

"No, of course not. It's obvious you're his first concern."

"Can we not talk about this now?" Lauren pointed at their father. "Things are bad enough."

"Sure. No problem. I was just mildly curious how you plan to raise these babies by yourself. But we have plenty of time to discuss that. So! Where the hell were you last night?"

"I told you. I went to that dance at the temple."

"Until three in the morning?"

Lauren blushed. "No, but I met someone, and we stayed up all night talking."

"*Oy!* Here we go again," her father muttered into his pillow. "God give me the strength."

"How late did you try calling?" Lauren ignored him.

"Until I finally conked out. I guess it was about three-thirty, four o'clock."

Lauren looked sympathetic. "What kept you up?"

"Oh, the usual. I'm pregnant with my sister's twins, but her husband abandoned her, but that's okay because she's already on to the next guy, Lord knows what a psycho this one is. Also, I finally found Matty Lieberman, on the Hutch Parkway of all places, then had the privilege to meet his lovely bride of Frankenstein, who happens to be Lieutenant Governor Armonk's daughter . . ."

"What?" Lauren cried out. "Oh, God! Tell me everything."

"You have to call him," Lauren pleaded after hearing the whole, bloody story.

"Why? What's the point? Did you call Avi and beg him to come back?"

"No." She bit her lip. "But your situation is completely different."

"How?"

"Because Matty really loves you, Shel. I'm sure of it."

"You don't know that."

"Yes, but you said the way he kissed you . . ."

"Oh, please. It was just a male ego thing. You know how they like to try to get you hot before they dump you."

"Girls, please," their father yelled. "I'm trying to get some rest."

"You don't believe that for a minute." Lauren continued to ignore him.

"I don't know what I believe. All I know is, right now I feel like I'm dying."

"Join the crowd!" he cried out.

"Hey. I've got an idea!" Lauren clapped. "Call him to ask about the car. That's a legitimate reason. You just want to know when the guy is bringing it back."

"Good thinking. That's not at all transparent. Hi. Remember me? You broke my heart yesterday? But forget about that. I just wanted to know if you heard from the Lexus dealer."

"So, come up with a different reason. It doesn't matter what. Just as long as you get to talk to him and tell him how you feel."

"He knows how I feel. That's what he's so afraid of."

"Maybe he just needs time, Shel. The poor guy was in shock."

"Hey, I was in shock, too, but that didn't cloud my feelings. He's the one I want!"

"I know what you mean." Lauren sighed. "I've been there."

"Several times," their father interrupted.

"Daddy, stop!" Lauren cried. "I'm trying to help Shelby with her problems."

"How about helping me with mine by getting the hell out of here. Go visit your mother."

"In a sec," Lauren replied. "So what are you going to do?"

"I don't know. My head is spinning, I'm depressed, I feel sick to my stomach . . ."

"Maybe this is good, Shel. I mean accepting the fact you finally found him, but he's not available. Now you can move on. Meet someone better. Like I just did."

"There is no one better," Shelby cried. "And shouldn't you at least wait until the body is cold before you get involved again?"

"I didn't plan it, Shel. It just happened."

"Why do people always say that? It sounds so stupid."

"But it's true. See, I was hanging around with Andrea and her friends, when I noticed this very cute guy staring at me. So I sort of waved, and he smiled, then I smiled . . ."

"I get the picture."

"Okay, so anyway, we got to talking, and it turns out we knew each other from high school. Do you remember Mark Siegel?"

"Sure. Pencil Pocket Boy. We were on the debate team together. That's who you met?"

"No, his younger brother, Danny. We were in the same home room in tenth grade, which I didn't remember, but then he confessed that's when he had this major crush on me."

"How romantic. What did that get him to? First base? Second base? A home run?"

"Shel-bee, stop. He's a very nice guy. He didn't lay a hand on me."

"GET OUT RIGHT NOW, BOTH OF YOU! AND DON'T COME BACK UNTIL YOU'RE BOTH MARRIED FOR AT LEAST TEN YEARS!"

Shelby and Lauren ran out the door. Even in his immobile state, he could still scare them.

"Man, is he ever grouchy!" Lauren closed his door.

"I know." Shelby shrugged. "I wonder if they gave him a new medication or something. So what's the story with this guy? Is he single, divorced . . ."

"Neither. He's a widower."

"Really? Isn't he sort of young for that?"

"Even younger than Daddy was when Mommy died."

"You know you're right?" Shelby nodded. "Here I'm thinking it's so rare . . . Was it cancer?"

Lauren shook her head. "Anorexia. She starved herself to death."

"Well, now there's something he wouldn't have to worry about with you."

"Shel-bee!"

"I'm sorry. I'm really, truly sorry. It just slipped out."

"I don't care. How could you say something so mean? I have feelings, you know. And this poor man was left with a two-year-old son, thousands of dollars in medical bills . . ."

"You're right. That was an awful thing to say. He's obviously suffered, and my heart goes out to him. So, you two really hit it off?"

"Yes. After the dance, we spent the whole night talking at his house."

"So that's where you were? I kept calling you to tell you what happened to me."

"I couldn't believe it when I looked at the clock, and it was five in the morning."

"So how much did you tell him about yourself?"

"The whole story. Starting from Allen, then Avi, the DES stuff, you, the babies . . ."

"You told him your husband left you and you're having twins, and he still didn't bolt?"

"He's a really great guy, Shel. He said he understood better than anyone how your life could fall apart in a heartbeat, and he really admired me because I wasn't sitting home dwelling on the negative."

"Okay, so either he's had loads of therapy, or he's in the business."

"Both, actually. He's a child psychologist."

"A noble profession, and there's always lollipops around. So now what?"

"I don't know. I guess we'll take it nice and slow. He's very protective of who he introduces to Jordan, and I've got a long legal road ahead of me. But I really like him, Shel. And as crazy as it sounds, I think we could really be good together."

"You know a man a total of twelve hours, decide you've got a great future, and this is taking it nice and slow?"

"Let's just say I'm taking it about as slow as you would if Matty called tonight, and said, 'Let's run away and get married.' "

"I'll shut up now." Shelby blushed.

"I like it," Ian announced, after he finished reading Shelby's revised draft of the wedding piece. "I do. It's pithy and fun. Say nothing of informative. Excellent job, my friend. I knew you'd deliver for Uncle Ian."

"Thank you," Shelby beamed. "I know it's not what we set out to write, but Warner fans are going to go crazy for it."

"So will the kids in sales. They can market a whole bridal advertising section around this."

"Not so fast, Uncle Ian." Shelby removed the pages from his hand. "Remember our deal? This was a two-for-one special. You have to approve my DES piece before I turn over my pithy little story to you."

"My dear, naive Shelby. Are you blackmailing me?"

"Of course not. I'm just telling you I've spent hundreds of hours on an extremely important investigation that uncovered . . ."

"Sob story after bloody sob story," Ian finished. "Especially the one about that poor woman who bled to death because the doctor misread her ultrasound and didn't know the embryo was lodged in her fallopian tube. Dear God, is that what you want us reading over our coffee and Krispy Kremes?"

Shelby just blinked.

"I'm simply asking, can't we uncover anything a bit more scandalous to spike the punch?"

"You mean other than the fact that the FDA, the most prominent medical journals, and dozens of pharmaceutical companies ignored the mounting evidence that DES was having tragic effects on millions of women and their offspring, and chose to continue marketing it anyway? You mean aside from the fact that if this sort of indifference had afflicted millions of men, the people responsible would have been indicted for criminal negligence? You mean aside from the fact that nearly 80 percent of DES daughters have benign precancerous cells known as adenosis around their vaginas . . ."

"Eegads." Ian shivered. "Can't you find a more pleasant way to refer to that region?"

"That region?" Shelby said sarcastically. "Sure. Maybe I could refer to it as the sunbelt!"

"Look, all I need to be happy is one little smoking gun. One aerial shot of a fat guy retired in Tahiti who is lounging poolside at his mansion, thanks to the moolah he made off this drug."

"The scandal, Ian, is not that one man got rich on blood money. The scandal is that thousands of knowledgeable medical professionals, top researchers, and multibillion-dollar corporations made big money and looked the other way . . . and are still looking the other way."

"So you're saying, basically, the guilty parties are just counting the years until all the victims are dead and buried?"

"That's right." Shelby fanned herself with the pages of her story.

"You're going for a Pulitzer, aren't you?" Ian swiveled in his chair

"I'm going for the truth, and if out of that comes recognition, yea for our team."

Ian formed a teepee with his fingers and bounced them against his lips. "It's not really our kind of story, you know. It's rather morbid and serious."

"You said it."

"And I've had more than my fill of hearing about deformed you-know-whats."

"Sunbelts?"

"Precisely. Although I must admit that the caliber of the writing and the reporting is par excellent. Pulitizer quality, in my humble but very experienced opinion."

"Thank you," Shelby bowed.

Ian hummed and swayed in his chair for a minute, then clapped. "Okay then! God help me, we run it as is. Although the suits upstairs will surely tweak my behind for this."

"Oh, come now. You'd love that." Shelby winked.

"You know me so well, darling."

Chapter Twenty-six

To celebrate the completion of her *Informer* assignments, Warner and Ian offered Shelby a night on the town, never expecting she'd beg off, citing limited free time. If only they knew that her free time was being spent moping around in pajamas.

A sympathetic Maria tried coming to the rescue with homemade soup, back rubs, and a constant array of bright, fragrant flowers that filled the guesthouse. Still, no smiles. "I'm tryin' my best, but the only thing gonna cheer this child up is a blessed phone call," she told Lauren.

It had been six long days since she'd seen Matty, and not one word from him.

"It's not like when we were kids and the only way you could stay in touch was to sit down and write a letter," Shelby cried to Lauren. "I gave him my screen name, my cell phone . . ."

"Maybe he's swamped at work," she offered. "It could be a real busy time."

"Maybe his child has taken a turn for the worse, and he's spending day and night at her bedside," Maria tried.

"No. He's sending me a message." Shelby sniffed. "Obviously, he doesn't want to see me."

That last possibility was devastating, but not completely unexpected. She and Matty had had strong feelings for each other as children, but he never made the effort to stay in touch then either. Why would he care about her now that he was a busy father and husband?

On the other hand, he wasn't the only one avoiding contact. Shelby hadn't called or e-mailed Matty because she simply couldn't bare her soul again, only to have him patiently explain that as much as he cared about her, he would never leave his wife. Nor could she take the chance of calling, then chickening out, then discovering the McCreighs had caller ID. She wondered if the whiz kids who developed that technology ever considered how their invention would foil love.

Shelby did, however, make other calls. First, she spoke with the service manager at the Lexus dealer, only to learn that once the car was up on the lift, they discovered several minor mechanical problems. They'd call her as soon as the parts came in, whenever that was.

Next, Shelby called her friend Mira in Chicago to pour out her heart and bitch about men.

"Tell me about it," Mira replied. "The men I date are like savings bonds. They take forever to mature."

Finally, Shelby called directory assistance for Portland and requested the residential and business numbers for Carol McCreigh. Odd though it was not to be referring to her as Mrs. Lieberman. And even odder that when they connected, the effusive woman was now considerably more subdued.

"Honey, I wish you luck. I really do," she said. "But the more I tried getting in between those two, the closer they got."

"Really? You tried driving a wedge between them?" Shelby forced herself not to giggle.

"Even at the wedding." Mrs. McCreigh laughed.

"Don't tell me you gave a reason why this couple shouldn't be joined together?"

"Actually what I said was, 'All in favor say aye!' "

"Oh my God. What happened?"

"Nothing. Everyone looked at me like I was a loon. And after the ceremony, Matthew refused to speak to me."

"So you understand how I feel," Shelby whined.

"Of course I do. And believe me, nothing would make me happier than to see you two together again. But, honey, my hands are tied."

"I know." Shelby sighed.

"There is one thing though," Mrs. McCreigh hesitated. "I'm not sure if it means anything."

"What is it?" Shelby's skin tingled. She loved hearing sources utter those words.

"I think it was two years ago that Gwen had an affair."

"With her best friend's husband?"

"Yes. I'm surprised Matthew told you about it."

"He didn't," Shelby said. "I happen to be an expert on debutantes. They either go for their best friend's husband or their husband's best friend. They never venture too far from the club."

"How convenient," Mrs. McCreigh said dryly. "Anyway, a few
months later they reconciled, and Matthew moved back home."

"Why are you telling me this?" Shelby asked.

"Because when I was in, Matthew happened to mention that
same best friend and her husband were filing for divorce."

"Did he seem. . . . concerned?" Shelby's heart skipped.

"Matthew never seems concerned, dear. That's part of his
charm. But if I was him, I'd be worried as hell."

It was the best news Shelby had heard in days. If Matty and
Gwen's marital boat could run aground once, then surely it could
sink. In the meantime she was treading in her own sea of confusion
and pain. Would Matty ever swim safely ashore, far away from his
stormy marriage?

Maria knocked on the guesthouse door, only to have to let herself in when Shelby didn't answer. Sure enough, Little Miss
Mommy-to-be was sprawled across the bed, looking peaceful at last,
after a week of walking around in a tearful fog.

"Miss Shelby, wake up child," Maria gently shook her shoulder.
"Wake up."

"Leave me alone." Shelby opened one eye and rolled over. "I'm
sleeping."

"But, Miss Shelby. You have to get up. There's a man here to see
you."

"You're kidding," she grumbled. "What time is it?"

"Just past eight. Here. I brought you some tea." Maria pulled
Shelby up with one, strong arm, and handed her the steaming cup.
"Oooh it's cold in here, child. The heat should have come up by
now."

"I turned it off," Shelby sipped the weak tea, sorry it wasn't Lauren's eye-opening brew. "It got so hot in here I couldn't breathe . . .
Who's here? And please spare me the lip about askin' not being your
job."

"I didn't have to ask. I could see plain as day. It's the man with your mother's car."

"How can that be? No one ever called me for directions. Where is he?"

"Out front."

"Oh, God," Shelby groaned as she threw on her long, flannel robe and slippers. "Why now? I finally fell back asleep . . ."

"You can't go outside like that." Maria stood with hands on hips.

"I can too! I'm just running out to give the guy a check. Then I'm going right back to bed."

"But it's November, child. You'll catch your death of cold."

"I'll take my chances, because I'm sure as hell not getting dressed, just so I can go talk to some greasy mechanic with bad teeth. Believe me, this guy didn't dress for me!"

But Shelby was wrong. And she knew it the instant she marched down the driveway. For there was no greasy mechanic waiting by the car. Not even highbrow Westchester auto dealers employed handsome, well-dressed men who came bearing flowers.

"Matty?" Shelby shivered as the wind whipped through her flimsy bathrobe, and her already disheveled hair blew across her face. "What are you doing here?"

"The car was ready. And you forgot these the other day." He gave her the wilted bouquet.

"Thank you." She sniffed the flowers. "What do you know? They're still dead."

"Yes, but I hear if you put them in a dry vase for a day, they get really good and dead."

"I'll remember that." Shelby tried to stifle a yawn.

"I'm sorry." He shuffled his feet. "Did I wake you?"

"It's okay. I have a million things to do today," she lied.

"You look beat. Have you been working hard?"

"Yes, that's it. Hard work . . . and no sleep."

"Same with me." He looked down.

"Why didn't you call to say you were coming?" She glanced down at her furry slippers and winced.

"For what? Directions?"

"Good point." Shelby smiled. "Okay, why didn't you call me at all?"

"I was afraid."

"Of what? My feelings for you?"

"No, of my feelings for you. Then I was afraid if I asked to see you, you'd say no."

"I would never say no." Shelby wrapped her arms around herself.

"Is there someplace we could talk?" Matty asked. "Preferably somewhere with heat?"

"Sure. I'm staying out back. It's nothing like the guesthouse at your place, but . . ."

He scooped her up and carried her across the backyard.

"Put me down. I'm too heavy for you," Shelby squealed.

"I'm sorry, ma'am." he laughed. "We can't take the chance of ruining those lovely slippers."

Shelby laughed, too, then cried, painfully aware a runny nose would only enhance her lovely image as a housefrau in flannel, with puffy eyes and morning hair. Trouble with her, she had recently discovered, was that once the faucet opened, it was a gusher.

When Matty gently put Shelby down, he wiped her tears with his hand. "I don't remember you being the crybaby," he teased. "That was my department. Remember?"

"Yes." She sniffed. "Everything made you cry. Like the time Wendy accidentally spilled her milk bottle on your head? We thought you'd never recover."

"I didn't. I still belong to a support group for people with dairyosis."

"You look fine to me." Her heart raced as she wondered how long she could just stand there without ripping the clothes off his irresistible body.

"This is a little awkward." He looked around, wondering where to sit. The only place without clothes strewn over everything was the bed. "And is it just me, or is it freezing in here?"

"I was roasting, so I shut off the heat." She rubbed his arm. "But I can heat things up."

"Please don't get the wrong impression, Shelby." He blushed. "I didn't come here to . . ."

"Yes, but in case you've come to tell me we can never be together, I want a consolation prize." She began to tug at his navy cashmere sweater. "Just once I want to see you naked."

Matty closed his eyes and smiled up at the heavens. "I want you more than you could possibly imagine, Shelby, but I really think we need to talk . . ."

"Absolutely." She threw his sweater on the bed and nimbly unbuttoned his oxford shirt, exposing his broad, muscular chest. "Let's talk." She fingered his dark curls.

"I take it you're happy to see me?" He caressed her face.

"I'll be happier when I see all of you." She unbuckled his belt, unzipped his fly, and let his pants drop to the floor.

"At the doctor's, they let me take my shoes off first."

"Well, this isn't the doctor, and you're not in Kansas anymore." She stepped back to examine her masterpiece. "You are beyond gorgeous." She stood on tiptoes to kiss him.

"So, I pass the test?" He actually looked worried.

"You're perfect," she whispered.

"Permission to stay?"

"I'm ordering you to stay." She quickly removed his shoes, then his pants, and gazed at the stunning man before her. His physique was so perfectly proportioned and strong, his maleness so alluring, no way would she be able to keep her hands off the merchandise.

"Is it my turn?" He nervously reached to untie the belt on her robe. "I've had a fantasy or two myself over the years."

She nodded yes, praying he wouldn't be turned off by her protruding belly. At least her ample breasts, tiny waist, and long, curvy legs remained hot items.

Slowly, Matty removed her robe, and lifted her nightgown over her head. Now it was his turn to gaze at his childhood friend, today a ravishing work of art, chiseled to perfection.

"I'm pregnant, remember." She bit her lip. "And I haven't even brushed my hair yet . . ."

"When I was about nine or ten I used to daydream about how you would look as a woman, and I had a hell of a good imagination. But never in my wildest dreams did I envision you this beautiful." He pulled her toward him and kissed her hungrily.

Shelby returned the kiss with the same unbridled passion, crying out when he caressed her breasts and licked her taut nipples. By now she was so aroused and flush with desire, she tore off his boxers and fondled him.

"It's been so long," he moaned. "I may not be able to hold it . . ."

"Shhh . . ." Shelby touched his lips. "I don't care."

Matty swiftly delivered Shelby to her bed. There he knelt before her, kissing her thighs and nibbling at her panties until they were wet with anticipation. Shelby pulled him on top of her.

"Are you sure about this?" he whispered. "Maybe we should stop."

"No way." She squeezed him until he cried for mercy. "When you come play at Shelby's house, you have to play what she wants, remember?"

"What I remember"—he laughed—"is that we played what you wanted at my house, too."

"Exactly. Now keep going, or else."

"Well if you put it that way." He laid her back down.

"There is one thing." She ran her hands down his warm, muscular thighs.

"Do I have a condom?"

"No, a cell phone."

"You thought of someone you'd like to call right now?"

"No, I want to make sure it's turned off."

"I left it in the car with my pager." He reached over to tease her clit with his middle finger.

"And what about a condom? Did you listen to your mother?"

"No," he groaned, falling back into the pillows.

"Bad boy." She smacked his firm ass. "You should always listen to your mother."

"Shelby, trust me, I didn't think you'd want to speak to me, let alone make love to me."

"Oh, what the hell?" She mounted him. "It's not like I can get pregnant."

"No, wait. We can't take any chances," he cried with anguish as he lifted her off. "I'd never forgive myself if I hurt you in some way . . ."

"I appreciate your concern, but what if I assured you every man I've been with was wrapped and double-wrapped?"

"Shelby . . . I can't give you the same guarantee."

"What do you mean?" She stopped. "How many other women have you been with?"

"Just Gwen," he stroked her hair. "But she's been with . . . another man . . . Let's be safe."

"Damn! You're right. We have to act responsibly. But I want you so badly . . ."

"Oh, believe me, ma'am. I'm at your service." He slowly ran his tongue from her naval to her sunbelt region.

"Oh! My! God!" Shelby cried out. "I'm melting . . ."

It was amazing how creative two motivated people could get when they desperately wanted to engage in risk-free orgasms. Exhausted, they lay breathless and limp, daring not to move for fear of altering the dreamlike state that had enveloped the room.

Still, even the most artful lovers need nourishment, and when they finally emerged, Maria was standing by, pleased to be called upon to whip up her famous country fried eggs. She had always been partial to handsome men with large appetites, but was even more gratified watching Shelby devour her cooking, as if she hadn't eaten in a week. Which she hadn't. *Kvell.* Yes, that would be the word Mrs. L would have used at a moment like this.

"Will you be needing anything else?" Maria asked. "I want to get my dusting finished."

"We're fine, thank you." Shelby could not take her eyes off Matty.

"Yes, I see that." Maria winked. "I'm thinkin' maybe I should switch car dealers," she mumbled. "I never got service like that before."

"So." Shelby sipped her coffee. "You said you came here to talk."

"I did. But then I was rudely interrupted."

"That's awful." She rubbed his foot under the table. "What did you want to talk about?"

"Hell if I can remember." He scratched his head.

"Maybe I can refresh your memory. Were you, by any chance, coming to tell me you'd realized you've been with the wrong woman all these years, and now you'd like to make a midcourse correction?"

"I wasn't going to put it quite like that." He laughed. "Although it is true that Gwen and I are having problems and . . . to be honest, she's asked me for a divorce."

"Yes!" Shelby clapped.

"Shelby! Stop!" He laughed. "You're not supposed to be happy when a friend tells you his marriage is over."

"I am when it's your marriage!"

"Call me psychic, but it seems you're in an awfully big hurry for us to be together."

"A hurry? You call waiting your whole life being in a hurry?"

"Well, hold on. Don't jump the gun," Matty smiled. "You don't know my whole story."

"Au contraire, my friend. I'm a reporter, remember?" Shelby leaned in. "This is what happens next. You're married to the lieutenant governor's daughter. Therefore, once the gossip columns get wind of a separation, they'll camp out at your doorstep for a few weeks and expect you to provide the coffee. Then after the story has been chewed up and spit out by the media, the lawyers will step in and it will get as ugly as a Ron Perelman divorce, complete with kinky allegations, mudslinging, and outrageous demands.

"Then there will the hotly contested, emotionally gut-wrenching issue of who gets custody of Emily, who gets the sailboat, and who gets the house on Martha's Vineyard . . ."

"Okay." He looked sullen. "You do understand my problem. But, it's not only the divorce that I wanted to talk to you about."

"What do you mean?"

"Look, once word gets out that Gwen is talking to lawyers . . . I didn't want you to read about it in the papers. I wanted to tell you personally."

"I appreciate that . . ."

"And I don't think it would be smart for me to get involved with anyone right away."

"Oh I agree. But I'm not anyone. I'm the girl who loved you when you couldn't tie your own sneakers, when you were afraid of the dark and needed me to hold your hand . . ."

Matty looked into Shelby's eyes. "Believe me I would be kidding myself if I said I didn't have strong feelings for you. I do. And what just happened here this morning? Frankly, I haven't felt that loved in years. But I'm tired and confused and hurt. I just need some time."

"How much time?" Shelby bit her lip. "A few days? A few months?"

Matty laughed. How could he have forgotten about Shelby's incredible determination? "I don't know. At the moment I just feel like running away. Maybe fly to Portland to visit Wendy and the kids, see some old high school buddies . . ."

"Could I come with you?" Shelby got down on her knees. "I promise I wouldn't be in the way. I'd love to see Wendy and spend more time with your mom."

Matty smiled, brushing the bangs from her face. "You want to spend time with my mom?"

Shelby's head bobbed.

"Well, that would certainly take the pressure off me having to do it."

"And you could take me to a Trailblazers game."

"You like basketball?" His eyes lit up.

"No, I like you." She kissed him tenderly. "And I would go anywhere to be with you."

Matty sighed. He was trying so hard not to cave, but Shelby could wear down a Kamikaze pilot. "I'm warning you. I'm no great bargain. I have to have my own remote control," he declared.

"So? I hate TV."

"And I hate being nagged about what I eat."

"Perfect. I hate being nagged about what I don't eat."

"I can be pretty grumpy in the mornings," he tried again.

"I can be grumpy all day."

"I hate parties."

"No big deal," she shrugged. "I hate people."

"After all these years, you honestly believe that you and I could work?" Matty stared.

"It has to work." Shelby laughed through tears. "It's the only thing I've ever wanted."

Chapter Twenty-seven

"It's a miracle." Irma Weiner clapped, referring to the wonderful news that Larry and Roz were about to be released from North Shore Hospital. "Just like the story of Chanukah."

Indeed, the timing was serendipitous. In this first week of December, Jews were celebrating Chanukah, a triumphant holiday commemorating when the Israelites prevailed during the darkest days of the year and were illuminated with hope by oil lamps that burned brightly, wondrously, for eight nights.

How fitting at this joyous time of year that Larry and Roz were finally well enough to be moved to Transitions, a nearby state-of-the-art rehabilitation center. There they would slowly rebuild muscle and mind, and try to prepare for reentering life, not as they knew it before the accident, but as they would know it now. A true miracle of miracles.

Eric's completed rehabilitation was another victory, as was his agreeing to reunite with his family after a yearlong journey through substance-abuse hell. In a few hours Lauren would be picking him up at JFK and bringing him back to North Shore, just in time for the little bon voyage party the fifth-floor nursing staff was throwing for the two patients who had captured their hearts and their prayers after being brought in through death's door.

Shelby was practically walking on air as she helped Aunt Roz pack up her hospital room. There were so many things to be grateful for, and so much to look forward to. In a few days, she would be flying to Portland to spend a week getting reacquainted with Matty and his family.

"It *is* like the miracle of Chanukah," Shelby hugged Irma. "Who knew the best gifts weren't from Toys "R" Us?"

"I wish she'd said that when she was younger," Roz said to Irma. "There wasn't a toy this child didn't ask for."

"And didn't end up getting." Shelby laughed. "I guess I was a little spoiled."

"A little spoiled?" Roz exclaimed. "My sister, may she rest in peace, spent a small fortune on the girls at Chanukah time. Between the clothes and the games and the books, the only miracle was there was any money left in the bank."

"Oh, puh-leeze. Daddy was loaded, and we knew it."

"Yes, well, riches come in many forms." Irma kissed them both good-bye. "And lucky for your family, you've been blessed with the most important kind. I'll be back in time for the party, but my dears, I have some Chanukah shopping to do myself. What do you get the man who has everything?" she wondered aloud.

"This sounds serious, Irma." Shelby nudged her arm. "What's the story with this guy?"

"Norman is a dear, sweet man," Irma blushed. "And, frankly, I'm having a ball."

"Good for you!" Roz nodded. "You deserve all the happiness in the world."

"Thank you." She waved. "See you later."

"It's about time she was lucky in love." Roz threw out get well cards while Shelby tossed her aunt's slippers and toiletries into a suitcase.

"Yes," Shelby agreed, wondering if Roz felt the same way about her.

"And the same goes for you, honey."

"Thank you," she replied. "Do you think . . . I was wondering . . . Never mind."

"What is it?" Roz looked over with a smile.

"Forget it. It was nothing."

"No, go on. You were going to ask me something. Please?"

Shelby hesitated. How she hated revealing her vulnerable side, and yet she was having nagging doubts about Matty. Who better to talk to than someone who knew and loved her since she was born? Someone who was the closest person she had to a mother? "I was just wondering," she began, "do you think I'm doing the right thing? Going to Portland?"

"Absolutely." Roz beamed. "I've always said when it comes to love, follow your heart no matter the odds."

"I know. But the thing is, Matty didn't ask me to go. I sort of invited myself, and now I'm wondering if that was a mistake."

"I think it's a wonderful idea, dear. You'll go, you'll have a good time reminiscing . . ."

"Yes, but he keeps saying how he needs some time alone."

"Honey, he's a big boy now. If he didn't want you to come, he would have said so."

"I don't know. He was never very good at saying no to me. And now I'm thinking maybe I should have butted out and let him go alone like he'd planned. Then he'd have time to . . ."

"Think about you?"

"I guess." Shelby looked away. "And the other thing is, I'm afraid one day he might come back to me and say that I was unfair to him."

"Because you didn't give him a chance to get over things first."

"Exactly. How did you know that?"

"Because I know what you're going through. You're telling me my life's story."

"I am?"

"Of course, dear. You don't think I was scared to death that your father would leave me? Everything with us happened so quickly. Your mother got sick, I got pregnant, she died, we got married, had Eric . . . I used to wake up in the middle of the night just to make sure Daddy was still lying there next to me. I was so sure he'd change his mind and accuse me of rushing him into the marriage, of never giving him a chance to recover from Sandy's death."

"Oh wow." Shelby's eyes welled up. "It is sort of the same story."

"That's what I'm saying. I know how it feels to fear regret. And to love someone so deeply you don't think you'll be able to breathe unless they love you back."

"I had no idea you felt that way . . . At least your story has a happy ending."

"Yes, it does. Although take my word. There were plenty of times I had my doubts."

"Why?"

"You of all people should know why. You made Daddy and me

miserable. You'd run around the house screaming how much you hated me, and that I messed up your life, and what right did I have trying to pretend I was your mother. . . . And I'd say to myself, maybe she's right. Maybe I made a mistake thinking I could take over where my sister left off. Maybe they would have been better off without me . . . You could really hit below the belt, my dear."

"I was only ten."

"Shelby, you were never ten."

She nodded, understanding for the first time the pain Aunt Roz must have endured, waiting all those years in the wings, then finally getting to be in a warm, committed relationship with the man she loved, only to be treated like the enemy by his daughter.

"But that's all in the past." Aunt Roz lifted Shelby's chin. "Like you said. The story has a happy ending."

"I am so sorry." Shelby started to cry. "Truly sorry."

"It's okay, dear." Aunt Roz hugged her. "Somehow we survived. It's like that nice song I used to sing from . . . what was the name of that show?"

"*See Saw*?"

"Yeah, *See Saw*. Remember? 'It's not where you start, it's where you finish.' "

" 'It's not how you go, it's how you land,' " Shelby sang. "I don't remember the rest."

"Me, either. I'm just saying what's important is we're together again, we're here for each other, we can be in the same room and not start a world war . . ."

"It is great." Shelby sniffed.

"And another thing. Your mother would be so proud of you right now. The way you overcame all your *mishegas* to help Lauren. The way you've been such a big help to us. Visiting every day, making sure the doctors and nurses did everything they could for us . . . she would be *kvelling* from ear to ear."

"I know."

"She loved you girls so much. You were her whole life."

"Did she . . ." Shelby started. There was something she was desperate to ask, even if she didn't hear the answer she wanted. "Did she love Daddy, too?"

Aunt Roz sighed. "To be honest? Not right away. But she learned to love him. Just like he learned to love me."

Shelby took Aunt Roz's hands. "I think he made a wonderful choice when he married you."

Aunt Roz's newly healed jaw dropped. "Thank you, dear. I never thought I'd live to hear you say that."

"Well thank God you did," Shelby kissed her stepmother on the cheek. "Thank God."

Having Eric home was not at all what Shelby expected. The boy who used to burp and fart in her friends' faces, the boy she used to call Porky Pig, was now a frail, quiet man of twenty-eight who looked as if he'd just returned from battle. Which he had. For the toll from his years as a cocaine addict was markedly clear. He was a shell of his former self.

Shelby even found it difficult to converse with him, as his attention span was limited and his interest in small talk only marginal. Nor did he seem to comprehend the enormity of what had happened to his parents, evidenced by the fact he continually commented on how nice they looked. The equivalent of mentioning to a Vietnam vet it looked like he lost a lot of weight, thinking he'd appreciate the compliment.

"Don't worry," Irma assured her. "He'll come around. It just takes time."

"But there's so much I need to share with him," Shelby argued. "About the accident, and the whole business with DES, and me being Lauren's surrogate, and finding Matty . . ."

"Fine. You'll tell him everything. Just not all at once."

"And what do you suggest that I say about who his real father is? In case you were wondering, he was right under your nose the whole time?"

"That I would handle a little more delicately, dear. It's possible he suspected it all along, but even so, it will be a big shock to his system. Maybe your father should be the one to handle it."

"No way," Shelby snapped. "My father had twenty-eight years to handle it, and didn't."

"Then I suggest you build up to it. Eric is very vulnerable now, and I'm not sure your style is well suited for breaking unexpected news."

"That is so not true," Shelby argued. "That's why newspapers pay me the big bucks!"

"Well then let's just say this isn't the time to be cold and blunt."

"Are you suggesting I don't know how to use discretion?"

"I wasn't even aware you knew the word."

Shelby wanted to clobber Lauren. Here she'd spent time ordering in a delicious dinner so the three siblings could sit around a kitchen table and get nostalgic. At the same time, she also wanted an opportunity to speak to Eric about his true birthright while he could seek comfort in the confines of his family.

Instead, Lauren, giddy with excitement, was monopolizing the whole conversation, going on and on about Danny, Danny's son, Danny's practice, Danny's love of antique cars . . .

"And what does good old Danny boy think about you being a mother of twins?" Shelby decided to lay her cards out on the table, along with the pasta primavera.

"He thinks it's great. He's a child psychologist," she explained to Eric. "He loves kids."

"Yes, but have you discussed my pregnancy in terms of how it might affect your relationship?"

"Shel, c'mon. It's not like we're engaged or anything. We just started dating."

"I know. But I also know how you get when you fall in love. You don't see anything. You don't hear anything . . ."

Eric pushed his food around on his plate.

"I'm not in love, okay? We're just good friends. Which is fine because I'm not ready for another serious relationship now, and besides, he's not sure he wants more children . . ."

"Excuse me?"

Lauren swallowed hard. "What I mean is, right now he's very happy with his one child. But he did say maybe one day in the future he'd want a bigger family."

"Eric, pay attention." Shelby shook his arm. "Did you hear what your sister, the brain surgeon, just said? She's not even legally separated from her husband yet, but she's already dating a guy who said flat out, no thanks to more kids, oh and about those twins your sister is carrying for you, what's her refund policy?"

"Shelby, stop! He said nothing like that. You're making too big a deal out of this. I still want the babies if that's what you're worried about."

"Yes, but what if a few months from now you realize you're hopelessly in love with him, and he refuses to commit to you because you're the mother of two?"

"I think I can get him to change his mind," Lauren whispered. "I still have a few months."

Shelby gripped the table and repeated the most inane comment she'd ever heard. But before she could rip into Lauren about her moronic plans to convince Danny Siegel he should be the next Mr. Brady Bunch, Eric finally spoke.

"It's been a long day for me and I'm kind of tired. I'm going to go upstairs now."

"No wait." Shelby added more pasta and salad to his plate. "Can't you hold out for another few minutes? Lauren and I had something important to talk to you about."

"I told you I don't like white sauce." He pushed her fork away. "You're worse than Mom."

"Sorry," Shelby retreated. "It must be my maternal instincts kicking in. Eat, *bubbeleh*, eat." But when Eric was not amused, Shelby tried to remember if he'd always been a picky eater, or if his appetite was just suppressed from his drug days. Trouble was, with the ten-year age difference, they'd spent little time together. Not to mention her resentment of his getting much of their father's attention didn't help matters.

"What did you want to talk about?" Eric stabbed a piece of lettuce.

"Um . . . how do you feel about being an uncle?" Shelby smiled.

"He'll be great," Lauren piped in. "As long as he's nothing like Uncle Marty."

"Wasn't he the worst?" Shelby said. "On Mommy's birthday he'd wait to see if we invited him out to dinner so he'd get a free meal at a fancy restaurant. But not once did he buy her a card."

"Did it ever occur to you he might not have had the money?" Eric sniffed.

"Oh, please. He always had plenty of money for booze and Belmont Raceway."

"Why are you so judgmental?" Eric glared. "You don't know what's in people's pockets, and you don't know what it's like to have an addictive personality."

Lauren and Shelby looked at each other. Even during his most stoned-out period, Eric had never been this sullen and cross. Obviously, he was still grappling with his demons and they'd have to tread lightly.

"I'm sorry, Eric," Shelby apologized. "Perhaps I did misjudge him."

"Oh, for Christ's sake. Stop placating me, Shelby. And stop talking to me like I'm a mental case. I'm a big boy now. If you've got something to tell me, spit it out."

"Fine!" Shelby was tired of walking on eggshells. "Brace yourself. It's really big."

"Shel, I don't know . . ."

"No, Lauren. The charade has gone on long enough . . . You ready, Eric?"

Eric stared at his plate.

Shelby took a deep breath. "Larry Lazarus is your father."

There. She said it. But where was the gasp, the look of horror? This was a major headline.

"Well, duh." He shrugged. "Of course he is."

"You knew?" Lauren's mouth opened. "Was I the only Lazarus out of the loop?"

"What do you mean did I know?" Eric looked at them as if they were crazy. "Why are you telling me this?"

"Because we didn't know you knew." Shelby was a little confused herself. If her father and Roz swore they never told Eric he was born their brother, and not their first cousin, then who did?"

"Why wouldn't I know?" He looked angry. "How stupid do you think I am? Larry Lazarus is our father, and Roz Lazarus is our mother. It's not a difficult concept."

Lauren and Shelby's eyes opened wide. It was worse than they thought. As far as he knew, he'd been born to Roz and Larry, as were his older sisters.

"Eric, honey . . ." Shelby started.

"No wait," Lauren butted in. "He's right. We're one big happy family. Let's leave it at that."

"Would someone please tell me what the fuck is going on?" Eric slammed his fist down.

"Okay, fine. But you have to listen good because this gets a little complicated." Shelby took his hand. "Daddy was married once before, to a woman named Sandy. He and Sandy had two daughters, who so happen to be Lauren and me. But when I was ten and Lauren was four, Sandy got cancer and her younger sister, Roz, moved into our house so she could take care of us. While Sandy was dying, Roz and Larry fell in love, and they conceived you. Sandy died in early December and you were born that May. At the time, we thought you were our cousin Eric because Roz was our aunt, and you were her baby. Then a year later, Larry and Roz got married and we were told to call you our stepbrother because our daddy was adopting you. But the truth of the matter was, you were really his son."

Eric's eyes told the whole story. He had absolutely no idea. "Holy shit." He kept shaking his head in disbelief. "Are you sure about this? Why didn't they ever tell me?"

"They didn't tell us either," Lauren cried. "Shelby figured it out by herself."

"See, the problem was," Shelby continued, "they never wanted us to know they were fooling around while Daddy was still married to our mother."

"I remember hearing stories about an Aunt Sandy. But no one ever told me she was your mother," Eric looked mystified. "I just assumed Mommy was."

"You mean you never wondered why I didn't call her Mommy?"

"Not really. You were such a bitch I figured you just liked pissing her off."

"Come to think of it, what *did* you call her?" Lauren asked.

"Nothing." Shelby sighed. "I really was a bitch, wasn't I?"

"Was?" Eric and Lauren said at the same time, then laughed.

"I gotta tell you. This is bizarre," Eric said. "To be living all these lies your whole life . . ."

"What do you mean, *all* these lies," Shelby asked. "Do you know something we don't?"

Eric laughed. Not just a chuckle, a knee-slapping belly laugh that brought tears to his eyes. Shelby and Lauren stared at him, then at each other. Was he still tripping?

"What's so funny?" Lauren furrowed her brow.

"I'm sorry." He wiped his eye with his napkin. "I was just struck by a funny thought."

"Please share." Shelby hoped she didn't sound too much like a twelve-step leader.

Eric collected himself. "Before I came in I was so worried about how I was going to tell you a secret that I've kept to myself for a long time. But then after hearing this, it's like what the hell? Big secrets run in the family."

"What's yours?" Lauren winked. "That you're gay?"

Eric flinched.

"You didn't know we knew?"

He shook his head.

"Well, duh," she mimicked him. "When Allen paid more attention to you than me at our wedding, I knew something was weird."

Eric blushed.

"Plus"—Shelby cleared her throat—"from what I could tell when I came home, you never had a girlfriend, you never read *Playboy*, and you liked shoe shopping even more than I did."

"Oh."

"Actually, I think I knew before you did. So that's old news. What else you got?"

Eric folded his arms. "This one you'll never guess in a million years. I have a companion. His name is Jamal. We met in rehab, fell in love, now we live together and are totally clean."

"That's great, Eric." Lauren touched her heart.

"I'm not finished." He held up his hand. "And since we both wanted to have a family . . . we decided to hire this woman . . . to be our surrogate."

"Oh my God. Are you serious?" Shelby grabbed hold of his hand.

"OH . . . MY . . . GOD!" Lauren squealed. "Are you pregnant?"

Eric nodded.

"This is unbelievable. When?"

"End of July, early August."

"This is unreal. Shelby's due in mid-July! Mommy and Daddy will flip out. They're going from zero to three grandchildren . . ."

"No." Eric laughed. "Make that four."

"Twins?" Lauren gasped.

"Yep," Eric winked. "And we are soooo excited."

Shelby was shaking. "How in God's name are you going to tell them?"

"I was thinking . . . maybe you could tell them."

"Me? Why me?"

"Because. You're the one in the family who breaks big news stories every day."

"Not this big!"

"You have to tell them," Lauren said. "They'll be so happy for you."

"Ya think?"

"I don't know," Shelby said. "Jamal's last name. It wouldn't by any chance be Goldberg?"

"Not even close."

"Is he white?"

"Nope."

Shelby looked at Lauren. "All in favor of keeping this a secret, say aye."

"Aye!!!"

I'll be honest. This wasn't the scene I envisioned when I said I wanted the three children to be together again. Naturally I'm thrilled they're all finally speaking to each other. But who could ever have imagined such craziness? Eric turned out to be a little fageleh who's using a surrogate like Lauren did with Shelby. Shelby's carrying twin babies for Lauren, but in the meantime is getting involved with a married man who doesn't know what the hell he wants. And Lauren is getting a divorce, but first she's dating a man who DOES know what he wants. No more children.

God help me. I'm way in over my head.

Chapter Twenty-eight

Shelby was still in shock. A few weeks ago she had no idea that Matty Lieberman was alive. Now she was flying to Portland, Oregon, as his date. Even better, his wife, Madame WASP, had asked for a divorce. So when the legalities and the fireworks were all over, Shelby's one true love would be open for business.

She was so glad she'd discussed her second thoughts about making the trip with him. He had actually laughed when she confessed that she felt bad about inviting herself. "What else is new? You always used to talk my mother into letting you stay for dinner, letting you sleep over, letting you go with us to the Jersey Shore. I can't remember. Did we ever invite you first?"

But then Matty got serious and said he had a confession as well. At first he wasn't crazy about the idea of Shelby tagging along. He really wanted time alone to do a marital postmortem, or at least meet up with some old friends to get plastered if the mood struck. "If you came with me, I'd have to be on my best behavior, and to be honest, I've just spent the past ten years on my best behavior."

He assured Shelby that he loved the idea of going away with her so that they could fill in the blanks on all the missing years. What he didn't relish was a reunion that took place under his mother's watchful eye. "I know her. She'll be listening through the wall with a paper cup."

But then after more pondering, he changed his mind again. If your life was falling apart, who better to talk to than your oldest and dearest friend? Besides, if Shelby didn't join him now, he'd have to spend the entire week explaining to his mother why.

Shelby was elated by his change of heart and couldn't wait to share the news with Lauren, along with a very exciting surprise. She'd felt the babies kick for the first time, and it was an extraordinary moment. A mixture of terror and jubilation, and the undeniable reality that she, selfish, cynical, tough-talking Shelby Lazarus, was hatching human life.

"Doesn't it feel weird?" She placed Lauren's hand on her belly. "It's like they're swimming laps or something."

"This is so unfair," Lauren cried. "Just when it gets exciting, you're leaving."

Or trying to leave anyway. The wall of traffic on the Grand Central Parkway was putting a damper in Shelby's efforts to make her flight.

"What happened to all those great shortcuts Avi taught you?" Shelby asked.

"That was to JFK," she cried. "He never showed me the ones to La Guardia."

"Just great. My ship finally comes in, and I'm stuck in the car."

"We'll make it, Shel. It's only another few more miles, and things usually open up after Shea Stadium."

"Did I mention I have to pee really bad?"

"Several times. Why didn't you go before we left?"

"I did. Three times."

"Should I stop somewhere?"

"No, just hurry. I really don't want to pull over to look for tissues and a tree."

Lauren turned off the radio. "Let's talk to keep your mind off things."

"Fine. What do you want to talk about?"

"Would it be possible for you not to have wild sex this week?"

"Excuse me? I plan to have nothing but wild sex this week. What's it to you?"

"I know you're going to say this is stupid . . ."

"Yes?"

"But if you're rolling around all the time, couldn't my babies get, I don't know, seasick?"

They're not your babies yet, Shelby thought. "Fine. I promise to draw the line at hanging from hotel chandeliers."

"I'm serious, Shel."

"Believe me, you have nothing to worry about. With this big belly, my George of the Jungle days are over."

Fortunately, traffic did let up, and a jubilant Shelby got dropped off at the curb, checked her bag with a skycap, hugged her sister good-bye, and marched triumphantly through the airport doors. She and Matty had agreed it would be easiest to meet at the gate, but Shelby knew she'd never make it as far as the metal detectors unless she first stopped at the ladies' room.

Once her mission was accomplished, she checked her makeup, checked to make sure she had all her belongings, checked everything but the flight board, which would have clued her in to the extensive delays occurring along the Eastern seaboard.

On the way to the gate, Shelby passed a bar in the terminal and was surprised to see such a large crowd. Who drank at eleven o'clock in the morning? Apparently a lot of people, including one guy who looked just like Matty. How funny was this? She hadn't laid eyes on him in thirty years. Now suddenly, everywhere she went, she was spotting men who were his mirror image.

But one thing wasn't funny. Shelby reached Gate 18 and the genuine article himself was nowhere to be found. Certainly if she could spot him on a busy parkway going 70 mph, she could pick him out of a crowd of passengers who were sitting quietly. Maybe he was in the men's room, or getting a magazine. Maybe he was buying coffee, or maybe that *was* him at the bar.

No, not his style, she thought. But just to be sure, she dialed his cell phone. No answer. She checked with the gate agent to see if there were any messages for her. There were none. She walked over to the newsstand, hoping to find him standing in line with a few car magazines and an Almond Joy. No such luck. Finally, her reporter's instincts kicked in.

Shelby covered his eyes and whispered, "Guess who?"

Matty jumped, but played along. "Sharon Stone in a short black skirt?"

"No," Shelby smacked his shoulder. "Someone even hotter . . . and younger."

"I like them hot and young."

"Yes, but do you like them thirty-eight and pregnant?"

"I'm totally turned on."

"Mind if I join you?" She sat on the barstool next to his.

"Come on in. The water's nice." He smiled, but it wasn't his usual, boyish grin.

"I didn't expect to find you here." Shelby went for eye contact. "Should I be worried?"

"I'm okay."

"Are you sure? Because I think all the okay people are sitting at the gate."

"I'm fine." He stirred his drink.

She looked at her watch. "Is it just my imagination, or did we come here to catch a flight?"

"Everything's delayed due to fog. Nothing's coming in, nothing's going out."

"Oh gee. I wish I'd known that an hour ago when we were sitting in traffic. I drove Lauren nuts. 'Hurry! If I don't get there in time, Matty will leave without me.' "

His face turned scarlet. Oh Good Lord, Shelby thought. I meant that as a joke. What is wrong with him? "You seem . . . uptight." She stroked his arm.

"I have a lot on my mind."

"Do you feel like talking about it?"

"No."

"Is it Emily? Are you worried about not seeing her?"

"I'm always worried about Emily."

"Is it work? The stock market? World hunger . . ."

"Would you stop?" he snapped. "I appreciate your concern, but I'm really not up for a big, long discussion at the moment."

"I'm sorry." She backed off. "It's the reporter in me. If I smell a story, I have to get to the bottom of it."

"Tell you what, then. When I'm ready to talk, I'll be sure to give you the exclusive."

"Jeez. You sound like me on a PMS day."

When Matty didn't answer, she closed her eyes. She wasn't big on prayer, but this seemed like a good time to start. But what to pray for? That whatever was on his mind didn't involve her? No. That whatever was on his mind didn't *affect* her.

"I'm sorry." He reached for her hand. "Forgive me. You're right. I'm feeling sick about something . . . We have to talk."

Noooooooo. Not *the* talk. Shelby's heart pounded. What could possibly have happened between last night when they spoke and now? He sounded so happy then. Didn't matter. She knew he was about to break her heart. God help her if he said that he and Gwen had decided to give it one last try.

"Fine. Let's talk," she said bravely. "But not in here. The smoke is getting to me."

"I know. I was thinking the same thing. Let's go find someplace quiet."

No easy feat in an airport overflowing with passengers milling about with time on their hands and big bags on their shoulders. If the two weren't bumping into giant carry-on gear, they were tripping over runaway toddlers and their in-pursuit parents.

But the longer it took to find a little piece of privacy, the more anxious Shelby became. Did she really want to stick around for the "You're a great girl, but . . ." speech? She'd heard it all before, just never from someone who mattered this much.

"I have an idea," Matty said. He grabbed her hand and led her through a crowded maze.

"Where are we going?"

"To the last place you'd ever expect to find a crowd."

"The chapel?"

"Great minds think alike."

Not that God isn't a big draw, but Matty was right. Save for one elderly gentleman who was lighting candles, they had their pick of pews. How sad and ironic, Shelby thought. God had brought them together, and now he was about to be a witness to the break up.

"Shelby, I don't know where to start."

"If I remember correctly, the first line is, 'Believe me. This isn't about you.' "

He raised an eyebrow.

"Then you say something like, 'You're an incredible catch, Shelby. Any man would be lucky to have you in his life, blah, blah, blah, blah . . .' "

"You're amazing." Matty smiled.

"Oh I know. But you still don't want me to go with you, do you?"

"It's not what you think."

"So then what's the problem?"

"I'm trying not to think of this as a problem. I'm trying to think of it as an opportunity."

"And I'm trying to follow you, but you're about three drinks ahead of me."

"How should I put this?" Matty brushed the bangs from her eyes and took a deep breath. "I woke up this morning and I had . . . I guess you could call it a revelation."

Oooh. A revelation. Not good. Revelations started world wars.

"I feel like I've spent my entire life being surrounded by people who tried to own a piece of my soul. My father abused me, my stepfather belittled me, my mother controlled me, my wife ignored me, my daughter . . . sometimes confuses me with the man who sells ice cream.

"I'm almost forty years old and I have no idea what it's like not worrying about how my words, or my actions, or my feelings are going to affect somebody else. I've never had the chance to wake up and say, Okay, what do *I* want to do today?

"I'm just tired of trying to meet everyone else's expectations. Tired of trying to be the perfect son, the perfect father, the perfect husband, the perfect lover. Because no matter what I do, someone is always right there to tell me that I'm not. But what I realized this morning was that the only person I've ever really failed was myself.

"So I guess what it comes down to is I want to finally enjoy some freedom. I want to see the Knicks play whenever they're in town. I want to buy a ridiculously expensive sports car for no other reason than I love the sound of the engine. I want to eat pizza in my underwear. I want to go to the great jazz clubs in New Orleans and be the last one to turn out the lights. I want to be Bar Mitzvahed and be counted as a Jew so I can fulfill my one promise to my grandfather.

"And I want to do all of this starting right now, because for the first time in my life, Shelby, there's no reason that I can't."

Shelby nodded, wiping her tears on her sleeve.

"Look, I know you think it would be so easy for us to pick up where we left off," Matthew continued, "but we were little kids then and so much has happened since. I had a lousy childhood and a difficult marriage. My daughter probably won't live to see her next birthday, and once my father-in-law finds out about Gwen and me, forget it. She'll tell him I'm leaving her, and he's such a vindictive son of a bitch, he'll exert all his power in Albany to ruin my reputation with the Department of Education, then my business will tank . . . I just need some time to sort all this out. Figure out where I go from here. Can you understand?"

"Yes." Shelby exhaled.

"Thank you." Matty kissed her hand. "Because you are the last person I would ever want to hurt. And I'm not saying that one day we won't be together."

"Just not right now."

He nodded.

"So we'll wait." Shelby tried to smile through tears. "What's another twenty, thirty years? Maybe we'll buy a retirement home together and . . ."

Matty pulled Shelby toward him and kissed her with all abandon. So what if she was feeling crushed, she could not resist his tender touch. It was the same warm, loving feeling she remembered as a ten-year-old girl. The same affection that kept her hopes alive for all these years.

"Why do you always do that?" Shelby touched her lips after they separated.

"What?"

"Kiss me right after you tell me you can't get involved with me. You did the same thing at the museum. You're so goddamn fickle it drives me nuts. I understand how conflicted you are, Matty. But Jesus Christ. It's so unfair to deliver an important message about how you want to test your wings, then interrupt the broadcast with a kiss that gets me so hot I want to rip off your clothes and fuck you until . . ."

"Shhh . . ." He laughed. "Don't say fuck in a chapel. It's bad luck."

"What the hell. My luck couldn't possibly get any worse."

"Shelby Lynn, do I have to wash that mouth out with . . ."

"You." She kissed him back as hard as he'd kissed her. "I know you love me."

"Yes."

"But I still can't come with you."

"No."

"Fine, but I'm warning you." Shelby looked deep into his eyes. "When you get back, if you feed me the line about just wanting to be friends again, trust me, it'll be a deal breaker. I can't be friends with a man I've seen naked. I can't be friends with a man who kisses me the way you do. I can't be friends with a man who touches me so deeply . . ."

"You honestly love me that much?"

"Yes." She could barely breathe. "And I always have."

Shelby sat in the waiting area and watched the gate agent shut the door. A minute later a panicked latecomer pleaded with her to re-open the jetway. He hadn't heard the boarding announcement that the flight was finally taking off, and if he missed this flight, he'd miss seeing his daughter's dance recital. Unfortunately, he was turned away. Flight 400 to Portland was officially closed for boarding.

So that was it for her, too. An incredible, lifelong dream had evaporated in the time it took to load an L-1011 with passengers. Matty was flying home alone, and from the sounds of his whole free-dom song, she could just envision him buying a catamaran and sail-ing the ocean blue. If she was lucky, she'd hear from him every year on her birthday.

What the hell did Warner Lamm know about fate and destiny? And what good was astrology if it couldn't accurately predict the out-come of the most important relationship of her life? It was all a crock. Life was a crock.

It was time for her to leave now. To call Lauren to come back and get her. And yet she couldn't even bring herself to reach into her pocketbook for her phone. Sadness and disappointment could be so immobilizing.

"Is there a Ms. Lazarus in the gate area?"

Shelby looked up. Of course she was hallucinating

"Is there a Shelby Lazarus here?"

Shelby spotted a flight attendant standing by the door to the jetway.

"Over here," Shelby raced to the door. Funny how quickly legs recovered when motivated.

"Are you Shelby Lazarus?"

"Yes," Shelby panted, certain she'd never run this fast even in her prime, let alone while she was carrying twins.

"This is totally going against federal aviation regulations, but I came back out here to give you a message from Lieutenant Gover-nor Armonk's office."

"You did?"

"It's from a Mr. McCreigh. He said if you're still interested in seeing Portland, you should catch the next flight out."

Shelby needed a moment for the message to register. "Yes, yes. Of course I'm still interested in seeing Portland. But what about taking this flight? It's still on the ground."

"Sorry, but we've already gotten the go-ahead to push back. Just speak to one of the gate agents and I'm sure they'll be able to get you on another flight."

"But aren't you getting back on?" Shelby persisted.

"Yes, but we're not authorized to allow any additional passengers on once we've completed the manifold . . ."

"I'm begging you," Shelby clasped her hands in prayer formation. "I'll name this child after you. I'll put you in my will. I'll, I'll . . . just drop dead right now if you don't let me board, and then it'll be this whole huge headline: UNCARING FLIGHT ATTENDANT CAUSES PREGNANT WOMAN TO DIE OF A BROKEN HEART, and it'll be a big scandal, and no one will ever want to fly this airline again, and . . ."

The flight attendant looked around. "Are you ticketed?"

"Yes." She fumbled in her pocketbook for the ticket and handed it over.

The flight attendant took a look, then saw Shelby's anxious expression. "Is this one of those now-or-never love stories you'll write a book about, and then they'll turn it into a movie, and one day I'll be on the leg from Newark to L.A, and it'll be playing on the monitors?"

"Exactly," Shelby jumped up and down.

The flight attendant looked wistful. "I sure did love *Sleepless in Seattle*."

"Oh, me too. But this story is ten times better, I swear."

"I could get in so much trouble for this." She looked over her shoulder. "But seeing as how you're in first-class and it's not even an upgrade . . . you have to promise to tell me the whole story from beginning to end."

"Thank you so much." Shelby hugged the woman. "Can I go get my pocketbook?"

"Yes, but hurry. You're holding up commercial aviation on the Eastern seaboard."

*   *   *

Shelby was right. The flight attendant and in fact the entire crew loved her story, especially the part about Shelby spotting her childhood friend on the parkway, setting off on a wild-goose chase, then getting pulled over by a state trooper.

"Oh, it should definitely be a movie." One of them sniffed into her tissue. "And with the babies and everything. You know who'd be great playing you? Jennifer Aniston. No wait. What's her name. That cute one from HBO. Sarah Jessica Parker. She'd be perfect . . . I'm such a sucker for this kind of stuff."

"Lucky for me." Shelby laughed. "Otherwise, I'd still be sitting at the gate."

Honest to God, I've never worked so hard in any of my previous lifetimes. But it was worth it, just to see the look of relief on Shelby's face when that nice flight attendant came back out to look for her. Poor lady will never know what on earth possessed her to bend the rules like that. And Matthew will remain clueless why he thought Shelby might still be sitting at the gate. Or more importantly, why he changed his mind, yet again, about having her join him.

What? You think I'd just leave my daughter sitting there, looking so sad and pitiful? Please. I'm her mother.

Chapter Twenty-nine

Shelby hoped that the turbulence and the subsequent nausea that caused her to spend a fair amount of the flight in the lavatory was not an indication of what the rest of the trip would be like. She so wanted for the week with Matty's family to go well, and for Matty not to have any regrets that he had changed his mind about bringing her home.

She was dying to ask what had caused him to reconsider. And come to think of it, why he assumed she would still be hanging around the airport after he got on board (even if it was true). But once they were airborne, Matty's spirits soared like the plane, and she saw no point in spoiling his good mood by rehashing the earlier events of the day. Besides, who had time for Q&A? Shelby was too busy running to the lavatory. Matty was too busy doting on her.

There also wasn't much free time once they arrived, as he had planned a week of nonstop action. Welcome home parties, dinners with old friends, golf outings, and a visit to his beloved tennis coach, who was dying of cancer. And as often as possible he took his sister Wendy's four kids to the park. Shelby marveled at how wonderful he was with children, even when they were clinging to his every limb screaming, "Swing me, Uncle Matt. No me first!"

Luckily, not *every* moment was spent with a crowd. Against his mother's objections, Matty booked a suite in a swank downtown hotel. There he and Shelby could continue what they began in the Lazarus guesthouse, with apologies to Lauren and the seasick twins. But by the end of the week, the poor guy was hinting that they needed to cut back on their lovemaking.

"What are you? Eighteen?" he teased.

"No, I just thought it would be fun to make up for every year we missed."

"Yes, but not all in one week!"

"You never could keep up with me." She patted his butt.

"True. But it's not just that, Shelby," he said in a serious tone. "You have to understand how strange this is for me. I was with Gwen for a long time, and now suddenly it's like I got traded to a different team."

"I understand. But at least now we're on the *same* team." She kissed his neck. "So let's play ball. Do you remember how I like my pitches?"

"Low and inside?" He unbuttoned her shirt.

"Exactly." She slowly unzipped his pants. "Are you sure you're not too tired?"

"Actually, I've never felt more alive."

On their last night in town, Carol McCreigh invited Matthew and Shelby over for an intimate send-off dinner with Wendy and her husband, Stephen. More than once the proud mother toasted the couple's bright future. "May you two never be apart again." She raised her glass.

Shelby was thrilled that Carol was in her corner. Other mothers might have encouraged their sons to lie in the bed they made, particularly when a sick child was involved. But that didn't seem to faze her. To the contrary, Carol seemed positively relieved to have Shelby back in Matthew's life. Maybe because she had a guilty conscience all these years for letting her ex-husband talk her into moving, which kept the close friends apart.

Or maybe not.

"You know what I always wondered?" Wendy asked after she filled everyone's coffee cups. "You guys were crazy about each other. Almost inseparable. But after we moved you never talked again. What happened? Why didn't you stay in touch?"

"Funny you should ask." Shelby looked over at Matthew. "I've always wondered the same thing myself. How come you never wrote to me?"

"What are you talking about? I wrote you all the time. There were some weeks I wrote you every day. You were the one who never bothered to write back."

"Are you serious?" Shelby replied. "Right after you moved, I wrote to you almost every single day and then never heard from you. It was like you decided what's the point in staying friends if we don't live on the same block anymore?"

"Why would I think that? I was absolutely miserable. You were the only person in the world I wanted to talk to. But when I never heard from you, I thought you decided who needs Matty? If I can't play at his house anymore, what good is he?"

"Wait a minute," Wendy sat down. "You both say you wrote to each other, but neither of you ever received any of the letters? How is that possible? I could see if maybe the post office lost one or two letters, but all of them? It makes no sense."

"You really wrote to me?" Shelby asked him.

"Yes, of course. And you wrote to me?"

"Not letters, volumes. In fact I remember this one day I made three trips to the mailbox because I had to tell you all about the awful family that bought your house. They had these two prissy little girls, Vanessa and Veronica, who'd call me every day to come over and play dolls. And I'd say, 'Play dolls? I haven't done that since I was four'!"

"This is so strange." Matty shook his head. "You have no idea how pissed I was at you for blowing me off. Remember, Mother? I'd keep asking you, Why isn't Shelby writing me back? And you'd say, 'out of sight, out of mind,' or 'I guess she's busy with her other friends.' "

"Other friends?" Shelby laughed. "What other friends? Matty was the only one who could put up with me."

An eerie silence filled the room. The enormity of the revelation was staggering. If these supposed letters had been received by the young lovebirds, the two might have stayed close and eventually reunited. Certainly they would never have let so many years go by without any contact.

"When you got older did you ever look for me?" Shelby asked.

"I thought about you a lot, but so many years had gone by already I couldn't imagine why you'd want to hear from me. And what was I supposed to say? Hi, remember me? Back in the sixties I was your neighbor in Manhasset?"

"Amazing! And I did nothing *but* try to find you! When I traveled on business, the first thing I'd do in the hotel room is look up any Liebermans in the phonebook. I did searches on the Internet. Once I paid a private investigator to track you down. And then a few months ago I ran into Stacy Rothstein at Waldbaum's, and the first thing I asked was if she knew anyone who might still be in touch with you."

"Really?" Wendy said. "I can't believe you thought about him after all these years?"

"But wait. This one's the best." Shelby smiled. "My Aunt Roz got something in the mail about a thirtieth nursery school reunion, and I almost registered just to see if Matty showed up."

"Temple Judea's nursery school had a reunion?" He laughed. "Gee. If I'd known, I would have gone just to see if Melinda Abrams still liked lifting her dress in front of me."

Everyone but Shelby laughed.

"Relax," he stroked her cheek. "It was a joke."

"I'm sorry. I feel bad that you never tried to find me. But at least you named your dog after me. That's something."

"Not exactly." He winced. "Emily loved watching the old *Lassie* reruns, so when we got her a dog, we got a collie named Lassie, which she had trouble pronouncing. It came out Lazzie instead. After a while we shortened it to Laz, and the name always reminded me of you."

"Ah-ha."

It was during this next dry spell in the already strange conversation that a rather unnerving thought occurred to Shelby. The normally gregarious, outspoken Carol had not said so much as a single word since this topic of conversation started. Nor would she look Shelby in the eye.

Oh God! Did Carol know anything about those letters? Shelby tried signaling Matty to look at his mother's pained expression, but he was too lost in thought. It would be up to her to follow her instincts.

"Isn't this whole thing strange, Carol?" Shelby cleared her throat. "Neither of us ever getting a single letter?"

Carol looked up. Her face was red and swollen.

"Are you crying, Mother?" Matthew asked.

She dabbed her eyes with a napkin and stood up. "Please excuse me for a minute. Wendy, do me a favor, hun. Go turn off the coffeepot."

"Sure." Wendy leaned over and whispered to Matthew. "What's with her . . . Should I put the cake away, too, Mom?"

"Yes, thanks."

"Let me help clear the dishes," Shelby offered.

"No. Sit." Carol said. "Both of you." She turned to Matthew. "I'll be right back."

When Shelby had returned home after the accident and sifted through the remains of her bedroom, she'd been saddened to discover that the essence of her young life had been reduced to three cartons and an A&S shopping bag. But never could she have imagined that the entire history of her long-distance friendship with Matty would be crammed into a shoe box that was kept inside of an old steamer trunk, which got stored in a dusty attic in a small two-story cape in Portland, Oregon. Carol McCreigh handed the box to her son. "I am truly sorry."

Shelby, a former Nancy Drew aficionado, knew before he ripped off the first piece of masking tape that the contents of the box would solve the mystery of the missing letters. What she didn't understand was why.

"Oh my God," Matthew cried out. "I don't believe this." He sorted through piles of unopened mail addressed to him, all with Manhasset postmarks dated January 1970. February. March. Each envelope had Shelby's signature red, S.W.A.K. seal, which had been hot stamped on the back. And there, underneath her letters, were his. Dozens of letters addressed to Shelby with large block lettering.

"How many of these did you save?" Shelby could barely breathe.

"Every last one." Carol sighed.

"But why, Mother? Why would you sabotage us like that? You knew how much our friendship meant to us."

"I . . . it wasn't . . . believe me . . ." she sputtered.

"I'm in shock," Shelby cried. "You purposely tried to come between us?"

"It's not what you think, dear."

"I don't know what to think. All that time we were pouring out our little hearts out to each other and . . ."

"It wasn't my idea. I didn't want to do it," Carol exclaimed. "But I made a promise."

"To whom?" Matthew and Shelby asked at the same time.

"To your mother, dear." She reached for Shelby's hand.

"My mother? There's no way! She adored Matty."

"Yes, but she had her reasons." Carol looked down. "It's a long story."

No one moved.

"However I say this, it's going to come out wrong," she said, waving her hands. "It doesn't make much sense now. I'm not even sure it made sense then. But Sandy made me promise on a stack of Bibles to keep you two apart. What was I supposed to do? It was the last wish of a dying woman."

"I don't understand," Shelby whispered. "What possible reason could she have had?"

"She was trying to protect you, dear. She knew that after she died you were going to feel totally abandoned. And then with us moving away so soon after, she told me she was afraid you might never recover. You were such a loner she thought you'd only try to lean on Matthew and not move on. I'm not saying I agreed with her, but I knew she was just trying to do right by you."

"I don't know what to say. I can't believe she actually made you promise not to give Matty my letters."

"Or to mail any of the ones he wrote to you."

"That's the stupidest thing I ever heard," Matthew exclaimed. "If your kid is in pain, you don't make it worse by keeping her away from the one person who can help."

"Oh believe me, I argued with her plenty," Carol said. "But, Shelby, you know what I'm talking about. If she made up her mind about something, you couldn't budge her for all the tea in China."

"Yes, but she had to know I would be crushed if I didn't have Matty to talk to."

"But you were kids, darling. We thought you'd eventually forget about each other."

Shelby took a deep breath. "When did she talk to you about all this?"

"A few weeks before she died. She had just come home from the hospital, and I came over to visit. It was awful. She was just lying there so pale and weak, groaning in pain."

Shelby cried at the recollection of those vivid images. The small, listless body. The nearly bald head. The faint voice. She had forgotten that other people might remember this last stage, too.

"I swear," Carol continued, "she practically made me put it in writing that I would carry out this request, and what was I supposed to say to her? 'No? I think this is ridiculous?' But she kept insisting that this was what was best for both our kids, and finally I gave in. I gave her my word."

Matthew shook his head. "I can maybe understand Sandy not wanting Shelby's letters to get to me. But why stop my letters from getting to her?"

"Because eventually you would have asked her why she wasn't writing back, and then she'd wonder what was going on and pick up the phone, and say, 'what letters?' Besides, the more I thought about it, the more I was okay with the idea. You were going through hell, your father and I were broke, fighting. It was a nightmare. So who needed you telling Shelby how bad everything was, and then having her blab it to the neighborhood that we were in trouble?"

"I still can't get over it." Matthew rifled through the box again. "Every letter that I wrote you never mailed? Every letter that she wrote, you never gave me?"

"Yes."

"But you saved them after all these years." Shelby sniffed. "Why?"

"Why does anyone save anything, dear? You just never know."

"Any regrets?" Matthew sighed.

"Regrets?" Carol looked at her son and Shelby holding hands, clinging to each for dear life, just as they had as kids. "I don't know. Who's to say what would have been? What's that expression? Sometimes you have to go around the world to go around the block? Maybe this was all *bashert*. Exactly how things were supposed to work out."

I know what you're thinking, and I couldn't agree more. It was a terrible idea trying to keep the kids apart. Certainly not one of my prouder moments as a mother. But didn't Carol do a great job of presenting my side of the story? What a good lady she is, defending me like that. Especially after I couldn't be bothered with her when we were neighbors. My loss.

Anyway, what's important now is that Shelby and Matty are together and happy. And maybe I can stop running around putting ideas in people's heads. Like that innocent question I had Wendy ask over coffee. I knew if she brought up the subject, Carol would gladly confess. The only reason she saved those letters all these years was that she hoped she'd be given the chance to return them one day. And God answered her prayers.

Actually, God answered mine, too.

It was a quiet, contemplative flight home. This time both Matty and Shelby felt nauseous, having nothing to do with turbulence or pregnancy. It would take a long time to recover from their twisted fate and the knowledge that their own mothers had conspired against them.

And yet they also knew it was their common bond. Both had spent their childhoods in the throes of turmoil and confusion. Both had been forced to grow up long before they were ready. And both had spent their lives struggling to understand a deep, unexplainable void that permeated their core.

"I guess Warner is right," Shelby explained. "It's all karma, baby. Learn the lesson, get the reward. Then destiny takes over, and you end up where you were supposed to be in the first place."

Suddenly Matthew understood. Their "chance" meeting on the highway might not have been chance at all. Destiny might have separated them, but it could also bring them together. And in light of that revelation, for the first time in years, his path was illuminated.

"I want us to live together," he proposed to Shelby over a tray of rubber chicken.

"I want us to live together, too. But where? You need to be in Westchester to be close to Emily, and I need to be in Manhasset because of Lauren and the babies."

"I know, but I might have a great compromise. I have a friend who's been trying to sublet her co-op on Madison and Eighty-fourth. It's a beautiful building. It's one block from Central Park and the Met. And it's halfway between Westchester and Long Island!"

"That sounds incredible," Shelby clapped. "Plus it's a quick cab ride to the office for me. You're a genius."

"No. Desperate." He kissed her hand. "I so want this to work. But before we go ahead with our plans, I want to get Larry and Roz's permission."

"Whatever for?" Shelby protested. "I'm a big girl. In fact a very big girl." She looked down at her enormous belly. "We don't need their approval."

"Fine. Then we'll ask for their blessing. I just need to know they accept me and my unusual circumstances."

"Are you crazy?" She laughed. "Given my circumstances, they would pay you to get me off their hands. Besides, you know how much they've always loved you."

Shelby was right, of course. When she and Matty drove over to the Transitions Center for Rehabilitation, they welcomed him with open arms.

"When the time is right, I promise I'll make her an honest woman." He hugged Larry.

"Is that a marriage proposal?" Shelby jumped into his arms.

"Not yet." He laughed. "Is she always in such a rush?" he asked his future father-in-law.

"Since the day she was born." Larry slapped him on the back.

"Anyway, my top priorities are to find a brilliant divorce attorney, and to do something I've been thinking about for years. I want to legally change my name back to Lieberman."

"Fantastic!" Larry laughed. "Because with that *schnozola*, you sure didn't look like a McCarthy or McGillicutty, or whatever the hell your name is now."

"I love the idea, too." Shelby clapped. "Then my initials would stay the same and I could keep all my monogrammed towels."

"That was my first thought, too." Matty laughed. "Saving money on towels."

Once Shelby and Matty figured out all the logistics and made arrangements to sublet the apartment in the city, Shelby hoped everything else would fall into place. Particularly with the babies. Now in her second trimester, if she wasn't feeling hot and tired, she was complaining about swollen ankles, indigestion, frequent trips to the bathroom, looking like a small baboon, and suffering through those humiliating visits to Dr. Kessler's office. "You'd think the Messiah was coming every time I had a weight gain!"

But the real problem was not with the surrogate, it was with the mother. Rather than being doting and attentive, and catering to Shelby's every need as she'd promised, Lauren was spending most of her time at Danny's house watching Jordan, slowly working her way into their lives.

"Not for nothing, Lauren, but don't you think you should be

spending less time over there and more time getting ready for your own children? You haven't even started picking out the layettes yet."

"I know. I will," she said. "I've just been so busy."

Busy my ass, Shelby thought. She could see what was happening. With Avi, the quest for children was the glue that had kept them together. But once he was out of the picture, even though Lauren looked forward to motherhood, the urgency dissipated. She wanted a family, but the timing had to be right.

When she met Danny, for the first time in her life she was involved in a tender, loving relationship that made her feel safe and nurtured. Unfortunately it was with a man who was adamant about not wanting the responsibility of a large family at this stage in his life.

"I'm not sure what you're doing," Shelby pressed. "I'm due in a few months, yet you're getting more and more involved with a guy who doesn't want kids. Where does that leave you?"

"I don't know." Lauren bit her lip. "I don't know."

"Do you love him?" Shelby held her breath.

"I think I do."

"And does he love you?"

"He says he does."

"So then what's the problem? If you love each other, you get used to his kid, he gets used to yours. What's the matter? He never heard about the Brady Bunch?"

"Oh, he's heard of them," Lauren cried. "He just doesn't want to be them."

"You have a major problem, Lauren."

"Ya think?"

Chapter Thirty

Monday, June 14, was a day like any other. Except at the Lazarus home, where friends and family were gathering for an all-day barbeque to celebrate the joyous release of Roz and Larry from rehab and the return to their home. One year to the day of the accident.

To commemorate the couple's miraculous recovery, *Newsday* ran their picture on the front page, and included an emotional sidebar by their daughter, famed journalist, Shelby Lazarus.

Roz complained about all the unnecessary publicity, but Larry was loving the attention, particularly when he found out the gardener who hit them planned to offer them a lifetime of complimentary landscaping services. "What some people will do for free publicity," Larry observed, laughing as he and Roz posed with Mr. Juan Pedro Martinez under their weeping willow.

"Can you believe it's a year already?" Lauren asked Shelby as they watched the photographer from *Newsday* shoot footage on their front lawn. "It just breaks my heart to know Daddy's going to walk with a limp for the rest of his life."

"Get real. At least he's got a rest of his life."

"I know you're right." She nodded. "Hey. In your wildest dreams, did you ever think you'd be back in New York, pregnant, and living with Matty?"

"Truthfully, no. I didn't see that coming." Shelby chuckled.

"Maybe we should name one of the babies after Juan Pedro Martinez. I mean obviously if it wasn't for him . . ."

"No way! You can't name your child after the man who mowed down your parents."

"Here you go." Matty returned from the bar with a tall glass of iced tea for Shelby. "Sorry, there was a run on cherry Kool-Aid . . ."

"Have you seen Danny?" Lauren looked around.

"Last I saw, he was trying to coax Jordan out of the pool to eat."

"Maybe I'll go give him a hand." Lauren smiled. "Jordie always listens to me."

"Whoa! Not so fast, Tonto." Shelby grabbed her hand. "I have to talk to you."

"Not now, Shel."

"Well when would be convenient for you? After the babies are born, and they're lying in the nursery waiting for their mother to pick them up?"

"Hey, guys." Danny joined them, unaware he was interrupting a broadcast in progress.

"Later?" Lauren pleaded with her eyes. "Please?"

"No, now," Shelby fumed. "This is the perfect time to talk. We're all assembled."

"What's up?" Danny, the resident shrink and ever intuitive one, asked.

"It's nothing," Shelby gritted. "We're just having some technical difficulties."

"What kind of difficulties?" Danny rubbed Lauren's arm. "Anything I can help with?"

"I don't know." Shelby massaged her belly, now an automatic reflex every time the babies kicked. "That depends on how you feel about having twins."

"Shelby, stop it!" Lauren's breathing became uneven. "This is between you and me."

"Not anymore. Look around." She pointed. "You're involved with someone, I'm involved with someone . . . Are you hyperventilating? Do you need a bag?"

"No." Lauren took a couple of deep breaths and slowly exhaled. "I'll be okay."

"If I could throw in my two cents here." Danny put his arm around Lauren. "I love your sister, Shelby. But we've discussed this whole thing ad nauseam, and she knows how I feel."

"I don't give a rat's ass how you feel," Shelby hissed. "This is not about what you want, or what you need. Almost nine months ago, against my better judgment, I agreed to conceive a child for my sister and her husband, and now that child is twins, her husband is *shtupping* some Israeli chick in the army, and Lauren is playing nanny to your child, which is a fabulous deal for you. You're saving a few hundred a week on a salary, and she's throwing great sex into the deal. I don't blame you for not wanting to mess with the formula . . ."

"Shelby, what are you doing?" Lauren looked as if she was going to pummel her. "You have no right to speak to Danny like that. He has done nothing to you . . ."

"Except give you an easy way to shirk your responsibilities and commitments . . ."

"I have done no such thing. And this isn't the time or place to . . ."

"No! Sorr-eee," Shelby gritted. "Time's up. Buzzer's sounded. What is my due date?"

"July 13." Lauren's eyes welled up. Shelby could be so impossible.

"And when is that?"

"Next month . . ."

"Exactly. And yet there seems to be a holdup. I told you to order the layette, and you didn't. I told you to line up a Lamaze coach, and you didn't. I told you to start thinking of names . . ."

"Oh sure. Now all of a sudden you're acting like the babies are my responsibility," Lauren started to cry. "But up until this point, you never let me forget you conceived them, you carried them, and you were going to call the shots . . ."

"What are you talking about? I did everything possible to include you."

"That is so not true." Lauren's whole body shook. "From day one you made me feel like I didn't matter . . . When I asked you not to go to Dr. Weiner's funeral, what did you say? You said I was being ridiculous, and as far as you were concerned, it wasn't my decision to make. Oh, and then yesterday? You didn't even tell me you had an appointment with Dr. Kessler."

"Because you were too busy playing Jordan's mother to show up for the last two visits. So I figured the hell with it. I'm not even going to tell her I'm going."

"Well why should I bother going when you act as if I'm not even there? When I told Dr. Kessler I wanted to know the sexes, you went nuts like, no way, forget it, we'll find out in the delivery room, we don't need to know that. But you never even asked if that was okay with me!"

"I didn't want you to know because I was afraid if you found out and were somehow disappointed, then you'd lose interest."

"Lose interest? That's the stupidest thing I've ever heard. When you got pregnant, it was like a dream come true for me. But then you acted like I didn't even exist. It was all about you."

"How could you even think that?" Shelby glared. "This has been the most unselfish act of my life. I had to get over my phobia of doctors, I had to stop dieting, I had to deal with excruciating back pain and swollen ankles, and still make it in to work. I have indigestion every night, oh and what about the fact I resemble a baboon? I mean I finally find Matty and look what I look like. And now you have the nerve to tell me I haven't been considerate of you?"

"That's right." Lauren took a deep breath. "Not considerate, and not honest, either . . . I know you didn't start out wanting anything to do with the babies, but that's not how you feel now. It seems to me, you'll be the one who is devastated if you go home empty-handed."

Shelby stared in disbelief. "You're just saying that so I don't accuse you of being fickle."

"It has nothing to do with me, Shel. I've seen that sad look in your eye when strangers ask you your due date, or the names you've chosen. I've seen how you can't stop smiling when the babies kick. I've seen you rubbing your belly, always so loving and caring. If we're being perfectly honest, then I think you have to admit that you're the one who changed her mind. Not me."

Shelby's jaw dropped. Was Lauren right? Was she so emotionally vested now, she was going to have a hard time parting with the babies, just as Matty had predicted? Admittedly, as her due date approached, she had gotten a little glum whenever she thought about the babies she'd nourished and safeguarded leaving her protective womb.

"Look," Danny ventured into the arena again. "I know this all started by your wanting to help Lauren, but you have to face the facts. They're not legally or even biologically hers."

"Oh, give it up already," Shelby cried. "We all know where you stand, so you can stop trying to pawn them off. Maybe you should face the facts. If it wasn't for you, everything would be going according to plan."

"Maybe it is," Matty said softly.

Shelby, Lauren, and Danny stopped bickering.

"The truth is, we're all here right now due to unforseen circumstances. No one expected Avi to leave, or Lauren to meet Danny at a dance that occurred on the very same day, or Shelby to find me on a highway . . . but that's exactly what happened. Maybe with good reason."

"What's your point?" Danny asked.

"That I've thought of the perfect names for the babies."

"Well, what good will that do?" Shelby put her hands on her hips. "That's like offering to clean the deck chairs on the *Titanic*."

"Maybe," he persisted. "But I still think these names would suit them perfectly."

"So what would you call them?" Lauren asked sweetly.

"I was thinking"—he hesitated—"that they should be called Liebermans."

"What?" Three heads turned.

"Are you crazy?" Shelby shouted. "Honey, these aren't cute little puppies you take home from the breeder, and if it doesn't work out you bring them back."

"I'm aware of that."

"What are you saying, Matty?" Lauren's face lit up.

"I'm saying rather than arguing over who did what to whom, we should take a step back and see that everything is unfolding the way it was meant to. These are Shelby's biological children, and if Lauren and Danny's future together would have a better chance without the burden of caring for two infants, then I say they should be raised by their mother . . . and me."

"Oh my God." Lauren and Shelby clutched hands.

"Do you really mean that?" Shelby's heart pounded.

"Yes, I do." His eyes welled up.

"But how could we possibly do this? We're in a tiny one-bedroom apartment, and . . ."

"You could live here," Lauren jumped in.

"What? In the guesthouse?" Shelby gasped. "I don't think so."

"No, I mean just this morning Mommy and Daddy told me they've decided to put the house up for sale because they'll never be able to manage with all the stairs. So, now you could move in."

Matty and Shelby looked at each other.

"How weird would that be living back on Majestic Court again, married with two kids?" Shelby cried.

"Actually? It would be awesome." Matty smiled. "It's like my mother was saying. We had to travel the world to discover what we really wanted was right in our own backyards."

"Oh my God." Lauren hugged Matty. "You are the absolute greatest. That way you'd be right here and I could see you and the babies every day, and I could baby-sit anytime you wanted . . ."

Shelby shook in disbelief. What has happening here? In the time it took to run a mile, the entire course of her life had just been rerouted. But is it what she really wanted? To be living in her old house, raising a family, and answering to the name Shelby Lieberman?

"What do you think, Shel?" Lauren eyed her cautiously.

"I don't know. I guess it's possible this is what I was hoping for."

"Oh my God! I thought so." Lauren hugged her so tightly. "I thought so."

"You sure about this, man?" Danny asked Matty, relief written all over his face.

"Let me tell you something, Danny. With everything I've been through, between my painful childhood, a rocky marriage, and having a terminally ill child, getting a chance to start over with the woman I love would make me feel like the luckiest man alive."

"What a sap you turned out to be, Shel." Lauren sniffled. "For all the grief you gave me about playing Barbie dolls, you ended up buying the whole package."

"That is so not true." Shelby blushed. "I have never driven a pink convertible, and I'm sure as hell never going to see that size waistline again."

"Yes, but it's okay because you're going to be a mommy," Lauren cried.

"So I am." Shelby joined her in a sisterly union of tears. "So I am."

"Hi, Shelby. How are you today?" Warner wheeled his chair over to rub her belly for luck.

"Great. Terrific. Couldn't be better. My ankles are the size of watermelons, I'm wearing a brace for my back, the babies are sitting right on my bladder so I have to pee if I even look at a glass of water,

I'm tired, I'm hot, I'm cranky, and I have another month to go. That's how I am."

"Oh bitch, bitch, bitch. But I know something you don't know that will cheer you up."

"Not now, Warner. I'm on deadline for a story Ian put me on, and look at all this fan mail I still have to answer." She pointed to another sack on her desk. "It's been a month since the DES story ran, and it's still pouring in."

"Well I can believe it, honey. It's the first time the *Informer* has ever run a five-part series on a serious matter, and thousands of people were affected by it. They just want to say thank you."

"It's nice to be appreciated." Shelby lifted the heavy bag of mail. "But how the hell am I going to respond to everyone?"

"Oh, pish tish. Stop *kvetching*. I have something very important to tell you, and I promise after I do, you'll use all those letters for confetti."

Shelby knew Warner would pester her until she played along, so to save time, she let him whisper in her ear. "Oh, my God!" she shrieked. "Are you absolutely positive?"

"Shhhh . . . no one is supposed to know yet. They're not announcing it until tomorrow."

"Oh, my God. I can't believe it. How did you find out?"

"You must be joking. The great Warner knows all. I predicted this. Remember?"

"Actually, now that you mention it, you went three for three!" She began to shake. "You said my parents would survive the accident, that I'd reunite with a long-lost friend under very bizarre circumstances, and that love would soon be in the air, and now this . . ."

"Did I say never to question me?" He planted a juicy kiss on her cheek.

"Hey, everyone," Shelby shouted. "Warner has a big announcement to make!"

"Wait, wait, wait. You know how Ian feels about people stealing his thunder."

"Tough! It's my thunder, and I can steal it if I want to!"

"Okay, Big Mama!" Warner stood up on his chair and whistled. "Yoo-hoo! Listen up every one. I have some big news to share."

"Barry Manilow said hello to you in an elevator?" a veteran reporter yelled out.

"It so happens, Barry is a very good friend of mine, you jealous little jackass."

"Tell them already." Shelby was jumping up and down, not a pretty sight.

"Okay, class. Here's the scoop," he clapped. "Our very own Shelby Lazarus, who wrote that wonderfully compassionate series on DES that helped thousands of readers, is going to be named one of this year's Pulitzer prize nominees tomorrow. Isn't she groovy?"

Suddenly the newsroom erupted, and everyone rushed over to Shelby's desk to offer their congratulations, at just the moment Ian returned to his office.

"What's the fuss?" He strode over to Shelby's cubicle. "Is it baby time already?"

"No, of course not," Shelby hugged Ian. "Warner told me about my Pulitzer nomination."

"Warner! Get over here, you little fairy tale." He pretended to put him in a head lock. "Didn't I tell you not to mention this until the news officially came from the committee?"

"Yes, but she needed cheering up right now, Ian. Look at her. Those are tears of joy."

"More like Buckingham Fountain if you want my personal opinion." He stared at the puddle on the floor. "Good God, Shelby. I think your water balloon broke. Everyone stand back!"

"That didn't come from me," Shelby looked around, hoping to discover someone had accidentally spilled a bottle of champagne. "I still have another month." But when she felt warm fluid running down her leg, she was certain it wasn't Dom Pérignon. "What's happening?"

"Well, what do you think is happening, sweet pea?" Warner laughed. "You're in labor."

"But it's too soon. We're not ready."

"Apparently they are." Warner patted her belly.

"Somebody get her a chair," Ian shouted. "Or a bed. What *should* we do with you?" He looked to Shelby for sage advice. "I've never done this before."

"I'm a little new at this myself." She thought for a moment. "But, here's the plan. First, someone needs to call maintenance to clean up this mess, then someone should take me to the ladies' room so I can clean myself up, then someone else should get on the phone for me."

"I'll make the phone calls." Warner clapped. "Whom should I call first?"

"Matty. Then Lauren. Then my parents. Then Irma Weiner . . ."

"Perhaps it might be useful to add a doctor to the list?" Ian suggested.

"Right. Of course. Call Dr. Kessler at North Shore and ask him what the hell I do now?"

"Aye, aye, Captain Shelby," Warner saluted. "It's all systems go."

But after ten minutes of working the phones, Warner feared the launch might have to be postponed. "Who's on your B list, honey? I can't seem to reach anybody."

"What do you mean?" a rapidly breathing Shelby returned from the ladies room.

"I called Matthew's office and his secretary said he's on his way to Connecticut to see his daughter. Lauren's not home and isn't answering her cell. Ditto with your parents. I paged Irma Weiner twice and she hasn't called back yet. And Dr. Kessler is away on a camping trip. But not to worry because the office said his partner is on call."

"His partner!" Shelby nearly fainted at the memory of her first examination with that dreadful man. "I hate that pompous son of a bitch. He's not laying a hand on me . . . Oh, my God. What am I going to do?"

"Don't vorry a think, darling. The great Warner is here." He gently placed his arm around her shoulder and grabbed her pocketbook. "I'll drive you to the hospital now, and I'm sure by the time we arrive, everyone will have gotten word."

"Thank you, Warner." She let him lead her toward the elevator. "You're such a doll I'm only sorry I didn't think to fix you up with my brother."

Chapter Thirty-one

Even though Shelby and Matty only attended two Lamaze classes before Shelby went into labor, she had learned enough to know she was in trouble. Not because there were any immediate complications, or even ominous signs. It's just that when she'd mentally prepared herself for this day, she never envisioned coming in four weeks early.

Nor did she expect on that day the intense heat and humidity would result in the mother of all thunderstorms. By 4:00 P.M., the sky was designer black, with lightning striking at close intervals rivaling, coincidentally, a pregnant woman's contractions.

Nor did Shelby expect to be alone with Warner in the birthing room. Seems Dr. Kessler had taken off to the Berkshire Mountains for a male bonding camping trip with his son. Her parents were spending a few, relaxing days at their Westhampton beach house. According to her son Brad, Irma was en route to an elder hostel in New Orleans with her new love, Norman. Lauren was treating Jordan to a day in the city to see the "biggy" dinosaur museum. And as for her future husband? Of all days for him to drive out to Connecticut to visit his daughter, Emily.

"This is a nightmare." Shelby was transfixed on the IV lodged in her forearm, wondering if the sight of the needle made others want to pass out, too. "No one is here yet, and with this weather, they may never get here!"

"Oh believe me, they'll get here, or my name ain't Warner Lamm." He mopped his brow while studying the fetal heart monitors. "Uh-oh," he shivered. "Here comes another one."

"I need drugs! Lots and lots of drugs!" Shelby shouted in pain as she squeezed his hand.

"I'm with you, babe. Although I think I heard the nurse say you're only two centimeters . . ."

"No way." She thrashed around. "Only two fucking centimeters? But I'm already dying . . ."

"Ooh. Sorry. False alarm." Warner took back his sore hand. "There are so many ding-dongs on this stupid machine, I thought it was a contraction. Where's the damn doctor? Isn't there an easier way to have a baby?"

"No." Shelby blew in and out. "That's why we must castrate men and make do with the people who already exist . . . Do you hear that?"

"Do I hear what?"

"The music. 'Silent Night.' "

"In June?" Warner stood very still. "I don't think so."

"I'm not kidding," Shelby closed her eyes. "I hear it loud and clear. And it's so strange because that was what my mother sang to me every night when she tucked me in."

" 'Silent Night'?" Warner laughed. "But aren't you Jewish?"

"Yes, but she didn't care. She thought it was a great lullaby. 'Holy infant so tender and mild, sleep in heavenly peace,' " Shelby sang. "You sure you can't hear it?"

"I have better hearing than my dog, but no."

"Well I do, Warner. What do you think it means?"

"What do *you* think it means?"

"Oh, please. Don't give me any of that latent, repressed, subconscious shrink shit. I hear the music, and it's not in my imagination."

Warner nodded. "It means, darling, that she's with you. Spirits often try to reach us with smells and sounds and sights. It's their loving way of letting you know they're here with you."

"Mommy?" Shelby started to cry as she looked around for another tangible sign so she didn't have to commit herself to a padded room when this was all over. "Are you here?"

Then suddenly the power cut out, shutting down the lights, the monitors, and the clock.

"Holy shit," Warner ran out to the hall, only to discover Shelby's room was the only one without electric. "She's gooooood." He ran back in, at the very instant the power returned.

It was perhaps no more than a ten-second blip, not enough time for the emergency generators to kick in, but long enough for Shelby to realize that even though her family had not yet arrived, she was not alone. And maybe never had been.

"Oh my God. In my life . . ." Shelby gripped Warner's hand. "You really think that was her?"

"Don't you?"

"I don't know. It looks like the end of the world out there. It could have been the storm."

"Hitting just your room?" Warner raised his eyebrows.

"Oh my God," Shelby whispered as she sobbed into her hands. "I'm so happy."

I've always wanted to do that. I'm just glad I waited until she would understand . . .

"When is everyone going to get here?" Shelby asked an hour later. But by the time Matty, Lauren, Danny, and her parents received word Shelby was in active labor, and raced over to North Shore, she was experiencing such painful contractions, all she wanted to know was when everyone was going to leave. "I want to leave too." She squeezed Matty's hand. "This hurts so bad."

"I know. But at least it's dry in here, and you're doing unbelievable, honey."

"When's Dr. Kessler getting here?" she asked again.

"The roads are flooded, Shel." Lauren rubbed her feet. "I'm sure he's doing his best."

"But he said he was coming, right?" She took two deep cleansing breaths.

"Yes," Lauren repeated. "Lucky for you his son got poison ivy, or you'd be stuck with Dr. I-Hate-Women. Has he even been in to see you yet?"

"Once." Shelby cried out in pain. "But he tried to do an internal, and I told him to get the hell away from me."

"Shelby, you have to let him examine you." Matty laughed. "Or else he won't know how far along you are."

"Yeah, well if he's so smart he should know where I'm at just by looking at me!" She collapsed. "That one was the worst. I don't know how much more of this I can take."

But Shelby was about to learn lesson number one of giving birth. Never ask when will labor end, for one will invariably find out. Not soon enough. In the meantime, she was able to gauge how much time had passed by observing the nurses had changed shifts.

Nurse O'Malley began her ten-hour tour of duty at 7:00 P.M., gasping when she marched into Shelby's birthing room for her appointed rounds. "Hold it, hold it, hold it!" She counted the number of people hovering over the bed. "What are all of you doing in here?"

"What do you think we're doing?" Shelby cried out. "We're trying to have a baby."

"I sure hope so; otherwise, you're about to go through hell for nothing. But only the mother and the coach are allowed in this room. Everyone else out!"

To Nurse O'Malley's dismay, her words fell on deaf ears, for Matty, now in charge of watching the fetal heart monitors, tracked a new contraction, and warned Team Baby to man their stations. "Pant and blow." He pushed Shelby's bangs out of her eyes. "You can do it, sweetheart."

With each subsequent scream, Roz fed her ice chips, Lauren massaged her, Danny counted the seconds of the contraction on his stopwatch, and Warner got Shelby to remain riveted to her focal point, a stuffed collie that bore a strong resemblance to Laz.

Finally, the contraction subsided, and everyone cheered, proud of their continuing contribution to the labor process. Shelby was at five centimeters now, and with their love and support, was somehow managing to hold on. Even in spite of her incessant cries, and her vacillating between begging for warm socks and wanting to rip off her hospital gown, only once did she demand a chaser of Valium and vodka. Then settled for a nice, soothing epidural.

"I swear to God, Cookie"—Larry wiped his brow as if he'd just suffered through that last contraction himself—"being here to watch you give birth is an absolute miracle."

Not swayed by paternal sentiment, or any sentiment, the determined Mrs. O'Malley barked orders. "Okay, we'll do this by process of elimination. Who are you?" She pointed to Lauren.

"Me? I was going to be the mother, but now I guess I'm more like the surrogate."

"Oh, really. Then who is she?" The confused nurse pointed to the woman in labor.

"I was going to be the surrogate," Shelby groaned. "Now I'm going to be the mother."

"So you must be the proud grandma." She pointed to Roz.

"No, technically I'm the aunt and stepmother of both the mother and the surrogate, so that makes me the great aunt, and the stepgrandma of the babies. I'm definitely qualified to stay!"

"And you?" She tapped Larry on the shoulder.

"Can't you tell?" he leaned on his cane. "I'm the proud grandpa. And, I might add, the recent contributor of a sizable donation to this institution in appreciation of the extraordinary medical staff. I doubt the board of directors would like to hear I was kicked out."

"We'll see about that!" Mrs. O'Malley was even more determined to pare down the crowd. "Who are you?" She pointed to Warner.

"This is your lucky day." He kissed her hand. "I am the great and powerful Warner Lamm."

"Really?" Her face lit up. "The astrologer from the *New York Informer*?"

"The one and only." He bowed. "And also in your midst"—he pointed—"is famed investigative journalist and Pulitzer prize nominee, Shelby Lazarus."

"Did he say Pulitzer prize nominee?" Larry asked Roz.

Roz shrugged. "Sounds to me like that's what he said."

"Well, I'll be." Mrs. O'Malley shook Warner's hand, not even acknowledging he'd just introduced her to an esteemed colleague. "I read you every chance I can, and you're amazing!"

"Why didn't you tell us?" Matty kissed her. "My girl's up for a Pulitzer prize! Wow!"

"Oh, yeah." Shelby grabbed hold of the metal bar on her bed. "The nominations are being announced tomorrow, but Warner got a heads up . . . Owwwww!!!"

"*Mazel tov!*" Her family offered up hugs and kisses. Could this day possibly get any better?

Mrs. O'Malley wondered the same thing. "We rarely have celebrities on the floor. Would you mind very much if I told the ladies that you were here?" she asked Warner.

"I'd rather you told the guys." He winked. "Actually, I must be going. . . ."

"No stay. Please," Shelby reached for his hand. "I can't do this without you."

"I don't know how to break this to you, darlin'. But with or without me, those cute, little buggers are coming out. Tonight's a full moon!"

"Jesus and Mary!" Mrs. O'Malley looked up. "Thanks for the warning. Things get crazy around here at full moon time . . . Okay, back to you." She eyed Danny. "What's your story?"

"Honestly? I'm not sure."

"Well, are you related to either the mother or the surrogate?"

"I hope to be one day." He smiled at Lauren.

"Then let me guess." She sized up the attentive man at the patient's bedside. "You must be the lucky husband."

"Nope." Matty swallowed his now-cold coffee.

"The father?"

"Not biologically speaking."

"Then I'm afraid you two will have to park yourselves in the waiting room down the hall." She pointed to him and Danny. "This party is for families only."

"Actually, I think I can remedy that." Matty looked around at everyone's fingers. "Who's got a ring I can borrow?"

"*Oy gutenu*," Larry shouted. "I almost forgot. Roz, get the ring!"

"Coming." Roz slowly made her way to the chair where her pocketbook was stashed under shopping bags full of deli sandwiches. "I put it in here somewhere." She ransacked the contents.

"What ring?" a groggy Shelby asked.

"Found it!" Roz handed the diamond in platinum setting to her husband.

"What ring, Daddy?" Shelby wasn't exactly her normal, patient self.

"Matthew?" He beamed. "If you are about to ask for my daughter's hand in marriage, I would be honored and privileged if you would present her with this ring."

Matthew studied the beautiful stone. "It's perfect." He smiled. "Where did you get it?"

"Let me see that." Shelby grabbed it from Matty's hand.

"It's gorgeous." Lauren peered over her sister's shoulder. "I've never seen it before."

"Yes, you have." Her father looked down. "You just don't remember because you were so small. But girls, this was your mother's engagement ring."

"It was?" Shelby clasped it in her hands. "Oh, my God. I can't believe it. Mommy's ring?"

"She would be so proud of you, Cookie. For coming to Lauren's rescue, for being so brave through this whole ordeal. And now look at you. You're enduring the worst kind of pain imaginable, and I know from pain, believe me. I thought if you wore it, it would remind you how much the two of you were alike. So much courage, intelligence, strength . . ."

"I love it," Shelby cried. "Thank you. But how did you know Matty was going to ask . . ."

"I didn't. It just so happens a few weeks ago I made the decision to give it to you for good luck. I thought if you wore it on your finger, you'd feel her looking over you . . ."

"Thank you, Daddy," Shelby said softly. "I do feel her presence. Before you got here I kept hearing 'Silent Night', and Warner said that's her way of letting me know she's with me."

"Isn't that something?" Her father nodded. "The day of the accident I was totally knocked unconscious. But somehow I kept seeing her face, and I knew I was going to live."

"Oh my God." Shelby grabbed his hand. "The same thing happened to me. The day of the accident I was sitting in Lauren's car in the hospital lot because I was too terrified to walk in here. Then I happened to look in the vanity mirror, saw her reflection, and completely freaked."

"What do you think of that, Mr. Lamm?" Larry asked. "Pretty incredible, am I right?"

"So many unevolved people, so little time," he cried into Matty's shoulder. "Of course it's incredible, but visits from the other side happen every day. Loved ones who pass over are even more alive than we are, just not in a physical dimension. Come on people. Get with the program."

"Isn't he incredible?" Nurse O'Malley swooned, letting her professional guard down for a moment. "Now where were we?"

"I believe I was about to propose." Matty took the ring from Shelby's hand. "May I?"

Shelby gripped the side bar and panted. "Yes. Don't let me stop you."

"Shelby?" He went down on bended knee. "I love you with all my heart, and I am eternally grateful that you chased me like a lunatic on the Hutchinson River Parkway. Right now I have never been happier or more fulfilled, and I hope you feel the same. So, if you don't happen to have any other major plans for the rest of your life, I was wondering, would you be willing to spend it with me?"

"You lost me." Aunt Roz nudged him. "That was your idea of a marriage proposal?"

"Yes." Matthew laughed. "But just so there's no confusion, Shelby, will you marry me?"

Shelby screamed loud enough to rattle the windows, a sign she felt another contraction coming on. Then she quickly panted.

"Is that a yes?"

Shelby squeezed his hand so hard he winced.

"It's a yes!" he shouted, carefully placing the diamond on her finger. "It's a yes!" he announced to Mrs. O'Malley, then kissed his beloved. "That makes me her fiancé. Now I can stay."

"*Mazel tov.*" They all cheered and hugged, grateful for all their bounty and good fortune.

"Oh, forget it." Mrs. O'Malley rolled her tearful eyes. "I can see I'm not going to get any cooperation in here." She walked out sniffing in a tissue. "Just keep it down to a roar!"

If only that was possible. For when she returned to take Shelby's vital signs, more visitors had arrived to wish Shelby and Matty good luck. Scott and Abby Rosenthal arrived with a bottle of wine, as did Dr. Glavin, and even Dr. Rhouhani, the emergency room doctor who had examined Shelby after she passed out. In fact, it seemed as if every doctor and nurse who took care of Larry and Roz, and who had subsequently gotten to know Shelby and Lauren during their long recovery, dropped by to revel in the family's joy.

The one doctor who had yet to make an appearance, unfortunately, was the hired gun. Seems Dr. Kessler had returned from his camping trip, driven straight to the hospital, and was now tending to two other patients in active labor. Indeed the full moon had triggered a babython.

"Do any of you brilliant specialists know how to do deliveries?" Larry inquired just in case Shelby progressed faster than expected. Fortunately volunteers were not needed, as a smiling but weary Dr. Kessler finally arrived, well enough in advance to take the helm.

It was 2:00 A.M., and the birthing room was strewn with sleeping bodies and food containers. Only Shelby and Matty were keeping vigil, not that they had much choice.

"How can they be sleeping through all the thunder and Shelby's screams?" He looked around the crowded room and laughed. "I heard her from the parking lot."

"Damn right!" She wanted to smack him. "You try having the immediate world stick their fingers up you every fifteen minutes while you're in the middle of a contraction."

"Other than that, how are you feeling?" He studied her chart and all the monitoring devices.

"How am I feeling? I'm exhausted, miserable, I hate men, I want this to be over . . ."

"I'd say she's between seven and eight centimeters." He nudged Matthew.

"See?" Shelby yelled. "What did I tell you? A good doctor knows how far along you are just by looking at you."

But even a med student would know what stage Shelby was in when she let out a bloodcurdling cry at 4:17 A.M. "They're coming. They're coming. I need to push."

"Breathe through it, Shelby," the nurse instructed. She held Shelby's hand as she was wheeled into the operating room that was set up for a twin delivery. "Breathe through it."

"Fuck the breathing!" she cried out. "I'm pushing! So get the hell out of my way. . . ."

"One more contraction, and then you can push till your blue." Dr. Kessler laughed. "Is she always this outspoken?"

"No," Matthew answered. "Usually she's worse."

Chapter Thirty-two

Shelby, caught between exhaustion and exhilaration, was overwhelmed by the sea of medical personnel on hand when she was wheeled into the OR. At first glance it looked like a scene from a Woody Allen film, with everyone gloved and gowned, busily preparing for the patient's lobotomy.

"Who are all these people?" She grabbed Dr. Kessler by his surgical scrubs.

"They're Santa's little helpers." He studied the ultrasound of her abdomen. "You can't have two babies without nurses, technicians, an anaesthesiologist, two pediatricians, and my chief resident, Dr. Mohar 'I've never dropped one yet' Singh."

Shelby and Matty laughed. Lauren had been right about this guy. He was the best.

"Shelby, my dear, it looks like you're in luck," he said.

"Why? They're holding hands and they want to come out together?"

"Not quite, but it appears as though they are both in the head down position and you can deliver vaginally. Many times Baby A is fine but Baby B is breach or transverse and we have to try to manipulate . . ."

Shelby let out a bloodcurdling scream and started to push and pant. This was no time for an Obstetrics 101 course. She was about to deliver the first baby.

"I love you." Matty grabbed Shelby's hand. "And I'm so proud of what an incredible trouper you've been."

"Shut the hell up and get this thing out of me," she cried.

"Yep, she's got Sailor Tongue. She's at ten centimeters." A knowing Dr. Kessler winked. "Shelby, on my count, let's give one good push. One, two, three . . ."

Shelby bore down, pushing so hard she thought her temples would burst.

"Baby A is crowning," Dr. Kessler finally announced. "At the next contraction, Shelby, let's give it one last unbelievably strong push. Then we can order out for pizza."

But miraculously only a quick push was needed, as Baby A seemed to be propelling itself out. And then there was the sound of that magical first cry, and a flurry of activity.

"She's a girl," Matty shouted. "A beautiful, little girl," he cried as he watched the doctor hand his daughter to the nurse, who then prepared her for the pediatrician's Apgar assessment. "You did so great." He kissed Shelby. "She's absolutely perfect."

"I want to see my daughter," Shelby cried, tears of joy streaming down her face. Understanding for the first time the immeasurable joy her own mother must have felt the moment she was born to her. "Who does she look like?"

"It's hard to say exactly." Matty wondered how Shelby would react when she saw her daughter's round face and jet-black hair. "I think she's got your . . . chin."

"My chin? Oh God. I knew it. She looks like Avi!"

Matty laughed. "To be perfectly honest, she looks more like an extra from *The Exorcist*."

As did their second daughter born, six minutes later. But at least this one showed the promise of looking like her fair-haired mother. And though Shelby was left exhausted and weak after almost fourteen hours of labor, she was overwhelmed with love and joy at the first glimpse of her children, regardless of whom they resembled.

There was further rejoicing when Dr. Kessler explained that although they were tiny and fragile, and would require neonatal care until they reached sufficient birth weights, as best he could tell, they appeared healthy. And awfully cute.

The proud patriarch was the first to hold his delectable twin granddaughters in the nursery only an hour after they were born. As he rocked with them, tears streamed down his eyes. How odd was his life? So full, yet bittersweet. So rich with love, yet also tragically painful. But more important, he was still here. Broken but alive, able to enjoy this greatest of gifts, the gift of life.

"You know what I was thinking, Shelby?" He rocked back and forth.

"What?" Her heart was full as she took in his prideful smile and the love in his eyes.

"One day you'll be in my shoes. And you'll understand what a parent wishes for for their child. Love and happiness, good health, opportunity, a little bit of luck in the stock market, and this." He nuzzled his bundles of joy. "The joy of having children. I only hope they bring you as much *naches* and pleasure as you did."

"Do you really mean that, Daddy? With everything we've been through?"

"Believe me. This is all the sweeter because of what we've been through. And you know what else I was thinking? This is the fourth generation of sisters on your mother's side. First was Granny Bea and her sister, Yetta."

"Who fought like cats and dogs."

"Then it was Sandy and Roz."

"Endless rivalry."

"Then you and Lauren."

"Catch a theme here?" Shelby rolled her eyes.

"And now it's Sari and Rachel. Do you think it was all part of God's plan?"

"What? That each generation should try to learn from the mistakes of the others?"

"Exactly."

"God help them," Shelby knelt to kiss her precious lot. "God help them."

I know those of us in the spirit world are no longer supposed to get caught up in the daily lives of our loved ones on the other side. But I must have some leftover human emotion bottled inside my soul. For at this very moment, I am feeling such an overwhelming sense of relief and joy for my family. Everything fell into place for them so perfectly, just not as I expected.

I guess it's true what they say. That man makes plans, and God laughs.

Perhaps it's just the nature of the human condition we spend a whole lifetime thinking we know what we want, what's worth striving for, only to discover what's truly best for us never even entered our mind. Until the damn thing falls right into our laps.

Like the two baby girls Shelby is happily nursing.

If only I could take credit. Turns out I had less to do with any of the events of the past year than even I suspected. I was recently made aware of this after my amateur attempts to alter the karmic lesson plans of my children were brought to the attention of the Higher Souls.

Basically someone ratted on me.

Do you know what I was told? I am a spirit, and this is my job description. I am to radiate the aura of God to humans, to comfort them on their passage to fulfillment, and to show them the path to kindness and compassion. For only then will I be given the energy to send the white light they need to complete their journey to enlightenment.

Pretty much everything else is a no-no. So no more trying to set accidents in motion, or causing oil to leak out of a car so my daughter would have to hitch a ride with the man she's been in love with her whole life. Which I don't care what anyone says, was a brilliant idea. No more turning lights on and off, although that certainly got her attention . . .

Still, I can tell you that things will be a whole lot less exciting for me now, but what's most important is my prayers were answered.

Shelby and Matty are head over heels in love, and completely crazy about their precious, twin daughters, Sari and Rachel, who, I might add, were named in memory of moi, and Carol's mother, Ruth. And are they ever happy making a life for themselves on their old stomping grounds, good old Majestic Court! Although I'm sure Larry and Roz were a tad surprised when they decided to gut the house down to the beams, and build something more to their liking.

What they didn't touch one inch of was the guesthouse, the magical place where their love story resumed. Today it is occupied by Maria, whose new role as nanny suits her to a tee.

As for Lauren and Danny, I'm happy to report this was truly a match made in heaven, just not by me. Danny is wild for her, and can't believe his good fortune in finding a loving, loyal woman who took to his son as if he was her own. One day, through the miracle of science, they hope to expand their family, but for now are content with their lot.

Thankfully, Larry and Roz have finally resumed a normal life, as normal as one could expect given that their physical injuries will have a lasting toll. Bowling is out forever, but they're so busy baby-sitting, and doting on their four granddaughters, they hardly notice.

Yes, I said four. Hard as it is to believe, two weeks after Shelby delivered, Eric and Jamal's surrogate went into early labor, too, and produced identical twin girls. So ecstatic were the proud parents, and so eager to share their bounty with family, they moved to Long Island.

Naturally at first Roz and Larry were on shaky ground when it came to understanding how a stranger who gave birth on behalf of their gay son and his lover could actually be bestowing new family members on them. But of all people, who were they to question the means by which children were brought into this world?

So all's well that ends well. My children are happy and in love, settling down, enjoying their families, and very important, not trying to kill each other anymore. Sure they have their little squabbles (you didn't expect Shelby to just roll over every time Roz annoyed her) but as best as they can, they are clinging to each other for dear life.

I ask you, what more could a mother want?

Further Information About DES And Surrogacy

If you or someone you know has questions concerning DES, contact:

DESAction USA
610 Sixteenth Street
Suite 301
Oakland, CA 94612
800-DES-9288
E-mail: DESAction@Earthlink.net
Or visit their website: WWW.DESAction.Org.

For information and on-line support about surrogacy, contact:

The American Surrogacy Center
E-mail: Support@Surrogacy.com
Or visit their website: WWW.Surrogacy.com

A Little Help From Above
HOT TOPICS FOR BOOK CLUBS AND GAL PAL DISCUSSIONS

A Little Help from Above covers a lot of emotional ground, especially as it relates to families who feud and the people who love them. Some of the experiences and feelings in the story may hit home. But even if they don't, nearly everyone has looked around at some point in life and asked, "Who are these people and what was God thinking when he threw us together?" To that end, perhaps you'd like to consider the following topics as a way to explore and share what you've learned about that which matters most in our lives—family and love.

DES
- Prior to reading this book, were you aware of the magnitude and multitude of problems affecting DES daughters and their families?
- Have you or anyone you know been identified as a DES daughter? How has your/their life been affected by its manifestations, such as infertility issues, illness and medical conditions, psychological problems, family relations, etc.
- Are there any prescription drugs on the market today that you or your family will not take because you believe that the risks far outweigh the benefits?

SURROGACY

- Have you or anyone you know ever been asked to be a surrogate mother? What was the outcome?
- If you were asked to become a surrogate for a woman you love, such as a sister, cousin, or best friend, what would be your reaction?
- What if you were asked about becoming a surrogate for a woman in your life who you are not close with, or worse, despise? Perhaps a sister-in-law, step-sister, co-worker, a family friend's child, etc. If your being a surrogate was the only chance this woman had of having a baby, and you were fertile and in good health, would your sense of obligation override your personal feelings about the individual?
- Would you ever consider being a paid surrogate for an infertile couple to whom you have no previous connection? How much money would you expect to be paid for this service, and would you insist on having a relationship with that child after he or she was born?

FAMILY FEUDS

- Why is it so hard for some families to keep the peace, while others seem to be so close-knit?
- If you have ever cut off communication with a family member, how did that affect you and other family members? Do you have any regrets?
- Have you ever been asked or stepped in to mediate a family argument? What was the outcome?
- What valuable lesson have you learned about family fights that you think might help others in a similar situation?

FIRST LOVES

- What is it about a first love that seems to color our future relationships, even if it ended badly?
- How do you feel about people trying to track down their first or former loves long after the relationship ended?
- What would you do if you discovered that your partner/spouse still had feelings for someone from their past?

MOTHERS AND DAUGHTERS

- As a daughter what is the most important thing you learned from your mother?
- If you are a mother of a girl, what is the most important thing you have tried to instill in your daughter? Is this different from what you would try to teach a son?
- Some women are best friends with their mothers, others feel a greater sense of obligation than love, and still others can't spend five minutes with their mother without getting into an argument. How would you describe your mother/daughter relationship?
- If you've experienced the loss of a daughter or a mother, what is a memory of that person that you hold dear?
- If you could give one piece of advice to a new mother, what would it be?

SISTERS

- If you grew up with a sister, how would you describe the experience and how did your relationship change, if at all, as you grew older?
- If you are now raising two or more girls, how would you describe their relationship to date? Do you sense that they've formed enough of a bond to remain close when they get older?
- Did you grow up with sibling rivalry? How did it affect your childhood? How has it affected your adult life?
- What is the difference between a sister and a friend?

KARMA AND DESTINY

- Do you believe there is such a thing as karma? Are you aware of the karmic lessons you were meant to learn in this lifetime?
- What role has destiny played in your life? Have you had experiences that you are convinced were meant to be?
- Have you ever had a psychic moment—a premonition, a dream, or feeling—that actually came true?
- Do you believe in psychics, astrologers, mediums, and others who say they can predict the future?

THE OTHER SIDE
- Do you believe it is possible for our loved ones to look out for us after they die?
- Have you ever felt certain that you had communicated with someone who had passed away? How did it make you feel?
- Have you ever felt like you've been given a little help from above?

THE WRITER IN YOU
- Everyone has a book inside them. Or two or three. If you could write at least one book that was guaranteed of being published, what would it be about?

Don't Miss Any of the Fun and Sexy Novels from Avon Trade Paperback